WILD BLUE U

FOUNDATION OF HONOR

THE OFFICER

WILD BLUE U
FOUNDATION OF HONOR

THE OFFICER

DOUG BEASON

WordFire Press
Colorado Springs, Colorado

ISBN: 978-1-61475-418-3

Cover design by Janet McDonald

Art Director by Kevin J. Anderson

Cover artwork images by Janet McDonald

Book Design by RuneWright, LLC
www.RuneWright.com

Published by
WordFire Press, an imprint of
WordFire, Inc.
PO Box 1840
Monument CO 80132

Kevin J. Anderson & Rebecca Moesta, Publishers

WordFire Press Trade Paperback Edition May 2016
Printed in the USA
wordfirepress.com

DEDICATION

*To the 33 United States Air Force Academy graduates
who were Southeast Asia Prisoners of War;
their goal and motto was to
"Return with Honor."*

ACKNOWLEDGEMENTS

I've received much help from reviewers, contributors of anecdotes, historians, former cadets, faculty members, editors, agents, friends, and a host of other people ... but all factual errors in the novel are entirely mine, and if not unintended, then were purposely inserted only as embellishment. Thanks to Kevin J. Anderson, Rebecca Moesta, Vivian Trask, Don Erbschloe, Vickie Erbschloe, Matt Bialer, Lori Peterkin and her book club, Lisa Ice, Ken Zeringue, Don Shepherd, Elizabeth Muenger, Joe Gross, Craig Hendrickson, Mike Heil, Bill Sabol, Jeff Dotur, Harald Dogliani, Gary Ganong, Jim Parsons, Bob DeBerry, Hugh Gordon, Deane Burbank, Dick Halloran, Phil Gronseth, Curt McIntyre, Jim Mateos, Chris Jaremko, Yvonne Kinkaid, John Paul Fraser Fisher, Don Cole, Ron Furstenau, Tom McNish, and Beast Beason. The editorial team: Mia Kleve, Holly Smith, Bob Vitas and Michelle Corsillo. Thanks also to my USAFA classmates for reviewing the flying scenes: Robert Massey, Lou Michels, Rick Sowers, George Patterson, Kevin Kenkel, Jack Casey, Kevin Roll, and Bill Ramsay. And of course, without whose love and support this series would never have been possible, Cindy Beason.

AUTHOR'S NOTE

Although this is a book of fiction, it is based on historical figures, events, and locations that are real. However, it is impossible to precisely reconstruct the thoughts and motivations of these historical figures and their actions. In addition, the author has taken liberty to dramatically embellish historical events. For example, although Soviet Ilyushin Il-28s were present in Cuba during the 1962 missile crisis, Chinese Il-28s were not. As another example, although I received pointers on the POW scenes in Vietnam, not all events herein occurred in the manner depicted. I did this not to denigrate, but only highlight and humanize the significance of these actions. In addition, although the cheating scandal of 1965 did occur, the discovery of the scandal did not happen in the manner depicted; "call signs" for Air Force pilots were not widely used in the 1960s and early 1970s, but for continuity I used them throughout the book; and High Country Construction, Colorado Technical Associates, and the USAFA's Department of Theoretical Mechanics did not exist. Finally, only to dramatize the novel, some anecdotes may be out of chronological order (such as an F-105 going supersonic over the Terrazzo, the Vietnam protests at the Cadet Chapel, etc.), the sole purpose being to not make this novel a dry chronicle of historical fact, but rather to show the true excitement of the evolution of a major American institution, the United States Air Force Academy.

www.DougBeason.com

DRAMATIS PERSONAE

Jean-Claude (Rod) Simone

Julie Phillips Simone—Rod's wife

Nanette Marie Simone—Rod's daughter

Major General Hank McCluney, US Army Air Corps—Rod's (deceased) adoptive father

Mary McCluney—Rod's adoptive mother

Washington DC

Ambassador T. Edward Phillips—Rod's father-in-law

Francine Phillips—Rod's mother-in-law

Colorado Springs

George Delante—Land developer and co-owner, High Country Construction

Elizabeth Delante—his wife

Fred Delante—his son

Jim-Tom Henderson—Co-owner, High Country Construction

Darius Moore—ex-El Paso County DA; Legal Counsel, Colorado Technical Associates

United States Air Force Academy

Captain Bobby Andrew—Executive Officer, Department of Theoretical Mechanics

Brigadier General Stanley C. Beck[†]—USAFA Commandant

Raf Garcia—waiter

Mrs. Gail McComas[†]—Cadet hostess, 1955 to 1977

Ben Martin[†]—USAFA football coach

Colonel Maas—Department Head and Permanent Professor, Department of Law

Brigadier General Robert F. McDermott[†]—USAFA Dean of Faculty

Brigadier General Robert W. Strong, Jr.[†]—USAFA Commandant

Colonel L. Bradford Whitney—Department Head and Permanent Professor, Department of Theoretical Mechanics

Rod Simone's USAFA classmates

Nino Baldacci[†]—Cadet (Poughkeepsie, NY)

Sylvester "Sly" Winston Jakes—(Boston, MA)

Jeff Goldstein—(New York, NY)

Manuel Rojo—(Albuquerque, NM)

George Sanders—(Fort Worth, Texas)

Other Locations

Captain Charlie "Rhino" Banner—Instructor pilot

"Beast"—Squadron Commander, 3525th Pilot Training Wing, Williams AFB

General "Speedy" Beaumont—Major General Hank McCluney's WWII wingman

Captain "Jazz" Ferguson—Rod's F-4 GIB (Guy-In-the-Backseat)

Major Tom Ranch—F-105 pilot, Rod Simone's ex-ATO and ex-AOC

Professor Clifford Rhoades—Professor of Aeronautical Engineering, Stanford University

Barbara Richardson—Stanford graduate student, newscaster

†—Denotes an actual historical figure

USAF Academy
Abbreviations and Terms

AMI—Any Morning Inspection, usually less formal than a SAMI

ASAP—As Soon As Possible

AOC—Air Officer Commanding

ATO—Air Training Officer

AWOL—Absent Without Leave

Blow—To rest, or to "kiss off"

Bomb—To do extremely poorly

BOR—Base Of the Ramp

Buy the Farm—To crash

Canoe U.—A small, inconsequential school that forms a suburb of the capital of Maryland with a campus partly on land and partly in the Severn River

CAP—Combat Air Patrol

CCQ—Cadet in Charge of Quarters

Clank—To freeze up; to royally goof-up

CDB—Commandant's Disciplinary Board

CIC—Cadet In Charge

Comm—Commandant of Cadets, a brigadier (1-star) general

Commshop—Commandant's office

CQ—used in place of CCQ

Crash—A landing in which the vertical velocity is so great and the time spent in reducing it to zero is so brief that the acceleration and hence the forces acting become so great as to result in structural failure

Cretin—That person disposed to doing acts of nominal coordination or acts requiring minimal thought

DF—Dean of Faculty, a brigadier (1-star) general

Doolie—That insignificant whose rank is measured in negative units; one whose potential for learning is unlimited; one who will graduate in some time approaching infinity

EI—Extra Instruction

FIGMO—Forget It, Got My Orders

Firstie—a Firstclassman, a senior (cadets in their final year at the Academy)

Fourthclassmen—Freshmen (first year cadet, known as Doolies)

FORM 10—Cadet administrative form for documenting infraction of regulations

FUBAR—"Messed" Up Beyond All Recognition

GIB—Guy-In-the-Backseat

Ground pounder—A non-flying officer

Hyper—An ultra-military cadet who is focused on military bearing

Hudson High—a small, inconsequential school [West Point] on the Hudson River distinguished by over 200 years of tradition unhampered by progress

IHTFP—"I Have Truly Found Paradise"; equivalently, "I Hate This Friggin' Place"

Intramurder—Athletic competition between squadrons; violent intramural

IRI—In Ranks Inspections

Magic—That name applied to the department of Electrical Engineering and all related hand waving activities

MAC—Military Air Command

MATS—Military Air Transport Service

NCOIC—Non-Commissioned Officer-in-Charge

Nino Baldacci—That individual having entered with the class of '59 and remaining until the present time, never having been off academic probation and never having taken a privilege. He is a perpetual turn-back, near and dear to all cadets.

ODP—Off Duty Privilege

OIC—Officer-in-Charge

ORI—Operational Readiness Inspection

OTF—Over The Fence, AWOL

PDA—Public Display of Affection

PE—Physical Education

PFT—Physical Fitness Test

Post—An order signifying to a subordinate that their presence is no longer needed

Rack—Bed

Rock—That superhuman who is free from female entanglements

SAC—Strategic Air Command

SAMI—Saturday Morning Inspection

SDO—Squadron Duty Officer

Secondclassmen—Juniors (third year cadets)

SIOP—Single Integrated Operations Plan

SOD—Senior Officer of the Day

Staff Tower—The level in the cadet dining hall (Mitchell Hall) where Wing Staff eats

Supt—USAFA Superintendent, a lieutenant (3-star) general

TAC—Tactical Air Command

TDY—Temporary Duty

Thirdclassmen—Sophomores (second year cadets)

Trash Hauler—Transport pilot

Truck Driver—the pilot of a non-fighter aircraft with more than one engine (bomber or transport)

Two!—A command to return the cadet to what he or she had been doing

UCMJ—Uniformed Code of Military Justice

VFR—Visual Flight Rules

Zoomie—That term by which a cadet is commonly known by jealous, and usually inferior, civilians

THE COMING AMERICAN

Bring me men to match my mountains,
Bring me men to match my plains.
Men to chart a starry empire,
Men to make celestial claims ...

Samuel Walter Foss
(At the base of the ramp leading to the USAFA
cadet area from 1958—2003)

Prologue

"Cry"

September 6th, 1952

Farnborough Airshow, England

The eternal stars shine out as soon as it is dark enough.

Thomas Carlyle

The first thing thirteen-year-old Rod Simone heard when the airplane door opened was the sound of rumbling engines. Thick, humid air rolled into the plane and he smelled jet fuel mixed with the scent of damp, ploughed ground.

Rod looked out the window and saw sleek, aluminized jets from France parked next to new, no-nonsense American B-47 bombers; a cargo plane from Germany was positioned near a collection of government aircraft from over 20 nations.

But his eyes widened when he spotted smoke erupt from a compact British jet starting its engine.

A fighter!

The flight line was crowded with all types of aircraft, but to Rod the only ones that mattered were the swift, nimble jetfighters; to him, they were the star of the airshow.

Every July, Farnborough hosted the largest collection of air-enthusiasts in the world, and the week-long air festival swelled the sleepy English village by 10,000 people who celebrated every form of manned flight, from bi-planes to jets to gliders. The airshow was nestled in England's green, rolling hills 15 miles southwest of London and was considered the Wimbledon of the aviation world.

The field was packed with civilian and military onlookers; they walked amid billowing tents, food booths, jugglers, and boot sales, making the crowded site look like an ancient medieval faire. His adoptive father had stressed on the long flight over that Farnborough was heaven-on-earth for pilots, and everyone who was anyone attended the yearly event. Here, aircraft executives negotiated million-dollar deals that determined the future of aviation for years.

Rod Simone walked down metal stairs behind his adoptive parents, Hank and Mary McCluney. They disembarked the C-54 transport, following Air Force's Chief of Staff, General Hoyt Vandenburg. Ever since 1947, when the Air Force had been formed from the Army Air Corps, the fledgling service controlled the nation's nuclear weapons, making General Vandenburg one of the most powerful men on earth.

Vandenberg's aide, a young second lieutenant freshly graduated from West Point, stuck to the general like glue. The rest of the entourage was a bevy of senior officers, all of them young, rapidly promoted because of the war. The casualty rate for pilots in World War II had been so high that some colonels—such as Rod's adoptive father—had been promoted to the dizzying rank of general before they were even 40. But unlike Vandenberg's aide, most of these men in the high-ranking entourage had nothing more than a high school education, having entered the Army Air Corps without a college degree or long-term leadership training.

The Air Chief Marshal of the British Royal Air Force headed up the official welcoming party and waited at the front of a reception line for the American delegation.

The Royal Black Watch struck up "The Star-Spangled Banner" when General Vandenberg reached the bottom of the stairs. Hank balanced his weight on a cane and grasped his wife's hand to keep steady; Rod stood at rigid attention. The anthem sounded especially patriotic being led by the Guard's pipes, and Rod thought the Brits played the instruments much better than himself, despite his four years of bagpipe lessons.

An aide whispered in the Air Chief Marshal's ear; the British general snapped an open-palmed salute as Rod's father stepped to the ground. "General McCluney. Welcome to the UK."

Hank returned the salute. "Aye, it's good to be back, sir."

The Air Chief Marshal smiled at his thick Scottish burr. "You sound as if you're returning home, general. Highlands?"

"Actually, I was born in the Lowlands, but I'm American now. My parents immigrated to America from Pitlochry when I was ten." He motioned to his wife and adopted son. "Sir, I'd like to present Mrs. McCluney and my son Jean-Claude."

The Air Chief Marshall bowed to Mary and solemnly shook Rod's hand. "Madam, Master Jean-Claude."

"My name is Rod, sir." Rod avoided his stepfather's eyes. Hank knew he didn't like to be called Jean-Claude any more—it was Rod now. It seemed like only yesterday that he'd come home from school with a bloody nose, scuffed pants, and torn shirt from fighting about his name. Jean-Claude was a sissy name for a boy to have in Southern California in the 1950s, and despite applying to officially change his name, Hank still managed to forget.

The Air Marshal drew himself up and nodded, a trace of a smile at his lips. "Excuse me, Master Rod."

Four silver stars glinted in the rare English sunlight as General Vandenberg walked back from leading the American entourage through the reception line; smoke trailed from his cigar. A portly, distinguished-looking gentleman in a three-piece suit walked next to him. Vandenberg placed his hand on the civilian's shoulder as he joined the Air Marshal at the bottom of the stairs.

"Air Marshal, do you know Professor Clifford Rhoades, chairman of Stanford's aeronautical engineering department? I've learned he's just completed a six-month sabbatical at Cranwell, and with his experience, he's just the person I need to help establish our own air academy."

"Yes, of course, I'm very familiar with Dr. Rhoades," the Air Marshal said. He shook Rhoades' hand. "Pleasure to see you again, Professor. Have you met General McCluney?"

"Yes, I have," Dr. Rhoades said. "Air University, 1948, at the first Air Academy conference." McCluney and Rhoades shook hands. "General McCluney is a living legend. He escaped from occupied France in the war by climbing over the Pyrénées, negotiating a nine-thousand-foot mountain pass. That was quite an accomplishment, especially on only one leg."

"I actually lost my leg to gangrene after reaching Esterri d'Àneu," Hank said in a soft voice. "But I would not have made it without Jean-Claude—excuse me, I mean Rod. My son helped me every step of the way along *Le Chemin de la Liberté*."

Rod's face turned red at the attention. His adoptive stepfather had saved his life by rescuing him from his burning home. Afterward, Rod had stubbornly refused to leave Hank's side, even after they'd made contact with the underground resistance.

"The Freedom Trail," Dr. Rhoades mused. "A highlight of allied relations. If I recall, the French Resistance helped over 600 American pilots escape from Saint-Girons to neutral Spain." He turned to Rod. "Not too many people have had the privilege to experience such a proud moment in history. Your father's a hero, young man. And it sounds as if you are as well."

Vandenberg took his cigar out of his mouth. "Damned straight McCluney's a hero. That's exactly why I'm twisting his arm to join General Fairchild's commission to establish our own air academy." He pointed his cigar at McCluney and Rhoades. "With you two on the committee, I know it will be a success."

"Well, well!" The Air Chief Marshall's eyebrows rose. "Good show, General. And to you, Master Rod!" He turned to Rod's father. "General McCluney, I'd be delighted to sponsor you for a lecture at Cranwell if you have the time before you fly home. You'd be a brilliant follow-on to Dr. Rhoades, and this would allow you to experience the British way of running a military academy."

Rod started to speak up but waited as a heavy transport aircraft thundered low over the airfield. His adoptive stepfather had told him that Cranwell was the world's oldest military air academy, but in contrast to the Brits, the US was still debating the necessity for even having an equivalent school for the Air Force—despite the fact that two-fifths of America's West Point graduates and a third of the Annapolis ensigns were being required to enter the fledging Air Force instead of their own respective services.

Hank spoke over the airplane's engines as he shook the Marshall's hand. "I'd be honored to accept, sir."

A young RAF escort officer wearing a silver epaulet around his shoulder appeared, almost as if on cue. "Madam, sirs—would you follow me please?"

The officer took Mary's arm and led her away as Rod and his father followed. They strode across the concrete tarmac, keeping pace with Vandenberg and Rhoades as they walked to a grassy field where colorful tents had been set up lining the runway.

Red, white, and blue canvas ruffled in the wind. Rod smelled roasting lamb, baking bread, and warm sour beer that contrasted with the distinctive tang of gasoline and kerosene-based airplane fuel. People mulled around aircraft sitting by the runway.

The Black Watch played bagpipes as they marched across the grassy plain in their traditional glengarry bonnets, black jackets, red tartan kilts, and white knee-high stockings. Rod felt a swell of pride as he watched their progress. His stepfather had spent the last four years teaching Rod the pipes and he appreciated the difficulty of playing while performing maneuvers.

High overhead a single plane roared out of a barrel roll and bore toward the ground. Its engines whined, increasing in pitch as the plane drew closer.

Rod turned to watch the brightly painted jet, the new British de Havilland DH.110 Sea Vixen. The plane continued to accelerate as the pilot tried to pull out of its dive.

Rod frowned. From the times he and his adoptive father had spent watching fighters outside of March Air Force Base, he knew the plane's angle of attack didn't look right; something was wrong.

Hearing the plane, Hank and General Vandenberg stopped speaking. They brought a hand up to shield their eyes from the sun as they searched the sky. The senior officers in Vandenberg's staff gawked at the accelerating craft.

The British escort officer muttered, "Blimey, look at that. Bloody fool's not going to make it."

"He's coming in at too steep of an angle!" Rod said. "He won't be able to pull up!"

Dr. Rhoades cocked his head. "How do you know that?"

"I don't know, sir. I just do." Rod turned back to watch the aircraft; he felt sick to his stomach. The plane was heading straight for the row of people and tents in front of them.

He heard Hank whisper, "My God, the lad's right! This is like what happened to my B-24."

Watching the plane accelerate to the ground, Rod remembered his stepfather's horrid account of when he had been shot down over France, nearly a decade ago.

It was almost as if time stood still; everything seemed surreal, out of place in the peaceful, bucolic countryside.

Rod shivered as if a cold chill had swept across the field. He looked around; no one seemed concerned about the plane. He felt his heart race. "He's going to crash! Run!"

Startled by Rod's voice, General Vandenberg frantically waved at the people on the other side of the grassy field. "Move away! Get the hell out of there!"

Rod saw a few individuals watch the incoming plane, but they stood transfixed, as if they thought the de Havilland would miraculously pull out of its dive. Hundreds of others continued to mill about, unaware of the descending plane.

Vandenberg's young aide, Lieutenant Whitney, broke away from the entourage and started sprinting toward the crowd; he screamed, trying to get their attention.

Rod immediately took off after the young officer, waving his arms and yelling as well. "Run! Get out of the way!"

"Jean-Claude!" Hank shouted behind him. "Stand down, lad!"

The plane started to shake; a high-pitched scream came from its engines. A cascading roar rolled from the jet as it strained to pull up its nose.

Suddenly, the plane tumbled and disintegrated, smashing into the grassy field just off the runway. The engine separated from the fuselage. It bounced into the air, and turned end over end as it careened into the crowd.

The plane's body shattered into pieces and swept through the throng; it mowed down the spectators like a scythe slashing through wheat.

Aircraft fuel sprayed from the tank in the fuselage and ignited. A ball of orange and yellow flame boiled into the sky. Smoke and streams of fire trailed after the tumbling pieces.

Screams mixed with the sound of explosions.

Rod and the young West Point graduate stopped and watched the carnage. Rod felt his breath quicken, blood pounded in his ears. There must have been fifty people killed in the blink of an eye.

A fireball roiled into the air, charring the grassy field and igniting the canvas tents.

Rod staggered back and held a hand to his face as he tried to mask the fire's heat.

Sirens from distant emergency vehicles wailed.

The Lieutenant grabbed Rod by the arm. "Get the hell out of here, kid!" He shoved Rod toward his parents.

Rod balled his fists. Why did the lieutenant do that? He was trying to help! People were hurt. They needed assistance! He started to retort, but the man left and dashed to General Vandenberg.

Rod breathed heavily and started jogging back to his parents.

As he approached he saw the lieutenant reach the entourage of senior American officers. The lieutenant turned and pointed to the field; he appeared to give an eyewitness account of the carnage.

A British officer ran up to the group, breathing in deep gasps. As he caught his breath he straightened and gave a flat-handed salute. "General Vandenberg! Air Chief Marshal requests your presence, sir."

"I can't leave these people!"

"You're not safe here, General."

"Screw my safety. These people need help!" Vandenberg threw down his cigar and started jogging for the crash site.

The RAF officer held out a hand, stopping him. "Sir, you must depart the area. Both you and General McCluney are in grave danger."

The heat from the fireball subsided, but distant screaming filled the air; the sounds of people shouting mixed with the low crackling of fire.

Black, kerosene-fueled smoke rose into the sky and boiled over the ground like a dark, rapidly moving fog. People stood in shock, others sobbed.

"I can't leave—"

"General, you *must*. Your safety is a national security concern for your country … and ours as well."

Rod saw that Vandenberg suddenly looked tired, as though the general realized the British officer was right.

But Vandenberg didn't move; it appeared as if he were wrestling with the need to stay and the need to ensure his own safety. As they waited for the general, Rod realized that no one had tried to help the injured people, except that testy lieutenant from West Point—and himself. Even the senior officers on Vandenberg's staff had been at a loss of what to do, perhaps overwhelmed by the disaster.

Suddenly, Vandenberg set his mouth. He turned and barked at his staff. "Listen up! Lieutenant Whitney and I are the only line officers present. I therefore delegate him my authority during my absence. He is in command."

He pointed at his young aide. "Lieutenant Whitney!"

"Yes, sir!"

"Coordinate the rescue. Your priorities are to ensure the safety of those not injured, attend to the wounded, and assist the British authorities."

The Lieutenant stiffened. "Yes, sir."

Vandenberg turned back to his staff. "Gentlemen, I'm appointing the lieutenant my site commander, delegated with my full faith. Assist him and obey his orders. Carry on." He turned his back and strode away, confident that his order would be accomplished.

Lieutenant Whitney turned to Hank. "I say, General. You and your wife move out of the way. And take this … this *child* with you," he said, raising his chin in Rod's direction.

Not waiting for an answer, he turned and immediately started assigning the higher-ranking officers details, appointing each one with a specific action: one to enlist volunteers, another to rescue those who may still be trapped, yet another to coordinate medical care, until the last general had been tasked. It took less than a minute for the senior officers to be transformed into a coordinated rescue team.

Rod stepped forward to join them, but the lieutenant drew himself up. "I *said* this is too dangerous for a kid! Stick with your parents." He turned to the group of officers. "Gentlemen, on my command, follow me at the double time, '*arch*."

Lieutenant Whitney started jogging to the burning wreckage as the group of older men trotted after him.

Rod felt his face grow red as he watched them leave. Within moments, the men fanned out as they approached the smoldering debris and started enlisting additional help from those who appeared not to be injured.

Rod reluctantly turned to join Hank and Mary, still standing by Dr. Rhoades. Warbling horns from emergency vehicles grew louder as fire trucks and ambulances converged on the scene.

Mary said in a quiet voice, "I'd always thought there'd be a disaster at one of these air shows. These pilots are such daredevils."

"It wasn't the pilot!" Rod said. "The jet started to disintegrate before it hit. I was watching. The pilot had bottomed out of his roll."

Dr. Rhoades stepped back and once again gave Rod a curious look. "That's a keen observation young man."

Hank shook his head as he stared across the field. "There will always be crashes. Flying is dangerous business, but these dammed fighter pilots think they'll live forever."

Rod felt a twinge of anger at the remark. Hank knew he loved fighter planes; he'd known it ever since he'd taken Rod to March Field to see the Air Force's new fighters fly onto the base. Why was Hank criticizing him?

A crew of firemen extinguished a grass fire as the American senior officers helped with the rescue. At the center of the chaos the young West Point graduate commanded the senior officers and volunteers.

Hank pulled Mary and Rod close as a British bobbie in a tall black helmet drove up in a yellow golf cart.

The vehicle slowed to a stop. "May I have your attention everyone," the bobbie said. "Exit the area. Step out quickly now!"

Dr. Rhoades walked up and conferred with the officer, then bid farewell.

Hank motioned for Mary and Rod to leave, but he drew himself up and stopped. He pointed with his cane. "Look. That young lieutenant. He's the only American out there who knows what he's doing. That's why Vandenberg delegated his authority. It's unprecedented for a junior officer to jump so many echelons in rank and have that level of responsibility." He stared as the lieutenant barked his orders.

Hank whispered as if he were thinking aloud, speaking to himself. "The chief knows Whitney has been trained to instantly assume leadership. That's not to say those senior officers aren't good men; but as non-line officers they simply aren't in the chain of command."

He struck his cane on the ground, as if he came to a sudden realization. "*That's* why we need an Academy: line officers, leadership, instantly reacting, doing the right thing. We need a West Point for the air."

Rod thought about the Air Chief Marshal's invitation for his stepfather to speak at Cranwell, Britain's air academy, and of the on-going debate in America about the fledging Air Force needing its own. Although he thought the lieutenant was full of himself, after seeing him coordinate the rescue, Rod thought that maybe his adoptive stepfather was right about establishing an academy.

Rod remembered his stepfather lecturing him about even greater challenges that this new Air Force would have to face: Russia's atomic bomb, enhanced V-2 rockets capable of reaching across continents, or even giant enemy jet bombers that might someday span the globe. When Hank had first told Rod about the need for an air academy, he'd said America needed airmen who could react to new situations, and who could be depended on to always do the right thing.

But in Rod's young mind, establishing an air academy wasn't just necessary to ensure an efficient chain-of-command, to graduate line officers, or whatever else Hank was talking about ... for Rod, attending an air academy would be the best way to accomplish what he'd wanted to do as long as he could remember: *fly fighters.*

Seven Years Later

CHAPTER ONE

"Mack the Knife"

June 23rd, 1959

Stanford University
Palo Alto, CA

The distance doesn't matter; it is only the first step that is difficult.

Marquise du Deffand, French noblewoman

Dressed in civilian clothes, Second Lieutenant Rod Simone sat near the front of the class, his notebook out and pencil at the side. Students filed into the steep lecture hall from the back, and after the first few people sat next to him and nodded a greeting, he felt relieved that he fit in.

Mentally he knew that no one would care that he'd graduated from the United States Air Force Academy three weeks earlier; nor would they have any reason to know. But still, after four years of being at the center of the national stage by being a member of the Academy's first graduating class—the only major military university established since West Point and Annapolis—he tried to keep a low profile and not bring attention to himself.

He hadn't cut his hair since graduation, and by wearing casual clothes he tried not to stand out. His old blue cadet blazer with

USAFA emblem, striped tie, and gray slacks would have been too conspicuous at Stanford, and part of his charge in accepting the Guggenheim Fellowship and attending graduate school at a civilian university was that he wouldn't alienate himself.

So as a new graduate, new husband, and especially as the new father of a two-week-old baby girl, he felt totally prepared to tackle any obstacle Stanford would throw his way.

The room grew quiet as a side door at the bottom of the lecture hall opened and the professor walked in.

Rod immediately reacted. "Room, atten'hut!" He pushed back his seat and bolted to attention. The metal legs of his chair screeched across the floor, and as Rod held rigidly still, it dawned on him that he was the only person in the lecture hall standing.

A nervous titter swept through the room. The professor glanced up and ignored him as he made his way to the podium.

Rod felt his face grow warm as he slowly lowered himself to his seat.

So much for keeping a low profile and not drawing attention to himself. Old habits died hard; his body had reacted by instinct, instantly responding after four years of cadet training. Rod's ears pounded with the sound of rushing blood, and he was certain that everyone in the room could sense his embarrassment.

The professor placed his books on the podium and ruffled through his notes. There were 250 seats in the lecture hall, arranged in the steep-ascending theater seating much like the F-series of rooms that Rod had used in Fairchild Hall, but that's where the similarity stopped. The Academy-centric military customs he'd followed as a cadet—such as calling the room to attention when an instructor came through the door—had to end, and end fast.

He was an officer now, and he needed to act like one. Otherwise, this next year of graduate school would be one giant *faux pas*.

The portly professor cleared his throat. He lifted his chin and looked at the class over reading glasses that hung low on his nose. Unlike the military instructors Rod had had over the past four years with their spit-shined shoes, immaculately pressed trousers, and buzz-haircuts, this professor looked as though he had stepped off the jacket photo of a literary novel. He was dressed in a brown corduroy jacket, maroon weave tie, and dark blue shirt; his white hair had a tan bald spot.

As Rod watched the man, he thought that the only thing the professor needed was a pipe to complete the stereotype.

The professor reached down to a drawer in the podium and pulled out a polished wooden pipe.

He looked up and banged loudly on his books. "Welcome to Aero 500, Special Topics. I'm Professor Rhoades. This class is designed to introduce the Aeronautical Engineering graduate student to a wide variety of cross-disciplinary topics, such as discussing if jet airliners may ever be commercially viable. Or if sustained supersonic flight is possible. We will have experts from the government and industry participate, interspersed with class discussion, and will meet every Tuesday afternoon for an hour and a half.

"Although I assume the majority of you are aeronautical engineers, I find it useful to introduce ourselves, especially since this class also serves as graduate credit for a variety of other disciplines."

He pointed his pipe to the young man sitting next to Rod. "Edward, since you're my student, please introduce yourself. Tell us your major emphasis and what your graduate goals are." He folded his arms and leaned back against the blackboard.

Edward said, "Thanks, Professor." He turned to face the class. "Edward Mark, Aeronautical Engineering with an emphasis in the new field of computational aerodynamics. I plan to do my thesis work at the Ames Research Center."

The professor pointed at Rod. "You. Go ahead."

Rod still felt flush from his earlier outburst. "Rod Simone, general engineering. I'll be finishing my degree without a thesis since I'm on a Guggenheim Fellowship, and I'm heading off to pilot training after my masters."

A murmur rippled across the room. The professor held up a sheet and squinted at it. "Simone?"

"Yes, sir?" Rod said.

"You sound French. Where are you from? The École Normale Supérieure? I don't remember you from any of my classes."

Rod squirmed in his seat. "The Academy, sir."

"The Academy?"

"Yes, sir. The United States Air Force Academy."

"Oh, yes." The professor smiled. "That explains your earlier enthusiasm. I'm glad to see your flying school finally got off the ground." The class laughed politely at his pun. "The experiment must have succeeded for you to have won a Guggenheim. Congratulations and welcome, Mr. Simone. I mean, *Lieutenant* Simone."

"Thank you, sir."

The professor hesitated, cocked his head and squinted at Rod, staring. He looked so long that someone coughed at the back of the room; a murmur ran through the class. After a moment the professor opened his mouth as if to say something, then thought the better of it. He looked around the lecture hall. "Who's next?"

Five minutes later the class had nearly exhausted reciting the schools that were feeding the graduate seminar: Stanford, CalTech, MIT, Princeton, Chicago ... although Rod had heard of all of them, he was the only one present with a national scholarship and the only one from an unknown school.

He felt good, heartened that the Academy would be able to compete with so many heavyweights, when he heard a low, husky voice from the back at the room that made him feel weak—

"Richardson. Barbara Richardson, from the Graduate School of Journalism."

Rod twisted his head and tried to search her out among the fifty or so students in the lecture hall. A torrent of memories roared through his head: That magical night with Barbara in San Francisco ... and a year later when he'd flown to Stanford on impulse, when his attempt to surprise her had turned to disaster. He'd relived both memories in his mind dozens of times, and wondered what he could have done different....

The professor took off his glasses and peered up at the back of the room. "Miss Richardson. You were in one of my seminars last semester."

"Yes, sir. I'm in aviation journalism. This is my second technical elective."

Rod spotted her. She was just as beautiful as when he'd last seen her two years ago. She wore her blond hair long over her shoulders; her ice-blue eyes bore into him from across the room. She was stylishly dressed in a white shirt, brown sweater over her shoulders, and a red-plaid skirt. She looked more self-assured and even more mature than before … and infinitely more alluring.

His hands felt clammy; it was difficult for him to breathe. He hadn't felt this helpless since basic cadet training.

"Welcome, Miss Richardson. Now, let's get started."

The professor picked up a piece of chalk. He turned and drew on the board. "Consider an infinitely-long wind tunnel with an inviscid, incompressible fluid flowing from left to right…." The sound of notebooks opening and pencils put to paper filled the lecture hall.

Rod barely paid attention, his head roaring with the memory of that first fleeting night with Barbara … her long arms and strong, tanned legs wrapped around him as they talked all night. Then the relationship had ground to a halt after he'd made a fool of himself at Stanford.

And he remembered his roommate, Fred Delante, constantly egging him to forget her.

Her face had matured. She was no longer a teenager. But she was just as fresh and stunning as she had been two years before, but even more refined. And incredibly more beautiful.

He tried to concentrate on the professor's lecture. Two sets of equations were written on the blackboard, underneath the words Rankine-Hugoniot. Rod shook his head and wrote the shock-jump relationship in his notebook. Now that he was married, and especially with a child at home, he couldn't afford to allow his mind to wander, think about other women.…

Ninety minutes later the class ended and the graduate students left in a bustle of noise. Rod didn't look behind him and purposely took his time placing his material into his leather briefcase, on which he had spent a good part of his first paycheck. He snapped the gold clasps shut and pushed back from the long table.

To his relief the students had filtered out of the room. He didn't want to interact with Barbara until he had settled down and put the memory of their encounters behind him.

Part of him wondered if she would even remember him. After all, it had been two years since he'd seen her.

But they'd also exchanged letters.

And then there was that beating he'd given to her professorial boyfriend.

There was no way that she would have forgotten about him, and eventually he'd have to meet her face to face.

He took a deep breath. He was married. And a father. Whatever had happened between them was in the past, and was far behind.

He climbed the stairs and started to leave when her voice came from outside the lecture hall. "Hello, Rod."

He turned. "Barbara." A helpless feeling enveloped him; he felt weak.

She held a notebook in her arms, crossed over her breasts. "Professor Rhoades was right. You still have your French accent."

He didn't know what to say. They looked at each other and he was lost in her ice-blue eyes. Time passed and neither of them spoke. He finally said, "It's been a long time."

"Yes, it has." A moment passed; then in a tart voice, "Have you assaulted anyone lately?"

He winced. He placed his briefcase on the floor. Her words cut deep.

Painful, disparate memories of his short temper flooded his head: seeing her with that older man, thinking that the professor had been trying to molest her ... fighting Fred Delante at the Honor Board ... and yet another memory, coming to blows with his father in that small plane as they flew over the Academy, almost causing it to crash....

Rod swallowed. "How have you been?"

She ignored his question and glanced at his left hand. "You're married."

He blinked and refocused. *Why had she noticed so quickly?* "And ... I'm a father, as well. Nanette was born just a few weeks ago."

Her eyes widened. "A father," she whispered.

"Do you want to see her picture?"

She shook her head. "... No. Not now. I ... I have to go." She started to turn then stopped. "So, what brings you to Stanford?"

"The Guggenheim."

She paused. "Is that all?" She stared; her eyes didn't waver.

He felt his face grow warm. Did she think he came here because of her? His mind raced for what to say, something, *anything*. "What about yourself? Graduate Aero seminars are pretty deep stuff for a journalism student."

She didn't answer.

After a moment her shoulders sank as the tension melted away. "Aero's the future. Remember?"

How could I forget. She'd lectured him about it the night they'd first met. "But why this? I thought you wanted to make a difference."

"I will. These seminars are the best place to discover where the action is, the new technologies. Couldn't you tell from the topics we're going to discuss? Commercial jets, supersonic flight, space travel." Her demeanor changed: ice-blue eyes shined as she clutched her notebook. She seemed so enthusiastic about the opportunities that it was almost as though she'd undergone a religious experience.

He glanced at his watch. "Look, I have to leave. My wife and my daughter...."

"Yeah." She nodded and started backing up. "I guess I'll see you around."

"Sure."

She turned and clicked away. Her footsteps echoed in the empty hall as she disappeared around a corner.

Rod stood silent. He ran a hand through his hair.

He was happily married.

He picked up his briefcase. Happily married. Now that he had resolved it with his head, he just hoped that his emotions would follow.

But he had to do more than that.

He had to be proactive, not put himself in a situation where his emotions and old memories would get the better of him. He vowed to avoid Barbara, and make sure he wouldn't say more than a few words to her every time he saw her.

Happily married.

He'd have to repeat the mantra a hundred times a day....

CHAPTER TWO

"Baby Talk"

August, 1959

Stanford University Married Student Housing

No, when the fight begins within himself, a man's worth something.

Robert Browning, *Bishop Blougram's Apology*

Rod scrunched over the small kitchen table that was covered with books, journal articles, pads of paper, pencils, and a cup of cold, stale coffee. He squinted in the dim light from a single overhead bulb and reread the problem set for his graduate mechanics class for the third time. He couldn't understand the words—or even concentrate on what they meant. Not with all the racket going on in the next room.

For the last two hours Nanette's screams had pierced the normally quiet married student housing. Julie had even turned on the kitchen and bathroom faucets to try to mask Nanette's shrill cries from the neighbors, but all that accomplished was to fill the small apartment with a cacophony of noise. With the distractions and loud sounds, it might have been better if he'd attended Columbia University in downtown New York City; at least with the traffic and taxicabs, they wouldn't be constantly disturbing their neighbors.

Rod raised his voice. "Julie! Did you burp her?"

"I've been burping her, rocking her, walking her, and swinging her all night … everything but giving her a shot of booze."

"Well don't do that! Do you think she's teething?"

Julie appeared in her pink bathrobe at the doorway, her hair in disarray, eyes bloodshot. She rocked Nanette in her arms. It was hard to imagine that such loud, frantic screams could come from something that small. "She's only seven weeks old, but I'm putting cold compresses on her gums in case she's teething early. Nothing seems to work."

"Then what else do you think is wrong?"

"Dr. Spock says its colic. If that's the case, there's nothing we can do. She may have it for another two or three months."

"Oh, great." It seemed as soon Nanette hit three weeks old, the screaming started every night at six on the button and lasted anywhere from three to five hours. Rod didn't know how much more of this he could handle. "Isn't there something else you can try?"

Julie stared. "You're kidding, right? You think I enjoy this? Why don't *you* quiet her down?"

Rod felt the veins on the side of his head start to pound; the past few hours of nonstop screaming was getting to him. "I have to study. This is my job, remember? If I don't graduate, then I don't go to pilot training."

"Well, screw pilot training. What about me? Aren't my goals just as important as yours?"

"I thought your goal was having a good time," Rod said.

Julie pulled back and her eyes widened. She turned and left the room, rocking Nanette in her arms.

Rod closed his eyes. He felt like a heel. He knew Julie was constantly watching Nanette, and if tonight's short time he'd been at home was wearing on him, he couldn't imagine what she was going through.

And now, look what he'd done. Although she'd never told him what she'd really wanted in life, what he just said still wasn't nice—or fair. He'd hit her below the belt.

He pushed up and walked into their small bedroom. Julie sat on the bed, looking dully at the floor. Nanette screamed while lying on the mattress, her eyes squeezed shut and her tiny fists clenched.

Nanette's crib was pushed up against the wall, next to Julie's side of the bed. Their clothes were stacked in cardboard boxes that served as a temporary chest of drawers. He wouldn't get flight pay until he started pilot training, so his $222.30 a month Second Lieutenant's salary didn't allow them leeway for extravagance—which for now was anything more than housing, food, and baby formula.

He thought of his former roommate's father, Mr. George Delante, and his caustic observation of how Air Force officers would be eking out a living, and how George Delante had urged his son, Fred, to quit the Air Force as soon as possible so that he could exploit his education for making money.

Well, Fred never had to make that decision since he'd been booted from the Academy on an Honor violation ... so it was Rod, and not Fred, who was experiencing the truth of Mr. Delante's prophesy.

"I'm sorry," Rod said.

Julie ignored him.

He reached for Nanette. He used a hand to support her head and brought the shrilling baby to his shoulder; he patted her back. He whispered in her ear, "That's okay, sweetheart."

He turned back to Julie, feeling like an absolute jerk. "Julie ... I didn't mean it—"

"Go to hell." Julie buried her head in a pillow.

Rod stood there for a moment. He thought he heard her sob, and his stomach felt sour. "Julie."

When she didn't answer he turned to leave, rocking Nanette as she continued to scream.

As he left the bedroom, he remembered that Mr. Delante had lectured him about this austere life when he and Rod were just a few, scant miles away in San Francisco's Fairmont Hotel—barely three years ago ... and on the same night he'd met Barbara Richardson.

O O O

October 1959

Engineering building, Stanford University

Rod glanced at his watch and was startled to see that nearly an hour had passed since he'd last looked at the time. It was eight thirty on a Wednesday night, and although five other graduate students sat next to him at the sprawling oak table, the library in Stanford's engineering hall was dead quiet; even the sounds of papers rustling seemed to be muffled by the surrounding bookshelves.

What a change from studying at home.

Rod turned his attention back to the two problems assigned during this afternoon's class. He'd quickly assimilated to graduate school, and compared to the hectic pace of life as a cadet, he now felt that he had an enormous amount of time to devote to studying.

Especially in contrast to the first few months with Nanette's colic, where he'd found he had to camp out in the engineering building in order to complete the horrendous problem sets that his professors kept assigning. But as opposed to his Academy homework, where he might be able to complete several assignments in the span of an hour, he discovered that sometimes it took that same amount of time just to comprehend what his professors even asked.

Thank goodness he'd reached an understanding with Julie: he'd study like crazy all week, and then watch Nanette over the weekend. Julie still did the heavy lifting, but at least he could give her a break.

Rod looked around the table. He recognized three of the students from this afternoon's class; he'd seen the other two in Professor Rhoades' Special Topics seminar, and assumed that they were all working on a similar problem set. Everyone was a first semester graduate student in Aeronautical Engineering, but no one had spoken in the last hour.

That was another reason for studying in the small engineering library annex, instead of the much larger library complex—there was almost no chance that Barbara Richardson would be here.

He turned back to his papers. He knew the purpose of these homework sets was to not only make graduate students apply what they'd learned, but to force them to use creative leaps in solving real-world problems.

Professor Rhoades had said the world wasn't just a series of homework exercises where you simply guessed at multiple choice answers; rather it was a complex, frothy, and ever changing exercise in intuitively connecting-the-dots, sometimes using unassociated, disparate information. And just as attending class brought new insight into solving problems, Rod remembered his most useful learning experiences as a cadet had come from participating with a group—with his squadron, or with his classmates in a focused study session.

He was tired of slogging it out alone, and with two months into graduate school, it was time to make a change. Civilian university or not, there was a better way to study and it was time to see who would join him.

Rod looked around the table and cleared his throat. "Excuse me. I assume you're all working on Dr. Ahluwalia's problem set in Methods of Theoretical Aeronautics?"

Most of the graduate students put down their papers; one ignored him, and another arched her brow. "So?"

"Since we're all working the same problem, why don't we solve it as a group? Use our collective knowledge to gain more insight into both what Dr. Ahluwalia is looking for, as well as the physical principles he wants us to learn."

"You mean solve the problem as a team."

"Right."

The female graduate student shrugged. "Sure. Seems okay to me."

"Yeah," another said. "Anything to help."

"It's called homework for a reason," said the lone student, still bent over his papers. "You do homework on your own."

Rod frowned. "You've never participated in a study group?"

The graduate student didn't look up. "Why should I? I've always been the brightest in school. I've never needed anyone's help. These problems are a piece of cake."

The female said softly, "Then why have you been here tonight as long as the rest of us?"

The loner looked up and glared, then returned to his problem set.

Rod gathered his papers and stood. "There's a small conference room next door with a blackboard. Why don't we use it to brainstorm?"

"Right." The others pushed back their chairs and gathered their material.

As they left, Rod stopped by the lone holdout. "You're welcome to join us."

The graduate student didn't reply.

Rod shrugged. "Just come on in if you change your mind."

Rod followed the other four students out of the engineering library and across the hall. They left the conference room door open as they started their discussion, in the chance that their fellow student might want to join them.

O   O   O

Two hours later, Rod and his classmates finished copying the train of equations they'd transcribed on the conference room's four blackboards. Rod felt that their discussions had given him more insight than he ever would have ever obtained by working alone. In addition, they finished in record time, allowing them to concentrate on their other classes; they made plans to meet after Thursday's class to start working on the next set.

The last one out, Rod closed the conference room door; a voice startled him.

"Lieutenant Simone?"

He turned. Professor Rhoades leaned against a doorframe, pipe smoke curled around him.

"Hello, Dr. Rhoades," Rod said.

"I heard your plea to form your study group."

Rod shifted his books from his left hand to his right. "We didn't bother you, did we?"

"No, no. My office is across the hall and I couldn't help but overhearing." He straightened and stepped toward Rod. "And I peeked in to watch your group's progress. Nice work, Lieutenant. I can see the Academy succeeded in its leadership training. Every time I try to persuade faculty members or students that study groups work, it's like trying to convince a herd of cats to all move in one direction."

"It didn't take much to convince the graduate students, sir. After two months alone of hitting my head against the wall, study groups make a lot more sense."

"Still, you managed to persuade your classmates; most of them, anyway. And from the way I observed you leading the group, I think you have a future in education. You're one of the standouts in my class."

He tapped his pipe and drew in smoke. "Why don't you stay at Stanford and complete your course work for a PhD. All you'd have left to do would be to conduct your research for your dissertation, and you could return to the Academy as an assistant professor. From what I've seen in my seminar, you have a natural talent for academics as well as leadership."

Rod straightened. He felt somewhat flustered at the praise, but he knew what he wanted in the short term. And it wasn't returning to the Academy, at least not soon—although someday it might be fun to go back and teach. "Thank you, sir, but I really do want to fly. I've wanted to all my life, and if I do well in pilot training, I'll have a good chance of getting fighters. It's been my dream as long as I can remember."

Rhoades smiled. "Ah, yes. Fighters. The future of the Air Force. Well, consider what I've offered, and even if you decide not to pursue a PhD, think about going back to the Academy to teach after your flying assignment. I think you'd enjoy it."

Rod lifted an eyebrow. "Yes, sir. I'll consider it." He'd never really thought about going back to teach, but now that Rhoades had mentioned it, he realized he *did* have a lot invested in the place. He couldn't say he'd always enjoyed being a cadet, but the incredible opportunities he'd been given, from flying to navigator training while living under the honor code, made him prepared for attending flight school.

Rhoades turned to leave, then almost as an afterthought, stopped. "Lieutenant, something's been nagging at me."

"Sir?"

"I'm sure we've met before. I don't know if you remember, but eight years ago I was completing my sabbatical at Cranwell when I attended the Farnborough Airshow, the one with that unfortunate disaster. You look very familiar, and I'm positive you're the young man who helped in the initial rescue."

Rod felt his face grow warm. The memory of the burning jet tumbling through the crowd of on-lookers was still seared in his memory. "Yes, sir. I was there. Hank McCluney was my father, and brought my mother and me to the airshow."

"General McCluney's your *father?*"

"Yes, sir—my adoptive father. He rescued me after he was shot down over Cahors."

Rhoades nodded. "So ... that explains your French accent. And yes, I do remember meeting you. You're a lucky man, Lieutenant. It's unusual for someone so young to experience Farnborough."

"I don't remember too much about anyone there because of the ... accident." He shook his head. "Sorry, sir. About the only one I distinctly remember was Lieutenant Whitney, who led the rescue." *And only because at the time I was impressed with his self-assurance, and not with the man he turned out to be.*

"Of course," Rhoades mused, "Field Marshal Whitney. Now *that* is a man who's a legend in his own mind. He was nearly as bad as that reprobate land developer who kept telling your father where to build the Academy."

Rod opened his mouth to disagree when he realized that Dr. Rhoades had put Whitney in his place, while simultaneously dismissing Whitney's inflated opinion of himself. *Well played, professor.*

But who was this so-called reprobate?

Rod frowned. "Yes, sir—but I'm afraid I don't know who else you're talking about."

Rhoades cocked his head. "George Delante. I'm surprised General McCluney never mentioned him. That man pestered your father throughout every phase of the Academy study."

Rod felt his face grow red. "He ... he had mentioned Mr. Delante, sir. They weren't exactly on the best of terms." Which was putting it lightly. His father couldn't stand the man, as Delante had tried everything from blackmail to extortion to force his father to build the Academy at an ill-suited site in south Colorado Springs. He was so slimy it wouldn't surprise him if Delante had even had a hand in his father's death....

Rod drew in a breath.

Now where had that come from? He hadn't seen Delante since graduation, when he'd spotted George and his son, Fred, with Captain Whitney in the stands.

But could Delante have been involved in father's crash? That would explain a lot—

He abruptly changed the subject; he didn't want to get into that whole mess with Dr. Rhoades. "Well anyway, thank you for supporting our study group, sir."

"Anything to help our best and brightest." Rhoades motioned him to leave. "Now you'd better get home. I assume your wife is waiting for you, Lieutenant, so this study group should free up time for you to return to her good graces. Heaven knows you'll have even less time to spend with your family once you get to pilot training. And, oh yes, please, give my regards to General McCluney."

"Yes, sir." Rod hesitated. "But he ... died in a plane crash this past spring."

Rhoades' face fell. "I'm sorry to hear that. I enjoyed working with him; we go back a long way. In 1948 we attended the first meetings at Air University to establish an air academy...." He grew quiet.

"The general who's heading up the Flight Accident Board was a good friend of dad's. He'll find the underlying cause of the crash." *And would that path lead to George Delante?*

"Good. Now if there's anything I can do, I'd be happy to help. Just put your mind to completing this year, young man. With your background and this degree, you have a world of opportunity ahead of you.

"But don't forget going back to the Air Force Academy—they gave you a world-class education, and hopefully produced the best officer they could, all on taxpayer expense. After flying, you owe it both to the Academy and the nation to return the favor, and pay it forward."

"Yes, sir. And thank you, that's good advice." Rod turned and walked down the long, empty hallway for home. Another seven months and he'd be through with this latest phase of his life.

He hadn't thought about his father for a few weeks now, and George Delante even longer. He hoped it wouldn't distract him from his studies, because Professor Rhoades was right, he did have a lot of opportunity—but right now there was something he wanted more than anything else in the world, and it wasn't teaching cadets: it was flying fighters.

CHAPTER THREE

"Good Timin'"

Nine months later
July 1st, 1960

Williams Air Force Base, AZ

We stand today on the edge of a new frontier.

John Fitzgerald Kennedy

It was *déjà vu*, all over again.

Just as he'd rushed from last year's Academy graduation to make Stanford's start of classes, after Stanford's June 23rd commencement he moved his young family to the southwestern town of Chandler, Arizona to meet his pilot training report date.

But the difference in last year's 20 days between graduating from the Academy and starting Stanford, was that he'd gotten married, Nanette had been born, and they'd moved from Colorado to the Bay area.

This year he felt as though they had an infinite amount of time to make the 20-day move.

And for himself, his greatest accomplishment was not in completing his Masters in Aeronautical Engineering, but successfully avoiding Barbara.

The Sonoran desert stretched out all around, punctuated by brown, rocky mountains. Dust swirled over the car as Rod drove his '59 station wagon up to the Williams Air Force Base gate. The outpost was situated miles from any sign of human presence.

A lone wooden guard shack sat next to the gate. Yucca and saguaro cacti dotted the bare landscape, and the flight-training base looked uninviting and bleak after living near the bustling San Francisco bay.

He pulled to a stop as he approached the guard shack. An air policeman wearing a tan uniform, pith helmet, a side arm, and a white armband with the letters *AP*, stepped out and bent his head to speak through the window. "May I help you?"

Startled by the loud voice, Nanette woke from her nap and started crying. She lay on the front seat on a pink blanket between Julie and Rod. Julie picked her up and frowned at the young airman.

Rod reached into the glove box and pulled out an ID and a sheaf of papers. "Good afternoon. I'm Second Lieutenant Simone, reporting for pilot training."

The guard studied the papers and seemed to straighten his posture as he read; he handed them back. "Welcome, Lieutenant," he raised his voice over Nanette's cries and pointed to a cluster of low brown buildings in the distance, barely visible on the shimmering horizon. "The 3525th Pilot Training Wing headquarters is about two miles straight ahead, on your left next to the flight line. Sign in there, then continue on this road to the housing area. During in-processing you'll be assigned base housing with the rest of your pilot training class, so there's no need to go to the housing office." He drew to attention and held a salute. "Welcome to Williams, sir."

Rod was taken back for a moment before he returned the honorific. It had been a year since he'd last saluted, and he knew he'd have to quickly transition from the relatively casual pace of civilian life he'd been living the last year while at Stanford. "Thank you, airman. Carry on."

He drove slowly from the gate as Nanette continued to wail. He felt a touch of pride at receiving the salute and being called "sir"; he'd just about forgotten the ever-present decorum found on a military base.

Julie rocked Nanette and spoke up over the din. "You'd think he'd try to be a little more quiet. Couldn't he see she was sleeping?"

Rod threw her a smile before turning back to look for the Wing headquarters. He couldn't see her expression through the sunglasses and white scarf she wore over her head, but her tone was unmistakably curt.

"Give him a break," he said. "The air policeman looked like he was just out of high school. And if he's guarding access to the base, the last thing on his mind is disturbing a napping toddler." He reached over and patted Julie's hand.

She stuck out her tongue and then grinned before turning her attention back to Nanette. Things had really turned around since Nanette had outgrown her colic and had become a toddler—although that had opened a whole new set of concerns, ranging from her playing with electrical outlets to finding her on top of the kitchen counter.

Minutes later he turned into the Wing headquarters parking lot. He spotted an empty space near the main door and pulled to a stop. "It may take a while to in-process if you want to take her for a walk."

She looked around. "Good idea. I'll find some shade. Just don't be too long; this heat is incredible, and no telling what Nanette will get into."

"Right." He gathered up his orders and ID from the glove box and walked quickly into the headquarters building.

A grey metal table was set up just inside the door, manned by young airmen and a brown-haired woman with streaks of white in her hair. Three other officers about his age were at the table, and Rod was motioned forward and told to start filling out paperwork.

Twenty minutes later he stepped out of the building and held a hand over his eyes to shade the glare. Sunlight reflected off concrete and brown stucco buildings; heat shimmered up from the black asphalt parking lot. He spotted Julie leading Nanette by the hand as they walked around in a small circle under an overhang at the end of the building.

He stepped up and helped them back into the car, then started driving further into the base, keeping his eyes open for the junior officer housing area. On the way they passed old, concrete buildings that looked as though they had been constructed out of cinder blocks during World War II. Every few hundred yards dusty signs pointed out the commissary, Base Exchange, base chapel, hospital, personnel services, maintenance, Wing and Squadron logistics, and airmen dormitories. Without exception the facilities were painted a mute brown, as if the Air Force was attempting to blend in the buildings with the ever-present desert and dirt.

Up ahead in the distance he spotted a sign on the right that pointed to FAMILY HOUSING. Reaching the narrow road, he turned onto the arrow-straight avenue.

They drove several hundred yards and a collection of dusty buildings came into view, materializing from a wavering mirage. He slowed and drew to a stop. In front of them he saw row after row of squat, one-bedroom, single-story coffee-colored houses lining the street. It looked as though an east coast slum project had been plopped down in the middle of the desert, without any of the trees, bushes, ponds, or foliage that might have existed in a more humid environment.

A lone tumbleweed blew across the road; heat rose up from the asphalt. Rod had an uneasy feeling that all the housing area needed was a garish SALOON sign to make it look as though they lived in an old west town instead of on the most technologically advanced air-training base in the world.

"Oh, my," Julie breathed. "Everything's so ... brown."

"They must have had a million gallons of this paint left over from World War II," Rod said. "Why else would they paint everything the same color?"

Rod drove forward; they drank in the sight in silence. Even the cactus looked dirty with the ever-present dust.

"And I thought Stanford married student housing was cramped," Julie said.

Rod nodded to a small playground at the end of the street, sitting in the middle of a dustbowl. At the center of the playground stood a metal swing set with three chain-link swings and leather seats, next to a metal slide that reflected intense sunlight. A dozen barefoot children, all covered in dirt, were on the swings, sliding down the slide, or running across the bare ground playing tag.

A row of women in folding chairs sat next to the playground's perimeter, young moms dressed in shorts and loose fitting blouses. Half the women held umbrellas to keep the sun off their head, the others wore white scarfs wrapped around their heads; all wore sunglasses and most of them were smoking cigarettes; a few held babies on their laps.

"This must be the social center," Rod said. "Do you want me to drop you and Nanette off while I unpack?"

"Fat chance," Julie said. "I barely got to see you at the Academy, and not much more at Stanford."

"Hey, I had less than a year to complete a Master's!"

She lifted Julie to her side and patted his knee. "And this year will be even worse. I'll have plenty of time to spend with the neighborhood wives. Let's get unloaded and put Nanette down for a nap."

Rod started the station wagon back up and turned down the row of identical houses. "I didn't know you were in a hurry to get the house in shape."

"I'm not," Julie said. She rubbed her hand along his leg. "I'm anxious to get you alone before you start flying."

O O O

The next day Rod sat in the flight physical and tried to control his heart from racing. *This couldn't be happening!* His mouth felt dry and cottony; it was difficult to breath.

He squinted at the eye chart, but he couldn't make out the details of line 9A.

"Don't squint," the doctor said.

"Yes, sir." Although he was in an air-conditioned clinic he felt as though he was burning up. If he failed the eye exam, he wouldn't be given a second chance and he'd be kicked out of pilot training before it even started.

He squinted again.

"I *said* don't squint, Lieutenant. Just read the last line."

"Yes, sir."

Rod stared at the eye chart and cursed himself for not having more light available during his graduate school studies. He hadn't had that trouble at the Academy; there'd always been plenty of light, from the desk lamp in his room to the fluorescent lights in the library. But in the cramped student housing at Stanford, after he returned from the library he'd tried to keep the lights low to avoid waking Nanette. If he'd only used more light he wouldn't be having this trouble now—

But wait, it wasn't fair to blame Nanette. He couldn't blame others for the choices he'd made. If he didn't put a stop to it now, then no telling who he'd blame if he screwed up and flunked out of pilot training. Now that he was here, succeeding in pilot training was up to him and no one else.

He straightened in the optometrist's chair.

"Read the letters on the bottom line," the doctor said. "We don't have all day."

"Yes, sir." He stared at the chart and tried not to squint.

The doctor tapped a pencil on the counter; it sounded as if he were attempting to telegraph his growing impatience via Morse code. The tapping continued. "Go ahead, lieutenant. I'm *waiting*."

Someone loudly laughed in the other room as something banged against the door; the optometrist turned at the noise. A slew of young officers were just outside the examination room, waiting to take the eye test after Rod.

As the doctor looked away, Rod saw his chance and squinted.

There, that was better. He started to make out the bottom line, and before it slipped out of focus he blurted out, "P Q H N V T."

"Correct." The doctor scribbled in Rod's medical records, swung his chair around, and called for the next lieutenant in line, all in one fluid motion. "Next!"

Rod grabbed his records and hurried from the room before the optometrist had a chance to change his mind.

The rest of the medical exam flew by, a piece of cake compared to the dreaded eye test. From turning his head to cough for a hernia check, to dropping his trousers and bending over the examination table, Rod detached himself from the mechanics of ensuring he was physically fit and instead mentally prepared for immersing himself in flight training.

O   O   O

Two and a half months later

Rod tried to focus and concentrate as hard as he could in case there was an upcoming emergency. Sitting behind him, his most cynical critic watched his every move and was prepared to berate him if he didn't get everything right—not to mention what would happen if he failed to successfully recover from the emergency. He wasn't sure what emergency he'd encounter, but he knew he had to perform flawlessly if he wanted to survive.

He sat upright in his seat and moved his hands and feet to keep the aircraft steady on final approach as he was preparing to land—

A sudden scream came from behind him. "Spin! Spin!"

"Spin recovery," Rod said in a clipped voice; he reacted as a machine. "Close throttle." He reached down and coordinated his movements as he recited the "Bold Face" emergency procedures from memory. "Clean up aircraft; ailerons neutral; retract flaps; retracting landing gear …"

"What are you doing? What are you waiting for?"

"Waiting for landing gear to retract to maintain hydraulic pressure … and retract speed brakes," Rod said without emotion. "Check turn indicator. Visually check direction of roll against turn indicator indication." He glanced up, and then back down. "Direction is the same; moving full opposite rudder to turn indicator; move control column forward until the spinning stops."

"The spinning has stopped! What now?"

"Centralize rudders," Rod said. "Easing out of dive, deploying speed brakes and taking it in for landing." He held up his hands. "Mission complete."

Julie grabbed him from behind and wrapped her arms around his neck while still holding a thick flight manual. She squeezed and almost made him topple from the metal folding chair. "You did it! Chair-flying an entire T-37 sortie from memory with three in-flight emergencies—without ever leaving the kitchen!"

Nanette laughed shrilly from her high-chair, probably mystified as to why her father had been play-acting by pushing on imaginary buttons, moving unseen control sticks, pushing against hidden rudders.

Rod sat directly in front of her; he leaned over and tousled her wispy hair.

She banged a spoon and giggled, unsure why Rod and Julie were so animated, but obviously enjoying the moment and her parents' excitement.

Rod stood and pulled Julie close. He whirled her around the small kitchen, missing the square folding-table, the wooden cabinets, the white O'Keefe and Merritt gas stove, and the bottle of vodka and orange juice sitting on the counter. "That's it! I'm ready for tomorrow's flight."

"Does that mean you won't need me for chair-flying anymore?"

"Nope." He bent her backwards and gave her a long kiss. "I'll have to chair-fly more often—with an IP on board, he'll be looking over my shoulder to catch any mistakes. Later, when I'm flying solo, if I screw up I may not recover. Especially when I transition to the T-33. And that's a real fighter." He pulled her upright. "But now, I'm ready for anything—even your mother."

"Then it's time to celebrate, Lightning," she said, using his call sign. She kissed him and turned to pick up her vodka screwdriver. "This will be the last time we'll be alone for a week."

Rod motioned with his head to Nanette. "What are you talking about? We haven't been alone for over a year."

Julie punched him in the shoulder and drained her drink. "She doesn't count. But mother goes crazy if she hears a pin drop—so what do you think she'll do if she hears me start moaning?"

CHAPTER FOUR

"Only the Lonely"

September 16th, 1960

Williams Air Force Base, AZ

Vice is its own reward.

Quentin Crisp, *The Naked Civil Servant*

Julie barely woke at the touch. Her head pounded and her eyes were closed with the remnants of a hangover, but she could feel his breath by her ear.

"I'll be home by two," Rod said.

"'Bye," she mumbled.

He kissed her cheek and padded lightly from the room.

She pulled up the blanket and rolled over. She looked blearily across the bed; the alarm clock's luminous hands read 3:45 AM. Good. She had another three hours until Nanette woke.

And then the fun would start.

Hopefully the headache would go away. Her mother was due in later this afternoon, but at least her father wasn't coming—he'd have gone through the roof if he discovered he'd have to sleep on their tiny, concrete living room floor. Their couch was much too small for him, and with the nearest motel over 20 miles away in

Mesa, Daddy would have turned around and headed straight back for Washington, DC.

As she closed her eyes, she thought that it hadn't taken Rod long to dissociate from family life after leaving Stanford. On early days he woke at 3:30 AM and guzzled coffee so he could roll into the training squadron for classes that started at 4 AM. He was home by 2 PM, but with studying for pop quizzes and tests, and memorizing checklists for upcoming flights, he was always exhausted—which meant that pilot training was like graduate school hyped up on caffeine.

What made it worse was that he was expected to participate in mandatory sports ranging from touch football to basketball to softball; attend myriad mandatory social events; and be at Happy Hour every Friday afternoon at the Officers' Club bar. All the officers stayed and no one left the club before Beast, their squadron commander, which meant Rod also lost his Friday nights; returning back home from the club at 2 AM resulted in him losing Saturday mornings as well.

Then there were the Dining Ins, those formal dinners that resulted in more evenings away from home; the formations on the flight line when general officers would fly onto the base; the parades … each item gnawed away at the time when he should be a husband and father.

As she drifted back to sleep, she thought at least she could attend the receptions at the various commanders' houses with him.…

O O O

Julie crossed her legs as she sat on the wooden bench in front of the metal carousel, watching Nanette and a dozen other toddlers, along with the rest of the young pilot wives in the neighborhood. She wore a pair of Jackie Kennedy sunglasses she'd bought from Sears, a wide-collar blue blouse, white shorts, and tan, leather thongs—the newest style she could find in open-toe sandals at Montgomery Wards.

Dressed in a sailor hat, diaper, and slathered with Sea & Ski suntan lotion, Nanette walked unsteadily around the carousel while holding on to the side. The other toddlers alternated between trying to climb onto the circular equipment to playing in the hot sand.

Julie shifted her weight on the towel she'd placed on the bench to keep peeling paint off her shorts as well as to insulate herself against the incredibly hot seat; it was still a few hours before noon, but the Arizona sun was harsh, even in September.

She poured herself another drink from her thermos, remnants of last night's pitcher of screwdrivers. Rod had had to fly, so she'd ended up drinking alone; she figured it would be a waste to throw the mixture away, and besides, it helped the day go by a little faster and a hell of a lot pleasanter, especially with her mother arriving later this afternoon.

A low buzz of excitement rocketed around the playground as the squadron commander's wife pulled up in her red Ford Galaxie. LizAnn's sleek, red muscle car gleamed from a fresh coat of polish, contrasting with the rundown, secondhand cars the lower-ranking student pilots owned.

Although there was a deep chasm in rank and salary between the second lieutenant students and their lieutenant colonel commander, LizAnn was down-to-earth, bubbly, and took the student pilots' wives under her wing. She treated the younger women more as sisters and girlfriends, as opposed to the strict, military courtesies that Beast demanded from their husbands.

And in contrast to the drab, spartan construction of the students' homes, LizAnn ran a vivacious support structure, and the student pilots' wives quickly bonded. As such, the wives congregated at the dirt playground, and under LizAnn's tutelage, established a rotating system of babysitting so they could participate in activities ranging from teas and brunches, to fieldtrips and hikes.

LizAnn stepped out of the car and waved. "Hi, y'all!"

"Howdy, darlin'!" the wives whooped and started to gather round their leader.

Julie gulped her drink and stood. She felt momentarily dizzy.

She held out a hand to steady herself; she must have had a lot more than she'd thought. Now that LizAnn was here, it looked like today's activities were about to take off, which meant she'd better lay off the rest of the screwdrivers. At least until lunch. More and more that seemed the only way she could put up with this hellhole.

o o o

Later that afternoon, Julie sat on the porch of their brown stucco home, waiting for her mother to arrive. Although the sun had moved just far enough so that half the porch was in the shade, the temperature still flirted with 90 degrees. At least the wait was bearable with the lack of humidity in the bone-dry, barren desert. And now that the buzz from her screwdrivers had faded, she'd mixed a concoction of cheap red wine, lemons, oranges, limes, and strawberries to cool in the refrigerator for sangrias.

The neighborhood was unusually quiet. The wives' gathering at the playground had dispersed into various homes to work on crafts, knitting lessons, and planning for the upcoming Octoberfest, while a few of the women had driven out to the museum in Phoenix. It seemed somewhat strange not to have any older children running around, but since the student pilots and their wives' ages were all within a few years of each other, the junior officer housing area was extremely homogeneous— newlyweds and a lot of babies and toddlers; all the older kids kept to the senior officer's housing area.

Nanette played in the corner, content to crash toy airplanes into each other, as she grabbed handfuls of Cheerios from a blue plastic bowl. She was always quiet after her afternoon nap, and it gave Julie time to catch up on reading *Life*, *Look*, and the *Saturday Evening Post* while Rod studied inside at the kitchen table. It was one of the few days that he didn't have intramurals or any of the other, myriad duties expected of student pilots, so by studying early, he'd be able to spend time with mother along with she and Nanette.

The telephone rang two short rings and one long ring; it was their house code for the ten-home party line. Rod's muffled voice came from inside. "I've got it."

A moment passed and the screen door opened; Rod stuck out his head. "That was the main gate. The Air Police are directing your mother's taxi to the housing area. She should be here in about five minutes."

Julie took a long, final drag on her cigarette and flicked the butt into the dirt. "Thanks." She stood and walked over to Nanette, sweeping her up; she held her upside down as Nanette shrieked with laughter.

Julie let her down in the yard and grabbed onto her tiny hand. "Let's go meet Grandma." They started walking toward the driveway, taking a circuitous route across the small patch of brown grass that lay on either side of the sidewalk. The student pilots tried to keep up the yard, but it seemed that no matter how much water they sprayed on the lawn, it turned brown almost as soon as they turned off the sprinkler.

The screen door slammed and Rod joined them in the yard. He wore his green flight suit, unzipped to his chest; his t-shirt was stained with perspiration from being on the flight line earlier in the day.

Julie spotted the yellow taxi a few hundred yards up the road as it slowed and turned into the entrance of the housing area; it crawled toward them, as though the driver was not quite sure where he was going.

"Remember the first time we saw this place?" Rod said. "I didn't think you'd ever get out of the car."

"Mother may not." Julie imagined the shock her mother must be having at seeing the dreary, brown houses and dusty playground for the very first time.

"At least the temperature is 20 degrees cooler than it was in the summer."

"It's still warmer than Virginia. I just hope mother isn't having an anxiety attack." She picked up Nanette and started to wave. "Say, 'hi, Grandma'!"

The taxi pulled up and a white shirted man wearing black pants, a black tie, and a cap jumped out of the car. He opened the back door and Julie's mother stepped onto the concrete driveway.

Wearing a pink pillbox hat, with matching jacket, skirt, white gloves, and high heels, Francine Phillips looked as though she had just walked off the pages of one of Julie's magazines. She drew in a breath as she looked around the neighborhood, her eyes wide as she took everything in. No one spoke.

Julie felt her stomach grow sour. "*Hello*, Mother. How was your flight?" She'd practically ignored her granddaughter.

Francine pulled back. "Julie! Why yes, dear, it's so nice to see you. The flight was fine, but long." A smile swept across her face as she seemed to notice Nanette for the first time. "And who is this little one? My, my, you've grown so much." She leaned toward Nanette and held out her hands.

Nanette clutched Julie's arms and wouldn't let go. Her lip quivered and tears welled up in her eyes.

"She wasn't quite a year old when you last saw her in California," Julie said. "Here." She picked Nanette up and held her out. "Go to Grandma, sweetheart. Grandma wants to hold you."

Nanette started wailing and buried her head in Julie's shoulder, terrified.

Julie tried to soothe her when she noticed the taxi driver standing by the car door with his hands behind his back; Francine's luggage was piled on the porch. She looked at Rod and nodded toward the driver.

"Oh, yeah." Rod took out his wallet and stepped forward.

Francine put out a hand. "Here, I've got it, Rod." She pulled a handful of bills from her purse and gave them to Rod. She turned back to Julie. "Let's get out of this horrid sun." She took Julie by the arm and led her and Nanette to the house.

Once inside, Julie put Nanette on the floor as Rod carried the luggage to the family room. Francine slowly took off her white gloves and without a word looked around the tiny living space.

Julie had draped the cinderblock walls with scarfs and pictures in an attempt to spruce up the featureless room, but the combination of poor lighting and bare concrete made the family room seem cramped and uninviting.

"This is much different than Stanford married housing," Francine said.

"The military doesn't believe in extravagance," Rod said. "Especially since we'll be here less than a year. The senior officer homes are much bigger. And nicer."

"I'm sure they are." Francine said, sounding unconvinced.

Julie raised her brows at Rod. "There's sangria in the refrigerator. Why don't you pour some, it will cool things down." *In more ways than one.*

Rod grunted and left the room.

Francine turned to Julie. "And how do you like it here, dear? How are you faring? This all looks a little … primitive."

Julie felt her breath quicken; she didn't answer. She patted the top of Nanette's head.

Nanette loosened her grip on Julie's leg, and with big eyes intently watched Francine, as if trying to decide if she could trust the strange, older woman. Sounds of ice trays being emptied, glasses clanging together, and water running came from the kitchen.

Francine said, "It looks as though you're living in a housing project."

"It's *fine*," Julie said. "Like Rod said, we'll be here less than a year, and with any luck we'll be assigned to southern California, perhaps near L.A."

"I see." She bent over and frowned at something on the floor. "What do you do with your time? Are there any cultural activities?" She straightened while continuing to look around the room.

Julie felt her face grow warm; she wasn't about to let her mother know how much she hated this place. "Some, but I keep busy chasing Nanette around. The squadron commander's wife organizes things for us, and we take turns watching the kids. We hardly see our husbands, even at night, because of everything from night flights to mandatory formations, so the wives are left to our own activities"

"Such as …?"

Julie bent over and encouraged Nanette to walk to her mom. Nanette took a few tentative steps and stopped to stare up at her grandmother; Francine squatted and smiled.

"Well," Julie said, "we've toured some historic sites in Chandler and Mesa, as well as the new museum in Phoenix."

Francine looked sharply up. "That's hardly very cultural, dear, visiting dusty, Western galleries—especially compared to what DC has to offer."

"I *know*, but like I said, we'll be moving next June." *And back to civilization.*

Nanette tottered to Francine, and then with a happy squeal, suddenly lunged out.

Francine laughed; she pulled Nannette in, and hugging her, stood. She cooed while gently kissing the top of Nanette's head. "That still means living in this god-forsaken place for at least another six or seven months. It's a good thing Edward didn't come on this trip; otherwise, he'd have you and Nanette out on the next plane."

She hesitated for a long moment. "Why don't you bring Nanette back east? We'd love to have you, and it would allow Rod to finish this pilot training without the pressure of having to juggle family responsibilities. Time will pass quickly."

Julie tried to keep her voice from shaking. "I said I'm doing fine here, mother, and so is Nanette. We're a family now, and I just can't run home at the first sign of adversity."

"This isn't an adversity, dear. This is a hellhole."

Julie clamped her mouth shut as Rod walked in the room carrying a tray of full glasses and the pitcher of sangria; he placed it on the table.

He looked from Julie to Francine as the room fell quiet. "Hey, don't stop on my account. I hope I didn't disturb you with all the noise."

"No, no, we didn't even hear you," Francine said.

Julie grabbed one of the drinks and quickly shot down the sangria.

She wiped her mouth and held the empty glass out to him.

He gave her a strange look; he took his time refilling it. "So … what were you two talking about?" He slowly handed her the drink.

Julie drained half the glass; she felt the alcohol warm her insides as it hit her stomach. "Just catching up. I was telling mother how thankful I am to be an Air Force wife."

Rod's eyes narrowed. He flicked his gaze from Julie to Francine. No one spoke. He shrugged and handed Francine a glass.

Julie lifted her drink. "I propose a toast."

"All right," Francine said. "To what occasion?"

Julie clinked glasses with her mother and Rod. "To the next step on my husband's path to general, where we'll *both* reach the top of the social pyramid."

Francine ignored her and squatted to smile at Nanette.

Rod stared.

Julie gulped the rest of her drink. Once again, Julie held out the empty glass—this time with an unsteady hand. "Hit me again, Lightning Rod."

CHAPTER FIVE

"I Fall to Pieces"

Six months later
March, 1961

Williams Air Force Base, AZ

We triumph without glory when we conquer without danger.

Pierre Corneille, *Le Cid*, II:2

Rod woke early the day before he soloed. He was eager to complete his last check-ride with an instructor so he could fly the T-33 alone, and finally "kick the tires and light the fires" to blast off into the wide, open sky without anyone else in the aircraft. He'd transitioned from the T-37 primary phase to the advanced phase, flying the single-engine T-33—a two-seat version of the USAF's first fighter, the F-80—and was anxious to fulfill his life-long dream.

He knew the F-80 wasn't one of the Air Force's first line fighters, and the T-33 was seeing it's final days as a training aircraft—at least in the U.S. But he also knew that this was the first step to him moving up to the F-100, or someday even to the new F-105 supersonic fighter that was just entering the inventory.

More importantly, the solo would be the first time he'd really be able to push the T-33 without an instructor pilot looking over his shoulder.

He pulled the station wagon into the deserted squadron parking lot long before the sun had risen. He was the first one there and he savored the privacy. The mountains were tinged with a pink outline and there were no clouds in the morning sky. Venus and Mars were all right tonight, hanging over the horizon, gleaming steadily and revealing no sign of atmospheric turbulence.

It looked like ideal flying conditions. With any luck, within a few hours he'd be back on the ground to wrap up his paperwork and would start prepping for his next major milestone since mastering the T-37: soloing in the T-33.

All he had to do was to complete his final check-ride; a piece of cake.

He grabbed his green flight bag from the front seat, slammed the car door, and headed into the white-painted, single-story building. He was the first one in squadron operations.

The flight scheduler's desk was elevated on a dark-paneled platform, guarding the entrance to the building. An arch over the desk was inscribed with the words "Hat in the Ring" and overlaid a mural of two T-33s jetting into a deep, blue sky. To the left, the glass door leading to the squadron snack bar was locked; to the right, a bulletin board was hung on the dark-paneled hallway that led to the Operations Center and Ready Room. Black and white photos of previous squadron training classes adorned the wall. On the opposite wall, facing the photos, were paintings of old trainer planes, going back to the bi-planes flown in World War I. A lot of history in here.

He padded for the back and sat at a table in the center of the Ready Room. He stifled a yawn, then spread out the Dash One, stiff yellow paper checklists, equipment logs, maintenance logs, and a host of other papers, manuals, texts, and documents as he prepared one final time, and focused, pushing everything else out of his mind and studied for the flight, changing his mindset from *thinking* to *reacting*.

For his Master's degree he'd pondered innumerable possibilities. The creativity he'd fostered at Stanford was in stark contrast to the rigid checklists he had to memorize for flying a high-performance jet. For if his plane tumbled out of control, he would only have a fraction of a second to respond, to perfectly follow a set of procedures—without making a mistake ... or he would die.

There was no time for him to intellectually dissect the awesome aerodynamic aberrations that might occur in a stall or in an out-of-control spin. He had to learn an entirely different mindset—one of instantly reacting and not thinking.

For all he'd been through, the intellectual, ever-questioning atmosphere at Stanford didn't prepare him for the by-the-book, no-deviation-checklist mentality demanded in pilot training.

So he was forced not to ponder, and instead to immediately respond by using the control stick and foot pedals; it was as though his muscles had to recognize the threat and function by themselves.

The mantra was "disengage brain, eyeball-to-stick."

It was an unsettling difference, but it was a metamorphosis he had to embrace.

He'd memorized the Dash One, the T-33's operating manual, to learn how to counter an uncontrolled spin, turbulent buffeting, or a loss of altitude. They all required specific actions performed in a precise sequence, and they all had to be practiced until he memorized them perfectly.

And today's check ride would be the final test before he soloed.

With the absolute adherence to rules, he'd come to learn why his adoptive father had always been such a black and white guy, no room for mistakes, with an unwavering view of the difference between right and wrong ... and he wished he'd realized that before Hank had passed away....

O   O   O

"Simone ... Frenchy!"

Rod's head jerked up. "Yeah."

His vision was blurred as a green flight suit swam into focus. The Ready Room was no longer vacant and was packed with fellow students.

The squadron scheduler stood in front of him, hands on his hips. "What the hell are you doing? You're first in line and you're late for your check-ride briefing. Get your butt to the briefing room!"

Rod struggled to his feet. "Yes, sir!" He grabbed his flight bag, scattering his papers in his wake; he shoved his material into his bag. Students flattened across the table to prevent their own papers from flying off the table as he stumbled to the door.

The scheduler called after him, "Room 101, Simone. You're tail number Zero Two. And don't forget to sign out the bird!"

Rod rushed into the hallway. He turned right and spotted 101 painted above an awning down the hall. The door was open. He sprinted into the briefing room ... and pulled up as he saw a portly man in a flight suit sitting behind a grey metal desk.

Rod frowned. It wasn't his flight instructor, First Lieutenant Oliver; this officer didn't look familiar. He wore two silver bars of a captain and was so large he could have used his stomach as a desk. He hadn't seen the captain around the building, so he was probably from another squadron. This must be the check pilot.

The officer didn't look up as he tapped a pencil on a green and white topographical map of the Chandler area.

Rod stopped a respectful distance from the captain, put down his flight bag, and saluted. "Good morning, sir. Lieutenant Simone reporting for check-ride."

The officer didn't look up and kept studying the map. "You're late, Lieutenant. Not a good first impression for the last check before you solo."

Rod couldn't read the officer's expression. Rod felt his face grow warm. For some reason, the ten-by-fifteen foot, wood-paneled briefing room felt stifling even with the air-conditioning on full blast. "Sorry, sir. I ... couldn't sleep last night and came in early. I guess my lack of sleep caught up with me." *That sounded lame*—but it was the truth.

"Settle down, Lieutenant. If you're this worked up over your last check, you'll be a mess when you solo."

"Yes, sir."

"And I should know." The captain looked up. "I did the same thing myself." He stuck out a thick hand and grinned. "Don't think we've met. Charlie Banner. I go by Rhino—but don't tell the Ops Officer. You're Devil 8 for the check ride."

"Lightning, sir," Rod said, shaking his hand. "Sorry."

"Forget it," Rhino waved him off. "I was here early myself. Olive Oil called in sick this morning and I told him I'd handle everything," he said, using Lieutenant Oliver's call sign; the senior officers frowned on the use of call signs, but Rod had learned the younger pilots were quietly embracing practice. "Gives me a chance to head out early. Taking the Boy Scouts backpacking up at Lost Dutchman this afternoon, so every minute counts."

"Yes, sir."

"Now pull up a chair and let's go over Motherhood."

Rod grabbed one of the grey metal chairs and for the next 45 minutes they reviewed weather, winds, active runways, frequency assignments, and procedures for mitigation of incapacitation, ejection commands, loss of communication with each other or the ground controllers, and other emergency measures. They then covered the flight profile in detail and laid out the mission maneuvers Rod was expected to execute.

Once Captain Banner was satisfied they took a short bathroom break then met at the ops desk where Rod signed out the trainer. They stepped through life support to suit up for the flight, grabbed their parachute and helmet, and left the training squadron at the back of the building.

The rear exit led directly to the flight line. When Rod opened the door the hot desert air almost slammed him senseless.

Heat rose off the tarmac. The horizon wavered as thermals rose into the air, making the cloudless, blue sky appear as though it were a giant heat sink. To the left, a line of T-33s shimmered in and out of view, a mirage in the dry, overbearing furnace. Rod spotted the number "02" painted prominently on the tail of the jet trainer closest to the building.

Rhino motioned with his helmet. "Lead on, Lightning."

"Roger that." They made a beeline across the hot concrete.

As they approached the T-33 Rod saw thick electrical cords that ran from an Auxiliary Power Unit to the jet. The yellow APU looked like a squat, triangular desk three feet high with the top lopped off. A blue pickup truck was parked next to the APU and an aluminum set of stairs was pushed up to the cockpit.

Two airmen dressed in drab green khakis worked on either side of the trainer. One connected a grounding wire to the jet and another inspected the concrete pad for any loose material that might cause foreign object damage, or FOD.

Captain Banner motioned for Rod to take the lead in inspecting the aircraft. "Never hurts to put a second pair of eyeballs on these birds. I'll follow you around the pre-flight."

"Right."

For the next five minutes the two officers walked around the silver trainer, looking for fluid leaks, ensuring all gaskets were tightened, and making sure that the aircraft was airworthy. At the front of the jet underneath the nose, Rod spotted a black, greasy substance on the pitot tube. He called the crew chief over and had him remove the gunk that had accumulated near the opening; the sergeant wiped it off with his handkerchief.

"Good catch," Rhino said. "About ready?"

"One more thing," Rod said. He squinted down the fuselage, and then reached up and pounded on the access panels to ensure they were all closed. He moved from panel to panel, thumping on metal but jumped back as the last one popped open. "What in the world!" He reached up and pushed the panel shut until the closing mechanism clicked. He turned to see Captain Banner grinning at him.

"Just as I said—good catch, Lightning. I was out here earlier while you were napping and set that up. The last two students didn't discover what I'd done and didn't get off on the right foot."

Rod nodded. "Thanks."

Once complete, they dug their helmets and oxygen masks out of their flight bags and climbed the portable aluminum stairs. Rod waited for Rhino to squeeze into the back cockpit position where the captain would oversee Rod's flying. A few minutes passed until two enlisted men had to help shove the overweight officer into the narrow seat; Rhino told them to use a crowbar if necessary and took the whole event in stride.

Rod eased down into in his seat, strapped in, and started tapping on the cockpit dials. One by one he watched the needles flicker, and once had to tap on the same dial twice. After he'd received the initial report about his father's crash from the Accident Investigation Board, he made it a habit to ensure *his* dials would never stick.

The control stick jutted up in between his legs. He waggled it back and forth. He worked the ailerons and ran a hand on either side of the cockpit, feeling for any loose cables. Finally satisfied that the jet was airworthy, he set the radio frequency and plugged in his headset. A hiss came over his headphones.

Rod adjusted his mike. "Captain Banner? Lightning."

"Lightning, Rhino. It's your aircraft."

"Roger that." Now that he'd been officially given command, he started running through checklist, calling out switch settings, fluid pressures, and electrical voltages. Rhino responded when called, but otherwise remained quiet and allowed Rod to complete the checklist unimpeded.

Rod raised a finger and rotated it around his head, then pointed at the airman standing at parade rest outside of the jet. The airman snapped to. A low sound came from outside the aircraft and dopplered up in volume. Soon, a high-pitched whine shrieked through the air as the engine caught. Black smoke boiled up around them.

Rod switched frequencies and checked in with ground control, using the squadron's sign. "Williams ground. Devil 8 request taxi with information Alpha."

"Devil Eight, taxi runway twelve."

Rod indicated that he understood. "Devil Eight." He switched to their dedicated internal channel. "Ready, sir?"

"You've got the stick."

"Copy."

Rod motioned outside the cockpit and threw several switches. The two airmen servicing the trainer drew to attention and saluted.

He returned the salute and eased forward on the throttle. The engine increased in frequency and the T-33 edged forward, away from the line of jets and the squadron training building.

The sun beat down, causing glint to reflect off distant cars and a row of metal, corrugated Quonset huts next to the flight line. Wind swirled into the cockpit as they rolled forward.

As they approached the end of the runway, Rod clicked his microphone. "Watch your hands, sir."

"Clear."

Rod flipped a switch and the cockpit canopy rotated down. As the canopy clamped shut the sound of the engine subsided. Rod could hear the blood pound in his ears. His hands felt sweaty, but it wasn't just from the heat; he felt the excitement lurking deep inside him, as though it wanted to burst out and reverberate throughout his entire body.

He steadied his breathing as they approached the end of the runway. So far so good for his last check-ride ... for after this was the culmination of everything he'd been studying for since he arrived, to *solo*.

He received final clearance from the tower, and within moments they were racing down the long, asphalt airstrip. Brown desert whizzed past, and he saw buildings sweep by, then the line of T-33s on the tarmac.

The jet bounced as it sped down the runway, and he felt himself being pushed back in the seat as they accelerated. Their velocity crept up and he started to feel the nose rise. He waited until they achieved rotation speed and he pulled back on the stick. They were airborne and started their smooth glide up.

When they were clear of Williams and reached altitude, Rhino ran Rod through a series of dual-only maneuvers of nose-high and nose-low recoveries, spins, power-on and nose-high stalls, and traffic pattern stalls. Rhino threw situations at him that demanded rote attention to detail and insisted Rod repeat back the checklist verbatim.

One by one Rod ran through the routines. He performed like an automaton, precisely moving through the motions. He lost track of time as he reacted ... and in less than an hour his headphones clicked.

Rhino's voice came over the internal comm.

"That's it, Lightning. Return to base. Approach final at five thousand AGL and execute a loop. Congratulations. You're cleared for solo."

"Rog, sir. Ah, I thought aerobatics that close to the airfield were forbidden...."

"It is. But it's a Willie tradition that will probably go away when we get a new Wing commander. So until then let's take advantage of it."

Rod clicked his mike and grinned. So that was it. In retrospect, the check-ride didn't seem that intimidating, and the loop was Captain Banner's way of announcing to the rest of the base that Rod had passed. Since Rhino didn't have any additional maneuvers for him to perform, Rod would be able to get him back on the ground in plenty of time to make his Boy Scout outing.

Rod obtained clearance from tower and pulled into a gentle bank heading toward Williams. He saw the rise of San Tan Mountain, with the Sonoran desert sprawling in the distance. The sky was unmarred by clouds and looked as though an immense, dark blue hemisphere stretching horizon-to-horizon had been placed over the parched desert ground.

For once he could enjoy the flight, in some ways act like a tourist, and not worry about having to perform. The upcoming solo didn't bother him; he knew his skills and wasn't worried about flying alone. In fact, he'd prefer being the only one in the cockpit, because he could push the jet to the limits of its endurance.

He approached the base and checked with tower one last time for permission to execute the inside loop. He was given clearance and came in just over 5,000 feet above ground level. The runway and training buildings spread out below him. He saw the housing area on the left, and knew that Julie and Nanette were probably out by the dusty old playground.

When he passed over the flight line he clicked his mike. "Here goes." He jammed the stick back and pushed forward on the throttles. The T-33 surged and pulled up into a tight, inside loop. The T-33 strained as he held the stick as far back as he could.

As they went over the top he saw brown desert below. It spread out in all directions through the top of his canopy. Above him the sky was a deep, dark blue, almost black.

The altimeter started to drop as he was pushed back in his seat. The pressure grew and soon the T-33 started to shake from the g's. He grunted from the g-forces; his vision narrowed, and all he could see out of the top of his canopy was brown desert, below. Rod eased up on the stick as the jet struggled to pull out of the loop.

At the top of the canopy he saw blue sky appear, indicating that they were bottoming out. The altimeter slowed its movement and when it started to creep back up he released the stick; the g-forces subsided. The runway was perfectly lined up a mile below him.

Rod started to click the mike when the control stick was ripped out of his hand. It slammed up against the front panel.

The T-33 dove to the ground.

Airspeed increased. The sound of wind outside the cockpit rose to a wail.

The control stick vibrated. The jet started to shake as it accelerated straight down.

Rod was pushed out of his seat, up toward the canopy by the sudden negative g's. He grabbed for the stick. He tried to pull back but the stick was stuck, as if Rhino was pushing it forward.

"Captain Banner!" Rod said. "Release stick!"

The jet screamed toward the earth. A brown and tan patchwork of fields and asphalt runway grew larger in the canopy; the ground rushed up to meet them. It sounded as if a train was roaring by.

The T-33 vibrated, shaking Rod, throwing him back and forth. The jolting slammed his teeth against his tongue, and he tasted the warm, salty sensation of blood.

"Release, Captain! Release stick!" Rod pulled as hard as he could but couldn't move the control stick back. Rod grunted as he strained. The trainer shook in an ever-sickening scream, and he thought he might break the yoke if he pulled any harder.

The altitude dial spun down in elevation as they raced through 2,000 feet. Rod clicked his mike as he was thrown violently from side to side. "Mayday, mayday, mayday!"

He raced through the emergency checklist as the ground rushed up. Nothing seemed to work. The stick wouldn't budge. It was as if Rhino was pushing his entire body against the stick even with the negative g's—

His entire body against the stick.

If Rhino's body was somehow jammed against the stick, there was no way Rod could pull back. Unless he forced Rhino to move out of the way—

He stomped down on the right pedal as hard as he could, almost standing in the cramped cockpit, and simultaneously pushed the stick forward and right. The jet started to rotate in the dive and rolled upside down.

As the T-33 turned, the negative g's shoved against him up against the canopy. The craft hurtled toward the ground as he alternated the pedals, rocking the jet.

Rod pulled back on the stick—it was free.

He jammed the stick back to the right and the trainer spun over.

He jerked back on the stick as hard as he could. The g's increased as he pulled out of the loop ... but this time less than a hundred feet above the ground.

He grunted, trying to stay focused as the periphery of his vision narrowed.

The T-33 shook as it strained to pull up, and Rod thought the aircraft might disintegrate. He tightened his grip and within seconds he was flying level, right-side up but only scant tens of feet above the bare, desert ground.

Unwilling to risk losing control once again, Rod pulled back on the throttles, lowered the landing gear, hit the speed brakes, and forced the aircraft down. The runway quickly drew up, and at the last instant, Rod pulled the nose up and flared. He slammed onto the runway just over the dirt end at 300 knots—he'd have less than 10 seconds to bring the jet to a stop.

Fire trucks raced down the end of the runway, falling behind him as Rod stood on the brakes to slow the jet trainer. He'd landed at almost cruising velocity and wasn't slowing fast enough.

He popped the canopy to give him more air resistance. Air screamed into the cockpit as it vibrated in the slipstream.

Smoke rolled up from the tires. The canopy cracked and flew backward, high into the air and tumbled over the back of the jet. A shrill shriek came from the brakes as the speed decreased.

The T-33 rolled past the end marker, and slowed to a stop just as the front tire left the asphalt and bumped onto the dirt.

The burning smell of rubber and metal-on-metal rolled into the cockpit. He disarmed the eject seats and quickly unbuckled. "Captain Banner! Rhino!"

The sound of sirens wailing grew louder as fire trucks approached the jet.

Rod turned and climbed to stand on his seat to see behind him.

Rhino's helmet leaned against the side of the cockpit. His body was twisted in the seat and blood dribbled from his oxygen mask.

Rod ripped off his mask. He threw his helmet to the side and scrambled over the top of his seat. He leaned into Rhino's cockpit and reached for the instructor's helmet, fumbling as he tried to unbuckle Rhino's strap.

An aluminum ladder was thrown against the T-33 with a loud clang. Simultaneously two additional ladders were flung against the opposite side of the jet.

A fireman in a silver fireproof suit stomped up the ladder. He put his arms around Rod and pulled him back. "We've got him, sir."

"He's hurt!" Rod struggled but the fireman tightened his grip.

Two other firemen climbed up, reached in, and removed Rhino's helmet.

His head rolled to the side, lifeless. The firemen checked his breathing and pulse before unbuckling the harness.

Rod felt his heart race; it seemed hard to catch his breath. He lurched forward to help but he was pulled back and admonished to clear the aircraft.

The fireman helped Rod down the ladder where a medic met him at the bottom and moved him away from the trainer. Two fire trucks and an ambulance were parked in the dirt around the jet, emergency lights rotating. Crackling sounds from radio static came from all three vehicles. A stretcher was brought up to the jet as a crew of firemen pulled out two hoses to cool down the brakes and tires.

Rod sat in the dirt with his head between his legs, next to the waiting ambulance. His ears were stopped up and he had trouble hearing.

Time seemed to pass in a haze for Rod as Captain Banner was removed from the aircraft and placed into the ambulance.

He couldn't think straight. He kept questioning what else could he have done, how else could he have helped Rhino. Could he have pulled out of the loop any sooner? Did he pull too many g's? Did he overlook anything?

He hadn't felt so distraught since he was told his father had died in a small aircraft accident, learning of the crash just days before he graduated from the Academy. At least with General Beaumont heading up the crash accident board, they'd get to the bottom of dad's crash ... unless that path pointed to some external cause, such as George Delante....

An officer in a flight suit squatted in the dirt beside Rod. He put a hand on Rod's shoulder and asked him questions in a low tone, having Rod recall the sequence of events from the time they'd approached Williams to when Rod lost control of the stick. As Rod related the incident, the grim-faced medic who had first attended Rod interrupted the officer.

The officer listened intently, stopping the medic to ask for clarification. Rod tried to listen, but their voices were too low for him to hear. As events came into focus, it dawned on Rod that the officer was their squadron commander, a young Lieutenant Colonel known by his call sign Beast; his wife, LizAnn, had taken Julie under her wing.

When the medic left, Beast said in a quiet voice, "You're lucky to be alive, son."

Rod looked up. The roar in his ears started to subside. "Captain Banner? How's he doing, sir?"

"Heart attack. The medic said he died quickly."

Rod closed his eyes.

Beast put a hand on Rod's shoulder. "I can't say for certain what happened until after the Accident Investigation Board, but it appears he slumped over when his heart failed. His helmet jammed the stick against the panel ... and if you hadn't rolled upside down to release him, you would have pranged into the runway." Beast paused. "You were less than thirty feet above the deck when you pulled out of that loop."

Rod opened his eyes as he heard the ambulance drive away with Captain Banner's body.

Beast straightened. "Good recovery, Lightning; that was one hell of a flight. I've never seen anything like it." He hesitated. "The big guy upstairs must have something huge planned for you—so whatever it is, don't screw it up."

CHAPTER SIX

"The Writing on the Wall"

Two months later
Late May, 1961

William Air Force Base, AZ

One never notices what has been done; one can only see what remains to be done ...

Marie Curie, Letter to her brother

During the last week of pilot training, Rod entered the training squadron, once again thinking that he'd pass Captain Banner's old office on his way to the student area. They'd cleared out his desk and belongings, but for now his side of the office remained empty.

So in a way, for Rod, the vacant area served almost as a memorial, and his passage past Rhino's old office space had almost become a rite, a way for Rod to silently remember the instructor pilot without drawing attention to himself.

As he entered the squadron area he saw his fellow officers crowding around the flight scheduler's bulletin board. He heard low-muted chatter; a sense of excitement permeated the air.

"What's up?" Rod said.

One of his classmates standing on his tiptoes answered without turning. "They've just posted the final order-of-merit!"

Rod felt a jolt of adrenaline. Finally! The results of every quiz, every check ride, and every flying evaluation over the past year had been combined into a single numeric score that would determine the final standing of each officer in pilot training. A single number that would set the course for the rest of his career.

He pushed through the throng. His fellow students jockeyed for position as they sought out their name. He heard an elated shout; someone must have gotten a higher position than they expected. Another officer cursed, drenched with a bucket of cold reality as he experienced a huge let-down.

Rod felt his heart start to pound. After all this time pursuing his dream, by overcoming the rigors of Academy and sweating through pilot training, it had finally come down to this. The entire year-long training effort would be wrapped up and summarized in a single number that would allow him to choose which aircraft he would fly: The smaller the number, the better the chance he'd be able to fly fighters—*any* fighter was all he hoped for now—the larger the number, the less chance he'd have.

Rod twisted past his classmates and peered at the typewritten sheet. His eyes flew down the list; nothing. He moved to the second page and felt his heart start to drop. He glanced at the third page and started to feel sick the further down he went—

He drew in a breath. Maybe they'd made a mistake; for some reason the Air Force still confused his given name with Rod, so maybe they were using adoptive parent's name. He decided to be more methodical and take his time. He looked back at the top of the first page, intending to go down the list one-by-one.

His name was listed first. Number one. And he'd missed it.

He felt lightheaded as he drew silently back. He moved away from the crowd and slumped against the wall. The sounds of his fellow students receded as background noise. Once again he'd beaten the odds and come out as the best of the best.

All he had left was to choose the aircraft he wanted to fly, a seemingly simple choice that would distill his life's ambitions and dreams. And as though it were the first swing taken in the golf tournament of life, his next decision would define the path he'd take for the rest of his career.

O   O   O

Two days later Rod sat in the base theater in his flight suit with the rest of his flying class, most of them Air Force Academy grads from the class of '60. The place hummed with anticipation.

Various types of Air Force aircraft were listed on a blackboard at the front of the theater with the number of available pilot slots written next to them. They were listed in the order of how past pilot training classes had bestowed the most prestige.

First were the bombers: the lumbering eight-engine B-52 Stratofortress, capable of carrying nuclear weapons, then the sleek B-47, followed by the aging B-36. There was a clear break before the list started again with fighters, followed by jet trainers, transport planes, refueling aircraft, and ending with a smattering of helicopters.

Everyone knew the top graduates would be allowed to choose their first choice; those who graduated with a lower rank-order in the class would have to settle for the planes that were left.

So everyone assumed it was a boring, anticlimactic selection-process backed by historical data, because student desires always matched the priorities listed on the blackboard.

Rod's name was called first. He stood and drew in a deep breath.

Everyone knew he'd pick the B-52, the flagship of SAC, Strategic Air Command.

SAC ruled both the Air Force and the skies. Flying for SAC was the quickest way to become one of General Curtis LeMay's legacies, one of LeMay's bomber generals. And as an Academy grad with a national scholarship under his belt, and now at the top of his pilot training class, it wasn't a matter of if he would make general, but it was a matter of *when*, and how fast.

All he had to do was to say "B-52" and his career would be set for life. After all, his father had flown bombers and the die had been cast.

But Rod knew what he wanted.

He'd known it that day he saw the rows of fighter aircraft sitting on the grassy field in Farnborough. He'd even known it years earlier, when he sat on the hood of his adoptive father's car, watching the fighters fly into March Field; and it had motivated him throughout his four years as a cadet. Once he'd wanted to fly the F-100, but now he had a chance to fly the hottest and fastest jet in the world, and there was only one of them listed for the entire class.

He blurted out "F-105!"

The silence was deafening.

Every officer in the base theater was stunned. The normally festive atmosphere plunged into dead silence.

Some students had spent the past two days calculating which aircraft would be available in the draw, negotiating deals with their classmates who had been undecided. A growing whisper swept over the pilots as they suddenly realized that the aircraft they might be able to pick could be entirely different from what they'd been expecting.

And what did it mean, that the training classes' number one graduate had forgone a sure path to being a general, only to choose a fighter? And a fighter-bomber at that! Would others follow in his path? Was Rod crazy? Was this a fluke, or was this a sign of changing times? Would someone destined for helicopters now be given the chance to fly something else?

This changed everything!

Excited jabbering erupted in pockets throughout the auditorium as everyone suddenly realized what had just happened: it was as though the room had been a tankful of man-eating sharks and Rod had just thrown in a bucket of raw, bloody meat.

Officers ran up to the blackboard, others scrambled out of their chairs to call their wives, others started negotiating with their classmates. It was feeding frenzy.

And people's careers changed on a dime.

O O O

Later that night after Julie rolled off him, Rod was wide-awake. He was on his back, his hands cradling his head and looking up at the ceiling, unable to sleep. He'd accomplished everything he'd set out to do in life at the age of twenty-three.

But after the stress of the last six years, he felt at least there should be a band playing, pretty girls throwing flowers in his path, crowds cheering. He should be able to walk to a balcony, lift up his arms, and have waves of adoration roll over him.

He'd accomplished far more than he'd ever expected. He'd beaten the odds and come out on top in everything he did. He'd graduated from the first USAF Academy class and won a prestigious Guggenheim scholarship; he'd completed a Master's degree in Aeronautical Engineering at Stanford and graduated first in his pilot training class; he was a new husband and father; and now he was assigned to fly the hottest fighter in the world.

But although he had accomplished so much, for some reason it didn't seem enough—in a way it almost seemed too easy.

He felt there was something else he needed to do, something just out of his reach that would make things perfect. There *had* to be.

Nanette sighed in the room next to them, her tiny voice breaking the silence. Julie turned on her side, and started snoring softly. He knew that there was something important that was missing in his life; he just wondered what would happen to make him discover what it was.

CHAPTER SEVEN

"Midnight in Moscow"

A year and a half later
6:59pm
Monday, October 22, 1962

Seymour-Johnson Air Force Base
Goldsboro, NC

*Hitherto man had to live with the idea of death as an individual;
from now onward mankind will have to live with the idea of its
death as a species.*

Arthur Koestler, *Peter's Quotations*

Rod walked out of the bedroom and stepped into the den of their small, one-bedroom base house. Nanette sat on the vinyl floor, thumbing through a picture book, *Policeman Small*, while Julie sat next to her, quietly smoking and sipping a glass of wine while watching their secondhand TV. They'd picked up the Philco Predicta on the day they'd moved in, because the family who was moving out had exceeded their household limit for an overseas assignment; it was cheaper for the departing Captain to part with the massive black-and-white Townhouse TV than to pay the overage, so on the spot Rod was talked into shelling out half a month's flight pay so they could own the noisy box.

Rod frowned; it was Nanette's bedtime and he had an early flight. "What are you watching? I thought Cronkite's News was over."

"Shhh," Julie motioned with her cigarette and kept her eyes glued to the 21-inch screen.

"Shhh!" Nanette giggled and returned to paging through her book.

"—We interrupt our regularly scheduled program to bring you this special presentation. Ladies and gentlemen, the President of the United States."

"What's going on?" Rod said.

"Open your ears and you'll find out."

The TV blinked and the image of 45-year-old John F. Kennedy filled the screen. Rod drew in a breath. The young President looked as though he'd aged, and it took Rod a moment to focus on his words.

"... it shall be the policy of this nation to regard any nuclear missile launched from Cuba against any nation in the Western Hemisphere as an attack by the Soviet Union on the United States, requiring a full retaliatory response upon the Soviet Union—"

"What's that mean?" Julie said.

"I'm not sure." Rod took a knee and stared intently at the screen.

"—to halt this offensive buildup, a strict quarantine on all offensive military equipment under shipment to Cuba is being initiated. All ships of any kind bound for Cuba, from whatever nation or port, will, if found to contain cargoes of offensive weapons, be turned back. This quarantine will be extended, if needed, to other types of cargo and carriers—"

"Other types of carriers," Rod said to himself.

Julie frowned. "Rod, does that include aircraft?"

The phone rang and Nanette jumped, startled at the sudden intrusion and her parents' stern demeanor. She started crying; Julie swept her up and started bouncing her on her knee.

Rod reached for the phone. "Simone quarters, Lieutenant Simone speaking."

"Lightning, this is Colonel Green."

Rod stiffened. "Yes, sir." The 335th Tactical Fighter Squadron's Squadron Commander never called—the lieutenant colonel went through either Rod's Flight Commander or the squadron's Operation's Officer if he needed to relay a message.

"I'm pulling you and Major Fischer up to squadron tonight for a prepositioning flight in case we have to launch against the Soviet Union. You'll fly two as my wingman; Fisher has four as Lieutenant Colonel Cox's. Pack for a week and show up at squadron ops for pre-flight as soon as you can, but no later than fifteen minutes. Got it?"

"Yes, sir," Rod's mind raced. Something *huge* was up. Cox was the squadron operations officer, and Major Fischer was one of the best pilots Rod had ever known. But although the squadron commander had just given him a direct order, the man had reached deep down through the chain-of-command and circumvented Rod's flight commander, his direct boss. "Sir, should I inform Major Stillman—"

"Stillman's in the loop. He'll be leading the rest of the squadron out later tonight, a few hours behind us. I need my best sticks with me on the first flight out."

"Copy. May I ask where we're heading?"

"You'll find out. The military went to DEFCON 3 five minutes ago."

Rod felt lightheaded. Strategic Air Command was normally at DEFCON 4, and now there were only two more levels remaining in the defense readiness condition before nuclear war was imminent at DEFCON 1. This had to be a show of force; this couldn't be real. "Yes, sir. I copy this is a ROUNDHOUSE exercise—"

"The hell it is! This is *real-world*, Lightning. Understand? Possible Emergency War Order. They're pulling out the crowd pleasers now and will be loading our birds as we speak. We'll be flying hot, VFR direct to our staging area—that is, if we aren't waved on to our target as soon as we rotate. Now get your butt in gear and get down to the squadron!" The phone slammed down.

Crowd pleasers. This was incredibly serious; that was code for the B-43, one of the two nuclear weapons the F-105D was rated to carry. Rod immediately hung up and walked back to the bedroom, unbuttoning his shirt.

Julie's voice drifted behind him. "What's up, Lightning?"

"I'm being deployed. Quick TDY." He shucked off his pants and rummaged through his closet for his flight suit. He pulled it on and decided to take the other suit as well, then turned and threw it on the bed.

Julie walked up and leaned against the doorframe, watching as she took a drag from her cigarette; she blew smoke up and behind her, out of the room. "The President's serious about those Cuban missiles."

"You've got that straight." Rod pulled out the top drawer on his dresser, grabbed a handful of underwear, T-shirts, and black socks. He missed as he tossed them onto the bed, and the socks skidded underneath the bedframe.

Nanette skipped into the room and saw the socks as they disappeared. "Mine, Daddy!" She got on her hands and knees and crawled under the bed.

"How long will you be gone?" Julie said.

"Not sure." He pulled out his combat boots and a small, green duffle bag from the closet, placing it on the bed. "Keep in close touch with Lieutenant Colonel Green's, Cox's, and Major Fischer's wives while I'm gone. Those guys are going with me, so at least one of us should be able to call. Just be sure to relay whatever you hear to the rest of the wives, and have them do the same."

"Right." She moved over to help him pack.

Nanette sprung out from under the bed, triumphantly holding up three pairs of black socks, "Daddy's feet stay warm!"

"Thanks, sweetheart." Rod took the socks and threw two of them in the duffle bag. He strode to the bathroom, pulled out a small travel bag, and dumped in his razor, toothbrush and toothpaste, and a comb. He hesitated and then threw in another razor; no telling how long he'd be gone.

When he walked back into the bedroom, Julie was sitting on the bed next to his duffle bag. She held Nanette on her knee and looked as though she might start crying.

"Will it be dangerous?" Julie said.

"I'll be fine." He zipped up his duffle, sat on the bed, and pulled on his socks.

"How long will you be gone?"

"Not sure; Colonel Green didn't say." He started lacing his boots.

"Where are you going?"

"Don't know, but it has to be somewhere there's a base...." he suspected it was probably one of the West German airfields, but didn't want to tell her that the location would be used as a staging point for warplanes destined for the USSR, although she could probably guess. And if the Seymour-Johnson storage depot was really moving the B-43 nuclear bombs to the flight line for them to load onto their fighters, if the Cuban crisis got any worse, he would probably be in the first wave of aircraft to pierce Russian air space.

He finished tying his boots and stood. Julie held onto Nanette tightly, as though Rod might be taking her with him; Nanette squirmed, trying to get down.

"I'll call you when I can. Just keep in touch with the other wives."

Julie nodded and didn't speak; her eyes brimmed with tears.

Rod bent and kissed her, then gave Nanette a quick peck on the head. "Gotta go. Wish me luck." He picked up the duffle bag. He swung it over his shoulder and left the room, not looking back. He had five minutes to drive the mile and a half from the housing area to the flight line. It was time to put his family behind him and focus on his job. He couldn't afford to be distracted when flying; too many lives were at stake.

Especially if he had to navigate over the Arctic and evade Soviet air defenses to drop his nukes.

O   O   O

Five days later
Saturday afternoon, 27 October 1962

Flight line, Alert Shack
McCoy Air Force Base, FL

The pilots from the 4th Tactical Fighter Wing clustered in front of the empty briefing podium in a building set just off the flight line, sixteen miles from Orlando. The crowded room was hot and humid, reeking with the odor of men who'd been pulling alert for three days straight, all on edge, all anticipating combat and the green light for Emergency War Orders, ever since CINCSAC General Thomas Power had elevated his forces to DEFCON 2 at 10:00 AM Washington time on 24 October.

An old, brown console TV remained unwatched in the corner of the room, and out the window, dusk had started to settle over the subtropical airfield. A flight of four F-105Ds was hot cocked at the end of the runway as they waited on alert: everything was ready to go, and all they needed was to start their engines, taxi, and take off.

As one of the more junior officers in the room, Rod sat in the very back row. He looked out the window, wishing that instead of seeing palm trees and sunny skies, he were sitting in an alert facility in West Germany. Although it was incredibly colder over there, that was where all the action would be if the balloon ever went up and they were sent to war. Over Europe, the sky would be darkened with fighters from East Germany, Mother Russia, and the rest of the Soviet Bloc, trying to prevent him from reaching his target. Flying in those conditions would stretch even the best to their limits.

But here, even if they spent time aerial refueling, they were so close to Cuba it would take less than a half hour at his max speed of 1,390 mph to traverse the 420 miles to the Soviet's Santa Clara missile site; the distance to the targets at Sagua La Grande in central Cuba wasn't much further. And aside from some Russian pilots who'd be taken out by the U.S. air-to-air guys, when it got down to it, here in Orlando, his mission wouldn't be that exciting.

But on the other hand, he had a much higher chance of coming out of this alive flying out of southern Florida rather than Germany—unless they really did start a world-wide, nuclear war....

"Room, atten'hut!"

Rod jerked himself from his daydream and bolted to his feet.

Colonel Perry, the 4th Tactical Fighter Wing Commander, walked into the room followed by his staff; smoke from his cigar trailed behind him. Lieutenant Colonel Green and the three other 4th TFW squadron commanders came in last and joined the group.

Colonel Perry had a mane of wavy, brown hair. Although large boned, he had fluid movements and projected a no-nonsense, commanding presence. He reached the podium as his staff lined up against the wall behind him. "Take seats." Chairs screeched across the black and white checkered vinyl floor; his staff remained standing next to the wall at parade rest.

"Gentlemen, the following is for your ears only. The first shots have been fired." He turned and pointed his cigar at a map of Cuba set up behind him. "Two hours ago, U-2 reconnaissance pilot Major Rudolf Anderson, Jr. was shot down over Cuba by a Soviet SA-2 ground-to-air missile during Operation Brass Knob, SAC's intensified aerial surveillance of Cuba that they'd taken over from the CIA." A murmur rolled through the room as the pilots straightened in the chairs. "Major Anderson was photographing suspected tactical nuclear missile sites erected near Guantanamo Bay Naval Station, and had been over the target area for an hour. His aircraft fell from a height of over fourteen miles and he is presumed dead. Major Anderson is the crisis' first death, and it may not be the last."

Colonel Perry turned from the map. "Thirty minutes ago another U-2 strayed into Russian airspace and was shot down over the Soviet Union. The status of the pilot is unknown." He allowed the news to sink in. "So where does that leave us?" He drew on his cigar as he looked around the room.

It was so quiet Rod felt as though his fellow pilots could hear his heart pound.

"As military officers we follow the President's orders. I don't know what's going to happen next, but the White House is currently waiting for recommendations from EXCOM. And when the President's Executive Committee has arrived at a course of action, if the President decides to invoke Emergency War Orders, that decision will be chopped through the JCS to SAC, where we'll receive our orders to execute. Until then, we'll continue at DEFCON 2, ready to deploy and engage in less than six hours. You've all been briefed on SIOP-63, and our orders are to flatten

Cuba, to ensure that no Soviet nukes survive.

"Because of these escalating events, I'm adding one more task to the 335th; Lieutenant Colonel Green will brief you on your orders, so stick around when you're dismissed. But before he speaks, intelligence will give a short update and a heads-up on a possible change in tactics if you encounter any bandits." Colonel Perry looked behind him. "Captain Hamilton?"

"Yes, sir." One of the few officers in the room not wearing a flight suit stepped away from the back wall and strode up to the podium. Hamilton pulled on a pair of black glasses from the pocket of his tan uniform shirt and read from a sheaf of papers. "Forty-five minutes ago, a U.S. Navy P-2H Neptune from patrol squadron VP-18 spotted a flight of four Soviet Ilyushin Il-28 'Beagle' light bombers in the mid-Atlantic, heading south-southwest at 415 knots at 40,000 feet. From radio intercepts, the flight is believed to be supplementing the other Il-28s already in Cuba, and interceptors from Langley have been scrambled to intercept their last known heading. Our best intelligence is that they're armed with four Nudelman NR-23 cannons, two in the nose and two in tail barbette, and may be carrying up to 6,600 pounds of bombs in their internal bay. It is not known if their payloads are nuclear, or if they will be loading atomic ordinance in Cuba."

Hamilton looked up. "And as the colonel said, you may also experience a possible change in combat tactics if you are engaged by the Beagles. This warning comes from a highly classified, strategically placed intel asset." He paused, his voice shaking. "I cannot stress enough how sensitive this source is. Do not speak outside this room of what I'm about to show you, as approval for presenting this only comes from the highest levels in our government."

Captain Hamilton turned and a lieutenant stepped up, handing him a manila envelope stamped with red markings. He tore open the envelope and pulled out an oversized, glossy photograph.

Hamilton held it up and slowly moved it from side to side so everyone in the room could see, then pointed to what looked like a fuzzy, overhead picture of an Ilyushin Il-28 Beagle sitting on a runway. The letters TS-SCI/TK/CORONA were stamped on the top and bottom of the photo.

One of the pilots leaned over and whispered, "That's from a U-2."

Another pilot said, "It can't be. I've seen U-2 photos and they look a lot better than that. Whatever took it was flying a lot higher than a U-2. Plus, they don't have those weird security codes stamped on them."

Hamilton said, "This was taken two days ago. You can barely make out markings on the wings, and the markings aren't the Soviet hammer and sickle—"

"I can barely make out the wings," someone said, and a titter ran through the room.

Hamilton pushed on. "We can't tell for certain what the markings are, but the point is that we're absolutely sure that this Il-28 is *not* a Soviet bomber—it's from a non-Soviet country, deployed with the Soviet air force. So if you engage any of these aircraft, they will probably not use the same tactics against you that you've been trained to counter."

The room filled with excited voices. Colonel Perry stepped up and growled, "At ease—let the captain finish."

Hamilton waited for the murmuring to die down, and then said, "Actually, that's all I have, sir. Are there any questions?"

A hand shot up. "How many Beagles have those markings?"

"At least one. We haven't detected any others, but that doesn't mean they're not out there."

Major Stillman, Rod's flight commander, called out, "How do you know these may be deployed against us?"

Hamilton hesitated. "The NSA—"

Colonel Perry cleared his throat.

Hamilton looked at Colonel Perry and the Wing Commander shook his head. Hamilton nodded and continued, "Uh, almost a hundred percent. All I can say is that there is a high probability they will be deployed because of its location."

"Was it Cuba?"

Hamilton shook his head. "No. And I'm not allowed to say. But we're fortunate that the analyst who spotted this was a young Air Force officer who knew enough about adversary tactics to realize that this might present an asymmetric threat; Lieutenant Manuel Rojo is assigned to a classified operating location near Washington, DC, and his discovery has created a firestorm at the White House."

Rod jerked up his head. *Manuel?* His Academy classmate! Rod felt a swell of pride; they'd lost touch after Manuel graduated from Princeton. So this is what he'd been doing.

Captain Hamilton said, "Are there any other questions?" He looked over the room, and when no one spoke, he turned back to Colonel Perry. "Thank you, sir." He stepped away and stuffed the glossy photo back in the envelope.

Colonel Perry moved to the front and took the cigar from his mouth. He stood for a moment, then his gaze moved from man to man, looking each of them intently in the eye before moving to the next officer. One by one, he moved down the rows without a word as he lingered on each of his pilots, making eye contact.

The room was dead quiet. Perry didn't speak for such a long time that Rod thought the room might boil over with the escalating tension. As time passed, for some reason he found it hard to breathe; a drip of perspiration flowed down his face. When Perry finally locked eyes with him, Rod felt a surge of emotion well up, a sense of incredible energy; he felt as though he could run out and do anything for the charismatic colonel.

Perry pulled up straight. "Men ... fellow officers." He looked around the room. "Brothers-in-arms ... fellow aviators. *This* is what you've been training for your entire career. We've invested millions of dollars to prepare you for this moment, this one point in time—your education, your training, your equipment, and your aircraft. I don't know how many of us will come out of this alive, but your family ... your brothers in this room ... your Air Force ... and your nation are all depending on you.

"You cannot fail. You *will not* fail. Our future depends on you successfully executing your mission. Do you understand?"

"Yes, sir!"

Rod felt his chest tighten, the veins in his forehead throbbed.

"You're the best of the best, and you'll step up to the task, no matter what the odds, no matter what those sons-of-bitches will throw against you. You won't give up. You'll keep on pushing.

You'll accomplish your mission. And you'll win. You'll do whatever you can to not let those Commie bastards succeed."

Perry lowered his voice, almost to a whisper. "Gentlemen, I'm honored to be your commander. I wouldn't be with any other group of men, or anywhere else in the world but here. I'll be flying lead when we launch, and I wish you Godspeed and good hunting."

The Wing Ops officer yelled from the back wall. "Room, atten'hut!" Once again the pilots bolted to attention.

His heart pounded so rapidly that Rod felt as though he'd just been injected with a shot of caffeinated adrenaline. He clenched his hands and breathed through his nose, trying to control his emotions.

Colonel Perry jammed his cigar in his mouth, turned, and stomped from the room, followed by his staff. When the last of Wing staff had departed, Lieutenant Colonel Green, Rod's squadron commander, stepped up to the front. "At ease, men. Chiefs, stick around; the rest of you are dismissed."

The officers of the 333rd, 334th, and 336th Tactical Fighter Squadrons queued up to leave as Rod and the rest of the pilots in the 335th TFS moved forward to fill the empty chairs.

When the other three squadrons had left the room, Green said, "You heard the Commander. This moment in time is probably the height of the crisis, and it could go either way. If CINCSAC orders us to go to war, we'll execute accordingly. If we're ordered to stand down, we'll do so as well.

"In the meantime, in addition to the alert birds we have poised at the end of the runway, Colonel Perry has ordered a flight of fully-hot D models to pre-position in a racetrack pattern in warning areas southeast of Key West. The 335th will be rotating through the warning areas with different Flights, flying two hour sorties in radio silence." He looked down at his notes. "We'll be armed with two B-43s, dialed to a 70KT yield, and will be leaving our Sidewinders at home. Unlike the rest of the Wing who will be sweeping from the northwest down from McCoy, we'll circle Cuba clockwise and come in from the southeast at 300 feet AGL using our terrain avoidance, R-14 search and ranging radar, to avoid detection for a radar low-angle drogue delivery. Our optimum solution is being preprogrammed on autopilot for a wings level, 4-g pull-up to auto-toss the bomb forward. After release, execute a slicing, 45-degree down-turn away from the bomb in full afterburner, to attain 550 KIAS down to minimum terrain avoidance altitude, to put distance between your jet and the blast."

He looked up. "We'll be the Wing's failsafe option in a southeastern approach to Cuba, in case those incoming Ilyushin Il-28s change their heading and take out McCoy before the rest of the D's can launch. Any questions?" No one spoke. "Okay, we'll be rotating through the flights with A-Flight at bat, B-Flight on deck, and C-Flight in the hole. First launch in 30 for warning area W-465B."

Rod felt flush; after all the wait, they were stepping right up to the brink. And he'd be on the leading edge of the first wave if the balloon went up.

Lieutenant Colonel Green spoke over the buzz. "D-Flight, get your crew rest. You're dismissed."

The pilots stood and excited whispers swept throughout the room.

Major Stillman, A-Flight commander, raised his voice. He motioned with his head and said, "Gator, Divot, Lightning—hit the head and grab your gear. The Flight call sign is Sniper. Preflight in five.

"Gentlemen, we're going to war."

O O O

Two and a half hours later

15,000 feet above sea level
Warning area W-465B, Northeast of Cuba

Rod kept his airspeed pegged at 315 knots as he followed Major Stillman and the other two F-105Ds in a loose trail formation. They were flying a monotonous racetrack pattern, and after nearly two hours of radio silence, he was starting to feel fatigued. They'd launched on afterburner for the failsafe spot, so now, despite their low speed and advertised range of over 2,000 miles, they were getting low on fuel.

The tankers were all either up north, supporting the heavy bombers—the Buffs and B-47s—or they were busy refueling the interceptors flying patrol, farther out to the east; so now, without the tankers, if they were suddenly chopped to Cuba to lay down their nukes, it would be a one way mission.

Rod's initial excitement at being part of the first fail-safe flight had diminished, and although he wasn't quite bored, flying in a giant, oval pattern over the Caribbean wasn't the most exciting mission he'd ever done. However, the fact that he carried two nuclear weapons, each capable of exploding with one megaton of energy—nearly 70 times more powerful than the Little Boy atomic bomb that destroyed Hiroshima—kept him alert.

The B-43 bombs he carried had a dial-a-yield capability to vary the explosive energy released, and both his weapons were set to 70 kilotons, 14 times less energetic than the maximum; but it didn't placate him. 70KT was still over four times more powerful than the Hiroshima device. And even though he'd toss his weapons in an airburst to destroy the most missile launchers possible, even with full afterburners, there was a good possibility he'd be swept up in the bomb's shock wave as he raced away from the blast.

The minutes crawled by and he tried to stay alert. He wondered how long this crisis might last, and how much longer they'd have to fly the racetrack pattern. He started to tick off things he had to do when he returned home ... when suddenly a call came over the radio.

"Sniper Flight, this is Romeo Ops. Your flight is to Return to Base. I authenticate Alpha Bravo with Tango."

Lightning glanced at his authenticator; this was a valid call from the operations center, so B-Flight must have attained its orbit in another warning area. Time to head back to McCoy.

Rod saw Major Stillman's F-105 bank out of a turn, followed by the other two fighters in long, graceful arcs. Rod gently moved the stick to the right, giving just enough back pressure to add lift to keep the plane level. His jet tracked the three F-105s as they each kept a two-mile separation in their loose trail.

They took a heading back to McCoy, the first of the fail-safe missions complete. With all the brouhaha earlier, Rod figured that things might finally get back to normal since nothing much was happening—

A glint of light flashed below him, to the northeast. That was strange.

He squinted and followed three, no *four*, silver objects that were arrowing on the same heading as his flight, but moving with much less speed. The four aircraft were so slow and low over the water it looked as though they were crawling across the waves.

No other planes should be in the warning area—at least no civilian aircraft—and he would have heard if any military flights were expected; after all, a naval blockade was going on, and the US and USSR were holding guns at each other's heads. And unless B-Flight was way, way out of their own staging area, and flying much lower and slower than ordered, then that left only one thing those objects could be—the flight of Soviet Ilyushin Il-28 light bombers that intel had briefed them on ... the same ones that Colonel Perry worried might take out McCoy, on a pre-emptive strike. The Beagles had last been reported flying at 40,000 feet, but they could have easily dropped altitude and changed heading to approach the mainland from an unexpected direction.

Rod spoke into his mike. "Sniper 4. Four bogeys, six o'clock low, five miles on the water, northbound tight box."

"Copy. Stand by." A moment passed, then Major Stillman's clipped voice came over the headphones. "Wing's notified, interceptors inbound. Our orders are to perform a show of force to wave off the bogeys—this may be a feint, testing our radar. Sniper Flight, hook right; two, go fighting wing."

Without waiting for confirmation, Stillman's F-105 rolled to the right and down to perform a split-S; Sniper 2 followed, while accelerating to trail Stillman 1,000 feet behind and to his side.

Sniper 3 came over the radio. "Three, go fighting wing."

Rod immediately pushed forward on the throttle and his F-105 jumped as it accelerated to catch up to Sniper 3. When Sniper 3 started to pull a split S, Rod jammed his control stick to roll and mirror Sniper 3's actions. Now inverted, he kept Sniper 3 in sight as they descended; the horizon rotated around him. He craned his neck around, searching for the four bogeys that should be coming into view. Time seemed to crawl by as Rod's fighter rotated back toward the direction they had been flying.

Suddenly, Stillman's excited voice came over the headphones. "Sniper One, talley four! Twelve o'clock low, four miles."

Rod felt relieved that Stillman had spotted the bandits.

Seconds passed, then, "Twop, talley four." Sniper 2 added a "p" to the end of his call sign to make his reply curt and crisp.

"Threep, searching, no joy. And bingo fuel."

Rod clicked his mike as the Ilyushins came into view. "Fourp, talley four."

"Sniper Three, return to base. Sniper Four, high cover. Sniper Two, push it up, tactical right side for a close pass. Regroup at 15,000. Copy?"

"Twop," came Sniper 2's voice.

"Threep." Sniper 3 sounded disappointed.

"Fourp," Rod said.

Still accelerating upside down in his split S, Rod shivered with an involuntary chill. Despite the subtropical heat outside the plane, he might as well have been in Germany; the cockpit felt as though it had been suddenly filled with ice. Now that Sniper 3 had been ordered back to base because of low fuel, Rod had been assigned to cover Stillman and his wingman as they flew toward the Ilyushins; with any luck their close pass would convince the Russian bombers to turn back.

His breath quickened as he bottomed out of the split S; his heart started to race. It hit him that he was in combat, and for the first time facing an enemy that was intent on killing his countrymen, as well as himself. But the only air-to-air weapons he had on board weren't any good for engaging another warplane at this distance. He'd have to fly closer to use his M61, six-barrel 20 millimeter Vulcan Gatling-type cannon; he suddenly wished they'd loaded Sidewinders instead of one of the nukes.

Sniper 3 peeled off for base as Rod gained altitude to fly high cover for Stillman and Sniper 2.

Sniper 3 flew out of view as Rod rose to his position. A wide expanse of water spread out underneath his fighter, reaching from horizon to horizon; below him, the F-105s and Il-28s seemed to advance toward each other in slow motion.

As the F-105s approached, Stillman's fighter suddenly broke to the left. He accelerated and turned on his side; wagging his wings, he roared past the flight of bombers, missing the formation by tens of feet.

Simultaneously, Sniper 2 split to the right for his close pass.

Almost immediately, the flight of Il-28 Beagles started to gain altitude and bank south, away from the US mainland.

Rod felt the tightness in his chest start to lessen, his heart seemed to slow. He clearly saw the distinctive red hammer and sickle on the Soviet Il-28's wings and tail as the Beagles turned to the southwest.

Rod pulled back on the throttle, slowing his craft as Sniper 2 rejoined Stillman, up and to the left.

Rod started to break left when he noticed that one of the Il-28s bore straight ahead, falling in altitude as it continued its flight toward mainland Florida.

What was going on? Had the Soviet pilot not seen that the rest of his flight had turned south toward Cuba? But that was impossible—this was the trailing aircraft in the flight, not even the second or third. He was bringing up the rear, much like Rod had been doing flying in the number four spot in his own flight.

Major Stillman's voice came over his headphones. "Bingo fuel; return to base Sniper Flight. Interceptors ETA is five minutes. Good job."

Up and to his left, Rod saw Stillman's fighter and the other F-105 still climbing as they turned north; they started to recede in the distance.

Rod clicked his mike as he pushed his control stick forward to drop in altitude. "Lead, four. One bandit still heading for US. I say again, one bandit did not break away and is still heading north. It's heading for the deck."

"Stand by one, four. Checking with Wing. Do not engage, copy?"

"Rog." As Rod clicked his mike, he felt as though time had slowed to a crawl. He seemed to stand outside of every movement he made, every thought that raced through his head. It was as though he had an infinite amount of time to study the options and consequences, as if his mind had been suddenly slammed into overdrive.

He continued to drop in altitude as the Il-28 drew closer, still crawling toward him; they now approached at nearly the same altitude.

He could have broken off in any direction, but he knew the Soviet warplane would fly on. This wasn't just a game of chicken; this was a real-world standoff, a duel between himself and some ticked-off Russian pilot who was taking things into his own hands.

He only had a few more seconds. This wasn't a feint; he had to do something, he couldn't just disengage.

He could disobey Major Stillman and take out the Ilyushin with his Vulcan cannon; if he did he'd down the Beagle, but that might ignite the Cuban crisis into an inferno starting World War III.

Yet, the Il-28 hadn't fired on him, so what was the Soviet thinking? What was he trying to do?

Whatever the Russian had in mind, he wasn't backing off.

Rod couldn't allow the Beagle to continue. The incoming interceptors might not be able to detect the Ilyushin once the Russian was flying low over the mainland; the Beagle could probably keep below a hundred feet over the Everglades, and would never be seen.

Rod had been trained to react, not just sit passively by—not with the stakes this high. He'd been ordered not to engage his weapons, but he knew one thing he *could* do.

He pushed the throttle full forward and kicked the F-105 into full afterburner.

The jet leaped forward and he was slammed back into his seat. He felt as though a pile of sand had hit him as his uprated J75-P-19W turbojet blasted out over 24,000 pounds of thrust. Rod's entire body felt incredibly heavy with the acceleration. He grimaced as the F-105 violently shook, speeding head-on toward the Ilyushin.

Passing Mach 1, he jammed the control stick as hard as he could against his crotch, and the F-105 lurched upward.

The Ilyushin simultaneously broke right, still heading for the mainland—

Rod barely inched over the turning Il-28, pounding the Beagle with afterburner exhaust and the sonic boom that emanated from his fighter.

Rod cut back on his throttle and glanced over his shoulder. It looked as though the Il-28 was just pulling out of a post stall gyration, probably due to over-controlling his aircraft while trying to avoid being hit and the turbulence caused by Rod's close, supersonic pass by the bomber—

And Rod was stunned at what he saw. The marking on the tail and wings wasn't the hammer and sickle of the USSR, but was instead a unique, five-pointed red star, the symbol of the Chinese People's Liberation Army.

The Beagle was Chinese, apparently flown by a Red Chinese pilot. The Ilyushin was a non-Soviet bomber using different tactics, just what his classmate Manuel Rojo had predicted.

Rod stared as the Chinese Il-28 slowly turned south to rejoin the three Soviet bombers heading for Cuba.

He lowered his airspeed as slow as he could go without stalling, to save fuel; with any luck, he'd at least have some fumes to fly on by the time he reached McCoy.

He clicked his mike. "Four, bingo fuel. Lone bandit vectored away from mainland, toward Cuba. I think that Beagle won't bother us. And ... and I have one heck of an intel report to file when I get back. You'll never believe what I saw."

"Copy, four. We saw the markings. Good job. Now get your butt to base before we all run out of fuel having to rescue you."

O   O   O

Three weeks later
21 November 1962

Seymour-Johnson Air Force Base, NC

The day after the naval blockade ended, Rod finally settled down in an office he shared with the rest of his flight back at the 335th Tactical Fighter Squadron building. Pictures of Soviet aircraft were hung on the walls and an empty bottle of champagne was in the trash, left over from the toast the flight had made just twenty minutes before. As the junior officer, Rod was finishing up the Flight's last minute paperwork on their arrival back at Seymour-Johnson yesterday afternoon.

"Lightning?"

Rod looked up and saw Colonel Perry, the 4th Tactical Fighter Wing Commander, standing in the door; both Lieutenant Colonel Green and Major Stillman stood behind him. Rod bolted to attention.

"Yes, sir!"

"At ease, Lightning." Perry walked into the room and held out a hand; he held his ubiquitous cigar in the other. "Congratulations, son." His massive hand enveloped Rod's. "Wanted to be the first to tell you that Tactical Air Command has approved your Distinguished Flying Cross—they accelerated it though the system and you'll be the first in the Wing to get it from the missile crisis. In fact, General Power wants to personally present you the award now that it's been approved. That was one hell of a job stopping that rogue Beagle from entering US airspace. Outstanding work."

"Yes, sir."

"We've got our eye on you, young man. You are one hell of a pilot, and you've got the right stuff. And with that, Air Staff is looking at just the right career-broadening assignment that will give you an opportunity to shoot up through the ranks. Something that will stretch you, and give you experience working in something other than fighters."

"Thank you, sir—I appreciate it. But if I may say, I really enjoy flying. Can this career-broadening be in another platform, say an air-to-air assignment, rather than something entirely different?"

Colonel Perry took the cigar out of his mouth and stared.

Rod felt his face grow warm. *Uh, oh—I hope I haven't stepped on it.*

Perry pulled on his cigar and blew smoke. "I understand what you're saying, Lightning, but let me give you some advice. First, you never make your own assignment; the Air Force will decide what's best for you, and will assign you a job to fill its needs. Since you've been marked as up-and-coming, I'll let this go and pass it off to your inexperience. But from now on, let me be clear:

The Air Force has its eye on you, and if we are going to put you in a senior leadership position in twenty or thirty years, the Air Force and the Air Force alone will decide where you go and what you'll do. Understand?"

"Yes, sir. I copy."

"Good. Second, because you're an Academy grad, I wouldn't be surprised if the Air Force doesn't send one of their rising stars back to the Academy on a career-broadening assignment, probably as an Air Officer Commanding. Got it?"

"Yes, sir."

"I thought so." He shook Rod's hand again.

"Congratulations again, Lightning. You're a good stick. And I hope that Chinese Commie who was flying that Il-28 is still trying to clean up his pants from the scare you gave him. I know I would be." Perry stuck his cigar back in his mouth and turned to go. "Carry on."

"Yes, sir. Thank you, sir."

As the officers stomped down the hall, Rod sat back on his desk. His shoulders slumped, exhausted from the exchange.

Maybe he'd use his Master's in Aeronautical Engineering from Stanford sooner than he'd thought. If he was going to return to the Academy on a career broadening assignment, he thought he'd like to go back as an instructor rather than as an AOC. Not that he wouldn't mind commanding a squadron of cadets; he enjoyed the time he'd spent as a cadet squadron commander.

It was just that he remembered what a great mentor that Captain Tom Ranch had been, and there was no way that he could measure up to him. The man had carried himself with some sort of incredible, otherworldly self-assurance, and had a deep sense of calmness, more than anyone he'd ever known.

Whatever it was that Tom Ranch possessed, he wanted it himself; and then he might be half the man that Ranch had been.

He still had another few years of flying fighters, and that was what he enjoyed more than anything else. The F-105 was one heck of a plane, and he was doing what he'd wanted to do all his life. But still, he knew Julie wasn't thrilled with living in Goldsboro, and they had some great memories of Colorado Springs; and his mom would love being around Nanette.

He couldn't wait to get home and surprise Julie that they might be heading back to civilization and Colorado in another few years.

CHAPTER EIGHT

"I Get Around"

Two years later
August 14, 1964

United States Air Force Academy
Colorado Springs, CO

We salute you, we who are about to die.

Gladiator

Nearly nine years to the day after he started classes at the Academy's temporary site at Lowry Field, Rod took a deep breath as he prepared to enter the classroom in Fairchild Hall as a faculty member.

No bells or buzzers announced that it was nearly time to start the 7:30 AM Theoretical Mechanics class. The corridors were silent throughout the academic building as the cadets waited in their classrooms, ready for the first day of school.

Rod straightened his tie, pulled down his tan jacket, and flattened his medals and silver pilot wings. Despite having reported in to the Academy six weeks earlier, it was going to take some time getting used to dressing in his Class-As again. He'd spent the past four years wearing a green bag, the flame-resistant flight suit, and hardly ever donned his tan short sleeve uniform, much less the more formal Class-As. And the year before that he'd worn civilian clothes at Stanford. But wearing a coat and tie was a small price to pay; he'd rather do that and teach at the Academy than push papers in a staff job at the Pentagon.

When they'd arrived in Colorado Springs, Rod's mother had urged them to live with her in the sprawling ranch house that overlooked the Academy. They stayed with her until their small two-bedroom house in Pine Valley on the Academy grounds was available and they treated the wait as a small vacation.

And now, on the first day of the 1964 academic year at exactly 0730, Rod yanked open his classroom door simultaneously with the rest of the instructors who were standing outside of their own classrooms throughout Fairchild Hall.

The sound of chairs being pushed across the newly waxed floor greeted the instructors as the officers entered the classrooms. Rod looked at the twelve cadets who had rigidly snapped to attention; he smartly marched into the classroom.

He clicked to a stop.

A red-haired cadet at the front of class snapped a salute. "Sir, section M-1A ready for instruction."

Rod returned the salute. "Thank you. Take seats." He turned and wrote his name, work, and home phone numbers on the chalkboard. "I'm Captain Simone, and you can schedule EI with me or drop into my office at any time. Feel free to call me at home if you're having a problem with your homework, but no later than 2200. Any questions?"

"No, sir." The class answered as one.

Rod walked to the front of the desk and pulled out the attendance sheet.

Every eye was on him. Rod could tell that they were sizing him up, wondering what type of instructor he would be. A hard ass? A push over? With the Theoretical Mechanic Department's no-nonsense reputation, he suspected the cadets thought the former. And with what Rod had experienced so far, the acting department head was trying hard to model the department after the Commandant's Office, or Comm Shop as the cadets called it.

In many ways the Academy hadn't changed from when he was a cadet. The Dean's instructors were typically more concerned with academics than the AOCs and military science instructors; the academic, or Dean's, side of the house was generally more relaxed than the Commandant's. But the Theoretical Mechanics Department had not had a Permanent Professor for several months now, and the acting department head, a heavyset Lieutenant Colonel named Norman LeCompte, seemed determined to have his faculty members concentrate on military bearing to the detriment of academics.

Rod knew the official reason was that Lieutenant Colonel LeCompte was trying to maintain discipline in the department; but the junior officers whispered that in reality LeCompte was positioning himself to be tapped as a Permanent Professor, a position confirmed by Congress that would assure his eventual promotion to Brigadier General upon retirement. LeCompte stressed uniformity so much, the rumor was that he wanted to be able to stand in the hallway and hear every Theoretical Mechanics instructor solving the same problem at the same exact time as every other instructor.

Rod looked over the cadets as they waited for him to jump right into the lesson. He remembered his first experience as a cadet, when Captain Whitney, the instructor, had been cold and aloof; these cadets seemed to expect him to be the same.

Instead, he sat on the edge of the desk and tried to put the cadets at ease. "Relax for a minute, men. Let me tell you a little about my background. I'm a grad, class of '59, and was in Third Squadron as a cadet. I won a Guggenheim and attended Stanford for a year where I got my Master's in Aero, then went to pilot training at Willie, outside of sunny Chandler, Arizona.

"Out of pilot training I was assigned to fighters and flew the F-105—" someone whistled. Rod smiled. "You're right, that's one heck of a jet: The Thud."

"Sir, did you carry nuclear weapons or did you fly intercepts?"

Rod smiled. "I can neither confirm nor deny carrying nukes, but later I'll tell you war stories about an intercept we made of Soviet bombers during the Cuban missile crisis. Anyway, my call sign's Lightning, and I was asked to come back and teach as a career broadening assignment. Any questions?"

The cadets shook their heads, visibly more at ease.

Rod slapped his thigh and straightened. "Okay. The way you gentlemen are going to learn Theoretical Mechanics is by doing the homework and demonstrating your knowledge with board work, quizzes, and GRs, or Graded Reviews. 'Thet Mech' underlies every engineering course you are going to take, so if you don't understand this material, gentlemen, I guarantee you will have difficulty with the rest of your courses. So with that, put away your books and get out a paper and pencil."

He didn't hear any groaning as he turned to write the START and STOP times on the board, but inwardly he grinned, remembering the shock he'd had nine years before at being given a quiz the first day of class.

But that was as a Doolie. So he didn't feel sorry for these Third classmen. If anything, after having already been at the Academy for a year, by now they should know to expect the unexpected.

O   O   O

The academic classes hadn't changed since Rod had graduated. The teaching schedule consisted of a two-day block, with each block consisting of an "M" day and a "T" day, seven class periods to a day. They alternated the blocks so that on the first week M-day classes would fall on Monday, Wednesday, and Friday, with T-day classes on Tuesday and Thursday; the following week they switched, with T-day classes held on Monday, Wednesday, and Friday, and M-days on Tuesday and Thursday.

As Rod walked back to his office he looked over the 14 available class times within the two-day block, mystified by how they had scheduled him to teach his five classes. He knew the cadet's schedule had been optimized to take into account the different labs and other activities that needed back-to-back two-hour time slots. But his five classes were just about as poorly scheduled as if someone had done it on purpose.

His early morning classes didn't bother him, although he was not really an early morning person—that hadn't changed since the

Academy. It was a fact of life that most USAF planes had a zero-dark-early wheels up, so he lived with the knowledge that when he was assigned to an operational fighter squadron he had to report at 0300 for a 0500 takeoff. So although he didn't like teaching the first period, early morning M- and T-day class times, he lived with it.

The real killer was that he also taught the same class—sophomore-level Introduction to Theoretical Mechanics—three other times over the two-day block: every day immediately after lunch, as well as 7th period on T day. So he not only got the sleepy heads in the morning, still groggy after marching to breakfast, but he also got the cadets right after they'd eaten a huge noon meal, when the infamous meal monster would sneak up and cause them to nod off.

Rod remembered how hard it had been for himself to stay awake after lunch, so he was convinced that he'd been given the prime slots because he was a first year instructor. He pondered the schedule as he walked through the sixth-floor office complex. He weaved through the cubicles, past aluminum-bordered, blue Styrofoam walls when he unexpectedly ran into an officer carrying a cup of coffee.

Rod pulled himself up short. "Oops. Excuse me." He noticed the silver leaves of a Lieutenant Colonel on the man's shoulders as the officer bent to wipe coffee off his pants. The Lieutenant Colonel then used a napkin to dab coffee that had splashed on the floor.

"Excuse me, sir," Rod said. "I wasn't paying attention."

The officer scowled as he straightened. "I say, things haven't changed then, have they, Simone?"

Rod's eyes widened as he glanced at the officer's face, then flicked down at his nametag. A cold chill swept through him. Oh crap; it was Whitney. The same Lieutenant Whitney who'd led the rescue at Farnborough … and the same Captain Whitney who'd terrorized him when he was a cadet. But now, it was Lieutenant Colonel Whitney; the only person in the world besides George Delante for whom he didn't have a shred of respect.

Rod stiffened. "Good morning, sir. How have you been?"

"Fine, until thirty seconds ago." Whitney dabbed at his coffee cup. He looked Rod over as if inspecting him for some uniform discrepancy. Seemingly disappointed that he didn't find anything wrong, he held up his chin, giving the same aloof look that Rod remembered years ago. "What brings you back to the Academy, Simone? Visiting, or are you one of the new Nazis over in the Comm Shop?"

Rod held back a retort, not yet knowing if Whitney's slam at the officers in the Commandant's office had been intended for him, or if he actually felt that way about the military instructors and AOCs. In either case, the slur was unfounded.

"I've been assigned to the faculty," Rod said. "Theoretical Mechanics. What about yourself? Are you still with the Engineering department? You've been here a while."

Whitney drew himself up. "Actually, I just returned to the Academy. I completed my PhD." He gave a hint of a smile. "A Doctorate in Mechanical Engineering."

"Congratulations, sir."

"Yes. And I suppose you heard the announcement this morning?"

"Announcement?" Rod frowned. "No, I haven't."

Whitney glanced at Rod's uniform and nodded coyly at his silver pilot wings. "NOTAMs—Notice to Airmen. You're a flyer. Don't you read them every morning?"

"Yes, sir, when I'm in a flying unit. But I didn't know the Academy posted NOTAMs—"

"Well, they do. But not for flight warnings. You should pay more attention. They're posted daily in the Theoretical Mechanics department to keep the faculty up to date on important activities and announcements. I suggest you start reading them."

"Yes, sir." Rod shifted his weight, anxious to get out of the officer's presence. Whitney had been arrogant enough when Rod had been a cadet, but now as an officer, Rod didn't have to put up with him. Since Whitney was in another department all he had to do was to avoid him.

Rod stepped to the side. "Excuse me, Colonel. I have to give EI." The charge to provide Extra Instruction to cadets superseded almost every other priority in the world.

Whitney lifted his chin. "I say, I'm sure we'll be seeing a lot of each other, Simone. Enjoy your assignment."

"Thank you, sir. I will." Instead of making his way to his own cubicle, Rod headed straight to the department head's office.

Two secretaries sat in desks at either side of the large, outer office suite. The far wall was covered with picture windows that looked over the Terrazzo, giving a spectacular view of the newly completed Chapel at the west end of the campus. The department chair's office was on the right with a similar wall-sized window view.

Rod rapped on the department chair's door and peeked in. The room was vacant, cleared of the books and memorabilia with which Lieutenant Colonel LeCompte had decorated his office.

Rod stepped back and glanced into the executive officer's office. The Exec had his back turned to the door and was speaking on the phone in low, guarded tones.

The front office was the nerve center of the Theoretical Mechanics Department, and Lieutenant Colonel LeCompte ran the department so efficiently that Rod was perplexed that he hadn't been told about the NOTAMs. In fact, he hadn't seen any sign of the postings on the department bulletin boards or common areas.

The Exec hung up and rolled his chair to the bookcase behind his desk. Rod tapped on the door.

Captain Bobby Andrew, the Executive Officer swiveled in his chair. "Hey, Lightning. You want to see me?

"Yeah, gotta minute?" Rod said.

"Sure, have a seat." Bobby waved Rod into the small room.

The Exec served as the office manager and executive assistant to Lieutenant Colonel LeCompte, and was plugged into everything going on in the department. He kept close contact with all the Executive Officers at the Academy, trading information and keeping everyone abreast of anything that might transpire. As a senior Captain, Bobby had taught in the department for three years, and his exec's job would insure him a choice assignment when he left next summer.

Rod shut the door and pulled up a chair.

Bobby grabbed a notebook off his desk. "Hey, Lightning, before you begin, I need to schedule you for an altitude chamber test up at Lowry."

"What for?"

"You're still on flying status, aren't you? We need to keep you current." He pushed the notebook over to Rod. "Pick a date, then we can sign you up to take cadets on their motivational rides in the T-33s." Pilots had to have a certain number of flight hours each month to keep their rating current.

"Thanks," Rod said. He flipped through the pages and signed up for an afternoon slot the following week.

Bobby placed the notebook on his bookshelf and turned to face Rod. "So, what's up?"

"Do you know anything about department NOTAMs?"

Bobby darkened. "How did you find out about that?"

"I ran into Whitney, from Mechanical Engineering. He terrorized me as a cadet."

Bobby shook his head and muttered something.

"Excuse me?" Rod said.

"Nothing," Bobby said. "I was just thinking to myself." Displaying his bomber pilot roots, Bobby's office was decorated in the vein of an SAC ready room. Pictures of Russian fighters covered the walls, with the words WOULD YOU RECOGNIZE HIM A HUNDRED MILES AWAY? printed underneath the photos. On his desk were pictures of him standing in front of a B-47 and B-52. Almost like a shrine in the middle of the wall, nestled carefully above enlarged wooden pilot wings and a picture of Pope Paul VI, was an autographed picture of General Curtis LeMay, creator and patron saint of SAC.

Rod said, "Why did you ask how I knew about the NOTAMs? Colonel Whitney said they're posted in the department."

Bobby sat for a moment as if he were debating what to say. Suddenly he pushed off the desk, walked around to a table, and picked up a stack of papers. "These are the NOTAMs, the first ones. I haven't posted them."

"What do you mean the first ones? Whitney said all the departments post them."

Bobby shoved a paper at Rod. "All the departments? Try just ours."

Rod picked up the NOTAM and shook his head, confused. "What am I missing?"

"Whitney ordered it."

Rod blinked. "Whitney? He can't do that. He's in another department. What's he thinking?"

"To make us more like a flying squadron."

"What!"

"You got it," Bobby said. "I think it's stupid as spit to pretend we're an operational unit. We're a military academy, for goodness sake, not an SAC unit getting ready for war."

"I agree. But how can Whitney order you to post these things? He's not even in our chain of command."

Bobby gave a wry smiled and nodded at the NOTAM Rod held. "Think again, Lightning. Your biggest nightmare is about to come true."

Rod glanced over the NOTAM. The quasi-official document looked like the real thing, but the contents were pure fluff, not on the level of flight warnings at all. They listed:

• Snack bar officers;

• Seating officers to check for attendance at football games;

• Extracurricular activities officers;

• Officers assigned to prepare coffee every morning;

• Officers assigned to check safes in the morning and at the end of the day;

• Officers assigned to ensure faculty desks were clean at the end of the day;

• Officers assigned to check that lights were turned off at the end of the day;

• Officers assigned to ensure trashcans were emptied at the end of the day;

and on and on and on....

Rod was about to give the NOTAM back to Hank when he read the last page:

THE PRESIDENT IS PLEASED TO ANNOUNCE THE SELECTION OF LTCOL (COLONEL, SELECT)

L. BRADFORD WHITNEY AS PERMANENT PROFESSOR AND DEPARTMENT HEAD, THEORETICAL MECHANICS, USAF ACADEMY, EFFECTIVE 14 AUGUST 1964.

He drew in a breath. The effective date of the appointment was tomorrow.

Rod looked up at Hank, feeling the color drain from his face. "So Colonel Whitney's ...

"You got it. Our new boss, the Thet Mech Department Head." He looked to the heavens. "The smoke has risen, a new ruler anointed. The king is dead; long live the king."

Rod slumped back into his chair. "Oh, great."

Bobby snatched the NOTAM. "Welcome to USAFA, Lightning. I bet you didn't think it was going to be like this coming back as an officer."

"This doesn't surprise me. We had a word for it when I was a cadet."

"What's that?"

"BOHICA."

"Excuse me?"

Rod pushed up to leave for his office. "A cadet term that probably showed how much we always expected to get screwed: Bend over, here it comes again."

CHAPTER NINE

"You Really Got Me"

August 21st, 1964

United States Air Force Academy
Colorado Springs, CO

There is no excellent beauty that hath not some strangeness in the proportion.

Francis Bacon, Essays, "Of Beauty"

Rod looked for Julie in the Officers' Club bar, downstairs from the main dining room. He pushed through the Friday night crowd, mostly younger company grade officers like himself, captains and some lieutenants. The older, field grade officers—majors and lieutenant colonels—made an obligatory appearance, but they usually disappeared, having children and families to return to. He felt right at home in the homogeneous group: college educated with at least a master's degree, mostly pilots, and all with young, attractive wives.

He spotted Julie sitting at a table with a row of whiskey sours lined up in front of her. Happy Hour's 30 cent drink specials ended in ten minutes, so Julie had spent three dollars for their evening entertainment.

She held up a drink, "Hey, Lightning *Rod!* Come charge me up, baby!"

A jukebox in the corner belted out the Beatles' "She Loves You." Some of the pilots were in their green cotton bags, but the majority of officers were dressed identical to Rod, in a Class-A tan coat and tie.

The noise in the bar reminded Rod of a cadet party, but that's where the similarity stopped. Not only were there more women here, but since most everyone was married, no one put the move on anyone's wife—unlike some fighter squadron parties he'd attended—which led to a completely different dynamic.

Rod slid in the chair next to Julie. "Hey. Did you miss me?"

She leaned over and gave him a long, wet kiss.

Someone behind them whistled, "Hey, get a room!" then laughter.

Rod pulled back and rubbed a hand along her side. "I need to be late more often."

Julie pushed a row of whiskey sours to him. "I thought this afternoon would never end. I'm looking forward to some adult conversation."

Rod looked panged. "Is that all you're looking forward to?"

"Save that for later, Lightning. I need a drink!"

He needed a drink as well after learning about Lieutenant Colonel Whitney's promotion, especially since the man was now his new boss. But he'd tell Julie that bit of news later. In the short time since he'd been back as an instructor, Rod had learned that any discussion in public that even hinted of criticizing the Academy would spread like wildfire and would eventually come back to bite him.

Rod tipped his glass in a salute. "Did Nanette drive you crazy?"

"It wasn't her. I dropped her off at the child care center this morning." Julie glanced at her watch. "It closes at eight, so don't forget we have to pick her up." She lit up a cigarette and said in a conspiratorial whisper, "It was the old ninnies from the Officers' Wives' Club."

Rod feigned a look of shock. "Old ninnies? You mean the Colonels' wives?"

"Worse, generals' wives. And retired generals' wives at that. You know how they can be. With the exception of Mary, that is."

"Mom was never the proper general's wife."

"Thank goodness for that; I might have never married you." She snuggled close and held onto his arm.

Rod shot down his drink. "Wow." He shook his head; the whiskey sour burned his throat. "So what happened at the Officers' Wives' Club?"

"We had a luncheon at the Broadmoor, and a speaker gave a presentation on the Cadet Chapel. Did you know that Cardinal Francis Spellman dedicated the cadet chapel last September?"

"Yeah, the Archbishop of New York. But I thought you liked that type of historical presentation."

"I do. Especially compared to the culture we had in Arizona."

"Culture? What culture?"

"Precisely. But I didn't mind the lecture; that was great. It was the seating chart."

"For the luncheon?" Rod picked up his second drink.

"That's right. They seated us according to our husband's rank."

"What?" Rod stopped his glass in mid-air.

"You didn't know that I'm Mrs. Captain Simone?"

Rod blinked. He put his drink on the table.

Julie took a long drag of her cigarette and blew smoke to the side. "They sat Mrs. Retired General so-and-so next to Mrs. Retired Colonel, who sat next to Mrs. Major, and so on, all down the table. I was placed at the end of the table, with the other Captain wives."

"That's crazy. You're not in the military."

"It gets better. I was actually seated ahead of the other Captains' wives, next to the Majors' wives—get this, because my husband is an Academy grad."

"Not because I'm a pilot?"

She dug an elbow in his side. "That would only matter if another Captain's wife had a husband who was a grad."

"Then you'd still be sitting next to the Majors' wives cause I'm a fighter pilot!"

"Think again, Lightning. I was told that bombers rule the air, no matter what their big-ego fighter pilot husbands think."

Rod laughed. "Why are they doing this?"

"Hell if I know. I'm still learning the rules. But when I do, they'd better watch out."

Rod drank his shot. "Do they know your father's an Ambassador? They should have put you at the head table."

Julie snuffed out her cigarette. "Rod, does it matter to people what you were before you became an officer?"

He paused. "It does if they know I was a cadet. That was obvious from the pecking order among your so-called Captain wives. But it doesn't matter to me."

"This is different. What matters now is my husband's rank, and not who I am, or what I do, or even if I'm from society. I was even given a book that explains all that when I joined the Officers' Wives' Club."

"You're kidding."

"You should read it; it's a hoot. *The Air Force Wife*. What's not in the book is that it really matters that you were a cadet. And a pilot, and even a Guggenheim Scholar."

Rod pondered that for a moment. "But those are my accomplishments. I'm the one in the military, not you. Why should you be treated any different than anyone else, just because of my rank or what I've done?"

"It doesn't matter what you think, Rod. That's the way it is."

"But my mother never experienced anything like this—

"Rod," Julie interrupted softly. She leaned close and kissed his ear. "Rod, your mother was the wife of a two-star general. Ask her what it was like when your father was alive, or even when he was on active duty. And remember, she is one of a kind."

"So are you!"

"I can handle this. Now that I'm learning the rules, I know exactly what I need to do to be accepted." She picked up her glass.

The strains of "Twist and Shout" erupted from the jukebox.

"Why didn't you tell me about this at Willie? Or at Seymour Johnson?"

"It didn't happen in those places. You were all pilots, and you were all lieutenants or captains, just like everyone else. There wasn't a pecking order."

Rod nodded. It didn't make any sense, but it seemed she understood the rules—if you can call them that—however crazy they might be.

But what mystified him was that knowing her society background, and how easily she'd been accepted in Europe and in the DC area when she was younger, then why wasn't breaking into the Officers' Wives' Club a piece of cake? Hopefully it wasn't because she was intimidated. He almost snorted at the thought, because that would mean she wasn't the same girl he'd married.

He gulped down his third drink. "Wow, I needed that." He held out his hand. "Join me on the dance floor, Mrs. Captain-Academy-Grad-Guggenheim-Fighter-Pilot Simone." He bowed. "Now that I'm back at the Academy, I feel like a cadet again."

Julie grinned and joined him on the dance floor. "Only if you promise to show me the same stamina you had as a cadet."

"Hey, I can still dance!"

"That's not what I meant, Lightning."

CHAPTER TEN

"A Hard Day's Night"

September, 1964

**United States Air Force Academy
Colorado Springs, CO**

Everything is funny, as long as it's happening to someone else.

Will Rogers

Six weeks later Rod had an opportunity to excel by performing one of the myriad extra duties required of Academy faculty: serving as the Officer-in-Charge of the cadet area.

When he was a cadet, Rod never wondered how they picked the OIC. The Officer-in-Charge changed every 24 hours so Rod had always assumed it was a duty rotated among the Commandant's staff. But every so often, the Dean of Faculty would help the Comm and volunteer one of his officers for the job.

So at 0200 hours, after starting his OIC duty some 8 hours earlier, and after walking miles around the dormitory area insuring that the cadets were indeed following the lights-out policy after taps, Rod closed the door to his small cubicle at the back of the

Command Post and prepared to get some sleep. He'd instructed the Senior Officer of the Day, a First classman serving the 24-hour shift with him, to wake him at 0530.

Although he was going to miss his class later in the day because of his OIC duties, he was thankful he wasn't serving on the weekend, especially two weeks from now. That was when the Academy played Navy at home, and every three- and four-star general in the Air Force would descend onto the Academy to confer about Air Force matters in an event called the Corona Conference—but in reality to cheer their team on to victory against the gutless Navy squids.

Corona was a much too visible time to be the OIC.

As it was, the Academy was almost a month into the football season and cadets swarmed over the campus at night, displaying their team spirit by pulling pranks—such as moving the Bell X-2 experimental plane from the Terrazzo to Arnold Hall. It had taken the USAFA Civil Engineer over a week to use a crane to pull the airplane out of the area. No one could figure out how the cadets had wedged the plane in the tight spot, much less how they negotiated moving it through the narrow halls, but it had been done nonetheless.

Rod neatly hung up his clothes and slipped under the covers, exhausted from his inspections. He needed to get some sleep, if for no other reason than to be prepared to keep on top of any nocturnal spirit activities. It wasn't a question of if the cadets would play a prank; it was a matter of when. And as much as he never would have believed it, life had been much easier as a cadet.

O   O   O

"Sir, wake up!" The Senior Officer of the Day stood at the door.

Rod sat up in his cot. *Time to get up already?* He rubbed his eyes and glanced at the clock. 0350. He'd been asleep less than two hours.

He pushed out of bed and strode over to the closet in his underwear. "What's the matter?"

"Sir, I ... I—"

"Don't tie up. What's the problem?" Rod looked through the closet, trying to find his clothes. He switched on the light and squinted from the glare.

"I was gone for just a minute, and when I returned, the door to the Command Post was open. I think someone snuck in while I was in the bathroom."

"Did they take anything?"

"No, sir. I did a quick inventory and the personnel folder is still present. So is all the telecommunications equipment. And I had the dorm keys with me the entire time."

"Good man. Get back up front. See if you can spot anything on the Terrazzo."

"Yes, sir." The cadet disappeared.

Now that his eyes had grown accustomed to the light, Rod turned back to the closet. Several overcoats, raincoats, and even a pair of athletic shorts hung in the closet, but his uniform was nowhere to be seen.

Rod ran a hand through the hangers. He glanced at the closet floor, thinking that his uniform might have fallen off the hanger, but there was no sign of his clothes. Only his shoes and socks remained underneath his bed.

A thought hit him. Someone must have taken his pants and shirt, his uniform. But why?

"Sir!" The Senior Officer of the Day's voice came excitedly from the front. "You need to see this! There are clothes flying from the top of the flagpole!"

Clothes? A cold chill ran through him. He slammed the closet door shut and raced to the door. The First classman ran up, his face flushed from the discovery.

Rod saw dark shapes dash past the Command Post. He heard muted laughter, the sound of feet running on the Terrazzo.

He looked up at the flagpole and couldn't believe what he saw. It was his clothes, his uniform flapping a hundred feet off the ground in the cool night air. Rod felt his face grow flush. "Get my uniform down from the flagpole! This place is crawling with cadets who know I'll be out of commission for a few minutes. Anything could happen."

"Should I call the Deputy Commandant? His instructions are to contact him if anything big happens."

Rod shooed him out the door. "Get my uniform. I'll call if we need him."

"Yes, sir."

Rod padded back to the closet. He pulled on blue athletic shorts, figuring he'd at least try to see was going on out on the Terrazzo. He rummaged around the closet for a pair of tennis shoes, but not finding any he quickly pulled on his black socks and black leather shoes. He knew he was helplessly out of uniform and looked like a crazy man, but he hoped that his presence would stop any pranksters before things got bad enough to call the Deputy Comm.

Ten minutes later, after helping the Senior Officer of the Day untie the flagpole ropes, Rod had his uniform back.

In the meantime, Rod had switched on the surrounding lights near the Command Post so that whoever was out on the Terrazzo would know that the OIC was awake.

He quickly changed and trotted out to the grassy area by the knoll. Nothing. He walked back to the Command Post, mystified as to why things suddenly appeared to be so quiet.

The cadet Senior Officer of the Day looked worried. "Should I call the Air Police?"

"Keep the APs out of this," Rod said. "These are pranksters, not criminals." He opened the drawer to the desk and pulled out a ring of keys. He picked up a walkie-talkie and switched it on; a burst of static came from the speaker and he turned down the volume. He tossed the device to the cadet. "Keep this. I'll take the other one and inspect the dorm. Call me if you see anything."

"Yes, sir."

Rod grabbed the second walkie-talkie and a flashlight before running out the door. In a way he felt ridiculous. Chasing cadets performing pranks was not his idea of having fun. Yet, the cadets knew they weren't supposed to be out of their rooms until reveille, no matter how infantile that may seem.

He also knew that the cadets just couldn't pick and choose which regulation to obey, no matter how crazy the reg might seem. Although he may not agree with every single regulation himself, he was duty-bound to enforce them. And if that meant chasing twenty-year-old men—boys, really—around a dark campus in the middle of the night, then so be it.

He remembered a time not long ago as a cadet when he was hitting golf balls off the top of Harmon Hall, so he knew the cadet mindset. But he'd matured, and now he was on the other side of the fence.

And to make things worse, what would the cadets do if he ignored the regs? They'd notice, that's for sure. They might think he was cool for allowing them to get away with what they thought was a small infraction, but would they later hesitate to obey him in a life or death situation if they weren't aware of the consequences?

An hour later the cadet area was still quiet. The display aircraft were still on the Terrazzo, none of the windows in the dorm had been soaped, Fairchild Hall was empty, and the immense granite Chapel Wall was unperturbed.

Rod felt perplexed as he swung his flashlight over the cadet area. He stood in the middle of the Terrazzo, having walked the entire cadet dorm, down to the gymnasium, and through the academic and administration buildings. No one was on top of Harmon Hall. The new planetarium and Arnold Hall were about the only other places he hadn't looked.

His eyes widened. The planetarium and cadet social building; why hadn't he thought of those places before? With a sudden cold shiver, he started jogging toward Arnold Hall. He ran across the Terrazzo and made his way past the honor court to the far, western part of the campus. He tapped down the stairs in front of Harmon Hall, playing his flashlight all around. Nothing.

He walked to the front of the cadet social center and ran his flashlight over the building; it looked untouched, no sign of any cadets.

He turned and illuminated the planetarium.

He nearly fell backwards at the sight.

The smooth, white hemispherical planetarium now had a large, red object sitting on the top, making the rounded mound look like a huge female breast, complete with an obscene, erect nipple.

"Oh, great," Rod muttered. Even with just his flashlight, Rod could see the gigantic nipple was painted bright red. There were no ropes holding it on, and in the context of being located on a nationally-recognized, federal landmark, it looked surreal: Demarcating the western boundary of the nation's newest all-male, military university was an incredibly large, female mammary gland.

Rod stepped up to the planetarium and placed the flashlight on the ground. He tried climbing on top of the planetarium, but was unable to gain any purchase on the steep, smooth sides.

He walked around the building for a good quarter hour, every minute growing more astonished at how the cadets had been able to pull off the stunt. It no longer mattered to him that he'd be reprimanded for allowing this to happen on his watch. He realized that his pants being run up the flagpole had been a deviously clever diversion, and that the night's real mission was to pay tribute—in a twisted cadet way—to the female anatomy. Despite the irreverence, Rod started chuckling; not at the nipple, but at the cadets' creativity.

He knew why the cadets pulled these pranks: to a man they were above average in intelligence; but compared to their peers at non-military colleges, they appeared incredibly immature, mostly as a result of being kept isolated in the cadet area.

The Air Force wanted its Academy graduates to be self-assured, to take the initiative and never give up. And this prank certainly demonstrated that.

But the cadets were receiving a mixed message. They were expected to be aggressive, to live up to their role models and excel as brash fighter pilots … yet their behavior was reined in by seemingly puerile cadet regulations.

To the cadets, the pranks were a way to blow off steam; but it created a chasm, in how the Air Force expected the cadets to behave versus what they actually did.

Rod remembered that just a few weeks ago a band of cadets had dressed up as commandos, painted their faces with green and black camouflage, and had hijacked a freight train that slowly chugged across the eastern Academy boundary. The chasm was made evident by the fact that the commandant had been furious, while the cadets had thought it was hilarious. It was too bad the cadet shenanigans were sometimes infantile themselves.

Rod's walkie-talkie filled with static. "Sir, this is the Senior Officer of the Day. It's a half an hour until reveille. Did you find anything?"

Rod clicked back. "Yes, I did. Call the Deputy Commandant as soon as possible. Ask him to meet me by the planetarium." Rod stole another look at the giant red nipple and shook his head. "And tell him ... no, just warn him he's not going to believe his eyes."

CHAPTER ELEVEN

"It's Over"

Two weeks later
September, 1964

United States Air Force Academy
Colorado Springs, CO

An Act of God was defined as 'something which no reasonable man could have expected.'

A. P. Herbert, *Uncommon Law*

Rod looked up from his desk at the knock.

Captain Bobby Andrew stood in the doorway. The department executive officer grimaced as he rubbed his hands together. "Head's up, Lightning. Did you pass the altitude chamber?"

Rod closed the textbook he'd been using to prepare for the next day's lesson. "Are you kidding? How could I flunk?"

"And you're current in the Thud?"

Rod was certain he didn't hear the Exec right. "You mean the T-33? Sure."

"No, I mean the F-105."

Rod frowned. "The Thud? Of course. It's only been a few months since I've flown it. But there aren't any Lead Sleds at Peterson."

Bobby lowered his voice. "Then just act surprised when Colonel Whitney asks."

Rod stood and moved close to the door. "Sure. What's going on?"

"The Corona conference started today; coincides with the football team playing Navy this weekend."

"Yeah," Rod said. "No kidding. I haven't seen so many generals in one place since I graduated. So what's that have to do with me being current in the 105?"

"A few of the four-stars wanted to fly back to Washington, DC in a fighter after the Navy game, so they're ferrying some two-seater F-105Fs out here. Most of the planes won't show until right before the generals are due to fly out."

"So?"

"The 105 pilots won't have enough crew rest to ride back with the generals, so they're tapping pilots on the faculty. Since generals aren't allowed to fly by themselves, you're one of the few Thud drivers that can help out."

"But why the secrecy? What's the big deal?"

Bobby sighed and stepped into Rod's cubicle. "Ordinarily it wouldn't be a big deal, but with you it is."

"Huh?" Rod blinked. "What have I done this time?"

"Remember that fiasco with the nipple on the planetarium? You're on Colonel Whitney's bad boy list."

"Come on. I just discovered it, I didn't do it!"

"But they had to blame someone. Remember, we live in a fishbowl. And since you're in Theoretical Mechanics, the spotlight's on our department. Now Whitney's afraid you're going to do something even worse. It's an open secret he's shooting to be Dean after General Mac retires, so I'm sure he thinks that if any of his faculty steps out of line, it will hurt his chances of getting that star."

"So I'm stuck between General McDermott wanting me to fly a four-star back to DC and Colonel Whitney not wanting me to go. Ten to one I know who wins that disagreement."

"You got that right. It's just a matter of time before Whitney agrees with the Dean. But you can also bet he'll keep you in the dark until the last minute. So keep this quiet, would you? Just act surprised when Whitney talks to you about flying the four-star."

"Are you kidding? When hasn't he surprised me?"

Bobby grinned and backed out of the small office. He pointed a finger at Rod and clicked it, as if it were a gun going off. "And do try to behave yourself, Lightning."

Rod gave a flat-handed British salute. "Right-o, Captain."

O   O   O

Early Sunday morning at Peterson field, the day after the Navy game, Rod walked around the F-105F Thunderchief and inspected the fighter during his pre-flight check. Floodlights illuminated the flight line. A yellow auxiliary power unit was pushed up in front of the jet, and at the side sat a portable aluminum staircase that led up to the cockpit.

Rod was dressed in his green flight suit as he visually inspected the fuselage. He ran his hands alongside the smooth under-surface as he checked for leaks, protruding metal, or anything that looked out of place. He reached up and grabbed the wing, then moved the flaps up and down. Satisfied that the fighter looked airworthy, he walked around to the front.

To the east a touch of red tinged the dark horizon over the prairie; sunrise was still a half hour off. JP-4 permeated the air and wafted over three other dual-seated F-105s parked on the ramp. It was a grand day for flying.

Rod adjusted his sunglasses and started climbing the cockpit steps when the enlisted crew chief stepped out from under the plane. Normally, the tech sergeant would have worn a T-shirt and fatigue pants because of the heat on the flight-line, but with the presence of so many general officers, the man wore a pressed fatigue uniform, shined combat boots, and a white scarf tucked into his shirt.

The crew chief wiped a wrench with a cloth and called up to Rod. "Good morning, sir. Looks like the general's convoy is approaching."

"Thanks." Rod climbed back down and stood at parade rest in front of the plane. A blue staff car flying a small four-star flag on the front bumper drove onto the flight line. Air Police guards standing on the yellow DO NOT PASS line brought their rifles up in a salute. Behind the car drove a two-ton truck with a tarp thrown over the back.

Rod waited as the staff car rolled to a stop. An airman jumped from the driver's seat, ran around the front of the car, and opened up the back door. There were so many stars on the general's flight suit that Rod almost couldn't count them. He stiffened as the man approached, and for good measure he threw in a salute.

The general returned the greeting. "Howdy, Captain." He stuck out a hand. "Glad to meet you; my call-sign's Speedy. The only thing you need to know is that I've got the aircraft unless I tell you otherwise. Just don't let me kill myself, got it?"

"Yes, sir," Rod said. *Speedy?* He stared at the general's nametag: SPEEDY BEAUMONT. His father's friend and wingman, and the man who'd given him the oath of office to swear him into the Air Force, five years ago.

"Good. As soon as they're finished loading my bags, let's kick the tires and light the fires." He trotted up the stairs.

"Ah, yes, sir," Rod said to the general's back.

"So, what's your handle, son?"

"Sir, I'm Rod Simone. Call sign Lightning. I'm ... I'm Hank McCluney's son—"

General Beaumont did a double take. He grinned wildly and bounded down the stairs. "You sure the hell are! Didn't see your nametag in the dark. How are you, son?"

"Fine, sir."

"And your mother, Miss Mary?"

"Doing well, sir. Still living east of the Academy. But you wouldn't recognize the place—they're building a golf course next to her property and she's not the only house out there anymore."

"Great to hear it." He hesitated, then placed a hand on Rod's shoulder. His voice grew quiet. "Look, Lightning, you know I headed up the Accident Investigation Board of your old man's crash."

Rod felt his face grow warm. "Yes, sir. I know. The way I read it, the report implied it was pilot error—"

"And that is bullshit, son. We couldn't find any real evidence Hank did anything wrong. There were a few bad gauges in the cockpit, but that's typical of aircraft that old. As far as we could tell it was a toxic combination of a stuck altimeter, a malfunctioning fuel gauge, and unexpected thermals."

"But the report didn't rule out pilot error!"

Beaumont twisted his mouth, as if he'd eaten something bitter. "This may come as a surprise, but unless a Board's findings are 100% certain, the government sometimes avoids admitting the possibility of a manufacturing error, which might result in retrofitting an entire fleet of aircraft. As such, there's tremendous political pressure not to explicitly blame equipment malfunction; millions of dollars could be at stake if anyone sues the manufacturer. So implying pilot error is usually the easy way out, no matter who the pilot had been."

Rod's breathing quickened. This was insane! His father had been a great pilot and was well respected throughout the Air Force; back in the early '50s he'd even been asked to help establish the Academy. In addition to serving on those commissions appointed by President Eisenhower, as a retired two-star general Hank had helped the Academy throughout its entire construction phase. And the only animosity he'd ever shown toward anyone was to the Delantes....

Rod frowned as he remembered the bad blood between the two families. It seemed as though his father had warned him about the Delantes for years, but that last run-in they'd had in the El Paso County Courthouse had severed their ties forever.

Unless the Delantes had somehow been behind those broken gauges in his father's plane....

Rod said slowly, "But maybe if someone had sabotaged his plane, they'd have gotten away with murder—"

"Now hold on, son. No one's talking about either sabotage or murder," Beaumont said in a sharp voice. "I said the Board didn't find anything wrong with the plane that would conclusively cause the crash. We even had an independent materials lab in Colorado check for anomalies. The Board's Executive Officer handled it himself, so we'd ensure we didn't miss any detail. So before you start jumping to conclusions, remember that the Board was charged with finding cause, not to fix blame or conjecture."

"I understand."

"All I know is that your old man was too good of a pilot to lose control of an aircraft, no matter how rough the thermals might have been." He slapped Rod on the shoulder. "Tell you what. If you're hard over for the details, I'll put you in contact with that lab. That way you can see for yourself, find where the facts lead you."

"Yes, sir," Rod said. After getting worked up about the possibility of learning what had really happened that night his father died, he felt suddenly tired—which wasn't good, considering the long flight ahead of them.

They quickly walked around the F-105 and pre-flighted the craft before Speedy climbed into the front seat, leaving the back for Rod.

As Rod started up the stairs leading to the cockpit, he heard the two-ton truck that had followed the staff car back up to the plane.

The crew chief stepped around the fighter and waved his arms at the truck. "That's close enough!" He spoke with the driver, then stepped over to the fighter and opened a side compartment.

Two airmen hopped from the truck and started unloading crates. They packed the compartment full of the cartons, then moved underneath the fighter, where they filled the bomb bay.

Rod squinted at the boxes. Each was stenciled with the name COORS in large, block letters. The crates were full of a local beer that Rod knew was brewed in Golden, a small town west of Denver.

The crew chief climbed up the stairs and insured that they were secure in their seats. The enlisted man removed the pin with the black and yellow tag from the explosive seat ejection system, and then slapped Rod on the shoulder. "All set, sir. Fly safely."

"Thanks. I'll have to with all this beer."

The crew chief paused, then grinned, showing gold-capped teeth. "Happens every time the generals fly out of here. Coors isn't distributed outside of Colorado. My sources at the Pentagon say it's the talk of DC."

"I bet."

The crew chief stepped down and wheeled the stairs away. Rod went hot-mike. "General? It's time to go over the checklist, sir."

"Copy."

Rod riveted his attention to the checklist. Hydraulics, fuel, oil pressure, idle RPM—everything looked good as they ran down the list.

Minutes later General Beaumont's voice came over the intercom. "Okay, let's haul ass."

Rod clicked twice, giving his concurrence as the canopy started to close. Although the general was supposedly only going along for the ride, and Rod was legally the aircraft commander, it was obvious that the general was in complete control.

The crew chief used two orange sticks to direct the fighter away from the tarmac, then popped to attention and snapped off a salute. Rod returned it, feeling a chill run down his spine, like every time he flew.

Although he knew he wouldn't do much during this flight, he still got a thrill knowing that once again he was seated in the world's most advanced fighter. All he had to do was to insure that Speedy didn't kill himself.

O O O

Later that day

Sometimes it's better to ponder an action before acting, especially if the repercussions haven't been well thought out.

Rod flew back to Colorado Springs in the F-105 he'd used to ferry General Beaumont to Washington and should have had plenty of time to think. This usually prevented the "Ready, Fire, Aim" syndrome of acting on instinct and charging off on a half-baked idea.

At 35,000 feet above sea level, the world stretched out as a mottled green and brown patchwork of colors, rising to meet the curved horizon ahead. The sky above diffused into a deep, dark blue so beautiful that it almost made his heart ache. It was times like this Rod enjoyed the most, literally miles removed from the nearest person. His wingman, another instructor who had also ferried a general back to Washington, DC, was flying in loose route formation at four o'clock and 5,000 feet behind him.

Rod had more than enough time to contemplate.

But performing deep, thoughtful analysis and flying a fighter were almost two mutually exclusive events—especially when controlling several tons of hot, screaming metal traveling nearly the speed of sound.

The idea hit Rod when he spotted the top of Pikes Peak emerge just over the horizon. Although the mountain was still over a hundred miles away, Rod should have had plenty of time to weigh the pros and cons, but the idea so excited him that the cons just … evaporated.

He glanced at his fuel gauge. He had plenty of gas for the short detour, as he was well under the F-105's 2,000-mile range. He scanned the rest of the console—everything looked great and the clock showed it was just before noon, local time.

The radio clicked and a voice came over his headphones. "Guzzles One and Two, this is Kansas City air traffic control. Handing you off to Denver Approach Control. Contact them on 278.9"

Rod keyed his mike and spoke to his wingman. "Guzzle go 278.9."

"Two."

Rod switched frequency and contacted Denver Approach Control. "Guzzle One, Denver Approach."

"Go ahead."

"This is Guzzle One. Request permission to deviate from our flight plan in order to fly over the Air Force Academy. I graduated from the first class and would like to display my aircraft to the cadets."

The controller said, "Permission granted, Guzzles One and Two. You are cleared for Visual Flight Rules to the Academy, then on to Peterson. We're awfully proud of you guys."

Rod confirmed the message with his wingman, and with eager anticipation hoped the timing would work out.

The ground crew at Andrews Air Force Base, MD, outside of Washington had turned their jets around quickly, unloading the boxes of Coors, refueling, and launching him back in the air for the quick trip home. And now, with the noon meal formation coming up, Rod knew that the cadets would be assembling on the Terrazzo, getting ready for First Call.

His plan was to approach from the south and fly in low enough to give the cadets an up-close view of their fighters. The second fighter, Guzzle Two, would come in close behind him. Rod remembered that properly timed, such motivational fly-bys could incite the Wing to a riot. And today, when the cadets discovered a grad was in command of the flight, it should excite them even more.

Rod banked to the south of Peterson Field after radioing that their ETA had been modified. He clicked his mike. "Guzzle Two, Lead. Keep your airspeed down and altitude up. Wait until I've cleared the cadet area before following me in."

His wingman clicked twice.

Rod didn't fly down to lower altitude until he passed over the red sandstone of Garden of the Gods; the rocky cathedrals looked almost surreal from above.

They followed a shallow glide path, and as they dropped to 1,000 feet above the foothills, the F-105 bumped up and down in the choppy air, turbulence created from cool air sliding down the Front Range mixing with hot air rising from the plains. Years before, supposedly severe turbulent conditions had gotten the best of his father.

He spotted the silver triangular cross-section of the cadet chapel nestled against the Rampart Range, up ahead in the distance. The controversial architecture was so space-age that cadets joked they didn't know if they should pray in it, pray at it, or pray for it. Light glinted off the tips of the aluminum spires.

His radio clicked. "Lead, Guzzle Two. Problem with my altimeter. Looks like it sticks."

"That's a rog. Stand by one." Rod craned his head around. Outside conditions were perfect. It might have been a little cool outside, but the sky was crystal clear, unchanged from this morning's take-off from Peterson. Rod knew that both he and his wingman had more than enough experience to do a VFR, or Visual Flight Rule, flyover. So even with Guzzle Two's uncertain altimeter they should be fine.

He clicked his mike. "Keep well above me, Guzzle Two. Stay behind in loose route. If there are any additional problems, immediately break off. Understand?"

Two clicks came over the radio.

He pushed the stick forward and dropped closer to the ground. He'd perform a classic combat maneuver, come in over the foothills, making him virtually invisible to the cadets on the Terrazzo, then pull up and roar over the Wing. If he timed things right, he'd give the cadets a thundering view as he flew overhead.

He passed over the north end of Pine Valley. His blood began to pound in his temples and his hands grew slick from sweat. He grinned at the excitement. The jet bumped through the thermals as he pushed the F-105 even faster; his breath quickened.

The hospital flew beneath him in a blur as he dove into the final valley before the cadet campus. Thickets of Douglas fir and aspen trees whizzed by beneath him, interspersed with granite boulders, a winding asphalt road and steep ravines. He felt a surge of adrenaline roar through his veins as he brought the fighter over the top of the final hill before the campus—

The Academy sat on the flat plain of Lehman's Mesa and looked like a picture on a postcard. Aluminum gleamed in the sunlight; waves of heat rose off the granite Chapel wall, the stone and marble Terrazzo. He bore in on a vector between the Chapel and Mitchell Hall.

The cadets were barely visible as a matrix of dots on the Terrazzo as the Wing lined up for the noon meal formation; they stood rigidly at attention.

Suddenly, the block of cadets started to undulate as they started jumping up and down. Some pointed at his jet, others pumped their fists in the air. Rod thundered across the Terrazzo and rocked his wings. He pulled up and looked behind him as Guzzle Two made his approach.

Rod felt his heart race. Guzzle Two was coming in too low and much too fast. Dust swirled up in rolling vortices trailing his jet. Debris filled the air, swept up behind the fighter. A dark, dusty cloud roiled across the Terrazzo and approached the campus like a haboob enveloping a desert city.

Cadets scattered as if chaff in a thunderstorm. Entire squadrons hit the ground and held their hands over their heads. Other cadets sheltered their face with their arms and staggered for safety. The jet looked as though it was flying lower than the top of six-story high Vandenberg Hall.

Rod screamed over the mike. "Pull up, pull up!"

Suddenly, Guzzle Two seemed to stand on its tail as the pilot yanked back on the stick and kicked in the afterburner. The fighter shook violently as it roared up, barely clearing the buildings.

Looking back over his shoulder, Rod saw the Academy campus dwindle away. The cockpit was still bathed in silence. Angry at what his wingman had done, Rod clicked his mike. "Guzzle Two! Report!"

"Ah, bad altimeter, lead. But that's not the worst of it."

"What?"

It took a moment before the reply came back. "My Mach meter reads 1.02."

Rod was stunned. His wingman had just reported that he had gone faster than the speed of sound, exceeding Mach 1. That would have created a dangerous sonic boom over the cadet area that could have injured people. Or even killed someone if there was any broken glass. But his wingman couldn't have been going that fast.

Or could he?

Something must be screwy with his wingman's console.

Rod yanked at his yoke and rolled out of the bank, determined to find the underlying cause. His face felt hot, as if the temperature had soared in the cockpit. He'd report the discrepancy when he landed and would insure this nonsense would never happen again.

He flew VFR direct to Peterson Field, angry at his wingman ... and himself.

O   O   O

Fifteen minutes later Rod pulled to a stop in front of Peterson Field Operations; his wingman taxied in behind him. Rod raised the canopy. Fresh air hit him as the sound of jet engines cycling down through the frequencies rolled into the cockpit. The enlisted man directing them brought down his orange sticks before moving an aluminum set of stairs to the jets.

Rod disarmed the ejection seat, unbuckled his straps, and climbed out of the cockpit. His legs felt wobbly as he climbed down the stairs, his helmet in hand. After nearly six hours in the cockpit, his quick jaunt out to the east coast and back reminded him just how tiring flying could be.

A blue staff car flying a flag with a colonel's eagle drove up to the tarmac. The car stopped and an officer wearing sunglasses and dressed in a tan, short-sleeved uniform stepped out.

Rod wanted to talk things over with his wingman, find out what in the world had gone wrong, but he needed to acknowledge the colonel first.

Rod saluted. "Good afternoon, sir. I'm Captain Simone, just returned from Andrews. Before my wingman's Thud is ferried back home, the crew chief should inspect the altimeter. He reported some screwy readings—"

"Are you Guzzle Two?" the colonel interrupted. Rod's wingman stepped up and saluted as well. The colonel didn't return their salutes, but instead stood with his hands on his hips.

"I'm Guzzle Two, sir," Rod's wingman said.

The colonel ignored Rod and turned his attention to the officer. "Young man, do you know you went supersonic over the Academy campus?"

Rod and his wingman stiffly held their salutes as the sound of sirens warbled in the distance.

"Yes, sir. That's why I'm putting the craft in for a maintenance check."

Two Air Police cars, their sirens wailing, screeched to a stop by the colonel's car. Four air policemen jumped out of the car.

Rod slowly dropped his salute. "Is anything wrong, sir?"

"I'd say the hell there is, Captain." The colonel whipped off his sunglasses and glared at Rod's wingman. "You broke nearly every damn window at the Academy, and several cadets have been hospitalized. You're going to be lucky if all you have to do is pay a few million dollars to replace the glass." He turned to Rod. "And you're in deep trouble, too young man."

"Sir?" Rod felt flush. The Air Police had walked up behind the colonel. Rod felt as if every eye on the flight line was on them.

"That's right, mister. You were in command of that flight. Depending on how your court martial goes, you could be looking at a stint in Leavenworth for enabling willful destruction of government property and endangerment of human life." He paused. "And you'd better be praying that none of those injured cadets dies—because it will mean life imprisonment for both of you."

O   O   O

Rod screeched to a halt in his carport. He tried to settle down as he waited outside their two-bedroom Pine Valley home, his heart racing, and his face flush.

His hands shook as he tightly gripped the steering wheel. He couldn't stay here long, otherwise the neighbors would suspect something was wrong. In some ways, living on USAFA grounds was like living in a fishbowl—all aspects of their lives were open for everyone to see.

He yanked his green flight bag out of the car and lugged his equipment into the house. The front door was open, and he heard the sound of the TV from the living room. The smell of cigarette smoke rolled from the other room.

"Is that you, Lightning?" Julie's voice came over the TV.

"Yeah," he said, heading for the bedroom. He threw his equipment to the side, next to the oak dresser and unzipped his flight suit; the bag rolled onto the floor, spilling its contents. He still couldn't believe his wingman had disobeyed his orders. How much clearer could he have been, instructing Guzzle Two to keep his altitude up and velocity down? He almost couldn't contain his anger—

Julie appeared at the door holding a long-neck beer bottle; a cigarette dangled from her other hand. "Want a beer?"

Rod sat on the end of his bed, unlaced his combat boots, and then struggled to pull them off. He threw them to the corner. "I've got to burn off some energy."

"What's wrong?"

It took an effort to keep it in, to not take it out on Julie. "I've ... been sitting too long in the cockpit."

Julie took a long sip of the bottle. She moved next to him and caressed his shoulder. "Nanette's next door. How about burning that energy off in bed?"

He twisted away. "Later. I've got to run."

She pulled back and cocked her head. "Are you okay?"

"I'm fine." He stood and ripped off his flight suit, then padded to his gym bag.

"How was the flight?" When he didn't answer she took a drag of her cigarette. "That general you flew wasn't an asshole, was he? I can't imagine being cooped up on a cross country flight with a jerk."

"The general was a gentleman." He jerked out a jock, short pants, white socks, black tennis shoes, and an old cadet blue-collared t-shirt that had SIMONE stenciled above the right breast. *The horse's rear end was my wingman, the guy who was supposed to be watching my six.* He couldn't get his mind off what this might do to his career, how everything he'd worked for the past ten years might be flushed down the toilet ... all because his hotdog wingman thought he'd pull something cute.

Maybe his father had been right all those years he'd spent badmouthing fighter pilots. Maybe they were an arrogant, self-righteous lot—including himself.

But he knew most fighter jocks weren't like that ... or in the past had he just been exposed to a much higher caliber of pilots?

"Then what's the matter? The Lightning I know doesn't turn down an invitation to bed."

Rod tied his shoes and straightened. He tried to keep his tone even. "Look. I've just got to get out and run. Burn off some steam. Later, all right?"

"Okay." She followed him to the front door. "When will you be back?"

"Later."

"Right. Later."

Rod started jogging west, toward the Rampart Range. He cut across the small cul-de-sac and followed the road as it turned north.

Cars whizzed past, and within minutes he came to a dirt road. He left the pavement and followed the path to the mountains. The ruts deepened, and soon it was apparent that only a jeep could make it up the rocky trail.

The path steepened as he ran into a grove of Douglas fir and aspen trees. Rod pushed himself, feeling his heart rate increase. Sweat dripped off his forehead and ran into his eyes. Step after step, he forced himself on, inwardly cursing himself for his stupidity as he ran. Afterburners. Why did his wingman disobey his direct order to stay above him?

They'd been cleared to fly VFR above the Academy so Rod himself hadn't done anything wrong; but still, as flight commander, it was he who was ultimately responsible.

He gasped for breath as he reached the top of the foothill. The Academy hospital was visible to the right; in front of him the cadet chapel stood out as an icon overseeing the cadet area. It hadn't been more than a few hours since the fly-by, but he knew his life had been turned upside down by the event. He could face prison time if the court martial didn't go his way, especially if they were looking to find a scapegoat. What did the colonel say, several million dollars of damage? And more importantly, he hoped no cadets, or anyone else on the Terrazzo, had been critically injured.

To the north the jeep path plunged down into a valley, where the top of Cathedral Rock peeked over a distant mesa. In front of the ridge he saw two smaller hills that he would have to traverse before reaching the cadet area. The hills were called the Three Bears, and he'd just conquered the largest of the three, Papa Bear.

The wreckage of his father's plane was at the bottom of a deep canyon, behind him, just below Eagle Peak. It was in such a steep location that no one had ever pulled it out.

He thought about running there, especially after remembering General Beaumont's explanation of the Accident Investigation Board report. Maybe there was something in the wreckage the Board had overlooked that would vindicate his father's name, and prove pilot error didn't cause the crash; after all, General Beaumont had mentioned finding a few faulty gauges.

And then he remembered that suspicion he'd had at Stanford about George Delante being involved....

But Rod had hiked to the wreckage before, and it would take a few hours to get to the crash site. He'd need a full day to go through the debris, and he also needed to take General Beaumont up on his offer to get in contact with that lab who performed the post mortem of his father's crash site.

There was too much to do and not enough time. For now, he decided to jog to the cadet area instead. Exhausting himself physically seemed to be the right thing to do on his path to mental repentance.

O O O

Two hours later Rod trudged into the house. The sun was setting over the Rampart Range as mountain shadows crawled toward the eastern plains. It would still be light for another hour, but he was glad to have made it back before he became a target for the cars whizzing along the Academy's winding, perimeter road.

The screen door banged shut behind him. The theme from the *Wonderful World of Disney* played on the TV, and the house smelled of cigarette smoke and stale beer. Nanette's high-pitched laugh came from the next room. He decided to shower and leave her with old Walt for a while.

He waited for steam to start billowing from behind the shower curtain. He threw his running clothes, sopping wet with perspiration, in the corner and climbed in the shower. Moments later, his eyes closed as he shampooed, he heard Julie's voice.

"How was the run?"

"Good." He turned into the shower to rinse his hair; at least the exercise had calmed him down.

"Speedy called."

Rod instantly stepped back from the shower spray.

"General Beaumont?"

"He just said Speedy." Her voice was slurred. "I don't know if this has anything to do with the mood you're in, but he left a message."

Rod was almost afraid to ask. "What did he say?"

"He'd heard what happened and told you not to worry about it. He said he'd ensure there was a full and open investigation. No one was going to get railroaded."

"Did ... did he say anything else?"

"Only that you're one shit-hot pilot." The shower curtain moved to the side. "But I could have told him that." Julie let her bathrobe fall to the floor. She stepped in. "I told him you'd gone on a run, and he said to be sure to settle you down when you returned." She started soaping his chest. "So have you settled down?"

"Yeah," he said, pulling her close. He drew in a deep breath; felt a surge of relief washed over him.

General Beaumont. If his dad's old wingman had called to reassure him, then his fears might have been all for naught. Maybe he would still have a career. "Funny how things keep working out."

She kissed his neck. "How's that?"

"I just keep waiting for the other shoe to drop."

CHAPTER TWELVE

"What Kind of Fool Do You Think I Am"

October, 1964

**United States Air Force Academy
Colorado Springs, CO**

*I seem forsaken and alone,
I hear the lion roar;
And every door is shut but one,
And that is Mercy's door.*

William Cowper, Olney Hymns, 33

Several hundred tourists milled around the entrance to the Academy chapel, moving in as many directions as there were people. Some climbed the wide steps to the main sanctuary, while others gaped at the amalgamation of gleaming aluminum, steel beams, and space-age architecture.

Rod held Nanette's hand as he pushed through the crowd, making their way to the low, polished granite wall that overlooked the cadet area. Soon, the Wing would march *en masse* up the inclined ramp to the chapel, and Rod had some time to kill before the two cadets they sponsored completed their mandatory Sunday church service. He sometimes wished they'd had the sponsorship program when he was a cadet so he could visit an instructor's home ... but with his luck he'd probably have been assigned to Captain Whitney.

Nanette tugged at Rod's hand. "I can't see, daddy." She stood on her toes but her head didn't come up to the top of the wall.

Rod swung Nanette up to his hip so she could look out over the Terrazzo. Various airplanes were on display, set on pedestals at the corners of the center grassy area, and positioned to look as though they were soaring through the air. The display craft ranged from an old P-51 to a modern jet fighter.

She pointed at the aircraft, excited that she could recognize the planes. Rod felt a swell of pride. He'd bought Nanette a different toy jet plane every time he went on a trip, and she'd become quite adept at recognizing the inventory of USAF fighter and bomber aircraft. Pretty decent for a little girl; she was nearly as good at identifying planes as Cadets Nelson and Wilson, the two Third class cadets his family sponsored.

Rod was scheduled to meet Nelson and Wilson after this morning's chapel service and he couldn't resist bringing Nanette here early to show her around. The sponsor program had been set up to allow cadets an opportunity to spend some of their off-duty time with military families, allow the cadets to have a home away from home, a place to relax and unwind, and experience military life in a family setting. It had been such a hit the year before that the Academy chaplains had aggressively blanketed the Colorado Springs military community and encouraged officers to take in as many cadets as possible.

Behind them, a majority of the crowd took pictures and gawked at the new cadet chapel, ignoring the rest of the campus. The chapel's seventeen spires jutted majestically into the blue sky, a futuristic structure constructed of metal and glass, looking as if a giant silver accordion had fallen on its side. Cadet folklore was that the seventeen spires stood for the twelve apostles and the five Chiefs of Staff of the US military services. Another urban myth was that the chapel held half the US's strategic reserve of aluminum— and that the Coors beer company would pay top dollar for every pound smuggled to its brewery to use for their cans.

They waited for their cadets and a flood of memories rushed over Rod as he gazed over the Terrazzo. With the newly built chapel, everything seemed so new. Yet in some ways things hadn't changed at all. If he hadn't been dressed in his officer's uniform, Rod felt as though he could march onto the campus and step right in to being a cadet; it was almost as if he'd never left.

He watched the Fourth classmen running on the white, marble strips like rigid, blue-suited robots. They ran at attention with their arms locked tightly at their side; they looked straight ahead and kept their backs straight, heads erect. Every so often an upperclassman would yank a Doolie aside and force him to stand at attention while being blasted for some gross disparity. Shouting echoed over the Terrazzo.

The Wing fell into formation, and once called to attention, started trooping toward the chapel ramp for the morning services. The strains of "Stars and Stripes Forever" reverberated across the campus as a blue block of over 2,000 cadets marched in step; the crowd turned chaotic as tourists wedged into every available spot to gain a good place to watch.

Air policemen backed the tourists away from the chapel entrance as the cadets came up the ramp. Most of the Wing split off to trudge up the steep steps to the main Protestant chapel, while fewer made their way to the basement for Catholic mass. The morning Chapel services were restricted to cadets with a later service open to the public.

The last of the cadets entered the Protestant chapel and the huge doors slowly creaked shut behind them like a medieval castle slamming its gate, keeping the tourists out while locking the cadets in.

Rod put Nanette down. "Let's look around, hon."

"Where are the cadets?" she said in her high-pitched voice. Her face scrunched up, not comprehending why all the pageantry had suddenly stopped; her dark eyebrows and thick hair came from his side of the family, and Rod imagined if his sister had lived long enough, she and Nanette would have looked uncannily alike.

"They're at church. We'll meet Cadets Nelson and Wilson after the service."

"Are we going to church, too?"

"Not today. We'll look around, instead."

They walked hand in hand through the crowd toward the chapel stairs. Twice, people pulled Rod aside and asked if they could take his photograph, as if they were unsure if Rod was a cadet or an officer. Now that the cadets had disappeared into the chapel, the tourists seemed eager to take a picture of anyone wearing a uniform.

Rod helped Nanette walk down the outside steps to a basement underneath the Protestant sanctuary.

A tour guide wearing a dark skirt, white blouse, and a red vest stepped up as they approached a set of closed wooden doors at the bottom of the stairs.

"I'm sorry, sir. The Catholic mass is closed to the public."

"We're not going to mass. May we look around the rest of the chapel?"

The young lady smiled at Nanette. "Certainly. Please be quiet though, and remember—"

"Mass is off limits. We won't enter the sanctuary. Promise."

"Yes, sir. Thank you." She turned back to guard the stairs like a moat dragon.

They entered the doors to the basement and stepped into a large vestibule to face the door to the Catholic sanctuary. They stood in the middle of a corridor that encircled the entire lower sanctuary. The floor was carpeted and the walls were painted with soft colors, making the basement look warm and inviting. Rod picked up Nanette and walked briskly around the corridor until they were well past the sanctuary doors.

Administrative offices ringed the outside hall. Paintings of airplanes in flight hung on the walls. The planes were shown flying high above massive cloud formations, and in one, a giant hand reached down from the heavens as if to help a damaged jet limp home.

They reached the Jewish synagogue at the opposite end of the great circle. As they passed, Rod thought he heard sounds coming from inside.

"What's that, daddy?"

"It's where the Jewish people worship, hon."

"Can we go inside?"

"No, they're in church ..." Rod stopped. He put Nanette down. "No, they're not. They worship on the Sabbath."

"What's that?"

"Just a minute." Rod stepped forward. He'd promised not to interfere with the Catholic mass, but this wasn't the Catholic chapel. He was curious as to what was going on. Maybe the Jewish cadets were holding a meeting.

Muffled laughter came from inside. That's strange. It didn't sound as if someone was conducting a meeting ... then he remembered that the Jewish cadets served as CCQ and in other official duties while their Protestant and Catholic classmates attended chapel. So there shouldn't be anyone in there; at least there shouldn't be any cadets.

He opened up the door and the noise abated.

Rod furrowed his brow. Nearly fifty cadets sat around in chairs, their Alpha jackets off, ties loosened. Several card games were in progress and he heard a pair of dice hit the wall. He smelled a faint odor of cigarette smoke.

"Room, atten'hut!" Someone had spotted Rod's silver Captain's bars.

Chairs pushed back as the cadets scrambled to attention.

The room was deathly quiet; all eyes were on Rod.

Rod surveyed the cadets. He felt his jaw tighten. They were obviously ditching either the Protestant or Catholic services. Both were mandatory formations, and if the services were skipped, it was punishable by serving time on the tour pad.

"Everybody's quiet. Are they praying, daddy?" Nanette tugged at his hand, her high-pitched voice echoed throughout the synagogue.

"They are now," Rod said. He remembered marching tours as a cadet and it hadn't been any fun at all; in fact, it had been a complete waste of his time. He'd received the punishment because he'd disobeyed cadet regulations, and the experience was so bad he still remembered the mindless boredom.

Now, as an officer, and especially as a member of the Academy staff, he had a duty to enforce cadet regulations. There was no question as to what he should do: line up the cadets, take down their names and squadrons, then report them to their AOCs—where they might then be marching tours for the rest of their cadet careers.

On the other hand, a few weeks earlier Rod had been granted an amazing amount of mercy through General Beaumont's intervention after his low-level flight over the Academy. The four-star had insisted that his wingman's F-105 be disassembled and inspected piece by piece to find a faulty part, the part that might have caused the F-105 to accidentally exceed Mach 1, and break both the speed-of-sound and nearly all the glass on the Academy campus. It had taken dismantling the fighter three times until another sensor beside the faulty altimeter was discovered, thus vindicating them ... so Rod knew from firsthand experience what it was like to screw up royally and be given a second chance.

But still, regulations were regulations....

Every eye in the synagogue was on him. He recognized two of the cadets from one of his classes. Sweat dripped off one cadet's forehead and splashed on the linoleum floor.

Once again Nanette broke the silence. "Daddy, I have to go to the bathroom."

"Not now, hon."

"I've got to go bad."

"You can't wait?"

"No!"

And it was suddenly apparent what he should do.

"Okay, I'll take you to the bathroom." He raised his voice. "Then I have to come back and start taking the names of these cadets ..." he hesitated, then said under his breath, "that is, whichever ones are still here." He swung her up and put her on his hip. "Let's go."

He was barely out the door when he heard frantic scurrying come from inside the synagogue. The sound of chairs being straightened, cards picked up, dice put away, ties tightened, and jackets buttoned, diffused into the sound of cadets tip-toeing out the door behind them.

When he returned a few minutes later, the synagogue was dark. He flicked on the lights; the place looked immaculate.

Nanette looked around, wide-eyed. "Where are the cadets?"

Rod closed the door and started the rest of the way around the basement perimeter. "Maybe they slipped into the Protestant or Catholic service, but I imagine most of them are probably hiding out. In any case, they learned a valuable lesson, hon."

Nanette twisted her face and looked up at him.

Rod smiled and squeezed her hand, suspecting that chapel services would be uncommonly packed next week.

CHAPTER THIRTEEN

"Suspicion"

October, 1964

United States Air Force Academy
Colorado Springs, CO

Discovery consists of seeing what everybody has seen and thinking what nobody has thought.

Albert Szent-Gyorgyi, *The Scientist Speculates*

Rod had a free Saturday for the first time since he'd signed in to the Academy and decided to put it to good use. He'd wanted to revisit the crash site of his father's plane before the first snow set in, and today looked like the perfect day to do it. He was lucky bad weather hadn't hit, and when it did he wouldn't be able to make the hike until late next spring.

Earlier in the day he'd dropped Nanette off at the Child Care Center so Julie could attend an Officers' Wives' Club social. He drove to the cadet area and parked his car west of Academy Drive in a dirt lot next to the hiking trail, then left a note on the windshield detailing who he was and where he'd be, and started hiking up Eagle Peak trail toward Stanley Canyon.

He struck out at a fast pace, eager to reach the site so he'd have time to rummage through the wreckage and associated debris. The sky was clear and deep blue, with a hint of fall coolness and the invigorating smell of ozone; a lone prairie falcon wheeled overhead in the thermals. Douglas fir towered on either side of the trail and he felt exhilarated, eager to reach the site.

The trail met up with Goat Camp Creek and he took an offshoot to the right that would take him north of Eagle Peak to a steep, desolate canyon. He kept a steady pace and felt like running up the mountain trail, but he didn't know if he'd be bringing back any items from the wreckage and he wanted to conserve his strength.

He passed a thicket of yellow aspen trees interspersed with granite boulders and patches of scrub oak. The scrub oak had turned a dull orange and would soon lose its leaves; in another week the aspens would be at the height of their color.

He rounded a small crest and stopped at the top of the canyon. To the right he saw two of the Three Bears he'd run a few weeks before, after returning from that disastrous flight over the Terrazzo when his wingman had blasted out windows in the cadet area; he winced when he thought of the damage and the injuries. To the left, Eagle Peak soared nearly 9,400 feet in altitude, standing over two thousand feet higher than the Academy grounds. The cadet area was behind him, and in front of him a canyon plunged down a good 500 feet, holding his father's crash site securely in its grip.

Five years ago he'd been fortunate to have his father's body evacuated from the site in spite of the steep terrain. Rod and his mother had agreed with the decision to allow the wreckage to remain where it lay, especially considering how difficult it would be to remove the scattered debris. An unexpected benefit was that the site would remain as a lasting memorial to his father's memory.

Rod turned and started climbing down the sheer drop, taking care to secure purchase with his hands and feet as he lowered himself down the canyon. He descended foot by foot, moving across rock and exposed tree roots to find a toehold on the path down. He remained patient and didn't try to hurry as he methodically descended the 500 feet to the canyon floor.

A bead of sweat gathered on his forehead; he paused to wipe it off. He'd made the climb twice before, once immediately after his father's crash, and the other right after he'd arrived for his teaching assignment.

It was peaceful here and eerily quiet. The canyon walls were shielded from the wind gusting down the Rampart Range as well as the noise from cars that constantly drove along the Academy perimeter. He was thankful that the site was so secluded; it was a fitting place for his father's crash site, and ensured that it would hardly ever be disturbed.

As he descended he heard the faint whoosh of a breeze rustling through the aspen. He smelled the scent of pine in the mountain air; water gurgled against rock in a stream bed below.

He reached the narrow bottom and strode off to the south, pushing aside brush and ducking under low lying tree limbs as he walked upstream next to a narrow creek. Shortly he spotted the wreckage on the east side of the canyon, twenty feet above the creek bed.

The plane had split in three major parts, with the cabin standing nearly vertical at the base of two large Douglas fir; the tail section and wing had ripped off and were embedded in pine trees mid-way up the canyon wall. The door to the cabin was open, left unclosed from when Hank's body had been removed from the craft immediately after the crash, five years before.

Rod held on to the trunk of an aspen and pulled himself up to the front of the fuselage. He looked inside. Nothing had changed from the time he'd been here back in June, a week after he'd reported for his teaching assignment. Hank's seat belt hung out the door; the front of the engine was implanted in the dirt, and a bird nest with leaves and dry straw sat just inside the cockpit.

Rod pulled himself up and balanced on the metal doorframe. A brown residue was smeared on the pilot's seat and controls. Hank's blood? Rod ran a finger along the stain, but nothing came off, just as the last two times he'd checked. It was as though the blemish was now a permanent fixture of the crash site.

He pushed inside the cockpit and looked around. Two of the dials, the altimeter and gas gauge, had been removed from the instrument panel during the Accident Investigation Board. Rod remembered General Speedy Beaumont's observation that the sticking gauges didn't solely contribute to the accident, which is why the crash had been ruled as pilot error. He'd even said that an independent analysis had been made by some materials lab here in Colorado.

But yet, if General Beaumont had been convinced as much as Rod that his father was a better pilot than that, and if the altimeter and gas gauge weren't proof enough for causing the crash, was there another contributing factor? Had something else triggered the crash? Was there a chance that the Accident Investigation Board and the independent lab had both missed the underlying reason?

It would be nearly impossible to pull the plane out of this steep canyon, and Rod doubted that another expedition would ever be mounted to comb over the crash site. In the scheme of things, he knew that this was a relatively minor accident, especially compared to having a first-line fighter go down, or a commercial plane with numerous civilian passengers. Still, his father had died, and the reason for the crash was a loose end that Rod wanted to tie up.

He spent the next hour methodically going over the cockpit, running his hands along the gauges, prying open the instrument panel and tracing the wires to ensure they were fully connected, and even working the steering column, rudders, and aileron controls.

Nothing.

He couldn't find anything out of the ordinary, and he was sure the Accident Investigation Board would have discovered the same.

He leaned back against the doorframe. He closed his eyes and tried to hypothesize what it would have been like for his father as he flew over the Academy grounds.

He remembered that it had been windy the night of the crash, because the flag lowering ceremony at retreat had been canceled. So instead of marching to Mitchell Hall and eating with his classmates, he'd driven down to Julie's apartment in Colorado Springs. In fact, the thermals and unusually high wind conditions had been highlighted in the preliminary accident report.

He imagined flying the small plane above the cadet area, banking in the air just before sunset. The plane would be buffeted, rapidly rising and falling as it hit pockets of turbulence. His father would know what to do—gain altitude, keep his airspeed up, and not lose lift; that would rule out relying on the altimeter.

He also knew the rudder and ailerons were responsive, as he'd just tried them. The steering column would have been responsive as well.

So where did that leave him? He furrowed his brow. Could there have been anything else? Hank would have been flying by visual flight rules, but in daylight and with no clouds, flying VFR would not have been a problem.

What about the engine? Could he have run out of gas? Even if the gas gauge had been sticking, Jim-Tom Henderson, the owner of Pine Valley Airport, had testified that his partner had completely filled the tank before the flight, and according to the flight logs, Hank had checked it as well.

But what if there had been a leak? A stuck gas gauge would not have shown that.

Rod opened his eyes. If there'd been a leak there'd be some evidence around the fuselage—streaks of gas, stains, a hole or something.

He grasped the fuselage, swung out, and looked over the bottom of the craft. Nothing but scratches from falling through the trees. He knew that six years of snow, rain, and weather might wipe away any evidence, so he decided to check the gas inlet.

He shimmied up the fuselage and balanced himself on the tree branches that held the craft upright. The panel to the fuel tank was open, so someone must have thought of checking this before.

Rod unscrewed the fuel cap. He pulled it out and stopped, stunned. Fumes rolled into the air and it was evident that the tank still had fuel in it, so there couldn't have been a leak; but he saw a white substance lining the edge of the cap, as though something had crystalized around the perimeter.

He hesitated, then touched one of the crystals, and brought it to his nose. Was it his imagination or did it smell sweet?

He touched it to his tongue. He tasted an overwhelming sensation of kerosene, but in addition, it also reminded him of … sugar? How could that be?

A thought struck him. He remembered in high school some kids putting sugar in a teacher's gas tank, and it had ruined the car almost immediately.

Could someone have done that to Hank's fuel tank? And if so, then who? His thoughts raced through the possibilities.

He felt his breath quicken. He'd had that random thought at Stanford, when he'd told Professor Rhoades about his father's accident; and he'd thought about it before he'd flown General Beaumont back to Washington DC when they were discussing the flight investigation board.…

Only one name came to mind, a name that his father had constantly berated, and who his father had admonished him to never have dealings with: George Delante.

He trembled as he pulled out his handkerchief and wiped the white reside from the fuel cap. He rotated the cap to get as much of the material as he could, then folded the cloth and placed it in his pocket. His hands shaking, he replaced the cap and screwed it on tightly.

He swung down from the fuselage and immediately started hiking back to the canyon wall with one goal in mind: to have the substance analyzed and contact General Beaumont about his suspicion.

Chapter Fourteen

"Pretty Woman"

Earlier that day
October, 1964

United States Air Force Academy
Colorado Springs, CO

There's a snake hidden in the grass.

Virgil, *Eclogue*, Book III

Julie Simone stepped into the women's powder room just after entering the Academy's Officers' Club. She'd timed things perfectly. The rest of the social committee hadn't arrived, and being here first allowed her to look her best, without giving the impression that she'd even visited the ladies' room.

She lit a cigarette, took a deep drag, and nonchalantly looked under the stalls. There was no one else in the bathroom or small lounge area except for herself. Good. She was alone.

She pulled a small flask from her purse, unscrewed the top, and quickly gulped two mouthfuls of vodka. She instantly felt a warm, soothing glow.

She basked in the moment; it was nice to be relaxed before the event. But she couldn't overdo it. She snuck a third drink, thought about it, and then a long fourth before returning the flask and taking a final puff on her cigarette. She glanced at her watch; she really didn't have as much time as she'd thought.

She smoothed her pink cocktail dress and brushed a hair off her shoulder. Pulling her long white gloves tight, she leaned forward and insured no lipstick was on her teeth. Her eyes were slightly red—Rod had that damn habit of waking up every other night and grabbing for her, but since she normally woke up around two or three every morning from the booze anyway, it was worth losing a little sleep to keep him happy.

She stepped back and turned partly to the right to look over her figure. She pulled in her stomach. Not bad. Chasing Nanette around their small house helped keep her trim. That was important. She'd learned in Washington that image was everything, and that was especially true while climbing the social ladder; and now she'd unraveled the Officers' Wives' Club unwritten rules, it was true here as well.

The Air Force was attempting to act society, and in some cases they did a fairly decent job—such as here, at the Academy, where there was enough public interest to force them to put on a good front.

But God forbid if she should ever have to live in a hellhole again like Williams, Arizona! Dirt and dust everywhere, and the only social scene had been beer busts at the O' Club and those wives-only outings to the Phoenix museums. Maybe she should have taken mother's offer for she and Nanette to live in Washington, DC until Rod had finished flight training.

And their assignment at Seymour Johnson, southeast of Goldsboro, North Carolina, wasn't much better than Williams. Talk about a backwater town.

She'd married Rod for the excitement, not the boredom; and the best way to have it was to marry someone from the first Academy class. Their assignment at Stanford, with its faculty parties and visits by heads of state, was probably the closest they'd come to experiencing real society, and the last time she'd really been happy. Because of Rod attending the Academy and his scholarship, they were the center of attention there, and even as a young mother, Julie thrived.

Being an Air Force wife implied the exhilaration of doing something different, of getting away from the life she'd been programmed to lead—of marrying some boring lawyer from Georgetown, raising his brats, and never leaving Washington, DC.

But now she missed the social life. She missed being the center of attention. She missed socializing with the politicos, and she didn't know if she could wait even more years until she was Mrs. General Rod Simone to achieve the stature she knew she deserved.

So until things changed, she was going to have to do it on her own terms.

They tried hard playing society at the Officers' Wives' Club. They put on the teas, they dressed up, they wore the white gloves, they put their husband's calling cards in a collection bowl at the beginning of every function, and they even sat according to their husband's rank in the military hierarchy. She, of course, was already an expert in a similar culture, having been bred as an Ambassador's daughter, so it came by instinct.

All she'd had to do was to decode the rules, and exploit them to make them work for her. And that meant immersing herself in the social activities and making herself indispensable.

People quickly found they could count on her to do the right thing, to invite the right crowd, and to impress just the right person, so that everyone felt so wonderful after the events she sponsored. And in doing so, her stature increased.

Because in the land of the blind, the one-eyed woman was queen. It didn't take long to regain the excitement she'd known when she was part of real society. And that was a very good thing, because she was really getting tired of being just a Captain's wife, near the bottom of the social ladder. She was getting to the point that if things didn't get better she'd have to make a change. A radical change. She wasn't sure what that was, but she knew things couldn't remain the same. It would drive her crazy.

She took a deep breath and stepped out of the Ladies lounge to greet the first of the social committee. She didn't have to wait long.

"Mrs. Jacobs, so glad to see you." Julie held out her hands and tightly grasped the outstretched hands of Mrs. Colonel Jacobs, the frumpy wife of the base commander. Mrs. Jacobs' husband was not a pilot, and this assignment was probably the highlight of his career. Rod had observed that the man was a good administrator, but he didn't have the vision to see beyond his own belly.

"Julie, dear, you always look so perky. How do you do it raising a little one?"

"That's why the Air Force invented child care centers," Julie smiled, then changed the subject. "I haven't checked on the meal. Should we?"

"Good idea." They walked back to the dining room and surveyed the area set aside for the luncheon. Waitresses in white blouses and black skirts placed salads on tables covered with white linen tablecloths. Tables were staggered throughout the room, with the head table set near a podium for the speaker. A wall-sized glass window on the north side of the dining room revealed a forested valley with a stunning view of the cadet dormitory, academic building, and chapel on the mesa.

The hostess stepped up. "How do you do, Mrs. Jacobs, Mrs. Simone. Would you care to inspect the kitchen? We are just about finished preparing the chicken fried steak."

"I'm sure it's fine, thank you," Julie said. She turned to Mrs. Jacobs. "Perhaps we should arrange the place cards for the head table. It's important the Mayor's seat be next to the podium so he won't have to walk around anyone before his talk."

"Oh, the mayor." Mrs. Jacobs blushed. "Julie, dear, I forgot to tell you. The mayor's office called yesterday and he won't be able to make it. The council is holding a special session today and he needs to give some sort of presentation."

"The mayor won't be able to come?" Julie stopped. She took a deep breath and forced a smile. Inside, her thoughts yammered, *What the hell do you mean he won't show up? Why do you think the Superintendent's wife made a special effort to be here?* She felt her face grow flush.

"No, but he arranged to have someone take his place."

"Mrs. Jacobs, perhaps you don't understand. We've had a record number of RSVPs because of the mayor. Who could possibly take his place, especially at the last minute?" She didn't settle for a used car salesman, did she?

"He's a state senator representing El Paso County and the entire Colorado Springs district."

The words set Julie back. "A ... senator?"

"That's right. The mayor said the senator will be running for Congress next year, so he should have an uplifting speech for us."

Julie felt her heart start to slow. At least the substitute sounded interesting. And he was sufficiently important that she might not lose any face with the luncheon committee, even without the Mayor's presence.

She needed the luncheon to be executed as a well-orchestrated play, with everything from the food to the speech overwhelming the guests, especially the Superintendent's wife. It was important to have this come off perfectly. And with the Superintendent's wife supporting her, it would open the doors to the social functions in Colorado Springs, where she hadn't been so successful breaking in.

Julie thanked Mrs. Jacobs and moved to the front door to serve as the official greeter as the women drifted in.

Within minutes two ladies entered, one dressed in a two-piece, pink Mort Schrader dress with matching headband, and another in a burnt brown Chanel dress, white gloves, and pill box hat, complete with oversized sunglasses.

Julie extended her hand. "How do you do, ladies. Welcome to the Officers' Club."

"Delighted," Pillbox said. She removed her gloves, finger by finger. "I don't believe we've met. Comm shop or faculty?"

"Faculty," Julie said. *Your turn, dear.*

The woman was trying to determine the pecking order, so Julie wanted to see how this fell out: *So does your husband work for the Dean or for the Commandant?* Which would lead to the next step in the dance: *What's your husband's job and rank?*

The woman smiled. "Yes, I see. No wonder we haven't met. I'm Mrs. Fitzgerald." She paused. "My husband's the ... deputy commandant?" She cocked her head.

"Yes, I'm sorry. I apologize," Julie said. Bingo: Mrs. Colonel Fitzgerald.

Mrs. Fitzgerald smiled.

Julie brought a hand to her chest. "We've only been here a few months. Rod was flying F-105s immediately after his

Guggenheim Fellowship at Stanford, and was ordered as an Academy grad to come back and serve on the faculty; we just haven't had the time to properly make the rounds. But I'm sure your husband knows him."

The women's eyes grew wide; Julie could almost hear their minds whirling as they elevated Julie's status because of Rod's credentials: fighter pilot, national scholar, and most importantly, a grad.

Mrs. Fitzgerald said, "Yes, yes of course! Welcome to the Academy, dear. We served a tour at the Point after Burt's first flying assignment—B-25's you know—and it took a while for us to get used to a nonoperational assignment, even though he was a West Pointer himself. Class of '43. I understand your situation completely."

They left their husband's calling cards in a silver bowl set by the ashtray at the entrance and turned for the powder room. Later, as hostess for the luncheon, Julie would go through the cards with the membership committee and mark off who had attended the luncheon. Those who missed two functions in a row would get a polite call from the vice president of the Officers' Wives' Club; three no-shows and her husband would be spoken to by the officer's commander. Social responsibilities were taken seriously in the Air Force.

A group of woman entered the Club all at once, and for a few moments they mobbed the front entrance. After being greeted they deposited their cards and Julie directed them to the luncheon.

Just as the last woman left, Julie spotted a blue staff car pull under the front awning. An airman first class dressed in a blue uniform coat and tie exited the driver's seat and ran around the car to open the back door. A willowy woman stepped out, dressed in a deep red, three-piece, brocaded cotton suit-dress with acetate jacket and side-zippered skirt.

Jackpot. Julie stepped out to greet the Superintendent's wife.

"How do you do, Mrs. Warren. I'm Mrs. Julie Simone—"

"Of course, I remember, Mrs. Simone. How is that precious daughter of yours?"

"Just fine, ma'am. Thank you for asking."

"She's such a precocious little child."

"We're fortunate the Air Force has provided us with outstanding childcare opportunities, ma'am." Julie took her arm and walked her up the stairs. "Do you need to use the powder room?"

"No, no. Please, I don't want to hold things up."

"Yes, ma'am. This way, please." Julie escorted her to the dining room. A buzz raced through the crowd as they turned the corner and someone spotted the Superintendent's wife. One by one the women stepped up and paid their respects, forming a line beyond the tight circle around the stately woman. Standing to her right, Julie basked in the attention.

As Julie watched dutifully over her charge, she noticed the hostess motioning to come her way. A man in a blue blazer, gray pants, and red striped tie stood looking confidently over the group of women, who now numbered at least two hundred. The man was suntanned with strikingly handsome blond features. He looked as big as a football player and his Beatle haircut was longer than any she'd seen in the military, making his presence even more alluring.

Mrs. Jacobs stepped up to the man and pointed him to the head table.

Julie touched Mrs. Superintendent's elbow. "Excuse me, ma'am. Our speaker is here." She brushed through the crowd and reached Mrs. Jacobs and the state senator.

Mrs. Jacobs beamed as she made the introduction. "Mrs. Simone, may I present Senator Fred Delante. We're delighted that he's agreed to stand in for the Mayor today."

Julie extended a hand. "Welcome to the Academy Officers' Wives' Club, Senator." She cocked her head. "Excuse me for being so bold, but you look familiar. Have we met?" She tried to place where she may have seen him before, but she couldn't quite think straight between the vodka and the Senator's penetrating eyes.

The man's eyes widened and he seemed somewhat taken back. "Mrs. ... Simone?"

"That's right."

He studied her for a moment, as if he were at a momentary loss for words. "I'm sorry. I was thinking about my speech, and

I'm afraid I allowed my thoughts to wander." He flashed a grin, showing strong, white teeth. "Thank you for inviting me. I'm looking forward to getting to know you."

"The pleasure's mine, Senator." A moment passed and neither of them spoke; she felt lightheaded, perhaps due to the vodka....

She suddenly drew back; she felt flush as she realized he'd been holding her hand the entire time. This wouldn't do! She glanced around but thankfully no one had noticed. Her heart began to slow. Any type of flirting by an officer's wife would immediately make the rounds of the base, and heaven knows what it might do to Rod's career. And of course, it wouldn't matter if she had instigated it or not; she had her image to maintain. And Rod's path to general.

Julie forced a smile. "I'll introduce you to the Superintendent's wife. We're about to get started."

As she moved through the crowded room, she felt as if all eyes were on her escorting the Senator to Mrs. Superintendent. After she introduced the two poles of power, Julie picked up a glass of white wine and took a sip.

No one looked her way, and she couldn't detect any whispers or murmuring about her *faux pas* with the handsome state senator. She felt as if a weight had been lifted from her shoulders. Things were going well; she couldn't imagine things going better.

CHAPTER FIFTEEN

"Do You Want to Know a Secret"

Later that day
October, 1964

United States Air Force Academy
Colorado Springs, CO

While to deny the existence of an unseen kingdom is bad, to pretend that we know more about it than its bare existence is no better.

Samuel Butler, *Erewhon*, Chapter 15

Rod hiked back to his car from the crash site and swung by the Child Care Center before going home. He signed Nanette out of the facility and walked her through the parking lot, listening to her jabber about all the new friends she'd made. Reaching the car, he opened the door and helped her step up into the white Chevy Parkwood station wagon that had carried them to Northern California, Arizona, North Carolina, and now back to Colorado.

Nanette scampered across the front seat and waited for Rod to walk around the other side. When he opened the door she patted the grey leather seat and smiled up at him. "Right here, daddy!"

Rod slid behind the driver's wheel. "Thanks, sweetheart." He pulled out of the parking lot and tuned Nanette out. He put his driving on autopilot, heading home to their small two-bedroom home in the Pine Valley housing area as he pondered what to do next.

He needed to contact General Beaumont as soon as possible. But aside from trying to call the four-star general at the office—where even on a Saturday, his staff would never forward his call, no matter how urgent it was or what story Rod would concoct—the only option was to call his mother and get the general's home number.

Fifteen minutes later he stood in his small living room and finished dialing General Beaumont. Nanette played in her room, having placed her dolls around an imaginary tea table to tell them about her new best friends. Julie was still out, so Rod could speak frankly about his concern of finding some unknown substance in Hank's plane, even over all these years.

Rod glanced around the room as the general's phone began to ring. Two of his father's airplane pictures from World War II sat on the floor, next to the purple and white flowered couch, a brown leather easy chair, and the new color TV. He felt a surge of annoyance as he saw the Zenith's Space Command remote control sitting on top of the console with the batteries out—he'd shelled out nearly a whole month's pay for the dammed noisy box, and it seemed the remote was always draining the batteries.

A voice interrupted his grousing. "Speedy!"

Rod straightened. "General Beaumont?"

"Speaking."

"Sir, this is Captain Rod Simone, Hank—"

"McCluney's boy! Of course, son. How ya doing, Lightning?"

"Great, sir."

"They cleared you and your wingman of going supersonic, didn't they?"

"Yes, sir, they did. And thanks again, General, for stepping up for us—"

"Anything for Hank's son, Lightning, you know that."

"Yes, sir." Rod was grateful that Beaumont remembered him, but he was also aware that as the quintessential general officer,

Speedy was used to dominating the conversation: he told you when to speak, he told you what to say, and he'd tell you when the conversation was over.

Rod spoke quickly. "Sir, I just returned from my father's crash site—"

"How's it look, Lightning? Have they moved anything?"

"No, sir." Rod shook his head. "They haven't touched a thing, even after five and a half years. It's in the same location—"

"Good. I told the Superintendent to leave the crash site undisturbed as a memorial for your old man. Glad to hear they're following my advice. Now what can I do for you."

"Sir, you told me you didn't think my father was to blame for the accident—"

"Damn, right I don't. Hank was a much better pilot than that. One of the best."

"Well, sir, I thought someone might have missed something during the Accident Investigation Board—"

"Impossible! The staff's attention to detail at that site rivaled a groom on his wedding night."

"Yes, sir, I understand. However, when I opened the fuel tank I discovered a crystalline substance caked around the seal. I think it may have been—"

"That plane's been out there in the weather for over five years, Lightning. Anything could have gotten into that tank."

Rod shook his head. "I beg to differ, General. The fuel cap was screwed on tight and I could still smell fuel—"

"The Accident Investigation Board took fuel samples, Lightning; the Board XO personally took care of that. If there were any abnormalities, it would have shown in the lab results." He paused. "Sorry, son. I understand your concern, but the Board's already covered that base."

Rod felt deflated. He'd gotten his hopes up that he'd found some concrete evidence that his father wasn't to blame for the crash. Detecting sugar in the fuel tank would have meant that the engine had failed and been sabotaged, and the accident hadn't been caused by pilot error.

His theory had seemed to make sense, and it all held together; Rod knew that George Delante's motivation would have been to get revenge on Hank for providing incontrovertible proof of his illegal dealings during the Academy's construction. But General Beaumont had just implicitly ruled out any evidence of anyone having a hand in the crash.

Now he was left at nothing and was back to ground zero.

Speedy's voice shocked him out of his funk. "Thanks for checking out Hank's site, Lightning. And keep in touch son."

"Yes, sir. Thank you, General—"

Speedy hung up before he finished.

Rod sighed. He padded to the kitchen and rummaged through the liquor cabinet. That was strange—they were out of vodka. Instead, he poured himself a stiff drink of bourbon and took a gulp. The alcohol hit his empty stomach like a bomb going off. He'd have to slow down and get some food in him, as well as hydrate from today's hike.

He ran over Speedy's conversation in his head and tried to think of what else he could do to get to the root cause of his father's crash. All the small aircraft's controls appeared to work, yet it didn't make sense those two faulty sensors would cause his father to crash. He refused to believe his father committed pilot error, but everything seemed to point that way.

He poured a second drink and looked in on Nanette. She'd cleaned up her tea party and was now placing toy aircraft in various locations in her bedroom. He felt a swell of pride that she played with the airplanes nearly as much as her dolls.

A fleeting thought crossed his mind. Would she ever want to fly? If so, he knew she'd have to do it on her own as a civilian, much like Amelia Earhart. She'd never have the opportunity to fly in the Air Force, much less attend the Academy. There was just no way they'd ever allow women to fly in the military or attend the all-male institution; even the WAVES in World War II hadn't been considered real military pilots.

But that suited him fine. The Academy was no place for a woman, and he'd be worrying about other, more critical things when she grew older, rather than her being a cadet.

He moved to the living room and plopped in the easy chair. He took another sip when the door opened, bringing in Julie and gust of cool fall air. Her hair was windblown, her cheeks flush; she looked radiant.

"Welcome home." Rod pushed up. "How was the social?" He spoke tentatively, knowing that she wasn't thrilled with Officers' Wives' functions, especially when Rod felt pressure from his department for her to attend.

"Amazing." She threw her purse on the couch and grabbed him by the arm.

He held up his drink to keep it from spilling. "Hey, watch out!"

She put her arms around his head and kissed him hard, drawing him tight. "Umm."

As Rod lowered his drink she broke off her kiss, grabbed his glass and shot down the rest of his bourbon. She kissed him again and pulled him to the couch. Her voice was low. "Now, Lightning. Right here."

"What in the world's gotten into to you?" He nuzzled her neck. "Nanette's in her room. She'll hear us."

Julie pushed him to the couch and straddled his legs. "Then make it quick! I'll keep my coat on—"

The phone rang.

"Ignore it," Julie said.

Rod rolled her to the side and whopped her playfully on the bottom. She giggled as she sprawled back against the cushions.

Rod grinned. "Hold that thought. If I don't answer this, Nanette will." He picked up the black handset and cleared his throat. "Simone residence, Captain Simone speaking."

"Lightning, Speedy."

Rod stiffened. "Yes, sir!" The greeting came as a shout.

Julie laughed at the surprise he'd shown.

"Mommy, mommy!" Nanette ran in the room and jumped on the couch. She squealed as Julie hugged her.

Rod felt a flash of annoyance. He turned to Julie and held a finger to his mouth, shushing them. He tried to tune them out as General Beaumont spoke.

"I've been thinking about that powder you found on the fuel cap," Speedy said. "I looked over my Board notes and I want you to check with the Accident Investigation Board's XO, a Major—"

there was a pause and the sound of papers rustling on the other side of the line, "—Whitney. That's it, Major Brad Whitney. He was on the Academy faculty back then, so you should be able to track him down. Copy?"

Rod shook his head. He felt a slight fog of comprehension from the bourbon. "You mean Colonel Whitney, sir? Colonel Brad Whitney?"

"Hell, I don't know, son. Or maybe he's a light colonel now. All I know is that the Superintendent assigned a Major Whitney to be our Executive Officer for the Accident Investigation Board. And I remember that little weenie was a short, arrogant son-of-a-bitch. He was responsible for inventorying our items and writing up our notes for the final report. Check with him. He'll know what happened to all the samples and can tell you if the lab found any anomalies in the fuel. Show him that white stuff you found around the fuel cap, understand?"

"Yes, sir. Thank you, General—"

"Keep in touch, Lightning. Let me know what you find out."

"Yes, sir—" Rod pulled the handset away from his ear as the line cut off.

Nanette thumbed through a Dr. Seuss book at the far end of the couch. Julie curled her legs beneath her and leaned back. She patted the cushion "What was that about?"

Rod sat next to her. He felt dazed as his eyes focused on the black Bell rotary dial telephone. "It was General Beaumont."

"Speedy? Wasn't that the guy who called after you broke those windows at the Academy?"

"I didn't break the windows, my wingman did."

Julie snorted and rolled her eyes.

Rod gave her a sideways glance. "Yeah, that's him."

"What did he want?"

"I called him earlier about some stuff I found out at the crash site that didn't make sense." He looked at Julie. She seemed somewhat confused and her eyes were bloodshot.

"So why'd he call back?"

"Something he remembered." Rod leaned back against the couch and closed his eyes. "I thought I'd figured out a reason for Dad's crash, and now I don't know what to think. He wants me to look into something and get back to him." He raced through the possibilities, trying to cut through the alcohol in his system and bring events into focus.

He was sure that his department head was the same Major Brad Whitney with whom Speedy had been so unimpressed. The general's assessment of Whitney being an arrogant little son-of-a-bitch summed up the man perfectly.

It made plenty of sense that the Superintendent would assign then-Major Whitney as the Executive Officer for the Accident Investigation Board. Rod remembered Whitney and his performance years ago at the Farnborough Airshow taking charge of rescue operations after the crash. In fact, that was one of the memories Rod had of first wanting to go to the Academy, ironically because of Whitney's quick-thinking reaction to the crisis, and attributing that to him being a West Point graduate.

But there was something else that nagged him about Whitney, something separate from being a supercilious senior officer. It had to do with the line of reasoning he'd been following earlier in the day, before General Beaumont had shot down his rational. Now what was that? Was it something to do with George Delante?

Julie nuzzled him on the neck and broke his chain of thought.

Rod opened his eyes and put his arm around her. He glanced at Nanette; she was absorbed in her book. He lowered his voice. "Your luncheon must have been a hit for you to come back so randy. Reminds me of our cadet days. Didn't any of the generals' wives show up?"

"They were there. And the luncheon went off well. Even the speaker."

"The Mayor?"

"No, some state senator. You wouldn't know him. Turns out he's running for Congress." She rubbed Rod's shoulder. "So what are you going to do for Speedy?"

Rod drew in a breath. He wasn't looking forward to approaching Colonel Whitney about the white substance he'd found caked inside the fuel cap. Although General Beaumont had specifically told him to have Whitney help figure this out, the general didn't have Whitney as his boss. And although Beaumont was a four-star general and Whitney was only a colonel, Speedy was back in Washington, DC, and Whitney was here.

"I have to ask Colonel Whitney to look into something for me, and he may not want to do it."

"Won't Speedy help?"

"Oh, he'll help all right ... but first I'll need to try it myself. If I call in General Beaumont, it will be using an atomic bomb for a flyswatter."

O   O   O

Two days later Rod stood at parade rest in front of Colonel Whitney's desk. He'd only been in the spacious office a few times, and always with a group of fellow officers.

A window stretching floor-to-ceiling looked out over the Terrazzo, giving a birds-eye view of the Chapel and the Rampart Range. Diplomas and educational awards covered the opposite wall; the bookcase next to Whitney's desk held textbooks and pictures of people too small to recognize. It hit Rod that unlike any other office he'd been into, there were no pictures of airplanes, no models of jets or rockets, or any other sign of operational experience, simply diplomas and academic accolades.

The department head frowned as he studied the white crystalline substance. Rod's handkerchief laid spread out on Whitney's desk, unfolded for the first time since Rod had gathered the material at the crash site.

Rod glanced at the wall clock as he waited for Whitney to look up and acknowledge his request. He'd asked for a meeting with the department head the first thing Monday morning, but Colonel Whitney's secretary had not called him in until just before Rod's seventh period class. He now had ten minutes to hurry from Whitney's sixth floor office down to his classroom on the second floor.

He decided he'd give him another five minutes and then ask permission to leave. Showing up late to class ranked slightly higher on the faculty's unforgiveable-sin list than cutting short a meeting with the department head.

Whitney rocked back in his chair. "I say, Simone. This is quite unusual. You must know the Superintendent ordered that crash site off-limits."

"I respectfully beg to differ, sir. The site is designated as a memorial. The Superintendent ordered the site to remain undisturbed and not to remove any material."

Whitney lifted an eyebrow. "Precisely. Meaning for you to have obtained this ..." he nodded at the white crystals, "material, you must have disturbed the memorial and gone against the Superintendent's explicit orders, which you yourself just told me." He leaned forward. "So what have you to say about your gross impropriety?"

Rod felt the veins in his face tighten. "Sir, all I'm asking is for you to grant me access to the lab reports from the Accident Investigation Board. This material from the fuel cap provides more than enough motivation to unseal the files."

"And why do you think I have access to those reports?"

"Sir, it's a matter of public record that you were the Board's Executive Officer." *Although I didn't know that until this weekend.* "Therefore, I thought you would know where they're located."

Colonel Whitney stared at Rod. He settled back in his leather seat and tapped his fingers together. "Captain Simone. Assuming what you say about the site not being off-limits, and that you somehow did not disturb the wreckage, I'm afraid I simply don't have access to the files. The report has been filed with the DTIC."

"DTIC?"

"Defense Technical Information Center. I'm surprised you haven't heard of it."

Rod drew in a breath. He glanced at the clock. He had eight minutes to class. "Yes, sir, I understand. But I'm not asking to see the Board's final report; I'm asking to see the lab's files, their analysis of the crash site." A thought struck him, something that General Beaumont had told him a few months ago on the flight line before he'd flown the general back to Washington, DC after the Corona conference. "The Board used a lab here in Colorado to analyze material from the site, including samples from the fuel tank. It should be straightforward to obtain their data."

Whitney narrowed his eyes. "How do you know the Board used a lab based in Colorado? That's not a matter of public record. That information had been sealed with the rest of the report."

Rod hesitated. He didn't want to bring General Beaumont into it right now. He'd rather use the four-star as an ace in the hole when he really needed help. "I—I assumed that the lab was based in Colorado, sir, both to keep down the cost and for expediency. You know how much pressure the Air Force is under to keep costs under control." He felt his face grow warm. It may have been a white lie, but it was still a lie ... and he was surprised how quickly he'd offered it up.

Whitney leaned back and tapped his fingers together. "Yes, that's correct. But the lab forwarded all supporting files to DTIC, including the data and lab analysis."

"Yes, sir." Rod's stomach churned as he glanced at the clock. Five minutes. He'd have to leave. "Sir, I'm teaching seventh period. I respectfully ask to be dismissed."

Whitney gave a hint of a smile and swiveled in his chair to rummage through a credenza sitting behind his desk. He withdrew a form and scribbled on it, then turned to push it across his desk to Rod. "If this is so important then it should go through official channels. I've noted your request for all the data, and once you've signed I'll forward this on to the Defense Technical Information Center. DTIC will process your petition and we should hear back from them in a few months, around Christmas. I assume this meets your approval."

"Yes, sir." Rod leaned over the desk and signed the form. He met Colonel Whitney's eyes but couldn't tell if the man was being straightforward or not. Although he hadn't heard of DTIC, he imagined that it must be some huge, insatiable bureaucracy that might swallow up his request and never be heard from again.

Whitney pulled out a blank sheet of paper. He picked up Rod's handkerchief and poured the crystals on the sheet. He folded the paper into fourths. "I'll forward this on to the lab. Colorado Technical Associates performed the original work for the Board, so they will be able to send their analysis to DTIC as an addendum."

He looked up. "This should put the matter to rest, don't you think?"

"Yes, sir."

He handed the handkerchief back to Rod. As Rod took the cloth, Whitney's hand hit a picture frame that sat at the edge of his desk, turning it toward Rod.

"I'll notify you when I hear back from either DTIC or Colorado Technical Associates."

Rod stepped back. "Thank you, Colonel."

"Carry on." As Whitney turned to place the folded sheet containing the crystals on his back credenza, Rod glanced once more at the clock—

And noticed the photo in the frame that Whitney had just disturbed.

It was a picture of Whitney in a captain's uniform, taken years ago, probably around the time Rod had been a cadet.

And standing arm-in-arm with the younger version of Whitney was a man whom Rod's father had admonished him to never trust: George Delante.

A hot, sour feeling churned in his gut, and he was momentarily short of breath. He felt his heart pound as he turned to go.

As he hurried from the office he recalled what he'd been trying to remember after his last conversation with General Beaumont: he'd spotted Captain Whitney standing next to George and his son, Fred Delante, in the Academy stadium after his graduation on June 3rd, 1959. He didn't know the extent of their acquaintance, but he remembered years earlier seeing hints of how close they'd become: Captain Whitney showing favor to Fred in class; Whitney's remarks about working with Fred's father in finding a lot for his new home.

As he rushed off to class he thought that whatever relationship Whitney had had with the Delantes, it wouldn't fair well for him.

He hurried three steps at a time down the four flights of stairs and ran into the hall just as his fellow instructors were entering their classes.

He flung open the classroom door. Chairs screeched against the floor as the cadets bolted to attention.

As he stepped into the room it hit him that in addition to sending his request into the DTIC abyss, he'd just given Colonel Whitney the only proof he'd had of what might possibly have caused his father's crash.

Rod saluted the cadets and instructed them to take their seats. Inwardly he seethed, and resolved to hold Whitney to his deadline at the end of the year. That should allow plenty of time for DTIC to produce those reports and for the lab to perform an analysis of that crystalline substance.

And if Rod didn't hear from Whitney after Christmas, then it was time to call in the big guns and engage General Beaumont.

Chapter Sixteen

"I Can't Get No Satisfaction"

Three months later
January 23rd, 1965

United States Air Force Academy
Colorado Springs, CO

The great consolation in life is to say what one thinks.

Voltaire

Rod, it's ... for you," Julie said, holding out the phone.

Rod put down the paper he was grading. "Do you know who it is?"

"Didn't say," she said, her voice slurred.

Rod jumped up. He hoped it was Colonel Whitney calling with news from either DTIC or the lab. Before Christmas he'd discovered that Colonel Whitney's assessment was correct: that the Defense Technical Information Center would take a while to respond. They dealt with a massive amount of reports, and his request had been entered in the queue along with everyone else's.

He'd also discovered that Colorado Technical Associates, the lab Colonel Whitney had used for the Accident Investigation

Board, was indeed a small business based in Colorado Springs. It did not list George Delante on any of their corporate information; so maybe he was making too much of the fact that Whitney and George Delante had been acquainted.

But if Colonel Whitney didn't come through soon, he was prepared to contact both DTIC and the lab himself.

For the past three weeks he'd tried to see the Colonel face-to-face, but he hadn't been able to get on his calendar, so he'd sent a detailed note reminding Whitney of his requests. It seemed the flurry of activity that accompanied the Wing returning after Christmas and the start of the new semester overshadowed all his efforts trying to pin down Whitney.

The amount of class work amazed him. Who would have thought he'd be swamped as a faculty instructor, grading home-work on a Saturday night, only two weeks after the cadets returned from Christmas break? With 5 classes of 13 cadets each, he would have figured that grading 65 papers would have not been that difficult. But he quickly discovered that each cadet had a unique way of solving the problems—which led to an incredible amount of effort on his part, because he had to reproduce each convoluted step the cadets had made in order to follow their logic.

Rod padded for the phone. "Be right there." He knew whoever was calling wasn't a cadet. He'd already picked up their homework assignment on Friday, so there was no reason for them to call. Also, the cadets had been drilled in telephone etiquette; they'd have said: "Ma'am, this is Cadet Third class Fratzenjam calling for Captain Simone," so maybe it was Colonel Whitney.

Julie pulled on her cigarette as she watched him speak.

"Captain Simone," he said.

"Is this the infamous sluggard from Weenie B-2?"

It was a voice from the past, his old roommate. "Sly! You old dog! Where are you?"

"Pete Field. I just flew in to pick up a reserve unit, and we're heading out tomorrow morning."

"Can you come over?"

"I don't have a car. I'm at the Visiting Officer's Quarters here at Peterson. Can you make it out here?"

"Sure. Just a moment." Rod put down the phone and turned to Julie. "It's Sly. He's in town just for the night. Want to meet him at the Club for a beer?"

Julie blew smoke. "Where are we going to get a sitter this time of night?"

Rod glanced at his watch. Like most pilots, he wore the biggest, fanciest watch he could afford—fancy in the sense of being loaded with practical stuff, such as time zone converters, stopwatch, and an extra-large, illuminated dial that he could read during night flights. "It's a little after six. What about dropping Nanette off at child care?"

Julie sashayed to the refrigerator. She pulled out a beer and held her cigarette in her mouth while she used a can opener. "They're probably full. Besides, she's got a presentation at Sunday school tomorrow."

"Don't you want to see Sly?"

"I'll see him next time he's out." She nodded to the phone. "Go on. I'll be fine."

Rod grinned and blew her a kiss. He spoke into the phone. "Hey, Sly. I'll meet you at the Club in forty-five minutes."

"That's a rog."

Hanging up, he gave Julie a quick peck on the cheek. "I'll tell him 'hi' for you." He turned to go change.

Julie called after him. "You owe me a dinner, Lightning."

"Whatever you want," he said as he rummaged through his closet for his flight suit.

Like all Officers' Clubs, there were two dress codes in effect at Peterson Field: coat and tie in the main dining room and flight suits in the bar. The bar was usually located on a separate floor from the more elegant dining area, and as far away as possible. Peterson was a flying base and catered to pilots, and at the O' Club those not belonging to the brotherhood were in danger of being ostracized. In addition, the noise, rowdiness, and chance of getting something spilled on him were in direct proportion to the number of flyers present, so there was no way that Rod was going to miss this experience by wearing civvies.

Forty-five minutes later he pulled into the Officers' Club parking lot. The place was jammed with Corvettes, Thunderbirds,

Corvairs, Shelbys, and even the new Mustang. There was a smattering of muscle cars, the type the Beach Boys sang about. It was part of the fighter pilot image; the leather-jacketed daredevil with a scarf thrown around his neck, just as at home on the racetrack as he was on the runway—and in the bedroom as well—since the self-confident, live-on-the-edge élan attracted pretty young things that were bored with nine-to-five lawyer or accountant types.

Rod took off his hat and stuffed it in the right leg pocket of his flight suit as he walked under the long awning in front of the Club's main entrance. He stepped inside and saw older men in dark suits and women in long dresses holding drinks and chatting outside of the dining room.

He took an immediate right and trotted down a set of red-carpeted stairs. Music and smoke drifted up from the basement and he heard the new Rolling Stones' song.

Rod entered the bar and peered through the smoky haze. There must have been a hundred people jammed in the basement bar, two-thirds of them wearing flight suits. The rest were young women, sitting on bar stools, or clustered around a pilot loudly telling a story. A jukebox at the end of the bar chugged the driving beat of "The Last Time."

Rod caught movement heading toward him from a table at the far end of the bar.

"Hey, Rod!" Sly carried a mug of beer; it sloshed on the floor as he gave Rod a bear hug.

They stood at arm's length, shaking their heads in amazement. "Can you believe it's been ten years since we were smacks?" Rod yelled over the music.

"Come on," Sly said, waving him to his table, "I'll buy you a beer." They weaved through the crowd to where Sly had ordered an extra mug.

Sly howled with approval as Rod shot down the first glass to kill his thirst; he poured another and brought the mug up in a toast. "Here's to the zoo."

"The aluminum womb!"

Rod settled back in his chair. He studied his old roommate. Sly had always been on the pudgy side, but he looked as though he'd gained considerably more weight. The naturally loose flight suit was filled out; it looked as though Carol kept him well fed.

"How are Julie and Nanette?" Sly said.

"Couldn't be better. Nanette knows more Doolie knowledge now than I ever did as a cadet. And without Julie, the Officers' Wives' Club couldn't function. What about Carol and the twins, Ed and Jack?"

"Crazy Eddie and Jack the Ripper? Two little hellions. Carol won't let me sleep next to her any more, scared we'll have another pair of twins."

"So how have you been?" Rod said. "You enjoying flying the Starlifter?" The C-141 was the new strategic workhorse of Military Air Transportation Service.

"Yeah, they're great. Join the Air Force and see the world. Where else can you catch some Zs and take a crap while flying a 12-hour mission? You can't do that in your fighter."

"You got it. I can't even stand using a piddle-pack. There's a lot to say about being able to get up and stretch during a long flight."

Sly grabbed at his fleshy waist pressing against his flight suit. "Only thing is that we sit around so much it's easy to put on the pounds—not that I ever had that problem." He eyed Rod's waist and slopped his beer at him. "You're keeping fit."

"Hitting the gym every day. Running like crazy."

"Don't they work you any at the Academy?"

"Not nearly as hard as flying. Or as stressful. But they do make us show up for retreat."

Sly's beer stopped halfway to his mouth. "That's it? The whole faculty?"

"Just Theoretical Mechanics. Once a week we line up on the north bridge to the Terrazzo to salute the flag. Then we watch the cadets march by."

"You're kidding."

"Nope. That's the only group activity we participate in as a department. Otherwise, all I do is teach, serve as snack bar officer, and make sure all the trash in the department is emptied at the end of the day."

"A lot of responsibility after carrying nukes on your last fighter. You must do something else."

"I wish we would; no wonder there's no unit cohesion."

"Well, it usually starts from the top. Who's your department head?"

"Colonel Whitney—"

"Whitney?" Sly's eyes bulged. "You mean pilot reject, AOC-hopeful, academically-hyper Captain Whitney?"

"The same one. But he's a full bull now, and from the way he's running the department, he's raging to become the next Dean. I swear, Sly, you'd think the faculty were cadets from all the silly stuff he does."

"That's his problem. He never had any real ops experience."

Rod clinked his mug with Sly's. "You got it. Pure academic track. He never set foot inside a flying wing, much less an alert shack or even a missile silo. He doesn't have a clue what the real Air Force does. Yet, he's running the department like it's a world unto itself. Morale has dropped through the floor and guys are scrambling to rotate back into an operational unit."

Sly poured the rest of the pitcher into Rod's mug and held it up until a waitress spotted it. "Another one, please." He turned to Rod. "Have you complained to anyone outside the department about what's going on?"

Rod darkened. "That would be going around the chain-of-command."

"Then why doesn't the Dean step in?" Sly said. "He's a one-star general, and the last I heard, generals still out-rank colonels, even Permanent Professors."

"The Dean's a one-star who came up from the ranks of the other PPs," Rod said. "And remember, by law, Whitney can remain a Permanent Professor until he's 65, so he's got that job for life. He's harder to remove than a hemorrhoid."

The waitress set a full pitcher on the table. "That'll be $3 even."

"I'll get it," Rod said. He dug in his pocket and handed her a five. "Thanks. Keep the change."

The waitress smiled and scooped the money onto the tray. "Thank you," and sashayed away.

Sly spoke while watching her leave. "That's a damn shame, Lightning—that prick Whitney making it all the way to full colonel."

Rod nodded. "He's climbing up to Dean on the backs of everyone in our department."

Sly took a swig of his beer. "Sounds like Whitney's still in it for himself."

"But it affects more than him; he's giving all the non-rated officers at the Academy a bad name, not to mention the other permanent professors. He's worse than a civilian."

"You got it." Sly lifted his glass. "Here's to the pricks in the Air Force—to those who've wormed themselves into jobs and you can't ferret 'em out."

"To the pricks!"

They clinked glasses and drained their mugs. Sloshing beer over the table, they tried to pour a refill. They laughed, oblivious to everyone around them.

Rod put a hand over his glass after he finished his third beer. "No more. I have to find my way home tonight."

"Just leaves more for me," Sly said. He poured another glass for himself. "Hey, have you been keeping track of the boys?"

"No. Up until this assignment I've been so busy I've lost track of what everyone's doing."

"Let's see: Captain Ranch finished at the top of my UPT class and was assigned straight to 105s."

"I heard that," Rod said. "Hopefully I'll run into him when I get back to the cockpit. And did you hear that Manuel Rojo finished his law degree at Princeton? After an assignment in the intelligence field, he snagged a White House Fellow. He's the only one besides you I've kept up with. The Air Force won't know what to do with Manuel next."

"Jeff Goldstein is flying BUFFs out of Minot, and George Sanders is flying Herky Birds, Hulbert I think," Sly said.

"Fantastic."

"Oh, oh—then did you hear that Sanders got hitched?"

Rod put down his drink. "You're kidding."

"I speak the truth."

"I thought Sanders was a rock! Who'd he marry?"

"Wendy Shelby. Carol was maid of honor. They wanted you and Julie there, but you were still at Stanford."

"Wow," Rod said. He sat back in his chair. "That's great; they make a good pair." He felt a warm glow as he remembered the easy-going cowboy and the thoughtful girl with incredibly deep brown eyes.

After Sly finished the pitcher, they exchanged work phone numbers and left the smoky bar. They walked out of the club into the cool, Colorado night and when the cold air hit them they staggered backwards.

"Wow," Sly belched. "I can't believe we only had two pitchers. I'm getting out of practice!"

"*You* had two pitchers. I stopped an hour ago. Remember the altitude. Colorado has more cheap drunks than anyone else in the nation."

"I don't remember getting this sloshed as a cadet!"

"That's because you're getting older." Rod reached for his car keys, glad that he stopped after his third beer. He helped Sly into the car and pulled out of the still-crowded parking lot, driving slowly until he pulled up at the Visiting Officer's Quarters.

Sly rolled out of the vehicle, slammed the door, and leaned into the window. "Hey, buddy, thanks for coming. Say 'hi' to Julie."

"Will do. Next time, give us a head's up so we can have you over. And bring Carol with you. I know Julie would like to see her as well. And the twins."

Sly slapped the car. "Next time." He turned and almost stumbled on the sidewalk.

Rod laughed and gunned his engine. He waited until Sly reached the door, and then turned to leave the base, keeping right at the speed limit. He headed straight down Platte and drove into the heart of the city, turning on Nevada Avenue, the main north-south street that would take him back to the Academy.

Chapter Seventeen

"Catch Us If You Can"

Later that night
0045 Sunday, January 24th, 1965

North Nevada Avenue
Colorado Springs, CO

The salvation of mankind lies only in making everything the concern of all.

Alexander Solzhenitsyn

Just as Rod was approaching the intersection he noticed three hitchhikers standing away from the street. That's odd. He'd think they would have stood closer to the curb and increase their chances of being picked up, especially this late at night. He glanced at his watch. It was 12:45 AM.

The three stepped under a streetlight just as he turned. They looked young, clean cut, were well-dressed, and didn't slouch as they walked. Cadets. Of course. They weren't allowed to hitchhike, but since they couldn't own cars until their senior year, how else could they get back to the cadet area?

Rod pulled over. He placed an arm on the back of his seat, reached over, and unrolled the passenger window. He called out, "Going to the Academy?"

"Yes, sir."

"Hop in, guys."

The three stumbled up, out of breath. One leaned his head through the window. "Can you drop us off at the north gate?"

"I'll do better than that," Rod said. "I'll take you to the dorm."

The three instantly opened the doors. "Wow, thanks, sir."

Once the cadets were inside, Rod set off. The two cadets in the back spoke quietly between themselves, snickering. The one in the front leaned back with his head against the seat. After a few minutes he closed his eyes and moaned quietly.

Rod glanced over. "Are you all right?"

The cadet just moaned again.

One in the back leaned over the seat. "He's had a little too much three-two beer."

"He's not going to get sick in my car, is he?"

"Oh, no, sir," the two cadets in back said simultaneously.

Rod sped up. The idea of having to clean up sick, underage cadets didn't appeal to him. He spoke to the two cadets in back. "What class are you guys?"

"Second classmen. We're juniors."

That set Rod's mind somewhat at ease. As Secondclassmen they had to be at least 19 years old, and the drinking age in Colorado for the relatively weak three-point-two beer was 18, so they hadn't done anything illegal.

The two in the back whispered quietly between themselves. One of them leaned forward and said, "You're not a grad, are you, sir?"

"Class of '59."

He waited a few moments for them to say something, but they kept silent; he tried not to laugh. The cadets must be sizing him up, wondering if he worked for the Comm Shop.

It was probably the first time they'd gone out this semester. He imagined the cadets using one of their rare privileges to try to get away, but now thinking they'd been picked up at the end of the evening by an AOC.

It was a classic cadet nightmare.

He bet they were wondering if he was going to report them for hitchhiking or breaking some other cadet regulation; they might even think he'd take them straight to Command Post and turn them in.

No one spoke as silence blanketed the car. Rod could almost feel the unspoken tension start to spiral up and become unbearable to the poor cadets.

He needed to put them out of their misery.

He broke the silence. "By the way guys, I'm not an AOC."

"Whew!" Any anxiety immediately melted away.

"Are you a flyer, sir?"

"Yeah. Pilot training in T-37s and T-33s, then transitioned to Thuds."

"All right!"

He couldn't tell if the cadets were more relieved that he wasn't an AOC or impressed because he was a fighter pilot. "But I teach Theoretical Mechanics now."

They didn't reply, but Rod saw in his rear view mirror the two cadets in the back seat exchange glances. He'd probably scared them again. Thet Mech wasn't exactly known as the easiest department at the Academy.

The cadet in front nodded off and his head slumped to his chest. The cadets in back asked him questions about what it was like in the old days, about attending the Academy when it was up at Lowry and his experiences as a fighter pilot. The drive passed quickly, and before Rod knew it, they approached the north gate to the Academy. He slowed the car and dimmed his lights as he rolled up to the guard shack.

An air policeman wearing a distinctive white dickey stepped from the shack. He stood at parade rest in the middle of the road, and then held out a hand, stopping them. He saluted and walked to the side of the car. "Good evening, sir. May I see your ID card?"

Rod dug his military identification out of his wallet and handed it over.

The air policeman studied the card with his flashlight, and then handed it back over. He sniffed the air inside the car and frowned. "Sir, I smell alcohol."

"I had three beers at the Peterson Club," Rod said, returning his ID to his wallet.

He shined the light into the car onto the cadets. "Do they have IDs?" He seemed to want to ask something else, but hesitated, maybe because Rod was an officer.

"They're cadets," Rod said, anticipating the air policemen's question. "I'll vouch for them. And if you're wondering, they're old enough to drink three-two beer."

"That's what I was going to ask." The air policeman snapped to attention and saluted. "Good evening, sir."

Rod smartly returned the salute, flicked on the car lights, and drove forward. He carefully followed the speed limit toward the cadet area.

Rod wound his way to the cadet area. He started to ask them about their class when something suddenly jumped out in front of the car and stopped in the middle of the road.

He slammed on the breaks and swerved to the right, causing the cadets to be thrown forward.

A white-tailed deer stood frozen in the headlights. A minute passed and a buck stepped slowly into the lights from out of the bushes; he must have carried a rack of fifteen points.

"Look at that!" The cadets bolted upright and stared at the magnificent animal.

The buck tapped across the asphalt to the white-tailed deer, lowered his head, and nudged it out of the road; the deer scampered to the side. The buck then turned and stood majestically in the middle of the road. Defiant, it raised its head at the car.

The cadet in front groggily shook his head. "Whoa, what's going on?"

Rod unrolled his window, allowing in the cool night air.

Seconds later, a troop of twenty deer moved cautiously onto the asphalt road. One by one they stepped out of the bushes, looking from side to side as they crossed the road. The buck watched over them as they passed, keeping his head up. The cadets were dead quiet as they watched.

Suddenly spooked, the deer bounded off, their white tails disappearing into the darkness. Rod stuck his head out the window to get a better look at the buck but it disappeared into the dark pines, following its herd.

"Wow." The cadets breathed.

Rod waited a moment before driving up to the cadet area, making sure no other deer followed. "You guys are really fortunate," Rod said. "I don't think I've ever seen so many deer at one time." They drove in silence, pondering what they'd just seen. At times like this the Academy grounds seemed more like a national park than the training grounds for the next generation of military leaders.

They approached the cadet area and the sereneness was broken by a cacophony of noise. Up ahead the dorm seemed to vibrate with energy. Although it was after one in the morning, Rod heard stereos blasting down from the hill. Music of the Beatles, Rolling Stones, and Beach Boys were mixed together in a jumble of sound.

Lights shone from the dorm windows. In some rooms it looked as if cadets were jumping up and down in time with the music, as though they were participating in a gang dance. In others, Rod saw shadows of guitars and bongo drums as cadets played in a band. He knew the energy level was always high after the Wing returned from Christmas, as if they were not yet ready to start the new semester.

Rod pulled around the corner and slowed to a stop before the far eastern stairwell.

The cadets in back piled out of the car. The cadet who had been in front stared wide-eyed at Rod. "Thanks, sir. You saved our bacon getting us back before taps." He turned for the elevator and staggered off with his classmate.

One of the cadets stayed behind. His close-cropped hair glistened as he reached in the window and solemnly shook Rod's hand. "We really appreciate the ride, sir. But may I ask you a question?"

"Sure," Rod said.

"When you told that air policeman that we were old enough to drink three-two beer, you didn't ask to see our IDs."

"I didn't have to."

The cadet frowned. "I don't understand.

Rod looked puzzled. "You're Second classmen. You have to be older than 18."

"But you didn't try to verify it."

"I believed you."

"But we could have been Doolies and only been 17."

Rod paused. "You're under the Honor Code. Of course I believed you."

"Wow." The cadet ran a hand through his hair. "That's weird."

"How's that?"

The cadet hesitated. "The word is out that the officers don't really trust us."

"Did you see that happen tonight?"

"No, sir!"

"Then what did you see?"

"What I saw was an officer who did ... the right thing. You trusted us."

Rod started his engine. "You guys get some rest. You'll be out of here in a few years, and you'll see the Honor Code is the best thing you can take out of this place."

The cadet drew himself up and saluted. "Thanks again, sir."

Rod returned the salute. "No problem." He sat for a moment, pondering why a cadet would ever think an officer wouldn't trust him. It didn't make sense—not with the Honor Code. That was one of the main reasons for even having a code, to gain and hold trust.

The cadet walked slowly, his classmates already having taken the elevator. As Rod began to pull away, the cadet turned and trotted back to the car. He waved his hand. "Sir!"

Rod stopped and rolled down the window. "Yeah?"

The cadet looked around, and then leaned into the window. He spoke quietly. "Theoretical Mechanics 305. You said you were in that department. Check it out, sir."

"Excuse me?" *What was this all about?*

"I've heard some talk." The cadet's eyes were wide and he looked nervously around, as if someone might be eavesdropping. "I'd have reported it, but ... but this is really serious. I almost didn't come back from Christmas break because of it. It's scary.

So check it out. Please, sir? Thet Mech 305." He looked quickly around and ran from the car, as if Rod's presence might somehow infect him.

Rod watched the cadet run up three flights of stairs before ducking into the dorm.

Just check it out. Mystified, Rod put the car into gear and drove slowly away.

Theoretical Mechanics 305 was a third year, or junior-level course. It was brutally tough, and one that all cadets had to take as part of the core curriculum. Rod remembered taking the class when he was a cadet and shuddered at the memory of being ordered to go to the board to work problems in front of his classmates. Hardly anyone did well and everyone had difficulty.

Rod drove down the hill, leaving the cadet area behind him. Shadows flashed past the side of the car, cadets running on the sidewalk trying to make it back to their squadron area before taps. They had to sign in from their off-duty privilege before the bugle stopped playing taps, or they would have to march off their punishment.

He passed the cadet parking lot and stopped at the intersection leading to the Academy's north gate.

Minutes ago he'd shown three cadets that he trusted them implicitly. It was one thing to say he trusted them, but it was quite another matter to actually show he trusted them. In any case, he'd done it. He hadn't questioned their age more than taking their word for it. And what had that accomplished? It had caused one of those cadets to ask Rod to look into Thet Mech 305.

What did he say he wanted Rod to check out—something he'd heard? It didn't make any sense. But whatever it was, it was something so bad that the cadet didn't want to come back from Christmas break; meaning a cadet was willing to either go AWOL, or resign and spend the next four years as an enlisted man paying back the time he'd spent at the Academy. Serious stuff. Incredibly serious.

A car drove up behind him as he remained at the intersection debating what to do. The car flashed its lights, and when he didn't move, whipped around him. Someone yelled from the car and he heard high-pitched laughing. The car was packed with girls, either leaving from visiting their cadet boyfriends at Arnold Hall, or dropping them off at the dorm after a night on the town.

Rod turned and looked up the hill at the Academy.

Lights blinked off in the long dormitory. Other lights glowed steadily in Fairchild Hall, the academic building. Behind them all, against the dark form of the Rampart Range, floodlights splashed against the cadet chapel, lighting it up in red, green, blue, and yellow.

It was one thirty Sunday morning, and now that he was sober, he knew what he had to do. When a cadet would take him into his confidence and ask him to investigate a matter, he had no other option but to do it.

He turned right at the intersection and drove on Faculty Loop around the parade field. Deer grazed on the lush grass and looked up as he passed. Overhead, stars burned brilliant in the clear, cold night.

He pulled underneath Fairchild Hall, parked in a visitor's spot, and walked swiftly to the Dean's elevator. There were three other cars in the vast, deserted parking lot, perhaps faculty members staying up late performing research.

The elevator took him to the sixth floor. He moved down the darkened hallway and entered the main Theoretical Mechanics department area.

Out the window, four stories below, the Terrazzo was lit in pools of light. Some of the light reflected up, bathing the office complex in a soft glow. Even in the near darkness, he could see the department area was immaculately clean. Every desk was bare—another sign of the strict discipline Colonel Whitney demanded of his faculty and staff.

Now how was he supposed to check out Theoretical Mechanics 305?

He heard a sound in the hallway. "Hello?" Rod walked briskly around the corner. "Is there anybody in there?"

No one answered.

He moved into the darkened hall and patted the wall, trying to find the light switch. No luck. He stepped down the hall, keeping his hands against the wall. He finally found the master switch and turned it on; florescent lights flickered and slowly brightened the area. "Hello?"

He stepped down the hall and looked into each office. Still nothing.

He heard a faint *click*. It was the sound of the fire door closing.

He strode to the stairwell and pushed opened the heavy metal door. He heard feet pounding down the stairs, then the sound of another door closing, several floors below.

"Hey!" He called, but no one answered. He thought briefly about following, but the person could have gone to any of the five lower floors accessed by the stairwell.

He frowned and walked back to the main department office area. He glanced around.

Now that the lights were on, he could see clearly around the suite's administration area. He spotted something that jutted from one of the file drawers behind the secretary's desk. He walked over, pulled open the drawer and a sheet of paper slid to the floor.

He picked it up. It appeared to be a cover sheet from this semester's first Thet Mech 305 Graded Review, or major test. That's strange. Why would it be out of place? The page looked as if it had been accidentally caught in the drawer. He opened the other drawers and found an envelope with the words THEORETICAL MECHANICS 305 GRADED REVIEW – MASTER COPY written in red ink across the front. He pulled it out.

The envelope's seal was broken.

He removed the exam and saw that the front cover page was missing.

"Oh, no," he breathed. Someone must have opened the envelope that contained the department's next major exam. Had they copied it?

An ice-cold shiver ran down his back. He rapidly went through the rest of the drawers. Everything seemed to be in place. The envelopes holding the other GRs were sealed, but he had no way of knowing if they too had been compromised.

What should he do? If this were classified material he'd call the Air Police. But this was an academic paper, and although it was serious stuff, it was not something the Air Police would handle.

The obvious choice would be to call the course director, the faculty member in charge of all aspects of the course.

He glanced at his watch. It was 0220 Sunday morning. This would really piss off the course director if Rod were wrong about the GR being compromised. He knew that this may turn out to be nothing, that the exam's front page might have been misfiled; but the GR's seal had also been broken—which meant that someone had opened the envelope.

Had they also copied the exam? He hoped that he was wrong, but there were just too many coincidences for him to be mistaken.

He walked to the dirty purple mimeograph machine that sat on a table against the far wall. The mimeograph machine was off; he placed his hand on the top. It was cool, room temperature, which it should be if it hadn't been recently used; plus, he couldn't smell the unmistakable odor of mimeograph fluid.

He looked through the copy log at the end of the machine and thumbed to the end. The last time anyone had made an entry was yesterday, Friday afternoon at four. It was the course director of Thet Mech 305. No one had used it since. At least no one who had logged their name.

He thought for a moment. Maybe they wouldn't use a mimeograph machine to copy the test; that would be too much trouble. It would be much easier to just copy it by hand.

He walked back to the secretary's desk and picked up a pad of yellow legal-sized paper. Squinting, he looked at the top sheet. There appeared to be indentations on it. He hesitated, then rummaged through the desk's top drawer, and withdrew a flimsy sheet of carbon paper. He placed it on the yellow pad and lightly scribbled a pencil across the top. Removing the carbon paper he saw the faint outline of words and numbered paragraphs.

Rod grabbed the Thet Mech 305 GR envelope and removed the last page. He compared the typed test questions with the hand-written questions from the legal pad—the numbered questions matched word for word.

He drew in a breath. Someone had copied the GR.

This must be what the cadet had wanted him to check out. If someone had copied the exam, then did they plan to distribute it? And if they did, then it meant that this just wasn't an isolated cheating incident. It involved more than one person.

And that meant it was a cheating ring.

If that were true, then this was a really, really big deal—and it was much too important for him to wait until tomorrow morning to tell anyone. He decided to call the course director, the officer in charge of Thet Mech 305.

He thumbed through the base phone book and found the officer's home number. He pushed the rotary dial as hard as he could, then counted the rings. On the tenth ring he hung up and dialed again, just in case he dialed wrong.

Nothing. No one was home.

He held his hand on the phone and thought for a moment. The course director must be out of town, perhaps skiing. Man, was he going to get a surprise when he returned.

Well, he had to let someone know. But the next one in line was the department head.

He looked up Colonel Whitney's home number and paused before dialing. *I hope I'm doing the right thing.* He started counting the rings. If the course director would be ticked at being called so late, no telling what Colonel Whitney would do....

"Hello?" Whitney sounded disoriented.

"Sir, this is Captain Simone," Rod said. He drew in a deep breath.

It sounded as though something fell from a nightstand. "I say! What are you doing, Simone? Do you have any idea what time it is?"

"Yes, sir. I apologize for calling so late—"

"Is this about that lab analysis from the crash site? For your sake it better not be, Simone!"

"No, sir. It's extremely urgent."

Whitney spoke with an edge to his voice. "This had better be good."

"Sir, I'm up at the cadet area, Fairchild Hall, in the department—"

"What are you doing there!"

Rod explained about the cadet, how he found the test, and the broken seal.

Colonel Whitney sounded bitter. "Simone, I cannot believe you called me about such an obvious matter. Did it ever occur to you that the secretary might have been in a hurry to get home Friday afternoon, and in her rush she mistakenly left the front page of that test in the drawer?"

"No, sir. But the seal was broken on the test envelope—"

"Or did you think that the course director might have tried to file the test but was interrupted and shut the drawer without thinking? And that caused the seal to break?"

Rod stiffened. "No, sir. But there is a pad of legal paper that has a copy of the test questions written on it—"

"Which was probably used by the course director for the secretary to type up! You're not thinking at all, are you, Simone? Or have you been drinking?"

Rod hesitated, and then said in a curt voice, "I was a few hours ago, sir."

"I should have known. Are you on one of your fighter pilot binges?"

"No, sir."

Whitney paused. "I haven't been impressed with anything you've done since you've come back to the Academy, Simone; from your classroom demeanor to that crazy stunt where you broke all the windows in the cadet area. Now leave me alone and get the hell out of my department. Do you understand?"

"Yes, sir. But with that cadet's story, shouldn't I call someone else?"

"No more buts. Period. That's a direct order. If you call anyone about this, anyone at all, then I'll haul you up on a court martial. Do you understand?"

"Yes, sir," Rod said. "I understand."

"Now go home and report to my office first thing Monday morning."

He winced as Whitney slammed the phone down.

Rod looked down at the test paper he still held. A sick feeling grew in his stomach. Colonel Whitney's direct order could not have been clearer—he could be court martialed, with the punishment ranging from being admonished to being confined. The Uniform Code of Military Justice demanded unquestioned obedience and left no tolerance for second-guessing.

It didn't matter if he was right or not, just that Whitney's order was legal. And the order was certainly legal. The classes he'd taken in Military Law as a cadet made that perfectly clear.

But he knew in his heart of hearts that he had probably stumbled upon a cheating ring, a major, and perhaps massive, violation of the Honor Code.

One of the reasons why security was so relaxed in the departments was because the faculty believed cadets strictly followed the code. He knew from personal experience that it was the basis for every aspect of cadet life.

He looked out the window to the Terrazzo. It was deserted, and most every room in Fairchild was dark. In a few hours, reveille would blow and the cadets would start getting ready for chapel. On the surface, things appeared normal and were running smoothly.

He doubted Colonel Whitney comprehended the seriousness of the situation. Rod had been trained all of his life to anticipate and to react, not to sit back and wait for bad things to happen. That was the mark of a loser, definitely not what the Academy tried to instill. It went against his very nature.

So faced with a possible court martial or doing the right thing, what could he do?

The letter of the law. Colonel Whitney had ordered him not to call anyone. As his superior officer, Whitney could not have been more legally clear.

But it wasn't right.

Angry at having his hands tied, he started writing on a blank sheet of typing paper. Whitney's order had been very specific, and Rod was not about to break it. He would not call anyone.

He composed the message in the military's formal "Subject—To" format, outlining his discovery and concern. When he finished, he turned out the lights and left the department.

He knew the Dean was out of town, so he drove to the Commandant's house, intending to wake him up and personally hand him the note, no matter what time it was.

It was never too late to do the right thing.

CHAPTER EIGHTEEN

"Eve of Destruction"

The next day
0815 Monday, January 25th, 1965

United States Air Force Academy
Colorado Springs, CO

His honour rooted in dishonour stood,
And faith unfaithful kept him falsely true.

Alfred, Lord Tennyson, *Idylls of the King*,
"Lancelot and Elaine"

H ey, Rod, can you come here for a minute?"
Captain Bobby Andrew, the department Exec stood in the conference room door with a worried look on his face. The department library filled one of the conference room walls. The other wall was lined with pictures of the faculty running back to 1955; blackboards covered the other two walls.

"Sure." Rod looked up from inserting a letter from Colonel Whitney into the packet of information for next year's follow-on course to Theoretical Mechanics 202.

He sat in the room with fifteen other junior officers, all instructors in Theoretical Mechanics. A half an hour earlier,

Colonel Whitney had pulled out all the Majors and Lieutenant Colonels in the department, leaving the grit work of putting together the course handouts to the Captains. Rod briefly wondered if it had anything to do with the evidence of cheating he'd found the previous night.

But there was no mention of his telephone call to Colonel Whitney or of the note he'd delivered to the Commandant. Instead, he was cooped up with the rest of the company grade officers who weren't teaching class, stuffing envelopes; busy work that didn't require any thinking, unlike the last time he had been in the large conference room....

In December he'd sat in this room right before Christmas, frantically grading the standardized Theoretical Mechanics 201 Final Exam along with the rest of the officers teaching the course. Major Forsythe, the course director, had sat at the head of the table, his jacket draped neatly over the back of his chair. Each instructor was responsible for grading a unique page of the final exam—nearly 300 pages of the same problems—so that they could give a standardized assessment across the entire class.

The instructors had written on the blackboard the status of how many pages they had graded; snack food covered a table at the end of the room. Each officer had been responsible for providing a portion of the buffet so the instructors wouldn't have to break for meals, and could grade until they were finished. It had been an all-day marathon that exhausted him just thinking about it.

Now, five weeks later, back from Christmas break, assembling the course material was the intellectual equivalent of chewing gum for the mind.

Rod pushed up and padded out the door to speak with Bobby Andrews. Bobby stepped into the hallway as Rod approached.

"What's going on?" Rod said. "Looking for me to fly another general back to Washington?"

Bobby rolled his eyes. "Not likely." He motioned with his head for Rod to follow him.

Rod lifted an eyebrow at Bobby's reaction. It was unlike the Exec to be in a reticent mood. He followed Bobby as they walked past his office. "Where are we going?"

"Dean's conference room."

Rod kept his face expressionless. *So it's begun.* Rod had arrived early this morning to schedule a meeting with Colonel Whitney as he was ordered, but it had quickly been canceled. Rod surmised it had to do with the note he'd given the Commandant early Sunday morning. Clothed in a bathrobe and standing on his front porch, General Strong had been visibly shaken when he'd read Rod's discovery.

Bobby and Rod walked briskly past the Dean's office and stood outside his conference room. Bobby put a hand on the doorknob and hesitated before he opened it.

Rod tried to sound upbeat. "Hey, thanks for getting me out of stuffing envelopes." He spoke quietly in a low falsetto, mimicking Colonel Whitney. "I say, if I read another cheery letter extolling the virtues of Theoretical Mechanics, I think I'd go crazy."

Bobby ignored Rod's attempt at humor. "Rod, do you know the name of that cadet who told you about the rumor concerning Thet Mech 305?"

Rod stopped cold. "How do you know about that?"

"I'm the Exec. It's my business to know."

Rod said slowly. "Colonel Whitney told me not to discuss that with anyone."

"This is different," Bobby said.

Rod shook his head. "I was ordered not to discuss it, Bobby. Not asked."

"Okay." The Exec sighed. "When you enter the room, sit in the back, keep your mouth shut, and don't ask any questions." He swung open the door and nodded with his head.

Rod nodded curtly and then stepped into the Dean's conference room.

The room was dark except for a light at the front. He slipped into the back and found a seat. The room was paneled with dark, polished wood and was filled with blue, overstuffed leather chairs that bore the names of the Permanent Professors on the headrest. It was an intimidating place for a junior officer.

At the front of the room sat a lone Second class cadet, dressed in his Class-A uniform; although he wore his Second class rank, for some reason his nametag was missing.

Colonel Maas, the head of the Law department and staff judge advocate, sat at the cadet's right. The Commandant, General Strong, sat at the cadet's left. The Dean was on sabbatical at Air University, so he wasn't present. Colonel Whitney sat next to Colonel Maas, and an officer who Rod recognized as an AOC sat next to the Commandant.

A chill ran down Rod's back as he recognized the cadet. It was the same young man who had asked him to search the Theoretical Mechanics department late Saturday night.

Colonel Maas nodded to Rod, then turned to the cadet. "Is this the officer?"

The cadet turned. His eyes widened when he saw Rod. "Yes, sir," the cadet said. His voice wavered but he sat straighter in his chair, as though he had somehow gained confidence with Rod's presence.

"Will you answer all the questions now?"

"Yes, sir."

Maas turned in his chair and looked at Rod. "Do you know why you're here, Captain Simone?"

Rod shook his head. "No, sir."

"This Second classman requested you be present before he answered any questions. But he said you don't know his name. Is that correct?"

"Yes, sir, that's correct. I gave this young man a ride to the cadet dorm, but I didn't ask him either his name or his squadron." Rod decided not to mention that there were two other cadets present on Saturday night. He'd bring it up later if needed.

Colonel Maas sighed, clearly impatient with the way things were going. "One of the stipulations of this interview is that we keep things that way for now. This is highly unusual, but the cadet has requested complete anonymity. He requested this meeting through his AOC and has promised some far-reaching revelation about your department. Do you have any questions?"

"Just one, to put this in perspective." Rod turned to General Strong. "Sir, does this have to do with that note I gave you Sunday morning?"

General Strong nodded grimly. "Yes, it does."

Now Rod knew why Bobby had wanted to know if he knew the cadet's identity: Keeping the cadet's name anonymous throughout the investigation would be the only way they'd learn about this possible cheating activity.

Rod glanced at Colonel Whitney. His eyes narrowed as they bore into Rod. His face was red and the veins on the side of his head seemed to pulse as he worked his jaw. In some twisted way he must be upset at Rod for discovering that the sealed test envelope had been opened. Perhaps he thought that if Rod knew the cadet's identity, the cadet would never have agreed to speak … and Whitney's department wouldn't be involved in a possible honor scandal.

"Very well." Colonel Maas turned to General Strong. "We're ready, sir. Colonel Whitney will conduct the interview since this involves his department."

Colonel Whitney tore his eyes away from Rod. He stood and straightened his jacket. "I say, Mr.—"

"No names," the Commandant admonished.

"Yes, of course." Colonel Whitney turned to the cadet. "Can you tell us why you want this particular officer present?" He waved a dismissive hand at Rod.

The cadet spoke in a low voice. "I trust him, sir."

"You trust him?"

Again, in a low voice. "Yes, sir. I know if he's here I'll get a fair hearing." He lowered his eyes.

"Why?" Whitney glared at Rod then turned back to the cadet. "He doesn't even know your name! How could you ever possibly trust a complete stranger?"

The cadet looked up and hesitated. "Because he … trusted me, sir. I've never had an officer demonstrate it so blatantly."

Whitney's face tightened. "Blatantly? What on earth did this officer do—"

The Commandant made a motion with his hand. "Focus on why he didn't want to return to the Academy, Colonel. Let's get moving."

"Very well," Whitney said. He worked his jaw as if he were attempting to calm down. He turned back to the cadet and drew in a deep breath. "Start from the beginning. Now that Captain

Simone is present, tell us why didn't you want to come back to the Academy after Christmas leave."

The cadet looked at Rod, his eyes searching through the dark room.

He wasn't sure what was going on, but since he knew that the cadet had asked that he be present, Rod smiled and nodded in encouragement. "Go ahead. You can trust us. All of us."

The cadet drew in a breath. "Sir, I need protection for my life."

"What!" Colonel Whitney turned to General Strong. "General, I recommend we cease this charade immediately and—"

The Commandant growled, "Hear him out." He turned to the cadet and his face softened. "Please continue, son."

The cadet stared at the Commandant. "Sir, I thought they were just rumors, but now I know for a fact that over a hundred cadets are involved in a cheating ring.

"And whoever knows about it has been threatened with death if they reveal its existence."

O O O

Rod straightened. Over a hundred cadets ... in a cheating ring? He'd suspected a few cadets at the most, but nothing this large, or this frightening.

The mere existence of just one cadet cheating and another knowing about it boggled his mind. *I will not lie, cheat or steal, nor tolerate anyone who does.* Not tolerating any cadet lying, cheating or stealing—classmate or not—was the fundamental bedrock of the Code; it had been unanimously approved by his own class, back in 1955.

The toleration clause in the Honor Code should have ferreted that person out.

But a hundred cadets? With death threats?

The cadet continued. The room was dead quiet except for his voice. "I heard several cadets had given information about the Theoretical Mechanics 305 final exam to other cadets. It wasn't constrained to one course or to one class. From the different classes involved, and the other courses, there must be well over a hundred cadets involved."

"Was this just during final exam week?" Colonel Maas said.

"No, sir. All last semester cadets sold copies of quizzes, GRs—"

"They obtained copies of the tests?" Colonel Whitney said. "How?"

"A cadet had managed to get around the lock on the sixth floor, and was able to access most of the academic department storage cabinets," the cadet said. "I had heard that Thet Mech was the easiest of all the departments to break into. They keep all their GRs by the secretary's desk in an unlocked drawer."

Rod looked sharply at Colonel Whitney. The department head scowled, then turned back to the cadet without mentioning Rod's midnight telephone call.

The cadet continued. "The stolen originals were sold to cadets called distributors. The distributors paid up to $200 for each GR."

"Stop right there, young man," the Commandant said. He leaned forward. "Now answer me carefully. Were you a distributor?"

"No, sir. But this was open knowledge. Otherwise, the distributors wouldn't be able to charge what they did."

"What did they charge?"

"Anywhere from $5 to $16 a copy, depending upon the demand, so they could recoup their initial investment."

"The demand?" Colonel Maas said.

"Yes, sir. If it was a difficult class, or if a cadet needed the copy to pass the course, then the distributor would charge more money."

"That's a hell of a lot of cash floating around," the AOC muttered.

"For some reason we had to pay by check," the cadet said. "The checks were always less than $10."

Colonel Maas wrote on a sheet of legal paper. Rod imagined the checks, as well as copies of the exams, would provide a way to trace the ring.

General Strong drummed his fingers on the long wooden table.

The revelations were truly shocking, and Rod felt as if he had just been let down by the entire Wing. It was though he had been personally betrayed; a perfidy of trust.

He felt a sharp, sour churning in his stomach as he tried to think of anything else that might strike him so deeply, something that he'd never suspect would happen and would disgust him to the core. He knew that Julie had never cheated on him, but he imagined that he would feel this way if he were to discover she'd had an affair; and he was sure she'd feel similarly betrayed if he did that to her.

Still, the cadet's revelation was nearly too disgusting to believe.

The Commandant pointed to the AOC. "Get a Wing Alpha roster and have this cadet show us who is involved, highlighting the ring leaders and distributors. I need to inform the Superintendent and the Dean, as well as the OSI, that our suspicions have been confirmed." The Office of Special Investigations was the legal investigating arm of the USAF. The general nodded to Rod. "Thank goodness you gave me a heads-up, Captain. We were able to get right on this and prepare for the worst."

He swung around in his chair to Colonel Whitney. "As for you, Colonel, your failure to recognize the severity of this situation could have ruined the entire investigation. And in case you still don't think this is serious, I order you to immediately start analyzing the results of all your GRs and quizzes to give us a trace back for fingering these cadets. Do it quietly so we won't tip anyone off, and work on a close-hold, need-to-know basis. Understand?"

Colonel Whitney lifted his chin. "Of course."

The Commandant reddened at Whitney's condescension. He leaned forward in his seat. "And lock up your dammed GRs!"

"Yes, sir." Whitney said. He sat and shot a scowl at Rod.

General Strong turned back to the rest of the officers. "Institute an immediate media blackout. Nothing gets out to the press until it's coordinated with Washington. I want to move quickly." He turned back to his AOC. "Get this young man out of the cadet area and off the Academy grounds, right now; don't return to his room. These death threats are serious and we need to make sure he's protected. Any questions?"

"No, sir," the officers in the room answered.

The Commandant stood. Everyone pushed back their chairs and joined him standing. He looked around. "This is a dark day for the Academy. Let's get to the core of this as quickly as we can. We have to excise the cancer." Grim-faced, he left the room.

Whitney lifted his chin in the air and followed, purposely ignoring Rod.

The sick feeling in Rod's stomach grew. The idealism from his cadet days was now shattered, he wondered if honor and trust could ever be restored in the Wing.

O   O   O

A few days later the Wing lined up for the evening meal formation at the end of a dark and cloudy afternoon. They stood at attention longer than usual after everyone was reported "present and accounted for" by the squadron commanders. A cold breeze blew over the Terrazzo, bringing a chill to the campus.

Before the command was given to stand at ease, every AOC, over half the faculty, and a cadre of OSI agents suddenly appeared from underneath the stairwells. They quickly moved through the Wing before anyone could react. Cadets from every squadron were identified and moved quietly away from the group, some more roughly than others.

In less than five minutes over 150 cadets had been whisked aside, escorted by security policemen and placed in solitary confinement away from the cadet area so they wouldn't be able to corroborate their stories ... or threaten any more cadets.

CHAPTER NINETEEN

"Help!"

February 4th, 1965

United States Air Force Academy
Colorado Springs, CO

Thus the devil played at chess with me, and yielding a pawn, thought to gain a queen of me, taking advantage of my honest endeavours.

Thomas Browne, *Religio Medici*, Part I

Rod put down the red pencil he'd been using to grade cadet homework and glanced at the clock in his office. It read 1450 on an incredibly slow Thursday afternoon. Twenty minutes had passed and he hadn't made a single correction … or looked at a single paper.

He heard murmurs down the hall, fellow officers dissecting the Superintendent's press conference that had been held yesterday afternoon. He smelled coffee wafting from the conference room where an independent team of officers from another academic department poured over the analysis performed on the Thet Mech GRs. General McDermott, the Dean, anticipated several lawsuits coming from cadets who had been dismissed, and he wanted to ensure that the investigation of the cheating ring had been conducted in meticulous detail. He'd flown in two nights before, cutting his sabbatical short, to personally supervise the analysis.

Try as he may, Rod couldn't concentrate on grading. He pushed the homework to the side and picked up this morning's *Denver Post*. The front-page story detailed accounts of yesterday's press conference with the Superintendent. There was no mention of the cadet who had broken the ring; only that an unnamed Second classman had been threatened with bodily harm, and that the Academy was railroading out cadets without giving them due process of law.

Rod fumed as he read the skewed account. He knew that he could never tell the real story. He remembered the times when his father had been forced to sit in silence while the distorted debates about his honesty were aired in the press during the Academy's construction. Any attempt to set things straight would have been viewed as self-serving.

The *Post's* article breathlessly recounted that 105 cadets had admitted to cheating, and of those, 29 were football players. Two of the cadets—the burglars—received dishonorable discharges. Four received general discharges and 94 accepted honorable discharges.

But the statistic that bothered Rod the most was that three Honor Representatives were involved in the ring—one Firstie and two Second classmen.

The revelation that the trustees of the Code would violate their charge disgusted him.

He remembered the day the Wing had voted on the Code when he had been a cadet, and the discussions led by Manuel Rojo of how it would be their code and not the Academy's— theirs to administer, theirs to uphold.

And theirs to lose.

Ten years later things could not have seemed bleaker for the Academy. Even the public was disappointed by the widespread violations.

Just two weeks ago, during Lyndon Johnson's inaugural parade, 600 members of the cadet Wing had been jeered and booed as they marched down Pennsylvania Avenue. And now, with General White, the recently retired USAF Chief of Staff heading up a high-level review of the Honor Code and all aspects of the Academy, the future looked uncertain for Rod's alma mater.

Rod didn't know what to make of this. On the one hand, he loved the institution dearly. Some of his earliest memories were of his father fighting to achieve his dream of establishing an air academy. Rod remembered going with Hank to Air University when he was just a child, and being in Washington, DC while his adoptive father testified before Congress. And as a member of its first class, he was proud of his heritage.

Yet, there were other foibles of the Academy that drove him absolutely crazy, such as the too-frequent change in top leadership, where over a 10 year span the Academy had rotated through five Superintendents, five Commandants, two Deans, and four athletic directors.

But the most disturbing trend was seeing the rise of officers such as Colonel Whitney, those who showed up for an Academy assignment early in their career but never left, propagating their own sense of military culture, when in fact they'd been disconnected from the real Air Force for dozens of years.

In his mind, what resulted was an insular system where constructive criticism was viewed as insubordination, exacerbated by a hypersensitive military chain-of-command.

Be that as it may, he needed to get past it.

He couldn't allow himself to be swept up in an artificial culture that wasn't aligned with the Air Force.

But yet, the Academy had been a major part of his life even before it had been established. He'd accompanied his dad to the initial meetings and site visits before the Academy was even built. As a member of the first class, he'd been part of establishing the traditions that were starting to be called the beginning of "The Long Blue Line." And now, as a faculty member, he was contributing to the education and maturation process of tomorrow's future leaders. He had too much invested in this place to let it drift from its noble purpose.

He knew he couldn't turn a blind eye to the problems made worse by the faculty's artificial culture and hope they'd go away:

Where would the Academy be if he'd ignored the evidence of cheating he'd discovered that night in the Theoretical Mechanics department?

That meant he'd have to confront Colonel Whitney about the status of the lab analysis of that crystalline substance he'd found at his father's crash site.

He could be respectful and courteous when speaking to his boss, but he couldn't ignore it, or allow himself to be patted on the head and told that it would be fine. It just wasn't right—

Captain Bobby Andrew stuck his head in the door, interrupting his thoughts. "Hey, Lightning. Put on your jacket and run over to the Dean's office. Speed out, buddy."

Rod folded the newspaper. "What's up? You're starting to make a habit of this."

"Who knows? Maybe Whitney's finally figured out a way to sacrifice you."

"Thanks." Rod stepped to his coatrack. "What a way to end the day." He pulled on his blue shade 84-service dress coat and straightened his tie.

Bobby stepped into the hall and followed Rod as he left his office. "Better hurry. They want you there by 1500."

"Why didn't you tell me sooner?"

"Would've if I could've; just got the call." He slapped Rod on the back. "Good luck, Lightning. And get moving!"

Rod stepped up his speed and made his way through the labyrinth of connecting halls until he popped out on the main north-south walkway on the west side of the building. At least he didn't have to run up any stairs, like his colleagues in the Physics and Chemistry departments who had their offices down on the second floor.

Twenty seconds later he stepped into the outer area of the Dean's suite. Three other faculty officers were present; they were all company grade officers, the same rank as Rod. The three captains congregated next to three Colonels who were probably their department heads. No one spoke as they waited.

Colonel Whitney stood alone by the window. When Rod appeared, Whitney crossed his arms and turned to look down on the Terrazzo, ignoring him.

Rod felt his hands grow clammy, unsure of what was going on. He recognized that one of the company grade officers, Captain Lastoneu, was from the Chemistry department, but neither he nor the others had been involved with analyzing the cheating scandal, so Rod assumed that for whatever reason they had been assembled it wasn't because of that. And from Colonel Whitney's body language it was clear that Whitney wasn't going to bring him up to date.

He caught the eye of his colleague from Chemistry. Lastoneu shrugged, indicating that he too was unaware of what might be transpiring.

It seemed somewhat crazy to be kept in the dark, so Rod decided to ask. He stepped toward Colonel Whitney when the Dean's Executive Officer appeared at the door. "Gentlemen, the Dean of Faculty."

The officers stood at attention as Brigadier General Robert McDermott stepped in the room. The Dean's service dress uniform looked as if had been tailored to his trim frame. He held himself upright and effused an almost noble-like presence. "Gentleman, at ease."

The officers immediately relaxed.

The Dean looked around and appeared to have trouble holding back a smile. "It's always a pleasure to announce good news, especially when the Academy is embroiled in such a critical, high-stakes crisis. And as your commander, bringing the good to pierce the veil of bad allows our comradery to flourish. So it is my great pleasure to announce that all of you have been chosen for promotion to major. Your name will appear on the promotion list when it's officially released by the Pentagon tomorrow morning. Congratulations, gentlemen. This is a well-deserved honor."

The department heads started clapping and turned to shake the hands of their promoted faculty.

Rod stood in silence, not knowing what to say. His ears pounded as a surge of blood rush through his veins.

There must be a mistake. He wasn't eligible to be promoted to major for another several years. He hadn't even been out of the Academy for six years. He couldn't believe it.

Rod glanced at Colonel Whitney. The man lifted his chin. Rod stepped forward to ask what was going on. Surely Colonel Whitney knew that he was much too junior to be promoted. They must have mistyped his commissioning date, or mixed him up with someone else … or was this some kind of cruel joke?

Someone grabbed him by the arm. Rod turned. It was General Mac, the Dean.

"Yes, sir," Rod said. He pulled himself upright as the pounding in his ears grew louder.

"Congratulations, Captain Simone." The Dean pumped his hand. "You were promoted an incredible number of years below the zone, far ahead of your peers! Amazing. We're all proud of you, aren't we Bradley?" He motioned with his head for Colonel Whitney to join them. "And on top of you breaking this cheating ring, you've clearly demonstrated your commitment to excellence."

Whitney stepped up. "Yes, Simone." He hesitated for a moment as he stared up at Rod. "Quite a feat."

"Thank you, sir." Rod turned to the Dean, "General. I … I don't know what to say. You're sure this isn't a mistake?"

The Dean laughed and put an arm on Rod's shoulder. "Of course not. You don't think my staff has made sure of these details?"

He steered him to the side, away from Whitney and the rest of the officers. "With this promotion, you've been put on the intermediate service school list to attend Air Command and Staff College at Maxwell Air Force Base this summer. Colonel Whitney has assured me that although you'll be a huge loss to his department, he should be able to get along without you. The needs of the Air Force come first, you know, and ensuring that our best and brightest are given the opportunity to receive the finest education for senior leadership is incredibly important.

"It's very unusual for a faculty member to leave the Academy after only teaching one year, but I've approved your transfer to Maxwell as soon as the semester is complete." He leaned over and said in a conspiratorial whisper, "And keep this close-hold; the Chief relayed that your follow-on assignment flying F-4s is being worked through the air staff." He stepped back and once again shook his hand. "Congratulations, Rod. You're on an incredibly fast, upward trajectory."

"Thank you, sir." He shook hands with the Dean, then the general moved to congratulate Rod's colleagues.

Rod turned to Colonel Whitney, at a loss of what to say.

Whitney pressed his lips together. "Yes, Simone. Just remember, you're still a company grade officer. And because you've been promoted so early, you're at the end of the promotion list, so you may not pin on your new rank for several years. *Years*, understand? And anything can happen during that time, correct? So don't get a big head."

Rod straightened. His cheeks burned. When had he ever assumed airs, or thought better of himself? That was a demeaning thing for Whitney to say—and for him of all people to say it. What did General Beaumont call him ... an arrogant little bastard? But no need to get into it now. He'd have to let it go.

Rod pressed his lips together. "Of course not, sir. I'm just stunned that I'd even be considered for early promotion."

"Yes, I can see." Whitney turned to go, but stopped. He gave a tight smile and moved close to Rod. He spoke so softly it took Rod an effort to hear the man over the conversation in the room. "That stunt you pulled with the Commandant," Whitney murmured. "You disobeyed a direct order, Simone. A direct order—and even you should know that's a court-martial offense. So I'll be watching you. You'd better not even think of straying over the line. Understand?"

Rod's breath quickened. He could barely believe what he'd heard. His mind raced with the thoughts he'd had just a few minutes earlier while down in his office, about being pushed into an artificial environment that didn't have anything to do with the laws and regulations for military matters. This wasn't right.

He struggled to keep his voice low. "Then I respectfully ask that you bring up charges, sir," Rod said. "Let's put this out in the open. You know I didn't disobey your direct order. And I did the right thing by informing the Commandant. I'll stand by my decision." His heart pounded.

Whitney drew back. His eyes narrowed. "You're at the edge of insubordination, Simone. You don't know what you're getting into."

"I beg to differ, sir. If you're threatening to court-martial me for an event the Dean just praised me, then I respectfully request to clear the record; let's put this behind us and move on, sir."

Whitney turned to face Rod. He stood only inches away and breathed heavily.

Rod smelled onion and black olives on Whitney's breath. He felt as though the heat in the Dean's foyer had suddenly soared.

"Is there anything else—Captain."

"Yes, sir." It was now or never. "The lab reports from the Defense Technical Information Center. And that crystalline sample I gave you. You said you'd have both results back before Christmas. It's been six weeks past the time you said you'd get back to me. Can I do anything to help expedite the process?"

Rod pulled back, certain that the Colonel would erupt in a tantrum.

Whitney stiffened. He stared at Rod and seemed about to speak, when slowly a smile came across his face. "Yes ... yes, I believe there is, Simone."

"Sir?" Uh oh, this was not expected.

Whitney lifted his chin. "I did receive a note back from DTIC, just the other day I believe." He put an arm around Rod's shoulder and pulled him away from the center of the room. Rod tried to shrug off the grip but the Colonel held firm.

They reached the window and Whitney dropped his grasp. He took on a knowing look. "I don't suppose you knew that your father and mine had similar backgrounds. They were a generation apart, but my father, as did yours, flew in the War."

Rod stopped. "Sir?" That was out of left field. Rod's BS detector swung into overdrive.

"That's right. But they flew in separate wars: General McCluney in World War II; my father in World War I. General McCluney was a pilot, whereas my father was an observer. An enlisted observer. I'm sure you remember from your Doolie knowledge what that meant—"

Where is this going? Most of what he remembered from Doolie year was how to survive.

"—Observers were considered expendable, not quite up to the status of a pilot. Not equivalent at all. Observers encountered quite a bit of resistance being accepted as Army Air Corps personnel, and they experienced quite a bit of disappointment after all they'd been through. Disappointment at not being fully accepted as part of the warrior ethos.

"And I've also experienced disappointment," he coughed, "yes, even I, despite my PhD. You see, I was medically discharged from pilot training, and that was quite a letdown, especially after achieving my high class standing at West Point. But I didn't allow that to stop me. I was the first in my class to obtain a doctorate, and the first to make full Colonel. You see, my father's disappointment and my own temporary setbacks have made me a much better man." He faced Rod directly. "You received this early promotion only because your father was a general and you're a pilot; so I hope someday, you'll remember this underserved, good fortune when you are disappointed."

Rod was at a loss of words, unsure where Whitney was leading him.

The Colonel looked down and sighed. "Captain Simone, I'm sorry to tell you this, but DTIC never received the crash data from Colorado Technical Associates. And as far as the analysis of that sample you gave me, well, I'm afraid I've learned that Colorado Technical Associates have gone out of business. They're bankrupt."

Rod stepped back. "Are you sure? Before Christmas, Colorado Technical Associates seemed fine; they even sent me a copy of their corporate information."

Whitney narrowed his eyes. "Of course I'm sure." He lifted his chin. "My secretary checked with the Colorado Springs Better Business Bureau and found a PO Box for the attorney dissolving their assets. She can forward that information to you if you wish."

Where just minutes before he'd felt uncomfortably hot, Rod now felt as if he'd been plunged in a bucket of ice. It was nearly too much for him to comprehend. After all this time waiting, some faceless government bureaucracy had said they'd never received the lab analysis performed on his father's crash. And worse yet, the same lab that was supposed to have analyzed the mysterious substance he'd found had gone out of business. Now what was the chance of that happening?

Rod slowed his breathing and tried to keep calm. "Sir, I don't suppose you still have that crystalline substance I gave you."

Whitney frowned. "Of course not. I just said I sent it to Colorado Technical Associates. But I assume that your sample was forwarded on to their bankruptcy attorney."

After the excitement of hearing about his unexpected promotion just minutes before, and now learning this, Rod felt as though he was riding an emotional yo-yo. "I'd ... really appreciate getting the attorney's contact information."

"Then talk to my secretary. She'll have the details." Whitney turned to leave, but stopped. "And Simone."

"Yes, sir?"

"My observation about ... insubordination. It still applies. Do you understand?"

"Yes, sir." Rod watched him carefully.

The Colonel stepped forward. He looked up and searched Rod's eyes. "Are you absolutely sure?" he said in a barely audible voice.

"Yes, sir," Rod said. "I understand completely."

O   O   O

Rod waited until Colonel Whitney had left the Dean's area before he walked over and congratulated his fellow officers on their promotions. Captain Lastoneu from the Chemistry department appeared to be in a daze. "Man, am I lucky!" he said. "As a chemist I never thought I'd be promoted past Lieutenant!"

Ten minutes later Rod left the Dean's foyer and found his way back to Theoretical Mechanics. He stopped by the secretary's desk and she looked up the contact information for Colorado Technical Associates' bankruptcy attorney; after a few minutes of searching, she told him she'd bring it to his office.

As he waited he called Julie and gave her the good news about the promotion. She told him to stand fast; she'd pick up Nanette from kindergarten at Pine Valley Elementary School and bring her up to his office before the end of the work day.

While he was on the phone, Colonel Whitney's secretary handed him a sheet of paper containing a PO Box address and a forwarding telephone number.

Rod hung up with Julie and dialed the number. On the third ring a bored voice answered, "Darius Moore."

"Excuse me?" Rod's mind raced. The name sounded familiar.

"I said, Darius Moore. Is anyone there?"

Rod felt as if he'd been hit by a two-by-four. A name from the past ... was this the ex-district attorney who had attempted to railroad his father for murder?

Rod drew in a breath. "Mr. Moore ... I'm calling from the Air Force Academy, about a chemical sample that was sent to Colorado Technical Associates."

"That company has declared a Title 11 Chapter 7 bankruptcy for liquidation, and I no longer represent the client. Who is this?"

Rod evaded the question. "Mr. Moore, do you happen know what happened to CTA's lab equipment or where any other of their material might be stored? We're trying to track down some work they performed for the Air Force five or six years ago, as well as some recent samples that had been sent to their lab for analysis."

"Their lab equipment was auctioned off and any government files in their possession have already been forwarded to the appropriate agency. All correspondence and deliveries have been returned to the sender per the owner's direction."

"And if any samples haven't been returned—"

"Then take it up with the Post Office. The owner has made it explicitly clear that Colorado Technical Associates will no longer accept any material. They're out of business."

"Thank you," Rod said. "And I'm sorry, I missed the owner's name. ..."

"High Country Construction was the sole shareholder. Now who is this?"

Rod clicked off. There was no way he was going to leave his name with the ex-District Attorney. He remembered all too well the bogus charges that Darius Moore had brought against his father, as well as the charade of bringing him down to the El Paso County courthouse in that abortive attempt to embarrass his father in front of the press. Hank had suspected George Delante was behind it, and later, after that run-in with the Delantes in the El Paso County Courthouse stairwell, his father's suspicions made sense. He just wondered how Moore could have fallen into this particular position.

Rod reached into his lower desk drawer and pulled out the telephone directory. He leafed through the white pages, found the number for High Country Construction and dialed. He glanced at the clock and saw he had a few more minutes in the workday—it would drive him crazy if he wasn't be able to speak to the ex-owner of Colorado Technical Associates until tomorrow.

The line was picked up on the first ring. "Jim-Tom Henderson."

Rod blinked. "Mr. Henderson ... of Pine Valley Airport?" Another surprise. He was certain this was the spry old gentleman who had owned the small airfield that he and his father had flown from numerous times.

"Not for a while. The government stole the airport years ago. Bastards took it by eminent domain. Gave it to that newfangled Air Academy. How can I help you?"

Rod sat up in his chair. "Sir, this is Captain Rod Simone, General Hank McCluney's son. You helped spread my father's ashes over the Academy nearly six years ago—"

"Well I'll be hogtied! Of course I remember you, young man. You were a cadet last time I saw you. How's Mrs. McCluney doing? Holding up well?"

"She's fine, sir. I'll pass along your regards."

"Great, please do. Now what can I do for you, Captain?"

"I'm trying to track down some material that was sent to Colorado Technical Associates, and I was told that High Country Construction was the sole shareholder—"

"Damn right about that, Captain, and a sad thing as well. Glad to finally dump CTA, even though all I got was pennies on the dollar. It was a terrible spinoff, a real goofy idea. It didn't have a single thing to do with either flying or land management. Tried to divest myself from that loss-leader for years. It was dragging us down, taking way too much time and effort. But George wanted it for some reason and ran it himself."

"So you weren't the owner?"

"Only on paper."

"Then you didn't run it?"

"Hell no! Why in the world would I have wanted to put up with all that federal due diligence and oversight bull?"

"Then who ran it? The bankruptcy attorney said High Country Construction was the sole shareholder. Isn't that you?"

Jim-Tom laughed but he sounded bitter. "No, it's not me, Captain. It's my partner—although not my partner by choice. The same person who literally screwed my sister out of her land and her fifty percent share of High Country Construction, back when you were still in diapers, boy: George Delante."

CHAPTER TWENTY

"Ticket to Ride"

February 4th, 1965

**United States Air Force Academy
Colorado Springs, CO**

*Integrity without knowledge is weak and useless, and knowledge
without integrity is dangerous and dreadful.*

Samuel Johnson, *The History of Rasselas, The Prince of
Abissinia*

Rod said goodbye and slumped back in his chair, shell-shocked, as realization sunk in. The so-called independent lab that had performed the forensic analysis of his father's crash was owned by the same man who had tried to frame his father for murder. What did Jim-Tom say, his partner, although not by choice?

How could this have happened? Who in their right mind would have contracted with Colorado Technical Associates to do this analysis if they'd had known about this relationship? It was as if the person who'd wanted his father out of the picture had been given the responsibility to rule on the cause of the crash.

So does that mean that George Delante might have been somehow connected with his father's crash? General Beaumont had insisted that the altimeter and fuel gauges were not functioning correctly, and that had strongly contributed to his father losing control of the plane ... but if something had been added to the fuel tank, and if that evidence had been suppressed, would that point to George Delante? Would that be reason enough for Delante to buy a forensic lab through a secondary layer, to somehow try to hide the evidence?

Rod hit the desk with his fist. In the original report, Jim-Tom had said that his partner had filled Dad's fuel tank! That would be motivation for Delante to divert any evidence to Colorado Technical Associates, where it could be conveniently lost or misanalysed.

And if that wasn't bad enough, was Colonel Whitney somehow mixed up in all this mess? After all, he'd been the Accident Investigation Board's Executive Officer and had been responsible for contracting a local forensics lab—conveniently owned by his friend George Delante. Everything seemed to fall in place, and it all hinged on analyzing that mysterious crystalline substance.

He pondered the implications when he heard a high-pitched squeal and the sound of tiny footsteps pounding down the hallway. He flipped over his notes, stood, and stretched. He needed to push this out of his mind, not burden his family. At least not right now.

Nanette ran into the room. She wore pink shoes, a dark-red dress, white tights, and a white parka. Rod walked around the desk and scooped her up. He rotated her upside down while she giggled.

Julie walked into the office, carrying his bagpipes over her shoulder. She held up a bottle of champagne, shook it, and sprayed the sparkling wine throughout the office. Frothy bubbles covered the desk, his bookcase, and the walls.

Rod held up a hand and tried to keep from dropping Nanette. "Hey! We're not allowed to have alcohol in the workplace!" He lowered Nanette on the carpet.

"And you're not allowed to be promoted this far below-the-zone, Lightning!" She laughed and continued to spray the bottle, soaking Rod's clothes and papers.

Nanette squealed. She clapped her hands and started jumping up and down. She opened her mouth, leaned her head back, and spun around.

Julie took a drink and gave the bottle to Rod. He swallowed a mouthful and pulled Julie close to give her a long kiss.

She broke off and held his head in her hands. "This is incredible! We need to celebrate."

Rod looked around his office; champagne rivulets zigzagged down the walls and pooled on floor. "I think we're doing a pretty good job."

She brought her mouth close to his ear. "I'll have Nanette wait outside your office, sit on the floor and color while we shut the door and—"

"And they'd pull back the promotion." Rod gave her a hard kiss and turned to the pipe bag she'd set by the door. He gave her a quick smile. "This is a great idea!"

He knelt and unzipped the bag as Nanette helped him assemble the instrument. He rummaged through the pockets and found a fresh reed, wet it and filled the pipes with air. A low hum grew from the instrument.

He straightened, swung the strap over his shoulder and began playing, starting off with "Scotland the Brave." Nanette started clapping and marched around the small room, stepping high and thrusting her tiny arms up and down.

Rod stepped into the hall as he played. Officers stuck their heads out of their office and gave him a thumbs up, some applauded. He moved to the main hallway outside of the department and immediately switched to "Highland Cathedral," then one hymn after another, as a crowd gathered down the long hall.

Nanette continued to march around him. After a few minutes, she finally tired. She sat on his shoe and held on to his leg as he played, watching as he covered and uncovered the finger holes on the chanter.

He ended with "Cock o' the North," then pushed the air out of the bag and put down his pipes. Several people cheered, a few whistled. His fellow faculty members came by and congratulated him, having heard of his promotion through the grapevine.

215

Rod shook hands and basked in the glow. He'd been on an emotional roller-coaster today, so ending it like this seemed somehow appropriate.

He turned and nodded for Julie and Nanette to return to his office. "Time to pack up."

Julie put her arm around him and laid her head on his shoulder while they walked. As they rounded the corner he saw Colonel Whitney standing by the door to his office, his arms crossed. He sniffed as Rod approached. His eyes surveyed Rod's wet hair and uniform.

Rod moved his pipes to one hand and swung them down. "Colonel Whitney. Do you remember Julie? We were dating when I was a cadet."

"Yes, of course." Whitney raised his chin. "The southern belle."

"Hello, suh," Julie said in a neutral voice. She stepped away from Rod, knelt, and drew Nanette close, away from Whitney.

"The last time we spoke you were planning to attend Georgetown." He glanced down at Nanette and a faint smile played across his lips. "Yes … patent law if I recall. So have you passed the bar?"

Julie narrowed her eyes. She set her mouth and slowly drew herself up to her full height. She stepped forward. "Why you little son-of-a—"

An alarm went off in Rod's head. Anticipating a firestorm, he shooed Julie and Nanette away and directed them into his office.

Whitney sniffed as they left. "I assume that smell is from your bagpipe, Captain."

Rod ignored the comment and placed his pipes on the floor. Today's revelations and small amount of champagne seemed to have a synergistic effect. "I spoke to Colorado Technical Associates' bankruptcy attorney."

"Good for you. Are you satisfied with our discussion from earlier today?"

"No, sir, I'm not."

"Then pray tell, Simone. What will it take to satisfy you?"

Rod drew in a breath and held Whitney's stare. "I also spoke to the sole public shareholder of CTA, High Country Construction."

"You did ..." Whitney paled. "The attorney gave you that information?"

"All I had to do was ask."

"And ... what did you find out?"

"What I suspect you already know, sir. I discovered that George Delante really ran the operation, and was the hidden co-owner. And since I've been asked by General Beaumont to keep him informed of the status of the lab analysis and DTIC report, I'll be calling him this afternoon to give him an update."

Whitney took a step backwards. "General ... Beaumont? The four-star on the Air Staff?"

"That's correct."

"I'm sure you'll give him my regards." Whitney's voice was barely audible.

"Yes, sir, I will. After I fill him in on all the details."

O   O   O

The next day, ten minutes before his first period class, Rod looked up as Captain Bobby Andrew stepped into his office. Bobby shut the door behind him, his face ashen.

Rod stacked his class notes and frowned. "You look terrible."

Bobby flopped into a metal chair in the corner. "I tell you, man, you should change your call sign from Lightning to Feline."

"What are you talking about?" Rod moved to sit on the edge of his desk.

"Lightning never strikes twice but felines have nine lives."

Rod glanced at the clock. "Look. I've got to head out in five minutes for class—"

"No you don't. You're heading home, ole buddy. Pack up your office and get the hell out of Dodge before Colonel Whitney returns from the Superintendent's office. And you'd better hurry. Between finding that nipple on the planetarium, breaking glass on your flyover, the cheating ring, and now whatever happened between you and Whitney yesterday, you've only got five more lives to go. So I'd be out of here before Whitney gets back if I were you."

"Okay, I give. Tell me what's going on."

Bobby leaned forward in his chair and looked under the door as if to see if anyone was listening. He sat at the edge of his seat and lowered his voice. "Colonel Whitney was ordered to attend a meeting with the Superintendent an hour before work started. He just called and told me to get you the hell out of his department, ASAP, if not sooner."

Rod stared.

Bobby looked apologetic. "His words exactly, not mine, Lightning"

"S'all right. But what for?"

"Midnight Mayflower: HQ Air Force assigned you local temporary duty to the Chidlaw Building starting Monday morning as special assistant to the four-star commander of NORAD."

"Where's that?"

"Just across town from the Academy in downtown Colorado Springs. You'll be there until your PCS orders come through to Air Command and Staff College, then on to F-4 upgrade training with a follow-on combat tour in 'Nam."

"What?" He'd never heard of anyone getting such a short notice assignment, especially followed by a Permanent Change of Station.

And then to Vietnam! Flying in combat was every fighter pilot's dream; he felt a surge of excitement. He was going to war! And flying an F-4. It was what he'd been training for all his life.

But why was he being pulled out of the Academy so quickly?

Bobby thumped on the wall. "Lightning! Focus! Are you paying attention?"

"Yeah, but it's happening too fast. And why?" Of course. Last night's phone call with General Beaumont....

"All I know is that you'd better be out of here before Whitney returns," Bobby said. "Sounds like he's getting his ass fried by the Superintendent. I imagine that if he wasn't a Permanent Professor he'd probably be packing for Shemya, Alaska right now to keep track of Russian missile launches."

Rod pushed up from the desk. "I think I know what happened." He turned for his bookcase and started pulling down textbooks. Some of the covers were spotted from yesterday's champagne shower. He wet his finger, wiped off the spots, and started piling the books on his desk.

"And ...?" Bobby stood to help him.

"And I don't think it's right for me to say. It's just too bad about Whitney. Because to a man, all but one of the Permanent Professors are outstanding individuals, really world-class."

"You're right—except for him. He's the oddball that slipped through the wicket. Just goes to show you that one malefactor can taint an entire institution."

"Well put." Rod picked up his class notes and handed them to Bobby. "Who's taking over my classes?"

"We'll double up today and then find five instructors to each take on an extra class so we can cover all of your sections."

"Thanks." Rod drew in a breath. General Beaumont had been understandably upset when they'd talked last night, but the four-star hadn't tipped his hand at all about what he was going to do.

It must have been paramount to get him out of the Academy. So he assumed that parking him as a special assistant was preferable to having him remain here for the rest of the semester. General Beaumont probably knew that the next altercation he'd have with Whitney might be bad enough to end his career.

They finished packing, and Bobby helped Rod place his items on a cart to take down to his car. Once they'd cleared the department area Bobby looked over his shoulder as if to ensure they weren't being followed. He slowed his pace and motioned for Rod to draw near as they walked.

"Just a heads up, Lightning. Before I was ordered to clear you out of your office, Whitney wanted me to contact some attorney that was handling the affairs for Colorado Technical Associates. He was pretty hard over that I track down a sample he'd sent them; said it had to do with an Accident Investigation Board he'd worked on a few years ago." He cocked his head. "I assume it has to do with your father's accident, right?"

Rod stopped in the middle of the hallway. "Did he say why he wanted it?"

"He's asked the chemistry department to pull out all the stops and expedite analyzing it once I track it down. He said both Headquarters Air Staff and the Superintendent want to know what that stuff is, and he's got until yesterday to find out."

"Wow. Keep me in the loop, would you?"

"No problem."

Rod felt a weight lift from his shoulders. It sounded as if General Beaumont hadn't forgotten his concern about that substance he'd found inside his father's fuel tank and wanted to put this matter to rest. But it was kind of weird that Whitney would be so cooperative, even with General Beaumont and the Superintendent breathing down his neck. Maybe this was an indication that Colonel Whitney really wasn't mixed up with George Delante and that sleazy attorney, Darius Moore....

As they entered the elevator to take them to the basement floor, it hit Rod that he hadn't bid farewell to any of his colleagues or his cadets.

"Wait. I just can't leave without saying goodbye."

"I'll tell the faculty you'll be at happy hour at the Club. We'll throw a good wake. And don't worry about the cadets—I'll tell them myself you're helping a four-star rid the world of Commies."

"Thanks, Bobby." They shook hands as the elevator opened. "You've been great."

"And you can buy tonight, Lightning." He pushed the cart out of the elevator. "Now get out of here. I wouldn't want you to lose another life by running into Colonel Whitney."

O O O

Two weeks later on an early Sunday morning Rod leaned back in bed and listened to the snowstorm belting his house. In the adjoining room Nanette played alone in the den, babysat by the TV blasting out *Rocky and Bullwinkle* reruns. He thought about calling her in, but he was too tired to function.

Although he'd left his flying duties and teaching responsibilities behind when he'd signed out of the Academy, Rod still probably averaged seeing his daughter only a few times a week. Working directly for the four-star NORAD Commander sucked up all his time.

Julie slept next him, her snores competing with the snow driving against the windowpane. A nearly empty bottle of gin and two cocktail glasses sat on the dresser, and next to the bed an ashtray was filled with Julie's cigarettes, remnants of the drunk-a-thon they'd had since Friday. It was a wonder he didn't have more of a hangover.

His mother had called earlier this morning, waking him and asking if they would be attending church. He mumbled an excuse, and she'd made him feel embarrassed that he should at least be going for Nanette, if not to thank God for his early promotion.

He shouldn't feel guilty, but this wasn't the first time this had happened.

They'd too easily slipped into the habit of drinking the weekend away and using Sundays to recover. Starting Friday nights with happy hour at the Club, they'd drop Nanette off with Rod's mother, and sometimes not pick her up again until late Sunday afternoon.

The Officers' Club encouraged the socializing as a bonding experience for the officers. The cheap drinks and mandatory membership was an additional incentive to frequent the facility, and it allowed him to keep in touch with the USAFA faculty while he was assigned to NORAD. That was usually an uplifting experience.

But this past Friday night had been the exception.

Captain Bobby Andrew had approached him with good news and bad.

The good was that he'd tracked down Rod's crystalline sample that Colonel Whitney had sent to Colorado Technical Associates. Five boxes of archived material had been sitting in a storage shed, and within a few hours he'd ferreted out Colonel Whitney's original envelope.

The bad news was that the USAFA Chemistry department had conducted multiple tests on the sample and they all came back as revealing not sugar, but a mixture of calcium carbonate and magnesium carbonate. They were both a white powder, but caused by the presence of water vapor in the fuel tank; so what Rod had assumed to be sugar was actually limestone, resulting from a naturally occurring chemical change in the tank over a six-year period. One of the professors who'd been promoted to Major with him, Captain Lastoneu, had explained that it may or may not be an indication that water had been added to the tank, but after all these years, it was impossible to know.

So he was back to square one of having no real proof that his father's crash had been caused by anything other than pilot error.

And with Colonel's Whitney's push to locate the crystalline substance and have it analyzed, there seemed to be no reason to link him with George Delante other than through a casual friendship. So whatever hidden conspiracy Rod thought he'd uncovered to cause Hank's crash, once again he was back to ground zero.

Rod lay back and stared up at the ceiling. He listened to the cartoon sounds of Boris and Natasha drift in from the den, mixing with the howling of the outside wind.

With all that had gone on in his life, something was amiss, and it wasn't not understanding why his father's plane had really crashed.

The early promotion should have made things better—especially when he knew that it was something that other officers would kill for. And the fact that he was now working for a four-star general before going off to school and flying fighters made it even better.

But still, he felt a void, just as he did when he'd graduated from pilot training.

Was he tied too close to the Academy, and somehow felt responsible for all the problems that were going on? For all his good fortune, he knew that he should be on top of the world ... yet, something was missing.

He'd already accomplished more than he could ever have hoped for, and still, he wasn't content. There had to be more to life.

Rod reached under the bed and pulled out his bagpipes. He'd played his heart out two weeks earlier when he'd been told of his promotion, but despite the reasons to be happy, he wasn't.

He carefully worked the connections and ensured the bag was primed, then left Julie in bed, and padded into the kitchen.

He looked out the window at the snow, and started filling the bagpipes with air. The sky was gray, gloomy like his mood, but swirling with flakes.

Within minutes the mournful wail of "Highland Cathedral" filled the house, competing with cartoons masterfully depicting thinly-veiled criticism of the growing Cold War.

CHAPTER TWENTY-ONE

"Magic Carpet Ride"

Three years later
June 2nd, 1968

21,000 Feet over North Vietnam

So faithful in love, and dauntless in war,
There never was knight like the young Lochinvar.

Walter Scott

Break right, break right, break right!"

Rod reacted instantly, rolling the aircraft hard to the right; then pulled the stick so hard to his lap it crashed against his crotch. The horizon rotated in front of him as the F-4D responded like a tiger pouncing on a kill.

He jammed the throttle forward to compensate from the loss in airspeed and altitude as the fighter's two GE J-79 engines pumped out 17,000 pounds of thrust. Rod flicked his eyes from the dials on the cockpit to the view outside the canopy. The mottled green and brown hills of Pack Six A, the combat area over Hanoi, stretched below, masking the MiG-19 Farmer he'd had in his sights just an instant before.

"Where is he?" Rod said over the mike.

Sitting in the seat behind him, Captain Jazz Ferguson, Rod's GIB—Guy-In-the-Backseat—twisted in his cramped seat, trying to look behind them. "Oh, crap, Lightning. A new bandit! He's at eight o'clock, coming up fast. Looks like a Fishbed!"

Rod's attention diverted from the target he'd acquired as his heart rate went into overdrive. The MiG-19 would have made an easy kill; he now concentrated on surviving.

The MiG-21 Fishbed had an empty weight of only 13,500 pounds, a sleek and fast fighter capable of accelerating to Mach 2. Compared to the 30,000-pound F-4—affectionately known as the "Smokin' Rhino" —the MiG-21 was reported by intel to be faster and far more maneuverable.

Reported to be.

Rod had a gut feel it was a myth.

As Rod slammed the stick back to the left, he also dove, picking up airspeed. "Tally-ho!"

He knew the MiG-21 would be directed by North Vietnamese ground controllers—actually they were Russians, a fact conveniently ignored by the media and the politicians running the war—and the MiG would be vectored to launch a heat-seeking ATOLL missile for the kill. Myth sometimes drove fighter tactics, and Rod instinctively took advantage of it.

"What are you doing?" Jazz screamed over his mike. The force from the diving turn threw his head against the cockpit.

"Hang on," Rod grunted, keeping the stick full to the left and buried in his lap. His wingman had turned back because of a fuel leak three minutes before. The rest of the flight was chasing down the two MiG-19 Farmers that had come up to intercept them.

An alarm went off in the cockpit. "Radar lock, he's launched a missile!" Jazz shouted from the back.

Rod pulled tighter into the turn.

"Lightning, pull out! Pull out! We're going to get hit—"

Fighting against the centripetal force, Rod strained to look over his shoulder. Just as he expected, the MiG-21 had rolled up after the launch, fully expecting Rod to pull out. After all, it was standard tactics. Rod immediately went to idle power to reduce his heat signature, counted to three, then hit the afterburners and jerked the fighter to the right.

The force from the afterburners igniting felt like a kick in the pants. The F-4 jerked and started accelerating into the roll.

Rod kept the stick as far to the right as he could. Alarms clanged in the cockpit, loud enough that Rod's ears hurt.

Suddenly, a streak of white shot past the F-4. The air-to-air missile rocketed past, missing the fighter by mere feet.

Jazz whooped in the back. "The ATOLL's tracking the other MiG!" The missile spiraled past, locking on the MiG-19 Farmer that Rod had had in his sights just seconds earlier.

Before the MiG-19 could react, the infrared-seeking missile flew up its tailpipe. The Russian-made fighter exploded in a fireball.

They continued to turn and soon the MiG-21 flew into sight. As if the North Vietnamese pilot suddenly realized that Rod was now in a superior position, it spiraled in a dive to get out of the way.

"No you don't," Rod said. Cutting back on the afterburners, he jockeyed the F-4 into position. He rolled his fighter left and right as he brought the MiG-21 into his sights. He flicked the trim button, flipped open the protector, and armed his Sidewinder. "Come on," he muttered, finessing the F-4 so that the agile MiG flew into the engagement box.

The MiG-21 veered to the right, then back suddenly to the left into his sights. Rod immediately punched the pickle button, launching the missile the same instant he drew a lock. "Fox, fox, fox!"

He felt the F-4 barely hesitate as the Sidewinder dropped from its mount. Seconds later, he watched a thin trail of white smoke corkscrew toward the MiG.

The missile clipped the fighter just in front of the engine. In a sudden flash, the MiG erupted in an orange-red explosion of smoke and debris.

Rod pulled up, avoiding the remnants of the engagement. Sweat poured off his face as he glanced down at the clock. Less than half a minute had passed since the time Jazz had spotted the MiG-21 until both planes had been destroyed.

A click came over his headphones. "Splashed him! Good show, Lightning. But scare the crap out of me next time, would you?"

Rod clicked his own mike. "Would you rather be a smoking hole in the ground?"

"Hell no!"

Rod clicked his mike twice, signifying he concurred. "Go to button two," he said. The flight had been pre-assigned communication frequencies, called buttons. Button two was the radio frequency his flight was using for the day.

"B-Flight, check."

"Twop." Said his wingman, Lieutenant "Basher" Morrison. He was on his way back to base with a fuel leak, but was still well within radio range; having graduated from the Academy barely two years ago, he was flying his third CAP and had missed all the action.

"Threep," drawled "Aussie" Foster, a lanky captain serving his second tour in 'Nam.

"Fourp." The final flight member, "Blade" Curtis, was the antithesis of a fighter pilot: quiet, studious, and focused on applying for astronaut training.

Thank goodness, everyone survived the MiG encounter. "Everyone but Basher regroup at 35, sector 22A," Rod said over the mike, keeping his words clipped and short. "Everyone okay?"

The fighters clicked their mikes, no one speaking. The flight presented an impeccable image, a poster child for pilots.

The taste of combat had quieted his usually rowdy flight, but on the other hand, the squadron commander wouldn't complain if he finally brought back a somber team.

Too many times in the past his flight had fueled their cocky reputation by flagrantly disobeying the rules. Last week Rod had been called during the middle of the night to show up at the central receiving facility, the air base brig, to bail out one of his airmen.

B-Flight prided itself on being the best, and Rod allowed his pilots to push themselves to the edge. He'd never thought being a Flight Commander would be so demanding, yet he was incredibly happy, even with his family still back in Colorado Springs.

Those last few months in Colorado had been tough. Thank goodness he'd been pulled to Vietnam, rescued from the Academy and its maddening ways; things had gotten so bad with

Colonel Whitney that he was lucky for being given the short notice PCS.

In the summer of '65, he was sent to Air Command and Staff College at Maxwell Air Force Base, home of Air University which he and his father had visited in the early fifties. Julie had hated the sweltering summer, the lack of culture in Montgomery, and the overt racism present throughout the south.

They'd lived in Prattville, a small town just outside of Maxwell, where he attended the twelve-month grooming school for mid-level officers. They were next-door neighbors to a cool, but polite German Air Force exchange officer who was attending the school, and Rod had thought that they allowed their son, who was a few years older than Nanette, too much freedom. He'd forbidden Nanette from playing with the rambunctious young lad, and both he and Julie were glad to leave the small southern town.

After graduation, they vacationed in the small mountain hamlet of Angel Fire, New Mexico, before PCSing to Vietnam; Angel Fire was the last time he'd been with his family before reporting for duty.

But instead of flying as a crew dog as he'd done years before in the F-105, within weeks of arriving in country he'd been frocked to Major—allowed to wear his new rank, but not paid the increase in salary—and was promoted to flight commander, commanding the flying unit that defined the essence of the Air Force. Since it was unthinkable to deploy nukes in the Vietnam conflict, the F-4 fighter was literally the weapon of choice, frustrating the long-time SAC proponents who were seeing their coveted B-52 nuclear bombers sparingly used to drop conventional bombs from dizzying altitudes—a mission unchanged from the carpet-bombing tactics used in World War II.

In the time he'd been here, he'd flown 71 combat missions in the new F-4 fighter. And as icing on the cake, he'd splashed, or shot down, four MiGs, just shy of becoming an Ace.

Rod was on top of the world and enjoyed every aspect of his Vietnam tour. The only bad news was when he'd heard that Major Tom Ranch's F-105 had been shot down over Hanoi a few months before he arrived. He grieved for his old mentor, but the rumor was that the war would be over soon; and he knew that if anyone could survive in the North, it would be Major Tom.

Rod's thoughts were broken when Jazz came over the open mike. He spoke in a clipped tone. "Wing just confirmed Lightning splashed a 21, gentlemen. I believe that makes him the first American Ace in Vietnam!"

Whistles and catcalls filled the airways. "Lightning! Way to go!"

"Beer, beer, Lightning. Open bar tonight at the Club!"

"Congratulations. We're all proud of you, boss!"

Rod clicked his mike. "Rog. Drinks on me tonight, but downtown. Fire Empire."

Whoops came over the radio. Rod heard Jazz relay the announcement of Rod's splash back to squadron headquarters, where the news would spread like wildfire.

The Fire Empire was renowned for its exotic dancers as well as for its wild parties. Rod figured that he'd be out several hundred dollars tonight, but he also knew that he only became an Ace once in his life.

The Flight deserved much of the credit, and Jazz had been just as worthy of the honor as he. Without everyone's help, he'd never been at the right place at the right time to make that fifth kill.

Back in 1966, North Vietnam announced that Captain Nguyen Van Bay had become the first Ace of the war, so at least the Americans were starting to claw back.

They rolled into the airspace over Saigon and were cleared for a combat landing. Flying at ten thousand feet, Rod rocked his wings before leading the flight down in a spiral over the airfield. The F-4s flew in at a tight bank, staying above the area controlled by the friendlies, and making it tough for a shoulder-mounted SAM to track them.

Rod greased his landing. He pulled up to the tarmac, opened the canopy, and allowed hot, humid air to tumble into the cockpit as he moved forward. The screams of their jet engines filled the air, audible even through his helmet headphones. The other jets crept behind him in a line as they made their way to their squadron area.

Rod reached down and cut the engines as they pulled up to their spot; the noise dopplered down in volume. An airman dressed in fatigue bottoms and stripped to the waist pushed an aluminum ladder out to the jet as another airman wearing headphones put down the orange sticks he'd used to guide them in and picked up a pair of wooden chocks to set behind the wheels.

Rod disarmed the ejection seat, removed his helmet, and unfastened his straps. He stood and suddenly felt chilled. His flight suit was soaked with perspiration, and the slight breeze actually felt cool compared to the closed cockpit.

"I hope you can afford this party, Lightning," Jazz said as he climbed out of the back.

"The bank's got plenty of money," Rod said. He zipped swiftly down the stairs to wait for Jazz when he heard someone shout his name.

He turned and saw the pilots from his squadron holding a long fire hose.

The Wing Commander directed them, hands on his hips and a cigar in his mouth. Colonel Robbie's long handlebar mustache curled up at the ends. He pointed at Rod and shouted, "Now!"

Someone used a crowbar to twist the top of the fire hydrant, and water shot from the hose, jetting straight for him.

Rod tried to duck, but there was no place to hide. The force of the spray nearly bowled him over. The pilots yelled, "Congratulations, Ace!"

Rod ran at an angle away from the water, but they kept the stream on target.

Water squished in his boots and dripped from his flight suit as Rod made his way back to the squadron area. It seemed that everyone on the base had shown up to pound him on the back and congratulate him. He kept his wet flight suit on during the post flight briefing, and the usual forty-five-minute brief stretched to three hours as different Colonels showed up to shake his hand and give him some sort of award.

The squadron commander uncorked a bottle of champagne. In the middle of the toast, the four-star commander of PACAF, Pacific Air Forces in Hawaii, called with words of encouragement; General Speedy Beaumont, now retired and living in Arlington, Virginia, was the last to call. Rod felt exhausted by the end of the briefing.

He left the squadron area and hitched a ride on the blue crew van that was making its rounds of the base. The flight hooted and hollered all the way back to their quarters. Even with the extended post-flight briefing, it was only late afternoon. That was one advantage of getting up at zero dark early to fly the combat missions: you could get back and hit the bar before it got too late.

Finally entering the multi-storied dorm that served as officer's quarters, he saw a pile of congratulatory notes stuck on his door. He pulled them off and started to read them, but thought better of it and piled them on his desk—he had less than an hour before the flight was going to meet him at the Fire Empire and he wanted to tell Julie the good news.

He took a quick shower, changed, and rapped on Jazz's door. He shared a small kitchenette with his backseater in the two-room suite. "I'll be in the phone room. Meet you out front."

"Rog," came Jazz's muffled voice through the door. "Ask Julie to give my wife a call and tell her I'll phone after tomorrow's mission."

"Anything else?"

"That's it." Because of the expense of long-distance calls, the Flight routinely passed messages from one wife to another when someone had the opportunity to call back to the states.

Minutes later, Rod sat in the phone booth at one corner of the recreation room. A torn pool table, an old Kenwood stereo, and a rack of outdated magazines were set in the room, interspersed with metal chairs and a brown leather couch. No one used the facility except for the maids when the squadron was out flying.

Rod spoke to the international operator and sat back, waiting for his call to go through. Someone ducked into the rec room, looked around then quickly left. In some ways the place reminded Rod of being back at the Academy. The officers were crammed together in a high-pressure situation, without any women but with plenty of energy to burn. But the resemblance stopped there. At the Zoo, the worst that could happen would be marching on the tour pad; here, friends could die.

The phone jingled; Rod picked it up. "Major Simone speaking."

"Sir?" The operator spoke with an accent.

"Yes?"

"I'm ringing."

Rod counted the rings. When it got to ten, the operator said, "Sir, shall I redial?"

"Let it ring some more," Rod said. He squirmed in his seat. Someone should be home. It was what, Sunday there, and nearly five in the morning. Where else could they be?

"Hello?" His mother's voice sounded weak.

"Mom? This is Rod."

"Hello, lad. Is everything all right? It's so early."

"Everything is fine, mom. How are you doing?"

She laughed quietly, "As well as you might expect. I am getting up in age, lad."

"You need to take care of yourself. I don't have long to talk. Is Julie there?"

"Oh, I'm afraid not. She hosted a fancy reception and dinner at the Broadmoor last night, and a freak spring snowstorm got so bad they closed all the roads. She called about midnight and said she couldn't make it back, so she checked into a room and promised to call this morning."

Rod shifted his weight in the cramped phone booth. "How bad is the storm?"

"It's still snowing, lad; three feet since last night. You know how the spring weather can be."

"Yes, I remember."

"Do you want to talk to Nanette? She started karate lessons yesterday."

"No, let her sleep."

His mother took a long moment to answer. "I think she's taking karate for you, lad. She wants to impress you. It won't hurt to wake her."

Rod closed his eyes. "If she's tired she won't remember the phone call anyway."

Another pause. "If you say so." She was quiet for another moment. "You take care of yourself, you hear?"

"I will, mom." He considered passing along the news about him becoming an Ace, but he wanted to surprise Julie himself. He blinked and discovered that for some reason his eyes were misty.

"Listen, tell Julie I'll talk to her tomorrow. And have her give Sally Ferguson a call—tell her that Jazz will call her tomorrow night our time, right after we return from our next mission."

"I'll tell her, son."

"And I have some great news; really good news. Just tell her I love her."

"You're not coming back from Vietnam early, are you?"

"No, but I wish I were. Give Nanette a kiss and I'll talk to you tomorrow."

"Very well, lad. Stay out of trouble."

"I will. Goodbye." He hung up the phone and remained in the phone booth. It felt weird, having some of the best news in a long time and not being able to share it with his wife. He could have told his mom, but he wanted to save it for Julie.

He pushed out of the booth and jogged down the hall, banging on the doors of his flight as he passed. "Hey, ho, let's go! It's time to celebrate, gentlemen!"

CHAPTER TWENTY-TWO

"Born to be Wild"

June 2nd, 1968

Fire Empire
Saigon, South Vietnam

That chastity of honour, that felt a stain like a wound.

Edmund Burke, *Reflections on the Revolution in France*

Rod peered through the smoke-filled bar as he tried to watch the floor show. He held up a hand to shield his eyes from the outside light that reflected on the tables in front of them, but the glare grew brighter the more beer he drank.

Worse yet, it was only six in the evening and his entire flight was already drunk.

A pyramid of beer bottles was stacked on the floor next to the table. If they drank as much beer in the next hour as they had the past two, the structure would reach the ceiling. But from the way the boys looked, they probably wouldn't hit their goal.

On stage a bikini-clad dancer gyrated on high heels to the pulsing beat of "Jumpin' Jack Flash," as she moved in and out of the multi-colored floor lights. Rod couldn't tell what she looked like through the smoky, purple haze—but it didn't matter because the point of the celebration had been to get drunk.

Jazz slumped over. His head hit the table. Basher reached over and started to prop him up, but Aussie intervened. "Leave him be. Otherwise, he'll slide to the floor."

Basher burped. "Good point." He let go of Jazz and his head hit the table again.

"Ouch," Rod said. "I thought Jazz could hold his liquor. I've never seen him pass out."

"Must have been the excitement of the dogfight," Aussie said.

Rod finished his beer and added the bottle to the pyramid. He gingerly placed it on the top, starting a new level. "Ta da!"

Basher whistled. "What a man! Not only can he fly and fight, he can stack 'em!"

Rod grinned and started to reach for another beer bottle, but there were no more on the table. Aussie said, "Hey, Lightning, how about another round?"

Rod he glanced at his watch. "It's after six, and we have an afternoon wheels up tomorrow. We should be knocking off pretty soon to sober up and snag some crew rest."

"You're just wimping out on us, Lightning!"

"Yeah, just because Jazz can't hold it doesn't mean we have to quit!"

Rod snapped his fingers and whistled for the barmaid. "Hey! Bring me the check!"

"Party pooper!"

Rod pulled out his wallet and counted out a sheaf of bills. When the barmaid presented him the ticket, he peeled off enough money to cover a tip, and then gave some more to Basher. "Tell you what. I'm heading back; I want to call Julie again. You guys have one more on me while Jazz sobers up. I'll meet you at the squadron tomorrow afternoon, but don't forget the crew rest."

"Go on and sleep it off, sir," Basher said. "We'll see you tomorrow." He put a massive arm around the barmaid. His biceps were as big as her thighs.

She snuggled up to him and giggled. "Hey, you too big for me, G.I."

"If you think that's big, take a look at this," Basher said. He reached down, but she twisted away and left the table. "Bring me another beer," he called after her.

Rod pushed up. He wobbled as he stood. "Wow, watch that first step." He felt lightheaded and steadied himself on the chair. "Catch you gentlemen on the rebound."

The guys lifted their beers in a salute. "Thanks, sir. We'll take care of Jazz. And congratulations, Ace."

Rod weaved his way out the door, moving carefully past tables of American military men in uniform. The place was nearly full, and as Rod moved past the stage, he caught a glimpse of just how vivid the young dancer's performance was turning out to be; but even with all the alcohol he'd had, her routine wasn't erotic, but clinical.

He pushed past a row of women standing by the door. The girls wore black, tight-fitting miniskirts, the standard dress for prostitutes in Saigon. One ran a hand against his back as he passed by. "Hey, Joe, what you say for some short time? Quicky, quicky?"

"No, thanks," Rod said, shaking his head. He stepped out into the street and was simultaneously almost blinded by the sunlight and bowled over by the fresh air. "Man, is this place evil." He was lucky to have only dropped a couple of hundred dollars in there tonight. He hoped the guys would be able to get back in time for their crew rest.

He walked down the street, stumbling as he tried to find a taxi that would drive him back to the base.

He passed by an outdoor market where skinned dog carcasses hung from ropes. Smells of garlic and onions frying in sesame seed oil wafted from tin-roofed buildings, and the odor reminded him of his boyhood in Cahors, of his father sautéing vegetables. A white-haired old lady, her skin mottled and dangling with age, squatted by a pile of dried rice. Barefooted children ran from the market and skipped up to him to beg for money.

He spotted the towering structure of the Saigon Intercontinental Hotel, a mainstay for high-level government officials when they visited Vietnam. The presence of such a lush hotel so close to the open air market made Rod wonder about the wisdom of flaunting so much wealth next to such squalor. It was something the Viet Cong would try to exploit, by pointing out such obvious incongruities.

The massive glass and marble hotel building came into view as he turned the corner. Taxicabs lined the street, waiting to be summoned to the hotel by the doorman.

Across the street, a crowd of people stood around a man holding a newsreel camera, the type used by TV reporters. A blond in a bright red dress stood with her back to Rod, speaking to the camera.

Rod set his mouth, wavering slightly from the alcohol. News media. In his mind, the war was being lost because of people like her. They were starting to flock to Vietnam with preconceived ideas and slanted the news to prove their point. If they only knew about the crap he and his fellow pilots put up with—flying pre-established routes, not being allowed to bomb SAM sites because of political agendas, politicians calling off bombing raids in the middle of a mission—he was certain they'd change their mind.

Even now that reporter was probably giving a distorted view of life in Saigon, showing the hotel where the politicians hung out and not actual Vietnamese homes, such as those who lived behind that open-air market. That was the type of distortion that would go over well with the bleeding heart liberals, and would play into the hands of the Viet Cong.

And she probably had the gall to stay in the same damn, up-scale hotel!

Rod breathed hard as he veered away from the line of cabs and walked unsteadily toward the reporter in red. He'd march right up to her while she was still being filmed, tap her on the shoulder, and ask her why the hell she didn't show a true picture of Saigon.

As Rod approached a young boy cycled toward the crowd, pedaling furiously on a beat up old bicycle. He kept his head down, concentrating on going as fast as he could. He veered right and left around people in the street. A car skidded to a halt and blasted a horn at the young boy, but still the youngster pedaled on.

Now almost next to the reporter, Rod started to raise his voice—

Through the fog of alcohol, something clicked in Rod's brain. What was the boy doing? What was he carrying in his basket? Why was he going so fast? He was so young; did he even know what he was doing? The whole scene didn't seem right; it didn't make any sense....

The young boy was now only feet from the reporter. He reached into his front metal basket and pulled out a package about the size of a loaf of bread. He tossed it at the cameraman and immediately took off, pedaling back the way he had come.

The package bounced once and landed in between the reporter and the cameraman. Startled by the noise, the man swung his camera down to the package.

Rod reacted instantly. "It's a bomb!" he yelled, slurring his words. He dove at the woman reporter. He hit her from the side and pushed her out of the way.

Lithe and weighing at least eighty pounds less than Rod, the woman was bowled over. She dropped her microphone and screamed in anger as she tumbled. Rod rolled on top of her, spreading out as far as he could and covering her with his body, as he yelled to the crowd. "Get away! Run!"

A few people pulled back, but the cameraman stepped forward hesitantly, keeping his camera focused on the package.

Suddenly, the bomb exploded in an orange burst of flame and smoke.

People screamed. The smell of burning paper, oil, and gunpowder rolled over them as Rod still protected the reporter, shielding her against the blast. "Stay down!"

Guards from the hotel ran out into the street, pulling weapons from their holsters. The crowd surged back and Rod heard people yelling. Someone gasped and started crying; a woman behind Rod started to shriek.

Rod looked up. The cameraman lay on his back, the camera knocked to the side. Blood ran from his mouth and gashes in his head, his stomach. Rod pushed off the reporter and scuttled to the cameraman on his hands and knees. The man's eyes were open, but blank. He put his ear next to the man's chest but couldn't hear a pulse.

A scream came behind him. "Randy! Where's Randy!"

Rod turned and saw the woman reporter crawl toward him, head down, the tips of her blond hair sweeping across the concrete. One of her shoes came off as she struggled to her feet. Her red dress was ripped in the back and covered with dirt and grime. She stumbled over; Rod and the cameraman were now encircled by on-lookers.

Rod turned back. He put his ear to the man's mouth and didn't hear him breathing. He straddled the man, locked his hands together, and started giving him CPR.

A dark complexioned man wearing a brown pinstriped suit stepped up and squatted next to Rod. He placed a finger on the cameraman's neck, waited a moment then pulled out a small flashlight and moved it over the man's eyes.

The man looked up as the female reporter approached. "He's dead," he said in a heavily accented voice.

Rod kept up the CPR, not willing to give up.

"How do you know?" The reporter demanded. She looked around frantically at the people milling around. "Somebody help him! Just don't stand there!"

"I'm a doctor," the man said. "There's nothing I can do."

"No!" The reporter tried to reach for the cameraman, but she stumbled.

The doctor straightened and put up a hand to keep her away. "He's dead." He pulled her back and spoke to Rod. "Sir ... sir, please. He's not breathing."

Rod stopped and stared at the cameraman. Could he have done anything else to save him? He heard the doctor speak to the woman reporter, "Take care of those cuts. They're just superficial; you'll be fine."

The doctor started to leave, but he squatted next to Rod. "Are you okay, sir?"

"Yes," Rod said. He pushed up and looked at the reporter.

She brushed back her blond hair, showing her face, and intense ice-blue eyes.

Rod felt his heart almost stop. His Third class summer ... San Francisco, the summer of 1956 ... and then graduate school at Stanford a few years later....

He swallowed. "Barbara?"

It took her a moment, but as she searched his face her eyes widened. She drew in a breath. "Rod? Rod, I—" She was at a loss for words.

A Vietnamese policeman pushed through the crowd, blowing a whistle. "Everyone leave. Leave now." He pulled out his sidearm and motioned for the crowd to step away. As the people moved back, he looked at the cameraman and the growing pool of blood. "What happen?"

Turning to Rod, Barbara Richardson said in a shaking voice, "This man saved my life."

CHAPTER TWENTY-THREE

"Scarborough Fair"

Later that afternoon
June 2nd, 1968

Sheraton Intercontinental Hotel
Saigon, South Vietnam

The follies which a man regrets the most in his life, are those that he didn't commit when he had the opportunity.

Helen Rowland, *A Guide to Men*

With a bandage on his face and his knuckles raw, Rod flexed his hand as he sat in the living room of Barbara's Intercontinental Hotel suite.

The décor was incredibly ornate. Tiny coconut trees were planted in two rows, demarcating the entrance from the door to the suite. A wooden bridge arched over a rock-lined stream that ran in and out of the room, and a ceiling fan rotated lazily, circulating air over scrubbed white walls, bamboo furniture, and fine pieces of museum art scattered through the room. One night in this place probably cost more than a month of Rod's salary, even with flight pay.

The shower ran in the bathroom. After the hotel doctor had attended her wounds, Barbara didn't want to be left alone. She'd insisted that he stay so they could talk.

Plates from room service were stacked on a cart covered with a white tablecloth. A half-empty pitcher of Mai Tais was set on a bamboo table; water from condensation clung to the pitcher's surface. A radio in the corner was tuned to 99.9 MHz, the FM station run by the Armed Forces Radio Service; Norwegian Wood played softly in the background.

Rod picked up his drink and stepped onto the porch that overlooked the city. Below, the smells of animal dung and outdoor cooking wafted up to mix with the opulence of the room. The place where the bomb had exploded a few hours before was now teeming with rickshaws, old women carrying packages. There was no sign of the disaster, no police tape to mark off the scene. It looked as though nothing had ever happened, as if the city had swallowed up the atrocities of war to keep its sanity.

Rod leaned against the door and sipped his drink; he moved the tiny umbrella to the side. The Mai Tai was too sweet for him, but it felt good as the liquor warmed his stomach. He'd have preferred a beer, but he made do with the pitcher of drinks that had accompanied the hors d'oeuvres she'd ordered from room service.

He turned as the bathroom door opened. Barbara walked out, dressed in a white bathrobe. She bent over and dried her long, blonde hair with a towel.

He caught his breath and turned back to the view outside. "How are you doing?"

It took a moment for her to answer. "Better." She sounded unconvincing.

He changed the subject, not wanting her to dwell on her cameraman's death. "It's hard to imagine you as a TV reporter. What happened to your writing career?"

"Opportunity." She picked up a drink and joined him in the doorway. She took a sip and played with the ice cubes with her tiny umbrella. The faint smell of White Shoulders perfume drifted past and brought back a rush of memories of the time they'd spent together....

He looked into her ice-blue eyes and felt out of breath.

He needed to leave.

He was feeling the Mai Tai and tried to think of a way out. "That's ... quite a switch, changing careers from aviation journalism to reporting the nightly news. You were always the idealist. I just didn't peg you as a liberal."

"Who said I was? And what if I were?"

Rod started to retort, but turned away, embarrassed at stereotyping her, of all people. He was being too confrontational. Her cameraman had just died for God's sake. But he kept silent and stared out the balcony at the city below.

She stood next to him and was quiet for a long time. "I've discovered a reporter can learn a lot just by asking the right questions, especially when you're being filmed for TV."

"Such as. ..."

"Such as," she turned him by the elbow and stepped close, "has anyone ever asked you how many people you've killed today?" She searched his eyes.

Rod pulled himself up. "Actually, yes," he said. "I was flying commercial from Denver to San Francisco, on my way to Travis to come over here."

"What did you say when asked?"

He hesitated, not wanting to get into an argument about why he was here, or even why the U.S. was involved in this third world country. That was so far above his pay grade it wasn't even funny. He needed to diffuse this and leave.

He forced a smile. "I said my quota was five ... but I'd only killed four and needed one more within the next few hours."

Barbara blinked. She brought her hand up to her mouth. A moment passed and she stifled a giggle. "What a comeback! What happened?"

"Nothing. He got real quiet and didn't speak the rest of the flight."

They were both silent for some minutes.

Rod finished his drink and placed his drink on a table. "Ah, look, Barbara. I'm sorry. I should have apologized years ago. That guy I beat up, your friend, the professor ... I don't know what got into me. I really thought you were in trouble." He stopped.

"And ... maybe things would have turned out differently if we'd have kept in closer touch. Who knows."

"Times change, people change." She turned away and grew quiet.

Yes, he thought, *people change.* He wasn't sure at all how things would have turned out if they would have kept in closer touch; but he remembered the times when he'd been dating Julie and his thoughts would drift to Barbara, and of the passion she'd had for making a difference in the world.

And now she *was* making a difference, reporting this war to millions of people, affecting their attitudes, changing people's minds.

She said softly, "Rod, that wasn't nice of me to ask you that question, about how many people you've killed."

He turned and studied her. "I deserved it after that crack about being a liberal. I didn't mean it that way."

She sipped her drink, and then swept her hair back behind her shoulder in a flowing motion. It was that motion that had captivated him so many years ago ... along with her intense, ice blue eyes.

She stood with her arms crossed, holding her drink and staring out the window. The sun was just setting. Lights blinked on over the city and Saigon lost its harsh edge in the growing dusk; it looked almost enchanting. Barbara nodded at the sight. "This is where the action is now, doing these pieces for the national news."

"How did you get into this?" Rod said. "It's so different from what you wanted."

"When I worked for McDonnell Douglas, I discovered a pretty face in a major aerospace corporation gets put in a lot of interesting situations, and not all involve writing."

"I can imagine," Rod said, remembering at the Academy when he'd been fighter pilot poster boy—doing everything, it seemed, instead of teaching cadets, such as flying beer out to Washington, DC for a general. He hesitated, then picked up the pitcher of Mai Tais and refilled their glasses.

Barbara said, "I started giving briefings for the executives, then they used me to speak to the news media." She shrugged. "It was an easy move after that, going from the one being interviewed to the one doing the interviewing. As a newscaster, the pay's much better than being a journalist, and I get a lot more publicity."

"And the prize is to anchor the national news."

Smiling, she raised her glass in a salute. He clinked her glass in a toast. She sipped on her drink. "Am I that obvious?"

"They'd be crazy not to make you a lead anchor."

"Walter Cronkite will never retire."

"He will someday," Rod said. "Or you can fill the void when either Huntley or Brinkley steps down. There's no doubt in my mind you'll be a real celebrity."

"What makes you so sure?" she said.

He drained his glass and looked away. He hadn't quite sobered up from the beer earlier in the day, and now his tongue felt thick with the Mai Tais. "Your ability to think quickly on your feet. Your intelligence. Your charisma." He turned to face her. "Some people have it all, Barbara. You're one of them. And better yet, you're at the right place at the right time."

"I was at the wrong place at the wrong time today."

"In this war, no place is safe in Vietnam; anyone can die at any moment. But when you're on TV, those people viewing the nightly news may watch you at first because you're a knockout, but they'll quickly see you're a good reporter. It shows. And you have talent. This war will make you famous."

Rod felt his ears burn. He'd probably talked too much, but at least he'd spoken his mind. And after all these years, he'd finally apologized for trouncing that guy he'd thought was molesting her back at Stanford.

He glanced at his watch. It was already dark and getting late. He needed to head back to get his crew rest.

Barbara watched him intently.

He hesitated, then said, "Excuse me, I have to get back to my Flight." He started to slip past her, but she stepped to the side, blocking the way out.

She didn't move. "Did you mean that?"

"What, that you're a good reporter ... or that you're quick on your feet?"

"Neither," she said. She placed a hand on his chest.

He pulled himself up. Time seemed to slow down, almost to a stop. He felt his heart beat faster, his face grow warm.

Barbara spoke softly. "When you apologized … and said that things might have been different between us…."

Even in the dim light he could see her ice-blue eyes search his.

"Yeah, I meant it," he said. "But who would have known twelve years ago when we had our chance?"

"Twelve years ago we were just kids, barely out of high school." She hesitated. "And then later, when I saw you at Stanford, the first day of graduate school—I was hoping you'd come there because of me. But when you told me you were married, and a new father …"

He drew in a breath and felt lightheaded. "I … wish things had turned out different, but they didn't." He started to leave. "Good night, Barbara. Like I said, you have it all. So good luck. Maybe we can get together before you head back to the states." He stepped forward.

She dropped her arm and said quietly, "You're wrong, Rod. That's my problem—I don't have it all."

He frowned.

She stared at him, hard. Slowly, she reached up and undid her robe, allowing it to drop to the floor.

She stood before him unclothed, her breasts rising and falling as she breathed. Her long legs were tan, accentuating the pale pubic region.

The blood pounded in Rod's ears. His mouth felt cottony. "I … I …" can't, he finished in his mind.

Thoughts of Julie, Nanette swirled around him. He felt giddy as she reached out a hand, and the time since he'd been away from his family seemed like forever.

He'd seen the skin shows with the boys, and the call girls had propositioned him nearly every time he'd come into town.

But he'd never wavered.

"You said that anyone could die at any time," she said. "Tomorrow it might be either of us."

He'd never had a reason to stray, and he never wanted to …

"But you have it all," he whispered.

She pulled him toward her.
She felt warm, soft, and fluid. "I don't have you."

CHAPTER TWENTY-FOUR

"Sky Pilot"

The next afternoon
June 3rd, 1968

Tan Son Nhut Air Base, South Vietnam

I am an American fighting man. I serve in the forces which guard my country and our way of life. I am prepared to give my life in their defense.

> Para I, The American Fighting Man's
> Code of Conduct

Lightning, do you copy?" Jazz's voice came over the headphones.

"Say again?" Rod shook his head. He looked out the F-4 cockpit to the crew chief, waiting for Rod's instructions. His mind must have wandered.

"Lightning!" Jazz said. "Wake up! The Flight's ready. Tower's just given us Rainbow Bright as the authentication code."

"Copy," Rod said. "Rainbow Bright." He had started to twist his wedding ring, but remembered that, like all jewelry, he'd left it back in the VOQ so he wouldn't inadvertently catch it on a switch. He keyed his mike. "Tango Flight, let's crank 'em." He looked to his right at the three other F-4's in his flight. In the fighter next to him Aussie gave him a thumbs up then reached up to start his engines.

Rod flicked a series of switches and started his own engines. Outside the fighter he heard the whine of the automatic power unit that gave his F-4 the preliminary current. Smoke belched from the yellow APU.

He glanced down and read from his checklist that lay on his knee. "Nav systems?"

"Rotating," Jazz answered from the back seat.

"Oil?"

"Check."

"Ejection seat?"

"Armed."

"Bombs?"

"Armed."

He ran through the rest of the checklist while the twin GE J-79 engines rumbled to life. The sequence was ingrained in his brain, he could have done it in his sleep ... and his thoughts drifted again to last night. The passion and hunger had seemed to last forever, as if their emotions that night they'd first met, 12 years ago, had been pent up, and finally boiled over.

He'd left the Intercontinental Hotel by taxi this morning and stared out the window as he passed old Vietnamese men dumping wash water into the gutter; women chattering as they strolled to market with plates of fish or bowls of rice balanced on their heads; children laughing as they kicked a tattered ball down the side streets. For some reason, in the midst of their poverty they seemed remarkably content.

Yet, the view out the window was absurd. He'd just left the marbled opulence of the ridiculously rich to travel through the squalor and bereavement of the incredibly poor, the ends of a spectrum measured not in miles but in billions of dollars.

The sight remained with him. In contrast to the destitution, he and Barbara had everything—she, the promise of becoming a national celebrity, and he, a bright Air Force future. Still, despite their passionate lovemaking, it seemed they'd both been searching for something, and were somehow not even as content as the poverty-stricken Vietnamese that now surrounded his taxi. He tried to put his finger on it, but couldn't.

When he'd kissed her goodbye, he didn't know if they would ever see each other again ... or if they should.

He felt a deep sense of guilt when he tried to call Julie after he returned to the VOQ. But she was still snowbound, and had not yet returned from the Broadmoor. Rod spoke to Nanette and promised that he would call as soon as he returned from today's mission. As he left for the ready room, his jaw worked as he tried to rationalize what had happened last night....

A click in his headphone ripped him out of his thoughts. "Lightning, I said tower's giving us clearance. Listen up!"

"Ah, rog."

Jazz's voice was low over the intercom. "We're not hot-mike, Lightning. Are you okay? I mean, it's my butt that's on a sling back here if you're not up to flying today."

"I'm fine."

Jazz was quiet for a long moment. "Look, if this is about you being grounded, look at it this way. The Pentagon doesn't want to risk anything happening to their newest Ace. You're lucky Wing looked the other way and allowed you this one last sortie—"

"I said, I'm fine," Rod said firmly. He keyed the mike.

Again, silence. "And you asked Julie to give Sally a call?"

"Roger that. But my mom will contact her; both Julie and Sally are expecting calls after this afternoon's mission."

Jazz clicked his mike twice.

Rod turned to the outside frequency and quick scan out the cockpit gave him the assessment he needed. The flight of four F-4s sat at the end of the runway, engines at idle, ready to punch into the sky.

Rod said in clipped tones, "Tower, tango. Say again."

"Tango, tower. Winds 220 at 10 cleared for takeoff runway 220."

"That's a rog." He flipped the frequency to his flight's. "Tango, lead. By my count, crank 'em and roll on a twenty second interval."

"Twop."

"Threep."

"Fourp."

Rod shook his head and tried to leave all the previous night's baggage on the ground. He was finally ready to get in the air. He had another life to worry about in the backseat, and didn't need the memory of Barbara causing him to make a mistake.

He kept his feet on the brakes and stood in his seat as he pushed the throttles forward. The F-4 started to shake like a rodeo bull injected with a barrel of caffeine.

Rod keyed the mike. "Ready, Jazz?"

"Rog!"

Rod kept the stick neutral, released the brakes, and punched on the afterburners. Flames thirty feet long exploded from the engines.

It felt as though a 500-pound bag of cement had been dropped on his chest.

The fighter accelerated down the runway, picking up speed. Rod's eyes flicked from dial to dial on the instrument panel, watching as the jet hungrily gulped fuel. When they passed the 3,000-foot marker, the airspeed indicator vibrated at 115 knots.

"Rotate." Rod buried the stick in his crotch and the snub-nosed fighter lifted into the air.

"Yahoo!" cheered Jazz from the back seat. "What a kick! Enjoy this last flight, Lightning!"

Rod turned his head to look out the cockpit as they accelerated up. Below them, the end of the runway melted into the mottled green brown jungle outside of the airbase perimeter. He watched the rest of his flight start their takeoff roll, then pulled to the right and climbed to twenty thousand feet where they would perform a rejoin.

An hour later, they rendezvoused with a KC-135 tanker over the South China Sea to refuel before flying CAP, or Combat Air Patrol, for a bombing mission scheduled to take place over Downtown, vernacular for the North Vietnamese city of Hanoi.

One by one the Flight nudged close to the boom that extended from the back of the 135's underbelly. When his flight had refueled, Rod pulled up and followed the director lights on the KC-135's belly.

The fuel boom looked like a long, narrow angel with tiny extended wings; it slipped into the F-4, directly behind the backseater on the spine of the aircraft. It always amazed Rod that the boom operator could so deftly maneuver the boom into the F-4's tiny fuel opening, all while lying on his stomach at the rear of the craft as they flew at nearly two hundred knots in formation with the military version of the Boeing 707.

A half hour later, fully loaded with JP-4, the flight peeled off to cover their area and patrol for MiGs.

Rod ordered his flight to deploy into a search pattern. Flying Tango 2, Basher slipped into position as Rod's wingman. They started the long wait to escort their brothers from the navy, flying A-6 fighter-bombers, who would come sweeping in from the sea to make their bomb runs.

Above them, the sky diffused into a deep black, devoid of any stars. The horizon stretched out before them, and distant contrails from the KC-135 tankers were barely visible.

Rod absently cracked his ring finger, once again bringing back the memories of the night before—

"SAM, SAM! Break left!" Jazz screamed over the intercom.

Rod reacted instantly, slamming the stick to the left and craning his neck to search for the in-coming missile. Ahead of them and to the right he spotted a streak of smoke that spiraled toward them. It had a lock on them, and jinking wouldn't break it.

"I've got it," Rod said in a cool voice. Instinct and years of training took over; he knew precisely what to do. He punched out a load of reflective metal chaff in the hopes that the Russian-made Surface-to-Air missile would break lock on their fighter and take a fix on the chaff. He grunted as the jet accelerated downward and to the left.

He pushed negative G's and heard excited chatter over the radio. He turned his head to spot the other two planes in his flight break to the right. In theory, their splitting maneuver should have confused the incoming missile's radar.

In theory.

The missile spiraled in a long arch and headed straight for them.

"Oh, crap," Rod breathed. He hit the afterburners, and the plane surged forward like they'd been kicked in the pants. He only had one more option, and it was risky.

"Incoming!" Jazz said. "Do something!"

Rod slammed the stick to the side. The missile had locked them in. No amount of maneuvering would cause it to miss. He'd have to wait until the last second, allow the missile fly close, then quickly pivot his wings by ninety degrees. If they were lucky the SAM wouldn't be able to react and would zoom on past. The moments seemed to stretch out forever as they watched the SAM approach—

Rod rammed the stick to the right; the F-4 pivoted, rotating around. For an instant he thought he'd done it, that they'd slipped by and escaped the SAM ... but the missile slammed into the right wing, punching a hole clear through the metal and fiberglass structure.

Rod saw a trail of debris spray out from the left, followed by a horrific explosion. Wind roared through holes in the canopy. Shards of metal peppered the dials.

Rod couldn't hear anything through his headphones except for static.

"Mayday, mayday, mayday! Jazz, anyone, do you copy?" There was no reply over the wind screaming in the cockpit.

He worked at the stick, but the plane barely responded. What dials he could read were pegged at zero. Hydraulics must have been taken out.

With an L over D less than a rock, the F-4 plummeted from the sky; Lift over Drag was a measure of how far the plane would fly, and now that was practically zero. He reached down and tried flicking first the emergency restart, then a series of other switches.

He ran through the "oh shit" checklist. All the time he called out over the radio, switching frequencies in the hopes that something would work.

Nothing did.

The fighter dropped toward the ground, still carried by its forward momentum. But despite his initial velocity, he knew they wouldn't get far.

The South China Sea lay somewhere behind him, and with his hydraulics Tango Uniform, there was no hope of turning around to try for the water; they'd have to punch out.

He tried to remember exactly where they'd been in their turn, where he'd be once he landed—if he survived—but he didn't like the answer that kept popping up in his head: North Vietnam.

The air screamed around him, tearing at his flight suit. He couldn't raise Jazz; he just hoped that his backseater had survived. It couldn't have been more than fifteen seconds since they were hit, but time seemed to stretch on forever.

Miraculously the fighter hadn't gone unstable, and with what little control he had left, at least they were upright.

But they wouldn't last that way much longer.

As the ground drew near, Rod decided to go. He couldn't risk getting any closer to the ground, despite not being able to raise Jazz. He just hoped that his GIB was cognizant enough to ready himself once he started the ejection sequence.

He clicked his mike. "Jazz! Bailout, bailout, bailout!"

Rod reached down, pressed his head against the back of the seat, and pulled the ejection handle. An explosive charge blew the canopy up and away from the fighter.

With an ear splitting explosion, Jazz's seat was ejected behind him. Time seemed to stand still for Rod, as if he could track every minute detail. The wind howled louder, slamming him back and forth against the high-backed seat. A half-second later his own seat was kicked out of the jet in a wild, high-flying arc. He tumbled and tried to keep his eyes open, but the world spun crazily around him.

He lost sight of the jet. Before he could gather his thoughts, another explosion kicked him away from the ejection seat.

His chute spilled open and long white cords whistled out of his parachute pack.

He felt a sharp, cutting sting in his calf, just as his parachute jerked him up. He spotted the ejection seat tumble away. A flash of pain seared through his leg; he looked down and saw that he'd been hit by the seat. His leg hurt like crazy but at least he was alive.

He remembered his airborne training, years ago when he was a cadet, at Fort Benning as he held onto the parachute ropes. He tried to get a bearing and spotted an area void of trees. He pulled up on the parachute cords and steered toward a collection of fields.

To his left, the F-4 arched toward the ground. It accelerated as it fell, but everything was weirdly quiet. Seconds passed and the jet disappeared in the thick foliage, looking as though the earth swallowed it up.

Seconds later a plume of black smoke and orange fire erupted from the jungle floor and roiled into the air. He started counting as soon as he saw the flames.

The plane's funeral pyre would act as a beacon for the North Vietnamese. He had to get as far away from the crash site as he could. He doubled his effort in steering for the open fields, but he didn't have the right angle to make it.

He drifted down in silence. Within seconds he heard the explosion's low rumble. He'd counted to twenty, meaning that the fighter had crashed four miles away.

He craned his neck around; he didn't spot Jazz's parachute. He tried to turn to get a 360 degree look, but as he rotated around there was no sign of a chute. His heart sank. With the way the day was going, losing his friend only twisted the knife that pierced him with guilt.

As he sank to the ground he prepared to hit the tall trees. He scanned the area; the closest clearing was miles away, and he didn't have enough forward velocity to make it. The pain increased in his leg as he drifted closer to the top of the jungle.

Standard operating procedure was to release the parachute as he hit the forest canopy and tumble to the ground; otherwise, his chute might catch in a tree and he'd hang from the high branches. Unless he could deploy his tree-lowering device he'd be a target for any Viet Cong who may stumble upon him. But with the way his leg felt, there was no way he was going to risk falling on it.

He pulled himself into a ball to reduce his exposure to the tree limbs, squeezed his eyes tight shut, and crashed into the upper branches.

CHAPTER TWENTY-FIVE

"Run Through the Jungle"

June 3rd, 1968

Somewhere in North Vietnam

To save your world you asked this man to die: Would this man, could he see you now, ask why?

W. H. Auden, "Epitaph for an Unknown Soldier"

Rod tumbled to the ground. He cried out as he rolled on his leg; he'd bruised or cut it bad.

He pushed up to a sitting position and unsnapped the latches from the parachute. The chute snagged in the tree, and he tried to pull it down, but it wouldn't give. He yanked again. Great. If anyone came along, the parachute would serve as a giant arrow, saying "hunt for me here!"

Grimacing from the pain in his leg, he pulled up on the cords and tried bouncing the chute out of the tree. No luck; the chute only rebounded like a sluggish rubber band.

His breath quickened, coming in short, sharp gasps. He rolled over in the dirt and looked up. If his leg wasn't injured he could scamper up the trunk and cut the chute free, but with the parachute looking like a gargantuan beacon, he needed to move as far away from the landing zone as possible.

He pulled himself up and almost fell; he limped away until the parachute was invisible through the foliage. Breathing hard, he winced with every step.

Blood dripped from his leg. He knelt; he scanned the area while pulling his squadron bandana from his thigh pocket. He wrapped his leg tightly and started to perspire.

Got to stay hidden. Keep quiet. Don't leave tracks. Throw them off course.

Escape and evasion training kicked in from the year after his BCT summer, years ago. Just last year, he'd taken the jungle survival course at Clark Air Force Base, required of all pilots going in-country, but it had not been half as memorable as that summer back in '56, when he'd been scared out of his wits in SERE, the Academy's mandatory Survival, Escape, Resistance and Evasion course.

He crept away and tried to identify as much of the flora as he could, realizing he may be living off the land for some time; he was thankful he'd paid attention during the survival training at Clark. He pushed past rubber trees, silky oak, scattered evergreen, Borneo teak, banaba bushes, and ironwood as he crept through the jungle.

He stopped in a thick thicket of banago trees, crouched over, and attempted to keep pressure off his leg. He looked around and tried to slow his breathing; he couldn't see more than a few feet in front of him. He should be safe, but he still pressed tightly up against a tree.

He patted his survival vest and inventoried his pockets: a .38 caliber pistol, mirror, compass, first aid kit with morphine, sugar, gum, string, knife, a two-way radio the size of a brick, compass, spare ammo, water, water distillation gear, and a waterproof map of Vietnam with greetings written in seventeen different languages, all promising a substantial monetary award if he was led to freedom. Another waterproof map was wrapped around thin sheets of gold, a down payment for the additional money his rescuers would receive.

He looked around as his eyes grew accustomed to the foliage, but still couldn't see more than a few feet through the jungle.

Again, he tried to control his breathing but he couldn't beat down the terror. He needed to find some water—at the rate he was gulping it wouldn't take long to empty his canteen and he'd soon be dehydrated. No telling where he was, or if any of his flight had gotten a fix on him when he punched out.

He extended the radio's whip antenna, pulling out the long black metal rod as far as it would go and twisted a knob on the radio's side; a crackle of static came from the speaker. He hurriedly turned down the volume and looked around to see if he'd been heard; nothing.

He brought the microphone to his lips and spoke in a hushed tone. "Mayday, mayday. Tango 1. Do you copy?"

He swept his eyes across the jungle. No movement, no sound.

"This is Tango 1. Do you copy?"

He repeated the plea, listening in between calls. When he didn't get a response, he turned off the radio and attended to his leg. It throbbed and was sensitive to the touch.

He unwrapped his blood-soaked bandana and gingerly unzipped the bottom of his flight suit. He almost fainted as he saw a gash that ran from his kneecap to his ankle. White bone was visible as a flap of skin sagged away.

He washed the wound with water before tearing open the first aid kit. His hands shook as he squeezed as much antibiotic as he could into the wound, then pulled the flap of skin up to cover it. Grimacing, he wrapped the leg in gauze and then wound tape around his leg. He was tempted to use the morphine, but he knew he'd need it later.

He zipped up his flight suit, rolled over, and grabbed for the radio. He had to take his mind off the wound; he knew that once the adrenaline rush and initial shock subsided, he'd be faced with excruciating pain.

He flicked on the radio. "Mayday, this is Tango 1. Do you copy?" He waited a minute and tried again. "Mayday, mayday!"

A voice crackled from the speaker. "Tango, this Rescue Alpha. We copy. We have a fix on your crash, but not on your LZ. Where are you, old buddy?" The drawl could have come right off the farm.

Rod straightened, fighting the growing pain in his leg. "Rescue, I'll find a clearing. Stand by." He dug through his survival vest and pulled out the three by five inch mirror. He picked up the radio and limped through the thicket. He pushed through the foliage, trying to spot a clearing.

After several minutes he came to an opening in the jungle. He listened for the sound of a helicopter, but couldn't hear anything except for the chatter of distant birds.

He dug out the compass and looked back over his shoulder. What direction had he come? Although he'd weaved a path through the jungle, he estimated he was northeast of where he had crashed. And if he remembered correctly, he'd landed to the south of his plane, which would place him southeast of the crash site.

He stayed at the perimeter of the clearing and leaned against a tree while speaking softly in the microphone. "Rescue, Tango. Try a clearing, football field sized, 135 degrees from the crash site."

"Rog, Tango," came the voice. "But we need authentication first, old buddy. What'cha got?"

Rod stopped, dead cold. He'd forgotten the code; the authentication code that Jazz had prompted him to remember back on the flight line, when he'd been thinking of Barbara instead of his upcoming mission.

A chill ran down his back. *What was it? Rainbow something— Night? Light? Sight? Kite? Come on, think!*

"Tango 1, we're waiting, ole buddy."

Rod brought the mike up to his lips. "I can't ... too many things are going on. I can't remember."

There was a long silence. "That's not going to cut it, Tango. Either give us the code or we're history."

"Wait ... wait." He racked his brain for something, anything that could make him remember. "Listen, it was Rainbow something." He waited, hoping. What was the damned code?

"Not good enough, ole buddy. We're countin' down, then we're blowin' this Popsicle stand—"

Rod felt a chill run through him. He understood why they needed the code; Viet Cong posing as injured airmen had downed other rescue helicopters. But he'd had it drilled into his head ever since he was a cadet that you never left your wingman. Never, no matter what the consequences.

He had a sudden thought. "Wait, wait. How about this: Are there any grads up there?"

"Grads?" There was some talking at the far end. The voice came back suspiciously. "What do you mean, grads?"

Rod hunched close to the ground, scanning the area. There was still no sign of any VC. "If there's an Academy grad on-board he'll understand. I was in the USAFA class of '59—the cadets had a code. For one of our dinner forms."

Again, it was quiet for a long, long time. Then the voice on the radio said, "An O-96?"

"That's right!"

A pause. "Go ahead."

"Fast, neat, average—friendly, good, good," Rod whispered.

A moment passed. "Okay … just a minute." Another pause. "What's a CDB?"

"Commandant's Disciplinary Board."

"Hold on." Another moment passed. "What's an RTB?"

"Red Tag Bastard—the class of '62 was the first class who used red as their class color."

The reply came back instantly. "That's a go, go, go Tango 1."

Yes! "I'll flash when you fly over."

"Roger that. Hang on, little buddy, we're on our way."

Rod withdrew his weapon and kept low, behind branches and just outside the clearing. He grit his teeth to push the pain away.

He simultaneously scanned the area and the sky, intently listening for any sound that didn't belong.

Within minutes he heard the unmistakable *chop, chop, chop* of the helicopter. He raised the radio to his lips. "Rescue, Tango. I hear you."

"We're searching, ole buddy. Stay with us, now, ya hear?"

Rod clicked the radio twice and moved to just inside the clearing. He flicked the mirror up and looked through the hole in the center; sunlight reflected into the air. He wasn't sure if he would see the helicopter first and then call them on the radio, or if they would spot the mirror's reflection, but he figured the more ways he got their attention the better.

The chopping grew louder. Through the hole in the mirror he caught a glimpse of the helicopter roaring over the edge of the clearing. He dropped his mirror and brought up the radio. "Rescue, rescue! You just passed over the clearing."

"Roger that. We'll pass over again."

Rod followed the sound of the helicopter as it wheeled around. He grasped his pistol; the handle felt slippery with sweat. His mouth felt dry, and despite the unbearable pain in his leg, his heart yammered with excitement, his hopes being lifted for the first time in hours.

The helicopter suddenly popped over the ridge of tree and Rod clicked his mike. "Rescue, Tango! You're in." A dull green HH-3E Sikorsky Jolly Green Giant, looking menacing with its fuel rod poking out the front, lifted its nose as it slowly dropped to the middle of the clearing. Wind from the rotors whistled through the trees and debris rotated up from the ground in a spiraling vortex.

"Head on out, little buddy. We'll pull you in."

Rod crouched and ran with a limp toward the center of the clearing. The HH-3E bounced once, then settled on the ground. A helmeted man in a flight suit jumped to the ground and urgently waved him on. Two other men brandishing machine guns clamored out and set up a defensive posture. "Move it!" They waved for him to hurry.

Rod felt overwhelmed as he limped on. Rescue was less than fifty yards away—

Rod heard a whistling sound and the helicopter exploded in a ball of black smoke and flames. Red and yellow fire roiled into the sky. Thick, black oily smoke belched from the underbelly of the Jolly Green Giant.

Sounds of rifle fire and automatic weapons popped from the jungle. The men who had hopped from the helicopter turned their weapons on the unseen shooters, but they quickly keeled over, their machine guns firing as they were slaughtered before Rod's eyes.

Rod stopped and dropped to a knee. Slowly, as if in slow motion the HH-3E crumpled to the side in an orgy of fire; its rotating blades dug into the ground and a high-pitched whine shrieked from the chassis as the engine suddenly died.

Rod felt a wave of heat roll over him as flames spread over the ground, coming toward him. "Oh, dear God." Where seconds before there had been hope, now there was only death.

He heard a noise from the jungle and turned. Half a dozen men dressed in ragged pants, dirty shirts, and carrying weapons crept from the jungle. Some wore rice paddy hats, but all were smiling as they jabbered to each other.

One trotted over to Rod.

Rod struggled to his feet and tried to stagger away, but his leg gave out underneath him. His gun and radio bounced to the ground and disappeared in the thick grass.

Rod crawled toward where he'd last seen the weapon, but a Vietnamese jogged up and stepped on it. He aimed his rifle at Rod's head.

A rapid-fire, high-pitched conversation rocketed between the men.

The one holding the gun on him grinned, showing crooked, yellow teeth. He started to squeeze the trigger when Rod heard a sound come from behind him—

Rod pitched forward into the dirt as he was smacked from behind with a rifle butt.

CHAPTER TWENTY-SIX

"Lady Madonna"

June 4th, 1968

**The Broadmoor Hotel
Colorado Springs, Colorado**

No one ever suddenly became depraved.

Decimus Junius Juvenalis, *Satires, II*

T he wind stopped howling as the worst of the late spring storm subsided. Outside the four-star hotel, away from the warmth of the log fires, low voices, and tinkling of champagne glasses, the snow fell straight down, softly blanketing the foothills.

Julie Simone stood at the window and thought it was an incredible change from just an hour ago, where the wind had been so fierce that the snow had been driven sideways into the windows. For nearly two days she hadn't been able to see more than a few feet outside the comfort of the magnificent, historic hotel.

She sipped her champagne and felt heady, even bold. The symphony fundraiser had exceeded everyone's expectations. And because of the blizzard, the party had been drawn out two days longer than anyone had imagined, bringing in the most money on record.

The city roads had been closed for 48 hours, and the hotel staff had risen to the occasion, accommodating their unexpected visitors with food, toiletries, and blankets. It didn't matter that everyone was wearing the same formal clothes two days straight—they were all in this together, and for those who needed their privacy, there were separate bedrooms, meeting rooms, or private hideaways in the labyrinth of corridors that permeated the grand resort.

She saw Fred Delante's reflection in the window as he stepped up behind her. She felt herself tense, well aware that even his innocent presence might start tongues wagging, and how whispered rumors might affect her reputation and even slosh over to hurt Rod's career.

Fred was dressed in a blue Nehru jacket with a short white collar that stood up like a priest's. The jacket and gold chain around his neck made him look as though he were a distinguished ambassador from India. He carried a tall, thin glass in one hand and a bottle of champagne in the other; he was just as handsome and suave as he had been when she'd first met him two years ago at the Academy's Officer's Club.

A fire burned softly in the fireplace behind them and cast a flickering glow throughout the room. Patterned furniture filled the room; oil paintings of mountains, aspen groves, and tumbling streams covered the walls. The wallpaper was subtly tinged with muted gold, not overpowering the ambiance. Music drifted in, and she recognized the strains of "Dr. Robert", the drug-laden Beatle song that seemed so appropriate in the early morning hours.

Julie crossed her arms and spoke without turning, "It's so peaceful. It's almost a shame that the symphony benefit will end." She was surprised that her voice sounded slurred. She didn't think she'd had that much to drink ... but then again, she hadn't participated in this type of marathon partying since her college days.

Fred stepped to her side and refilled her drink. "This is the most successful benefit we've ever had. You've done a great job, Julie."

"It's not too difficult when you have a captive audience." She drank deeply from her glass and turned to face him.

His presence was almost overpowering. He had a large physique, and from his muscular build, it was obvious he'd worked out with weights. Unlike Rod, who ran to keep in shape and was lanky, Fred Delante carried himself as though he still played football for the University of Colorado.

Fred smiled and showed perfect teeth framed again his sun-tanned blond features. "Except you've kept up a constant, passionate plea for help. And it moves people when it comes from such a beautiful young woman."

"More likely because they're trapped at the Broadmoor and can't get away from me."

He filled her glass again, and then topped off his own. "No, because you're so passionate."

She blinked and turned away. What did he mean by that? She studied his reflection in the window, but he didn't reveal any emotion.

He sipped his drink. "My son lives for days like this," he said. "They canceled school, and in another few hours he'll spend the rest of the day outside with his buddies, hurtling down hills, digging tunnels in the snow." He laughed. "He works harder on his days off than he ever does in class."

"How old is he?" She turned unsteadily. She wavered, and then put her drink down on the windowsill. She'd have to slow down.

"Fred, Junior? Nine. He'll be ten, next month."

"Nanette's age." She held a hand up to her head. The room started to reel.

"He was born when I was starting Law School," Fred said. Setting down the bottle, he steered Julie over to the couch by the fireplace.

She leaned back against the soft fabric, grateful to be off her feet. She must have thought she was in college again, staying up for days on end. At least she felt comfortable alone with Fred. She reached over and lightly touched his arm. "I know what it's like to have a child born while you're in graduate school. It adds an incredible amount of pressure."

"That's probably when Marie and I started to slip apart. I was concentrating on surviving Law School, and then on passing the bar."

"That doesn't sound so bad; every lawyer's had that pressure."

"But after that it was making partner, and then the political campaigns." He shrugged. "When those fell through, it was gaining favor with the Administration and lining up a political appointment in the State Department."

"So it was drawn out."

"Longer than I liked." He sipped his champagne. "I may go back into politics someday, but I need to do something noteworthy at State, first. Move up the ranks and make a splash. Get name recognition. And if I'm lucky, become an Ambassador."

"One thing after another," Julie murmured, looking into the fire. Strange how it so much paralleled her own life. Striking out for one goal after another, but there was always something in the way, holding her back.

Except that in her case it was Rod's goals, not her own: first graduate school, then pilot training, and finally fighter lead-in training. Even after flying fighters, it was returning to the Academy to teach as an instructor.

And now it was Vietnam, a sure path to his next early promotion.

So what was next? Rod making general? Being a general's wife would put her at the top of the social ladder. But for Rod to make general it would involve more years of sacrifice, several more years of moving and pulling up roots, just when she'd gotten her home into shape, or when she'd put up the last picture. And worse, it meant still more years of being the dutiful Air Force wife, perhaps another decade of continuously starting over ... and it became more and more difficult with each assignment, at another location with new people to impress.

And it was harder the older she grew.

Maybe that's the reason why these symphony benefits meant so much to her. They weren't connected with the Air Force and their unique social ladder. It was her own way of making a mark, her own way of making a difference.

But lately she'd felt that she'd risen as high as she could in the Colorado Springs social circle. Monied here meant old money—really old money—dating back to Palmer or the Tutts. Even being a general's wife wouldn't allow her access to the real inner circle.

She'd once told Rod that she wanted to enjoy life, to party, and to have fun.

Well, she wasn't having fun now. And the spark that was once there had vanished.

She looked at Fred.

He brought his champagne glass up in a toast and smiled at her. "Are you back?"

"Excuse me?"

He turned on the couch. "I lost you for a moment. I thought you were either going to fall asleep or stay immersed in your thoughts."

She ran a hand through her hair. "Was it that obvious?"

He nodded.

She leaned forward to pick up her glass. She drained the rest of the champagne and unsteadily held it out; he refilled it.

She kicked off her shoes, tucked her feet beneath her, and looked into the fireplace. She ran a finger along the rim of the glass. "So where's Marie?"

"She and Fred, Jr. are with her mother."

"She's missing the highlight of the year."

"That seems to be happening more often. She doesn't really care for these benefit functions. One of these days I suppose she'll sell one of her artworks and then she'll accompany me. But until then, she's content to work herself to death, painting until she finds herself."

"Sounds like you and I."

"Painting?"

"No," Julie said, shaking her head. "Finding ourselves. Like Marie, trying to find herself—or at least it seems we're trying to find what's missing in our own lives." She paused. "Isn't that why we're here? Each of us trying to discover what's really important? Otherwise, we'd just write the symphony a check and pass this by."

They grew silent. The only noise came from wood popping in the fireplace, snow brushing against the window, and the faint sound of another song that drifted in the room.

Fred said quietly, "You know that Rod and I were roommates at the Academy."

"Of course." Once again she drained her drink "How could I not know?" She placed the empty glass on the long table in front of them. "I didn't remember at first, but it was inevitable. Your lives revolve around that damned place, even after you leave."

"Did you tell him we've met?"

"Why should I?"

"I ... was just wondering. It's been years since I've seen him. Ever since...."

"The Courthouse stairwell?"

He looked startled. "That's right, you were there."

She turned and stroked his arm. "Whatever happened in the past is between you and Rod. It's none of my business." His presence felt warm—and strong. She continued to stroke his arm. She almost didn't say it, but the words came out. "Just like what happens ... between us."

He looked up. His eyes flicked from side to side, searching her eyes.

She drew in a breath, and felt a rush of anticipation. Her heart beat faster and she was short of breath; she hadn't felt this way since college. And Rod had been gone for over a year—

No, this is crazy.

She shook her head, and pulling her feet out from under her, tried to stand. She wavered and Fred stood to steady her. He put a massive arm around her waist, and she felt the nearness of his presence, his strong but gentle grip....

"Are you all right?"

She turned and placed a hand on his chest. Her breathing quickened. "Please, help me. I'd like to lie down."

"I'll walk you to the door."

She stopped and looked into his eyes. The world seemed to shrink down to just the two of them. Whatever had happened throughout the years between him and Rod didn't matter anymore. She needed to be touched, to be held, and to feel needed. It had been so long since anyone had cared about her, and not about what she could bring to a career.

"No," she said, "I meant to your bed."

CHAPTER TWENTY-SEVEN

"The End"

June 5th, 1968

Somewhere in North Vietnam

Of all I had, only honor and life have been spared.

Francis I

Rod drifted in and out of consciousness. It was a nightmarish journey of bouncing in the back of a truck, being blindfolded, tied up, and screaming in pain whenever he landed on his throbbing leg; of stopping in villages where people jabbered in Vietnamese as they crowded around the vehicle; of smelling urine and decaying food with the overpowering scents of roasting meat, and of the agony of someone prodding his leg with a stick—

"Out you go, Joe."

He gasped as he was shoved from the truck; he fell to the ground, sprawling. His face and side felt as if they'd split open as he hit the dirt. He couldn't see because of the blindfold. He rolled over, trying to ease the pain.

Someone kicked him in the leg and he screamed.

Hands brought him roughly to his feet. Rod gritted his teeth and moved his shoulders back and forth, shaking off the hands. "Stop it!" He tried to jerk free, but he was yanked back and pulled upright.

Someone scurried forward in the dirt. A second later he was hit in the stomach with a pipe. "Oof!" He doubled over, gasping for air, the wind knocked out of him.

A foot kicked him in the back of the knees, and he slumped to the ground. His leg felt as if he'd been sliced with a hot knife.

"Up! Up!" said a sing-song voice.

Again, he was jerked to his feet. This time Rod remained docile when he was shoved forward.

He stumbled and limped ahead, but he tried to hold his head up and not bow.

Excited voices jabbered around him. He heard children run up and laugh, dogs barked, women chattered. The sounds swirled around him, mixing with the voices of the men who accompanied him.

Rod tried walking, but every few feet he stumbled and tripped over stones, potholes, and uneven ground. He tried to keep from crying out, but the pain in his leg just wouldn't go away.

He couldn't understand the language or what people were saying, but their tone was unmistakable. He was on parade, being displayed as a trophy of war, the arrogant pilot, untouchable while flying miles above the ground, who with a flick of the finger could rain death upon their villages. But now he was reduced to something less than human.

The crowd suddenly started to jabber, rising with excitement. Rod heard the patter of feet, a high-pitched laugh.

He was struck in the groin by a stick. He doubled over, his dog tags clinking as he gasped for breath. People on either side of him forced him to stand and didn't allow him to seek the sanctity of resting on the ground.

His legs trembled. He forced his head up and tried not to show subservience.

Finally, after what seemed a half hour, he was thrown in the back of the truck and the men climbed aboard. They started the engine and people cheered, laughing as they hit the side of the vehicle. The truck sputtered, then bounced off to another village where he was paraded yet once again.

O   O   O

Rod lost count of the times he was led on display. A few hours into the ordeal a bowl of foul-smelling liquid was shoved at his face. He hesitated and turned away, but someone slapped him and said something in a singsong voice. His stomach growled and he slowly lowered his head to the bowl, where much to the amusement of his captors he lapped it up, but the liquid and morsels of unknown vegetables and meat warmed his stomach.

In village after village he tripped and fell. He tried to get up but was unable to put weight on his wounded leg.

A crowd gathered around him. Finally, after much heated discussion among his captors, he was picked up and carried for some distance until they entered a stale, musty building.

They left his blindfold in place and he was laid on a pad on a raised table. Small, dainty hands pushed his shoulders to the mat. Overhead fans came on and swept away the dankness, cooling the room. He smelled the faint odor of alcohol, heard the sound of long dresses swishing.

Someone elevated his leg and he heard people gathering around the foot of the table.

They unwrapped his bandage. Rod yelped as someone pinched up and down his leg.

He tried to sit, but hands held him down. A discussion occurred in the same singsong language.

People scurried in and out of the room. He heard the noise of something being placed on the table, the sound of jars opening. The pungent tang of sulfur and alcohol wafted through his nose.

"What are you doing?" Rod said. His voice was hoarse, barely audible.

Someone slapped him.

They forced Rod to lay on his back, unable to see. He waited, not knowing what they were going to do to him. He felt sick to his stomach; he started shaking and couldn't stop.

He remembered his adoptive father's leg injury—had it been

only twenty-five years since Hank had been wounded after being shot down over France? Even with a severely wounded leg, Hank had rescued Rod from his burning home, only to succumb to gangrene. And then he'd had his leg amputated after crossing the Pyrénées into Spain—in a civilized country, not some backwoods excuse for a third-world nation, and especially not in a remote village.

"Hey. Hey! What are you doing?" Rod raised his head and shouted hoarsely at the unseen people in the room. "What are you doing?"

He was smacked on the side of the head. Hands forced him down.

"What are you doing? Tell me!" His voice broke, a deep feeling of dread swept over him. He shook as the tears started. "Tell me. Just show me, please. Oh, God, please let me see. ..."

Someone forced his head to the pad and a rush of memories roared through his mind: from becoming an Ace, to trying to telephone Julie, to rescuing Barbara, to the emotion of their lovemaking; and from being shot down, to luring in the rescue helicopter. He sobbed as he realized how many lives he had ruined, and he broke down when he felt a knife slice at his wound.

He screamed in pain, smelled the overpowering odor of sulfur. They were going to cut off his leg.

They forced his head down. He struggled and turned his body back and forth. Someone smacked him again on the head.

Wracked with guilt and feeling more pain that he'd ever felt in his life, he cried for help, for anyone, and anything to save him and make it all go away....

Chapter Twenty-Eight

"White Room"

`July, 1968`

**The Hilton
North Vietnam**

A man can be destroyed but not defeated.

Ernest Hemingway, *The Old Man and the Sea*

Rod's eyes fluttered open.

The room was dimly lit and smelled musty. He was in a small cube, no more than 10 feet on a side and just as high. The ceiling and walls were constructed of some kind of off-white plaster or mortar that crumbled along the corners.

He lay on a hard cot and was dressed in striped, faded red pajamas, but they weren't the soft, comfortable pajamas he'd worn as a child; rather they were made of a coarse, itchy cotton material.

Movement caught his attention. A cockroach ran along the edge of the wall and disappeared under a wooden door. The door had splinters and looked thick, intimidating. A small opening was carved in the top, inset with three thick bars. The opening was just large enough for someone to peer through, and the bars were spaced close enough to prevent even a hand from reaching through.

Although his neck was stiff, Rod craned his head and squinted at the light coming from behind him. A long, narrow window with bars was set about chest high from the floor. Noise drifted in, sounds of metal clinking, men shuffling their feet in dirt, low muttering, and the unmistakable singsong voices of Vietnamese. He smelled something sour and the room reeked of urine.

He was in prison.

He rolled to his right and winced as he put pressure on his leg. His leg!

He struggled to an elbow; he felt sore and weak, but was relieved that he even still had the limb.

He looked down and ran a hand over his right leg. It was wrapped in a crude bandage and didn't feel that bad, considering what he had gone through....

He swung his feet down to the damp concrete floor. He had to urinate. His leg felt good enough to put weight on it—he must have been taken to a crude hospital on that last stop before this prison. He had a hazy recollection of bouncing in the back of the truck and being passed from person to person after the operation, but nothing really clicked.

He spotted a large tin cup sitting in the corner. Was this his urinal or his water supply?

He scratched an itch, then brought his hand up to his face and patted a scraggly beard. Just how long had he been out?

He straightened and felt stiff; he held a hand to his back and limped over to the tin cup. It was half filled with water. He glanced around and didn't see a hole in the floor to use as a toilet.

He shuffled to the window, dragging his bandaged leg. Outside was a dirt courtyard lined by nondescript, low slung buildings, all constructed of the same material as his cell.

In the middle of the courtyard a rock-lined well was set into the ground. Two Vietnamese guards wearing tattered uniforms and military caps stood by the well and smoked cigarettes, rifles slung over their shoulders. The sky was overcast, hazy.

He heard the constant sound of metal clinking against a wall coming from somewhere within the compound. There was a low hum of traffic in the background, as if the prison was near a busy street or in a city.

The door rattled.

Rod turned and saw eyes peering through the small slit, flicking back and forth. The eyes disappeared and a key was inserted into the lock; the door swung open.

A guard stood in the opening and pointed a rifle at him. The man said something in Vietnamese and motioned him out of the cell.

"Bathroom?" Rod said. His voice croaked. "I need to go to the bathroom."

The guard growled and angrily motioned with his rifle.

Rod raised his hands above his head. The guard motioned again and Rod limped out of the cell and into an unlit, low-ceilinged corridor. Cell doors stretched on either side as far as he could see. The guard prodded him with a rifle and urged him to move down the long, dank hallway.

He dragged his bandaged leg as he walked. The faint clanging of tin cups preceded his path as he passed each door, almost as if news of his passage was being heralded from cell to cell; but there were no voices or whispers to indicate that anyone besides the guard knew that he was in the hall.

They approached an open door at the end of the passageway; the guard said something in Vietnamese. Rod stopped. The guard said something again, this time in a louder voice. When he didn't move he was shoved through the opening.

The guard motioned to sit on a one-legged stool in the middle of a vast, concrete-walled chamber. Wooden crossbeams were set into the ceiling, at least thirty feet above the floor. But as opposed to his cell, a single light bulb hung from a wire in the middle of the ceiling, along with a pulley threaded by a long rope.

The guard motioned him to stay. He kept his rifle trained on Rod as he backed out of the room. He slammed the door as he left and Rod heard the unmistakable click of a lock.

In front of the stool, the rope dangled from a pulley screwed into a crossbeam. To his right, a wooden desk and a chair were pushed against the wall.

Rod remained on the stool. At first it was easy to balance his weight, but he soon discovered that unless he kept perfectly still the one-legged stool would start to wobble.

He spread his feet to keep balance. That helped, but he felt pressure on his legs; a tight sensation crept up his thigh and his muscles started to burn as he fought to stay upright. He was uncomfortable and needed to urinate.

How long were they going to keep him? What were they trying to accomplish? He started wondering what was going to happen next.

He really needed to pee, and his bladder started to feel pain from not being able to go. He thought about getting up and to see if there was some sort of hole in the floor or at least a container he could use, but he had an uneasy feeling that someone was watching him. He couldn't tell where the people were, but there was definitely someone watching, either by peering through a tiny hole in the wall, or perhaps looking down from the ceiling.

Minutes passed, maybe an hour. He didn't know how long he sat, but he didn't move.

His back began to ache and didn't know how much longer he could stay balanced on the stool. He couldn't lean back or relax, but had to remain positioned just right, with his feet planted in front of him in order to keep upright.

He studied the walls, the ceiling. He strained to hear something, anything, but there wasn't any sound; it was as if the concrete walls were insulated and made sound proof.

Time passed, and the need to urinate grew greater.

That's it; enough was enough. He couldn't stand waiting any longer. He slowly rose and limped stiffly over to the desk, hoping find something he could urinate in. He opened the top drawer—

The door was kicked open.

Rod stopped and looked up, startled. He drew his hand back from the desk.

"So you are thief as well as war criminal?" A short, stocky man with distinct Chinese features stood in the doorway; this was no Vietnamese. Unlike the guard, the man didn't wear a uniform, and instead wore an unusual combination of an old-style, solid white shirt with a wide, open collar, and black, baggy pants. He looked as though he'd stepped from the early 1950s. Rod could see muscles ripple underneath the man's shirt; he reminded Rod of a fireplug.

It took an effort, but Rod straightened. "I need to urinate. I was looking for a container."

Fireplug pointed to the floor. "Knees."

"What …?"

Fireplug's face tightened. "Kneel down!"

Rod hesitated, and then slowly lowered to his knees.

Fireplug turned his head and said something in Vietnamese to someone outside the door. He moved aside and a thin, uniformed guard walked briskly in the room. The man moved quickly to Rod, drew back his palm, and slapped Rod across the face.

Rod's head turned at the smack.

The guard started to slap him again, but Rod threw up a hand and caught the guard's arm.

The guard kicked him in the right leg, his bad one.

Rod collapsed, unable to move.

"Sit," Fireplug said.

"I … can't stand up."

"Sit."

The guard started to kick him again.

"No, wait," Rod said. He lowered his hands to the floor and crawled on his knees to the stool. He straightened it, and favoring his good leg, used the stool to pull himself to a squat. He rotated the stool around and sat, exhausted.

The guard moved behind him and pulled back his arms, jerking his entire body off balance. His leg throbbed as his hands were roughly tied behind his back. The guard then stooped in front of Rod's stool. He slammed Rod's ankles together, and then tied them together with coarse, brown rope.

Fireplug walked slowly around the room. He dragged the chair around and sat behind the desk, where he opened a drawer and removed a pad and pencil. The guard walked behind Rod and stood close enough that Rod smelled a curious odor of soy and fish mixed with the man's body odor.

Fireplug folded his hands on the desk. He stared at Rod. "Who are you?"

Rod drew in a breath. So this is it.

He'd heard the rumors of torture, but they couldn't be officially verified. During his prisoner-of-war training the Air Force had taught him to suck it up, steel it out; to only reveal his name, rank, date of birth, and serial number. He didn't know what they'd do to him physically, but if being a POW in Vietnam was anything like what the North Koreans had done, they wouldn't touch him ... but they'd screw with his mind.

At least he knew that Fireplug wouldn't harm him physically. The Vietnam War was too much of a media circus, and with the nightly news broadcasting film all over the world, the Vietnamese would never dare to harm any POWs; otherwise, their atrocities would be exposed to western journalists and there'd be an international uproar.

That meant he'd do what he'd been taught and tough it out.

Deep down he knew he couldn't be broken, not with the resistance experience he'd had in SERE. He was too tough; they'd never break him.

He'd been drilled on the Geneva Conventions so he answered formally. "My name is Roderick J. Simone, Major, United States Air Force, 20 January 1937, service number 77231A."

Fireplug stared. A minute passed and he wrote on the pad. "What your unit?"

"My name is Roderick J. Simone, Major, USAF, 20 January 1937—"

"You told me that. What your unit?"

"My name is Roderick J. Simone—"

"What airplane you fly?"

"My name is Roderick—"

Fireplug slammed his palm to the desk. "You are criminal!" He tapped his pencil on his pad and nodded to himself, as though he were going through an internal checklist. "Major Simone, I understand your commitment to code of military conduct, but code not present here. Your code on lawyer's desk at Pentagon. So I ask you again, what your unit?"

Rod lifted his chin. "My name is Roderick J. Simone, Major, USAF, service number 77231A."

Fireplug folded his hands and nodded to the guard standing behind Rod.

Without warning, Rod was smashed on the back of his skull. He was picked up from the stool and thrown forward though the air, knocking his forehead against Fireplug's desk.

His head throbbed like crazy. White dots of light swirled around as he gasped for breath. He tried to roll over when the guard struck him with his rifle across his legs.

"Stop it!" Rod screamed. The pain reverberated up his back and he jerked sporadically on the concrete floor. He rolled over and ducked his head, trying to keep the guard from hitting him again. Emotionless, the Vietnamese guard held his rifle butt high in the air, as though he were about to smash it down on Rod again.

Fireplug sat with his hands folded and asked in a monotone, "What your unit?"

Rod breathed heavily, sucking in as much air as he could; his heart raced. He stared at the man. There was no emotion in Fireplug's eyes. He's not going to yield.

But neither was he. He was tougher than this son-of-a-bitch amateur. "My name ... is Roderick J. Simone ... Major, United States Air Force, 20 January 1937, service number 77231A."

Fireplug kept his eyes on Rod and said something in Vietnamese.

Rod flinched when the guard approached, but instead of hitting him, the man dug a long finger-nailed hand into Rod's arm and jerked him to his feet. He roughly pulled Rod to the rope hanging from the ceiling by a pulley. Setting down his rifle, the guard turned Rod around and yanked his elbows together behind him.

Shards of pain shot through Rod's arms. "Stop, stop it!" Rod said.

The guard looped the rope around Rod's elbows. He drew the rope tight until it cut into Rod's skin.

Rod gritted his teeth. The rope hurt, but it was better than being hit while he was on the floor.

The man then looped the rope over Rod's head.

Stepping back, the guard tightened the slack.

Rod felt the twine dig into his neck. He had to stand on his toes in order to breathe.

"Your unit?" Fireplug asked without emotion.

Rod spoke past the rope digging into his throat. "My ... name is Roderick J. Simone ... Major—"

"Geneva convention not for war criminal." Fireplug motioned with his head.

The guard pulled on the rope.

Rod was jerked into the air.

He swung by the back of his elbows. Incredible pain shot through his back, his chest, his neck, and his arms. He gasped and tried to keep his head up, otherwise the rope would tighten, and he'd choke by his own weight.

"I ... I can't breathe!" Rod struggled to keep his legs down and his head up, which allowed him to gasp for breath—but it worsened the pain in his back and his elbows, making it even more excruciating. He screamed as he heard a pop and felt his arms separate from his sockets.

His shoulders burned, the pain white-hot, searing his vision red; his ears pounded with the rush of blood and he gasped for breath. He swung just inches from the floor, a minute distance but the difference between living and dying.

The rope twisted slowly, clockwise to counterclockwise, turning him as he hung. His entire existence focused on the pain, the incredible agony as he tried to keep from choking.

He lost control of his bladder. He felt warmth run down his leg, soaking his pants. Urine dripped from his pajamas and a sour stink rose from the floor.

Fireplug picked up his chair and walked slowly in front of him. He placed the chair on the floor and climbed on the seat, moving his face next to Rod's; he spoke in a low voice. "What your unit?"

"I—I can't." Answering the man went against everything he'd ever trained for, everything he believed in. From the time he was a basic cadet, to the briefing rooms in Vietnam, everything was focused on duty—completing the mission, keeping his honor.

Rod strained to hear Fireplug as the man spoke softly through the pain. Rod felt as though his pounding ears were stuffed with cotton.

The man was barely audible, his voice competing with the sound of the pulley as it squeaked, slowly rotating Rod back and forth; it vied with Rod's own gasping for breath as he fought to keep conscious.

Fireplug whispered, "Tell me about yourself, Jean-Claude Simone. Tell me about your Tactical Fighter Wing, how you fly your F-4D from Tan Son Nhut airbase in South Vietnam to kill Vietnamese children. Tell me about your F-105 intercepting Ilyushin Il-28 in 1963, and your cowardly fight against that much, much better pilot. Tell me about graduating from Air Academy and scholarship to Stanford. I already know all there is to know about you!"

Rod panted. "What—what do you want?"

"You tell me. Confirm this, so I can believe you and set you free. I want to believe you."

Rod felt the blood rush from his face, his breathing increase as he spun slowly around the room. Fireplug's face rotated by, alternating with the guard who stood holding the rope with both his hands, his feet spread and watching emotionlessly.

Had he already given up, told them everything? How does he know all these things? Why was Fireplug doing this?

What does he want?

Blood roared in his ears, pounding; his eyes stung from sweat rolling down his forehead. His sight grew dim, brown around the edges.

The rope tightened as the guard jerked on it, spinning him higher above the floor.

Fireplug's voice pierced the haze descending over him, like a knife cutting through a layer of fog. "Tell me, Major," he whispered. "Tell me how you crash your F-4 Phantom. Tell me how you kill your backseater. Tell me. ..."

"Oh, God, save me!" Rod choked and struggled to breathe, tried to stay conscious, tried to live.

He'd never survive if he passed out ... but yet anything was better than this, even dying....

CHAPTER TWENTY-NINE

"Hey Jude"

July, 1968

The Zoo
North Vietnam

People will not readily bear pain unless there is hope.

Michael Edwards

T apping.
It wouldn't go away.

Rod moaned.

He was still alive, but he was afraid to move, afraid that if he showed any sign of life, that the rope would tighten and the pain would come roiling back.

His arms throbbed; his neck burned from the rope; his head ached from the blows; his leg throbbed in pain. His teeth hurt and he could barely think through a red-tinged headache.

And his ribs—he felt as though he had been kicked, and as he tried to remember what had happened, he shuddered, anticipating being struck again.

He faintly remembered being bundled and thrown in a truck, taken somewhere else; a different prison from the Hilton, where he'd undergone his initial interrogation and torture.

Even with his eyes closed, he could tell he was on a dirt floor. His nose was smashed into the ground; he smelled urine, blood, decaying fish, and clay earthiness. Spittle drooled from his mouth.

The faint sound of tapping came from the wall behind him.

Movement, and he felt something on his face. Flicking open his eyes, he saw a cockroach scurry over his nose.

The room was dimly lit. In the corner of his eye he saw the legs of a cot.

They'd thrown him in a new cell.

His cell.

He didn't know how long he'd been imprisoned, but within seconds he'd already accepted the cell as being his.

His neck burned from the rope. He tried flexing his arm; it ached, although he had not even lifted it.

His clothes felt damp, his crotch was wet, soiled.

He must have urinated and defecated over himself. When? On the ropes, in the truck, or after they'd thrown him in here? He couldn't remember.

His stomach growled and he was suddenly very thirsty. His headache wouldn't go away and his mouth felt cottony. If he hadn't known better, he would have thought he'd woken from a nightmare after a drinking binge.

Outside the cell, the sounds of someone speaking in Vietnamese drifted in from the courtyard. Someone walked up and down the hallway on the other side of the door.

The tapping continued, a faint clinking.

Rod rolled over and faced the wall. He put out a hand and tried to trace where the tapping originated. He scooted closer, and with an effort he placed his ear next to the decaying plaster.

The tapping sounded loudest three inches from the floor, as if someone was lying on the other side of the thick wall, a mirror image of him, tapping "shave and a haircut."

He started to knock, but pulled back and hesitated. What if it was Fireplug, somehow trying to mess with his mind? He hadn't seen any other prisoners since he had arrived, although he'd certainly heard screams; those primordial cries for mercy could have come from any human, and not just a fellow US citizen. But "shave and a haircut" was uniquely American.

It took an effort as he rapped on the wall twice; nerve damage from the ropes made it difficult to move.

A clatter of taps came back in response.

He listened for a moment. The new tapping came in groups, as though there was some sort of pattern. It didn't make sense; he couldn't understand what it meant. Was it a code? He tried to concentrate, but his head hurt.

A sound outside the door made him roll back over. He flung his arm out in front of him and tried to retain the same position as when he had been thrown into the cell.

The door jiggled and quickly opened. He heard someone place something on the floor, then leave. The entire encounter had not taken more than fifteen seconds.

Rod counted to a hundred, and when he didn't hear any sound from outside, he rolled over to face the door.

A tin cup sat just inside the doorway.

Rod pushed forward on his stomach and scooted across the floor. He pulled the tin to him and peered inside. Water.

He gripped the can and tilted it up, eagerly slurping the water to his mouth. It was warm and smelled stale, with the ever-present fish smell that permeated everything, but he drank deeply.

His gut tightened as the water hit his empty stomach. Feeling strengthened, he ignored the pain in his arm and pushed up so he could finish the water. Within seconds he'd drained the can.

He leaned back and breathed deeply. Slowly, his headache lessened, and moved to a persistent yet low-grade, background throb. He felt better and he was still hungry, but at least the cottony taste in his mouth was gone.

He placed the tin cup back by the door and rolled to the wall.

The tapping started again. It was in the same pattern that came in groups of two, followed by a series of taps. He counted the groupings, the taps.

Something was familiar but he couldn't put his finger on it. He couldn't decide if it was the lack of food or that he'd hit his head, but whatever the case, he couldn't understand, couldn't decipher the code.

He was disappointed when the tapping stopped. Time passed and nothing more came of it.

Was it Fireplug, lying on the other side of the wall? Or was it another prisoner, perhaps an American who was trying to get in contact with a fellow pilot? He was scared to tap back, remembering the beatings and being jerked off the floor by the ropes.

He hesitatingly reached out and made the smallest sound on the wall—

A staccato of tapping exploded from the other side of the wall. The entire pattern repeated itself, and then it was suddenly silent.

Rod tapped twice. Again the pattern repeated, this time more slowly.

Over and over Rod mimicked the code, repeating the tapping sequence. It was almost like Morse code, except it was more complex, with more structure. It started out with two taps, followed by a single quick tap; the series ended with two groups of five taps followed by 25 quick taps.

If there had been 26 taps, it would have been obvious that it was the alphabet, one tap for each letter. But 25 taps didn't make any sense. What type of code would consist of 25 taps?

The tapping pattern started once again.

He tried to concentrate, but his head hurt and his mind felt enveloped in a fog. A code. A way to communicate; a way to transmit information with using the alphabet.

And then it hit him. Nobody really uses all of the letters in the alphabet; surely missing one of the letters wouldn't matter. And if so, then this sequence was the alphabet, minus a letter. It had to be.

The first number was the row, and the second number was the column; the matrix element corresponded to the letter of the alphabet: "1-1" must be an "A." That was verified by the one quick tap, meaning it was the first letter in the alphabet.

"1-2" was "B" and so on, until "5-5" meant "Z."

He quickly tapped "2-3" then "2-4"—"H-I"—and waited for an answer.

Instantly a reply came back: "W-E-L-C-O-M-E".

A simple word.

A word normally said in passing, without thinking twice, or without expecting a reply.

But it was a word that communicated across the gulf of separation, bridging a chasm of despair; it was an icon for Rod that defined the very essence of hope.

Even more importantly, it was evidence of another human being; one who cared enough to patiently teach him a code. A code where he didn't have to see the person in which to communicate, or even know what the person looked like, how he sounded, or if he was injured or whole.

Rod lowered his head and couldn't stop the tears. Despite all that Fireplug could throw at him, he knew that he had won. He wasn't alone.

O   O   O

A day later Rod had mastered the tap code so efficiently that he could pass messages nearly as fast as he could speak. At first he questioned the personal information he was being asked, but at the end of the day he discovered the purpose: his answers were being relayed by tap around the camp to confirm that Rod was who he said he was, and was not a spy planted by the North Vietnamese.

It was then he received his biggest shock since he'd arrived as a POW. As soon as his identity had been confirmed, the man in the next cell finally tapped out his name. It took a moment for it to sink in: T-O-M R-A-N-C-H.

It couldn't be. Rod felt his heart rate rise; he didn't want to be disappointed. He tapped, D-E-T-A-I-L-S.

The tapping came back and reconfirmed Rod's growing hope.

Tom Ranch! His ex-ATO and mentor as a cadet!

Feeling excited as a surge of adrenaline rushed through him, Rod rolled over and started tapping as quickly as he could: *I thought you had died! Are you injured? How long have you been here? Who else is here? What do you know about the camp? How have you survived?*

Tom patiently tapped back answers to Rod's growing questions—too slow, in Rod's mind. Soon, Tom tapped for him to wait—Rod needed to hear what Tom had to transmit: Tom tapped on and on, detailing who had been captured, including each officer's rank.

Tom then insisted he tap the entire list back verbatim, in order to ensure that if anyone was ever released, then a detailed and accurate list of all prisoners would make it out. It was tedious work, but the fact that his ex-ATO was in the next cell almost made life bearable.

Days later, when Rod's excitement had subsided and his questions had been answered, Rod scrunched to the wall and tapped: "H-O-W D-O U K-E-E-P S-A-N-E"

"H-O-P-E" Tom tapped. "F-R-O-M G-R-A-C-E"

"H-O-W C-A-N U H-A-V-E H-O-P-E H-E-R-E"

"E-A-S-Y W-A-N-T T-O K-N-O-W M-O-R-E"

"Y-E-S" Rod hurriedly tapped.

Over the next few days, Tom patiently detailed the good news that had propagated around the camp for years, the incredible news that kept their spirits lifted, their hope alive, and made their faith steadfast even in the face of such incredible adversity. And when Rod finally understood that it was something he could never attain on his own, the void he'd felt for so many years finally disappeared.

And for the final time, he left his old life behind.

CHAPTER THIRTY

"Liar"

November 2nd, 1968

The Zoo
North Vietnam

Things are entirely what they appear to be and behind them ... there is nothing.

Jean-Paul Sartre, *Nausea*

Rod rolled over when the door was kicked in.

The routine was growing old.

Rod placed his feet on the floor, stood, and bowed. He looked down in an outward sign of obedience. It appeared that he was being subservient to the Vietnamese guards; he was a model POW. But inside he seethed with alertness, always looking for a chink in the seemingly invincible armor that cloaked his captors.

The ropes ensured all the prisoners in the compound the POWs called the Zoo acted this way—at least externally.

The camp's name reminded him of the Academy. The cadets called it the Blue Zoo. While attending USAFA, the cadets perceived that they were being mercilessly locked up and mistreated. But in reality, at the time he didn't know how good he'd had it, especially compared to the harsh torture and random cruelty inflicted by the North Vietnamese guards.

Rod waited for the sound of his daily ration of tepid water and rancid portions of rice to be placed on the floor. He tried to draw no attention to himself in the hopes that he wouldn't be hauled off to the ropes. For several weeks, for days on end, Fireplug had called him out of the cell and hung him from the ceiling in the small torture chamber, extracting a miniscule amount of information from him, one piece at a time.

He'd been broken that first time back at the Hilton; he'd felt defeated and worthless. If he'd had a knife in his cell he might have committed suicide because of the enormous guilt, the shame that wracked his soul.

It may not have seemed a big deal to anyone else, but to have admitted to Fireplug that he'd been an F-4 pilot went against all his training of not yielding an iota, or even a quantum of information. It had been drilled into him for years not to give in; but what the North Vietnamese were doing was clearly against the Geneva Convention.

Rod soon discovered that Fireplug and the rest of the guards regarded the Convention as an ethereal concept. The Vietnamese called them criminals, and not prisoners of war, so the Geneva Convention was just as remote as the Declaration of Independence: Rod's inalienable right to the pursuit of happiness was as much of a fantasy as a nightly massage.

After being moved to the Zoo, the nightly tapping from Tom Ranch helped him keep his sanity. And just as Tom had mentored him as a cadet, Tom now patiently answered all of Rod's questions.

He didn't know if he could survive without Tom's daily encouragement, of Tom's detailing of Christ's grace, forgiveness, and redemption that made more and more sense when faced with the daily rigors of the rope, and him forsaking classified information ... or from the guilt of his affair with Barbara and causing Jazz's death. He'd learned to survive—and most importantly, to forgive himself.

Tom continued to tap out POW names. He started including those passed from other camps so Rod could memorize the entire list of U.S. prisoners.

He'd stopped when the name of Jeff Goldstein was included. Was it his Academy classmate, the tall basketball player from the Bronx? The same Goldstein that had double-dated with the Playboy bunnies when they were cadets?

When Rod excitedly inquired about Jeff, it had taken a while for Tom to get back that Goldstein hadn't been heard from in nearly two years. The news that his classmate might have died in prison sent Rod in a deep funk for days.

Listless, Rod slumped back against the wall. He couldn't move, couldn't think, as he struggled with his re-found faith.

Why did he find out about Jeff, only to discover his classmate might have died in prison? And why did he learn about it now?

What did it mean? Was this a premonition of his own death? Night and day, throughout his anguish Tom tapped encouragement, trying to lift his spirits … when suddenly the tapping stopped.

He heard the faint sound of keys jangling down the hall. Rod felt his breath quicken. The keys. Were they coming for him? He prayed the guard would pass him by—the fearful clinking could come at any time, a precursor to torture.

The guard stood in the doorway, leaving the cell door open after the food and water had been placed on the floor. In his peripheral vision Rod could see that the Vietnamese's rifle with fixed bayonet was pointed at Rod's chest.

Rod remained sitting, not knowing if he would be shot or forced out of the cell for another session with the ropes.

The guard didn't waver, didn't show any sign of movement. Was the guard just playing with him? Rod sat as still as he could.

Finally, the guard motioned with his rifle. "Up."

Rod slowly straightened, his back stiff. As he shuffled out the door he was thankful he'd gotten in the habit of rising early to pray and urinate into his can. Otherwise, he'd have been taken away with a full bladder and would be forced to soak in his urine while on the ropes. It was a small way to deal with the atrocities, but it brought order to his life.

Rod tried to think why he was being pulled out again, especially since there was nothing more they could wring from him. Was it Fireplug's way of messing with his mind, ensuring that he was entirely broken? The lashes were bad enough, but he prayed that he'd be kept from the ropes, and steeled his mind to accept the pain—not if, but when it would happen again.

After his ankle chains were fastened he was prodded down the long, dark hallway. The chains rubbed against his leg, opening scabs that had formed from wearing the metal bracelets. He passed cell after cell and heard coded displays of encouragement, passed not through tapping, but by rhythmic coughing and clearing of throats as he shuffled past.

At the end of the hall he started to turn right, toward the inevitable torture chamber when the guard barked at him in Vietnamese.

Rod stopped and felt the rifle muzzle press up against his back, urging him forward, into the open courtyard.

He stepped into the sunshine and brought up a hand to shield his eyes. The smell of dust, feces, and cooking oil rolled over him. He stepped uncertainly in the dirt, taking small steps as he relished the sunshine. The warmth felt incredible, and he just wanted to sprawl out in the light and bask in the sun's rays.

But the guard's gun against his back pressed him on.

They walked past an old French swimming pool in the center of the square; they called it Lake Fester. The prisoners had discovered that the Zoo was an old French film studio whose buildings had been subdivided into cells.

The dirt square reminded Rod of a European plaza, but this was lined on three sides by prison cells, and plugged on the fourth side by a long, one-story windowless building. Through his small window, Rod had seen prisoners escorted to the long structure.

They walked toward the featureless building and he heard the growing sound of coughing and clearing of throats coming from the thin slits that served as windows in the cells. Little by little the sounds grew louder. He couldn't quite make out the message, but knew that they were words of encouragement, meant for him. He squinted and tried to discern Tom Ranch through one of the narrow slits, but he couldn't recognize any faces.

The guard pushed him into the building where they entered a well-lit hallway. Unlike the hall that connected the cellblocks, this one had fresh paint, clean floors, and even the faint smell of flowers.

A Vietnamese nurse dressed in a ubiquitous white uniform motioned him to step into the first door. Inside, two orderlies, also dressed in white, quickly pulled his pajamas over his head, leaving him naked and feeling more vulnerable than he had ever felt with Fireplug. Rod felt a chill as he saw what appeared to be an operating table at the far end of the room.

The orderlies wrinkled their noses as they gingerly stuffed his old clothes in a woven bag, and then led him to the back of the room. The nurse turned on a shower set in a corner. Steaming water splashed on the sloping floor that allowed water to flow into a drain. The nurse motioned him under the hot water.

The sensation felt incredible. Months of stress, sweat, dirt, blood, urine, feces, vomit, and tears washed away as Rod experienced the first bath he had taken since he'd been captured. He stood under the shower and tried to scour away the dirt.

The nurse turned her head as she handed him a squat, yellow tube, then pantomimed for him to wash his hair.

Minutes later, they cut off the water. He stepped from the shower and was quickly toweled down. The nurse circled him, clinically inspecting him like he was an animal up for auction. She knelt down and ran a finger along his leg, inspecting the scar he had obtained from the makeshift operation after he had been captured.

Finally, seeming satisfied with his condition, the nurse stepped away and jabbered in a high-pitched language. She washed her hands in a sink at the side of the room as the orderlies handed him a new pair of striped pajamas.

Rod slowly pulled the fresh clothes over his head. He bowed as one of the orderlies stepped up to him with a brush. He noticed that several of the plastic teeth were missing as they quickly combed his hair, and then gave him a quick haircut and a shave. Immediately after he was finished with his makeover, the guard who had been waiting at the door stepped up and motioned him back into the hallway.

They took several turns and entered another door where Rod felt a cool breeze waft from the room. Air conditioning! He was almost chilled after the recent shower.

The guard opened a door and motioned Rod to enter. He drew in a breath and shuffled in, his ankle chains clanking.

Scents he hadn't smelled for months rolled over him: perfume, aftershave lotion, dry-cleaned clothes, and food.

A heaping plate of fresh fruit, cheese, crackers, rolled meats, and sweets spilled over a long table set at the side of the room. An array of liquor bottles, complete with neatly stacked glasses and a bucket of ice, lined another table.

In the back of the room Fireplug stood behind two movie cameras. His arms were crossed and smoke rose from a cigarette he held in his hand.

A movie screen was set in front of a black, two-reeled 16mm movie projector at the opposite end of the room. Caucasian men and women milled around the food at the side.

Rod felt his heart begin to pound. Were they Americans? He'd heard rumors passed by tap code that every so often a contingent of reporters would show up at the prison. But instead of being shocked at the squalor of their treatment and living conditions, word around the camp was that the reporters leered at them, called them war criminals.

And now, to Rod, his whole shower experience made sense: His captors wanted him presented as being freshly scrubbed and humanely treated, and from the food being displayed, well fed.

Rod's stomach growled at the smells coming from just a few feet away.

The reporters picked up cameras when Rod entered the room. They started clicking away, and the three movie cameras swung to focus on him. A sound technician held a boom with a microphone over Rod's head.

Fireplug called from behind the cameras, "Please, Major Simone. You please help yourself to drink and fine food. Take as much as you want, just as you always do! Eat, eat!"

As much as he wanted to rush over to the table and stuff his face with handfuls of meat and fruit, Rod didn't answer, but merely stood in the center of the room.

Fireplug explained smugly to the visitors, "Look! He just eat and not hungry. You see by his actions he fed well, healthy. Would he not have gone directly to food if he starved, as some of your biased reports have said? See how benevolent we are."

A blond-haired man dressed in a brown, double-breasted suit with a wide lapel and a gold tie brought a microphone up to Rod. The man spoke in a clipped German accent. "Good afternoon. What is your name?"

Rod looked at Fireplug who was smoking silently by the movie screen. He said quietly, "My name is Roderick J. Simone, Major, USAF, 20 January 1937, service number 77231A."

"Major Simone, how are you being treated?"

Rod kept silent, refusing to lie despite his well-washed appearance, and he was not about to give any information that might later be used against him by Fireplug. Yet, there had to be a way he could communicate to his superiors he was being mistreated.

"What do you think about President Johnson's announcement yesterday? Do you support it?"

Whatever had been announced, there was no way Rod would have heard about it—not this soon. And he certainly couldn't comment on it, either way. Instead, he folded his hands and extended his middle finger in the classic American gesture of Flipping the Bird.

"Major Simone, do you understand me?" The German reporter frowned.

"My name is Roderick J. Simone, Major, USAF, 20 January 1937, service number 77231A."

Not getting cooperation from Rod, the reporter turned to Fireplug. "His service number agrees with our records. May we show him the motion pictures?"

Fireplug glared at Rod, then nodded, and waved for them to proceed.

The reporter put down his microphone and stepped back. He motioned to one of the crew.

A small, wiry man wearing a Jefferson Airplane T-shirt dragged a chair to the center of the room. He positioned the chair facing the screen.

The reporter spoke to Rod. "Please sit, Major Simone. We have a movie clip that you might find interesting."

Rod considered ignoring the request, but there was nothing to be gained by remaining standing. Keeping his middle finger extended, he sat as the movie cameras filmed him.

One of the reporters turned on the movie projector. Someone dimmed the lights and a jerky picture splashed on the screen.

Rod tried to show no emotion as a picture of the U.S. Air Force Academy chapel filled the screen. The camera dwelled on the tip of one of the 17 spires, showing a perfectly blue, cloudless sky. Rod felt a pang of longing for home; it appeared the picture had been taken during a crisp, cool Colorado morning. The camera slowly panned back, showing the front of the Academy chapel.

At first the scene looked peaceful, but then it was replaced by a view taken at a different time. Sounds of people shouting came from the projector. The screen was filled with a mob of angry people, pushing and shoving at a group of air policemen who lined the top of the long stairs leading to the Protestant chapel. Denim-clad protestors, some with long, greasy hair hanging down to their shoulders, screamed insults. They shook their fists; some threw rocks and cans. Two nuns and a priest had handcuffed themselves to the metal railings.

Rod's eyes widened. He felt the veins in his forehead start to pound as he watched the crowd surge forward, breaking past the Air Police and spilling into the Protestant chapel. The camera followed the protestors as they charged into the quiet Sunday service.

He saw cadets and their guests turn in the wooden pews at the intrusion. At the front of the chapel the chaplain stood behind the white marble washing-machine podium; an astonished look swept over his face.

Two of the protestors wrestled their way out of the policeman's grip and ran down the center aisle to the altar. They took wineskins hanging from around their necks and sprayed what appeared to be blood on the altar.

Over the shouting and cursing, Rod heard the crowd chanting, "Stop the War! Stop the War!"

The scene switched to three young Air Force officers, neatly dressed in their class-A uniforms, reading a statement in front of a crowd of reporters. A hand-printed sign, written on long sheets of green-lined computer paper, hung behind them:

USAF ACADEMY FACULTY AGAINST
THE VIETNAM WAR!

Lights flashed from cameras. Rod could make out only part of the officer's press statement over the confusion:

"—an immoral act—"

"—I am a conscientious objector—"

"—our pilots are war criminals and should be tried in international court—"

The cameras in the room remained focused on Rod. He tried to keep his face stony, showing no emotion, but it was difficult ... throughout it all, he kept his middle finger rigid.

The reporter stopped the movie projector. The lights went up and the cameras filming Rod moved in for a close-up.

Another man moved in front of Rod, squatted down, and said softly in a German accent, "So, Major Simone. What do you think about your own cadets calling you a war criminal?"

Rod stiffened. "They weren't cadets."

The reporter raised an eyebrow. "Oh? They were at your Air Academy."

"They weren't cadets," Rod said.

"Who were they?"

Rod remained silent. He'd already said too much. Could Fireplug have gleaned any information from the exchange?

This interview was a sham. He was certain the Germans didn't know the Vietnamese had duped them; they'd probably been promised an exclusive interview with an American POW and had jumped at the chance.

Rod could just imagine the glee his captors must have had when they'd been approached by the television crew. The Vietnamese couldn't have found a better way to extract information from one of their so-called war criminals than by having a foreign news group show up and perform an internationally-telecasted interrogation for them.

He'd been presented as a well-groomed and manicured pilot; and despite his gaunt and skeletal look, the Vietnamese tried to convince them he was well fed from the display of food on the long table.

But if anyone were to watch the interview, they'd see his unspoken gesture of defiance.

Which gave him another idea.

He started blinking as the cameras zoomed in for the close-up. He concentrated on making short and long blinks, to communicate dots and dashes; not in tap code—that would give their communication path away—but in Morse code.

He blinked:

—

— — —

· _ ·

—

· · _

· _ ·

·

Torture.

He repeated the sequence even as another reporter stepped up.

"Are you a war criminal, Herr Major? You've just seen your fellow Americans say you are. What do you have to say?"

Rod kept blinking and stared straight ahead, refusing to be drawn in to either inadvertently confessing anything or compromising his oath.

"Major Simone, what do you have to say for yourself?" The reporter paused. "Does your silence imply your guilt?"

Fireplug stepped forward. "Yes, it does!" he said, unable to restrain himself.

The first reporter, now standing next to Fireplug remained unconvinced. "Or, perhaps it doesn't."

Fireplug reddened. He smiled broadly and extended a hand back to the table of food. "Please, help yourself to more delicacies. Major Simone is tired, so he will rest.

"I personally escort him to quarters and bring back another war criminal." He said something in Vietnamese and the guard opened up the door from where Rod had entered.

Fireplug held out an arm, showing Rod the way out. "Please, Major."

Rod turned without emotion and shuffled toward the door; he refused to acknowledge the reporters or Fireplug. The contingent of Germans turned back to their projectors and cameras to prepare for the next POW who would be paraded in front of them.

Once Rod was in the hallway, a guard stepped up and led him through the labyrinth until they reached the center of the prison. Rod entered the courtyard and he was pushed violently from behind. He stumbled forward and barely managed to keep from falling.

Fireplug stepped from behind. He waved an angry arm at the guard, yelled something in Vietnamese, and strode quickly off.

Rod felt a rifle muzzle push him forward and he hurried his pace, following Fireplug. But instead of turning for his cell, he was led past the rope room to a small, low-ceilinged chamber that had manacles hanging from a hook in the ceiling. A wooden chair was positioned under the manacles, and two bamboo poles were propped up in the corner, next to a rubber strap that looked like a severed fan belt.

Rod's heart began to race; the sticks and strap were commonly used as whips.

He was shoved into the room, and he caught himself, trying not to sprawl to the floor. He'd been beaten before, but the Vietnamese had always laid him out on a concrete slab, or lashed him to the ground. And it always seemed like they were in a hurry, as if they might be reluctant to inflict the punishment—except for when the handful of Cubans at the camp participated in the torture, and then they never rushed.

Now, Fireplug took his time.

Fireplug turned to face him as the guard slammed the door. Beads of sweat stood out on his oily skin. He narrowed his eyes. "Why you no answer my guests?"

Rod remained silent.

Fireplug raised his voice. "Why you no take food? Are you not hungry?"

Once more Rod refused to answer.

"How did you know those people on movie were not cadets? Do you lie? Do you make me look foolish, make me lose face before my guests?"

Fireplug smacked his hands together and angrily motioned for the guard.

The guard placed his rifle against the wall and approached Rod. He walked behind Rod and ripped his pajama smock down, leaving his back bare. He shoved him under the manacles, and Rod caught himself.

Rod's face felt incredibly hot and he couldn't help from shaking.

The guard pushed the chair across the concrete floor until it was positioned behind Rod, then climbed up on the seat.

Fireplug stepped close to Rod. He motioned with his hand. "Hands up."

Rod kept his eyes fixated on Fireplug's eyes as he slowly raised his hands high over his head.

The guard grabbed his right arm and jerked it back. He slapped one of the manacles over his wrist.

Rod winced as the shackle tightened.

The guard grabbed his other arm and roughly slapped Rod's wrist into the shackle. Rod had to stand on his tiptoes in order to keep the metal cuff from cutting into his wrist.

The guard stepped down and dragged the chair to the side. He picked up his rifle and walked behind Rod.

Fireplug thrust his face close to Rod's.

He saw blackheads on the man's pores, and he felt an urge to retch as he smelled a sour, fishy odor. His arms stretched over his head, he felt his calves start to cramp.

Fireplug's eyes were wide, inflamed. "Why you no take food? Why you no answer questions?"

Because you'd parade me in front of the other prisoners and use me for propaganda, Rod wanted to scream. He felt totally helpless. The metal bit into his wrists as he tried to relieve the weight on his toes; it was hard to concentrate on what Fireplug was saying.

He drew in a breath and closed his eyes. He didn't have anything left in him, nothing more he could do. He silently mouthed a prayer ... and suddenly, a weird calmness swept over him and he stopped shaking....

"Why you make me lose face!" Fireplug said.

Rod opened his eyes.

When Rod didn't answer, Fireplug suddenly stepped away and stormed to the corner of the room. He picked up the rubber fan belt that was frayed at the end, resembling a cat o' nine tails. He smacked it against his hand, and unblinking, slowly walked over to Rod.

He walked behind Rod; the single bulb in the ceiling cast a distorted shadow of Fireplug in the floor.

Rod felt his blood pound in his ears as Fireplug's shadow shifted on the floor. He swallowed. He tried to dissociate, think of anything else but the here and now, to take his mind off the mounting tension and the pain that was sure to come. He vowed to try and count the lashes....

Suddenly, the shadow raised the strap over its head, and Rod saw quick movement—

He screamed as a searing bolt ripped through him. Intense pain reverberated through his body. It felt as if a live electrical wire had sliced through his back.

Fireplug whipped the rubber strap. Once again Rod jerked back as he was hit, screaming, praying for the pain to go away....

Fireplug walked to his front and breathed hard. He thrust his face into Rod's.

Rod closed his eyes and tried to turn from the sour, fishy smell.

Fireplug pinched Rod's face between his fingers, forcing him to look at him. "You talk now? Everyone know you war criminal. You pig dog. You kill babies. You kill mothers. Your own president fear us with yesterday's announcement! Now you talk." He moved to the side, reared up, and struck Rod's back.

Rod lurched, but Fireplug bore down, again and again.

Rod heaved in a dry vomit. Thirty? Thirty-five lashes? He tried to twist away but Fireplug pinched his face even tighter. The pain in his back throbbed and he felt something run down his waist and drip to the floor. It felt as if the upper part of his body would fall away.

Fireplug moved to his front. "You talk, criminal! You just like everyone else! You weak. You talk!"

Rod groaned, then worked up what saliva he had in his mouth. Pursing his lips, he pushed forward and spat. A wad of spit hit Fireplug's cheek.

Fireplug pulled back, his eyes wide and mouth open. He wiped the spit away with his forearm and then roared. He thrashed out and violently whipped Rod's chest, his shoulders, his arms and legs. He moved behind Rod and continued, one lash after another.

Rod threw his head back and cried out. "Stop it! Anything! Just stop!" The pain seared through him, and his back felt like ground meat, but like a madman, Fireplug continued the beating.

The room started to blacken. He lost track of time; he became dissociated from the torture.

He couldn't concentrate on what was happening, and he'd lost count as the lashes approached four hundred—and as consciousness slipped away, a pleasant, cool calmness washed over his body. He felt serene, and in some ways he felt as if he were floating up, through the air ... and Jean-Claude left the pain far, far behind....

CHAPTER THIRTY-ONE

"Bad Moon Rising"

Two Years later
November 23, 1970

The Zoo
North Vietnam

Without measureless and perpetual uncertainty the drama of human life would be destroyed.

Winston Churchill, *The Gathering Storm*

od slid across the concrete floor and tapped on the wall: "T-O-M P-L-E-A-S-E T-A-L-K."

No answer.

Tom Ranch still didn't respond.

He tapped again and put his ear to the wall, straining to hear at least the faint sound of scratching, or perhaps Tom shuffling across the floor ... or even moaning.

Still nothing.

He picked up the tin cup and tapped three times: "R U T-H-E-R-E?" It was the dead of night and they tried to save tapping with the can to when the guards weren't present; but with Tom still not answering, Rod threw caution to the side and tapped furiously "T-O-M T-O-M T-O-M T-O-M!"

Earlier, it had been common not to hear from Tom for days on end, especially after a session with Fireplug. But two months ago, after the death of Ho Chi Minh, treatment had greatly improved and torture had decreased to nearly zero.

Now, the North Vietnamese seemed to have had forgotten their newfound benevolence, and had returned to their old ways of beatings and torture. It didn't make any sense.

Two nights ago they'd dragged Tom away when it sounded as though the air war had resumed. The turnaround was so quick that Rod felt himself slipping into a deep funk, reminiscent of the depression he'd felt in early '69, when word had spread throughout the Zoo that President Johnson had both unilaterally and unconditionally halted the bombing of North Vietnam—a decision that Rod learned later was completely driven by politics, just before the U.S. elections; it was the announcement that those German newscasters had asked him about when he'd been hauled before their cameras.

It had been two days since Rod had last heard from his old ATO and AOC. Rod had kept tapping, anticipating that Tom had been brought back to the cell when Rod was either not awake or had been dragged off for his own round with Fireplug—

The door was kicked open and light from a bare overhead bulb streamed into the cell. The wooden door slammed against the wall. Rod pulled back and dropped his can. He hadn't heard the telltale jangling of keys that usually preceded a guard's presence.

"Queeky, queeky!" the guard said. He motioned Rod forward. "Move!" His face was bright red and his eyes wide; beads of sweat covered his forehead. He looked over his shoulder as he motioned Rod out of the cell.

"Hurry now!" The guard stepped into the cramped room. He raised his rifle and pushed the barrel up against Rod's chest. "Out! Now!"

Rod felt a chill; his heart began to pound as he heard other cell doors being kicked in, guards screaming at the prisoners. Their frantic nature paralleled the purge and widespread torture that followed the failed escape attempt by Atterbury and Dramesi in May of '69.

Was this a precursor of returning to those dark days? Why else were they being pulled out of their cells in the middle of the night? He remembered the lashes being so brutal that Atterbury had died from the endless punishment.

Did someone else escape … and this time, were they successful?

Rod drew in a breath. He tried to stop shaking as he held out his arms to be handcuffed. The guard slapped on the metal cuffs and then shoved him forward. Rod sprawled from the cell. He stole a glance to his left.

In the dim light he saw all the cell doors were open. POWs shuffled out of their rooms, some holding their hands over their eyes; others feigned humility, as though they were expecting to be beaten.

It was one of the few times in his years of captivity that Rod had ever seen more than two prisoners together. A lump of emotion grew in his throat, tears moistened his eyes. He wanted to rush over and embrace his comrades, hug his fellow officers with whom he'd had so much in common and had endured so much pain—but he knew they'd be severely beaten if he tried.

Was that in store for them anyway?

Next to him, Tom's cell door remained shut. Rod glanced at the men limping down the hall as they hobbled away. He looked quickly behind him. No one was there; Rod's cell had been the last in the long, narrow building. He turned back; ahead of him the guard had disappeared around the corner.

He stepped up to Tom's cell and peered into the cold, dark chamber—

The room was empty. The concrete pad that served as a bed looked as though it had not been slept on; he couldn't even see the ever-present tin cup that served both as a water cup and a bucket for their liquid and fecal waste.

Rod inched closer and put a hand up to the bars. "Tom?" He whispered hoarsely. "Tom!" Where was he? What had they done with him? They must have taken him away, but when? And where?

Rod felt the hard point of a rifle muzzle push up against the small of his back. He flinched, expecting to be beaten.

"Quick!" It sounded more like "queek". The guard shoved him away from Tom's cell.

Rod stumbled forward, barely keeping his balance. He turned the corner to join the tail end of the POWs, and kept a good three feet away from the man in front of him as they entered the courtyard.

Guards lined a pathway leading outside the compound and prodded the POWs to hasten their pace. They shuffled through an archway, its thick, wooden door swung wide, open to the jungle.

Three two-and-a-half ton trucks, their beds covered with green canvas, were parked on a street alongside the compound, motors running and emitting fumes. Guards encircled them, illuminated only by soft moonlight peeking through the clouds.

Two guards stood at the rear of each truck, rifles leveled. They urged them to board. "Queek!"

One by one the POWs shuffled up to the truck. They lowered their heads and a guard blindfolded them. The prisoners then stepped up onto a wooden pedestal to be shoved inside. Some of the men sprawled into the truck bed. Unable to see with their blindfolds, others stepped cautiously toward the front, filling in whatever free space they could find.

The man in front of Rod stumbled; a cloud of dust billowed around them as he fell to the ground. Although he was still cuffed, Rod bent to help him.

A guard ran up. He lifted the butt of his rifle to hit the fallen POW.

"Wait!" Rod held out his cuffed hands. "I'll help."

The guard's eyes widened; he struck Rod with the rifle butt. "No!"

Rod winced at the blow and staggered back.

The guard turned to the fallen prisoner and kicked him in the torso. "Up!" When the prisoner lolled back and forth on the ground, the guard turned to Rod and motioned him forward. "Up!"

Rod stepped around his fellow POW and lowered his head so he could be blindfolded; coarse cloth cut into him as it was pulled tight across his forehead. He twisted his head to ease the pain, but someone slapped him on the cheek. "No move!" Rod stopped resisting.

"Up! Up! Hurry now, quicky, quicky!"

Someone pushed him from behind; he almost stumbled, but he caught himself and stepped onto the pedestal. Hands shoved him into the truck.

Unable to see, Rod tried to move to the front of the truck without stepping on any of the men. He worked his way around, and when he reached as far forward as he could, he eased himself down onto the wooden truck bed.

Once the POWs had boarded, it sounded as if a guard swung on board. "Criminals no talk! Stay down!"

The engines revved. Rod smelled smoke as it belched from the tailpipe; a loud clank reverberated throughout the jungle as the gear was engaged and the truck lurched forward. It gained speed and the men were jostled from side to side as the truck drove along a road pocketed with holes and furrows from erosion. Dust roiled into the truck, and soon the men started coughing.

The POWs sat on their haunches, their arms over their knees with their wrists still cuffed. Being at the front of the truck bed, Rod leaned back against the passenger compartment at the front of the truck. Although Rod could sense dim moonlight coming from the blindfold, he couldn't see a thing.

"Criminal no talk!"

Rod reached out his foot and pressed it against the POW sitting next to him. He tapped with his foot. W-H-A-T I-S G-O-I-N-G O-N?

His fellow POW rotated around until his cuffed hand was next to Rod's knee. F-I-N-D-I-N-G O-U-T. Rod heard the man push his foot against another POW.

Rod did the same, and within minutes the men in the truck had established a communication link. Information began to flow around the truck, and although the POWs communicated in tap-code, the truck was dead silent except for the sound of the engine, the wheels bouncing on the dirt road, and the swish of leaves as the truck drove close to branches that extended across the path.

Every few seconds the truck would hit a deep hole, and a resounding "oof" echoed underneath the canvas.

The senior American officer in the truck was quickly identified without tipping off the guards. They'd be beaten if discovered; the Vietnamese were well aware of the danger that communication lines could bring from their own time serving as prisoners underneath the French in the first IndoChina War, preceding the American military buildup in the 1960s.

The clandestine feature of tap-code communication provided a way around the Vietnamese restriction of keeping the senior officer from organizing the POWs. So in the truck, as in the camp, the Americans circumvented the guard's strategy of isolating the men. Once they established the chain-of-the-command, they relayed the orders from the senior officer as quickly as they could.

But despite the speed that the men organized themselves, no one knew why they were being moved, or why their expedited departure was being accomplished blindfolded and cuffed in the dead of night. It appeared the entire camp had been evacuated; and although the men were now united in the sense of having a third of the POWs together for the first time since their captivity—all in the back of the truck—no one could guess where they were going ... or what might happen once they arrived.

Rod received news and retransmitted it, pressing his fingers against the man on one side of him, and tapping with his foot against the man in front of him. He felt a sense of despair as the lack of specific information rocketed around the truck.

Would they be executed away from the Zoo so that no trace might be found of them?

He doubted they'd be released, for the guards hadn't tried to conceal evidence of their beatings or starvation; any sane civilization, even the Vietnamese, would at least try to pretend they'd treated the POWs humanely. He recalled Fireplug's laughable attempt to convince the German reporters of his supposed benevolent treatment, so he knew they weren't being released.

And if they were simply being moved to another camp, then why would it take place so quickly, and under the secrecy of night? Especially after things had slowly gotten better at the camp since the beatings following Atterbury and Dramesi's escape.

The only rational explanation then was the one that Rod and the rest of the prisoners had faced from the minute they'd been shot down: they knew there was a possibility they may have to die for their country; they'd all known that from the minute they'd volunteered to fly.

And that time may be quickly approaching.

O   O   O

The truck swayed from side to side. Rod's eyes fluttered open and he pulled himself awake, raising his head from nodding beneath his knees. He tried not to wake his fellow prisoners as he straightened. His thighs were stiff and his back sore from sleeping bent over, but it was nowhere as bad as waking after an extended period of torture.

He bent over and placed his blindfold against his knee, trying to push it up. After a few tries, the cloth moved, and a small slit appeared below his left eye; he could barely see out of the bottom of the fabric.

The truck had slowed, and he saw streetlights; the first he'd seen since being at the Zoo. It was still dark, but he could tell they were near a town.

He tilted back his head and strained to see. In the dim light he caught glimpses of crowded streets, automobiles, concrete buildings, and billboards. He heard the faint sound of cars, horns honking, people jabbering outside the truck; he smelled distant scents of lemongrass, ginger, mint, long coriander, bird's eye chili, basil leaves, and the incredibly delicious aroma of chicken being roasted. Another, pungent odor mixed in with the smells of gasoline and fumes—was it dog meat?

They must be in a city. Hanoi? He knew it held the largest collection of people in the North, and from all he heard, smelled, and saw, they were in no small village.

The truck slowed even more, and soon all the men were awake.

Now that there was faint light under the canvas, they could no longer be so overt as to keep a hand on a fellow prisoner's knee, or rapidly tap a finger where it might be seen. Instead, to communicate they discretely placed their hands behind their neighbor's back, or underneath his foot.

They re-established contact throughout the truck, and Rod's suspicion of being in Hanoi was confirmed by someone who had seen the Long Biên Bridge as they drove into town.

Minutes crept by. They passed what appeared to be lights illuminating a power plant, and the truck slowed before grinding to a stop.

The guard stood. He kept his rifle at the ready as he looked outside. He appeared to be waiting for something. More time passed, then he straightened as three people clamored on board.

Moving among the POWs, they reached down and untied each officer's blindfold. "Criminal no move!"

Now that he could fully see, Rod blinked in the dim light. He looked blearily around the truck; all the POWs looked drained and dead tired.

A hand appeared at the end of the truck bed, accompanied by the appearance of a shaven head, white shirt, and dark slacks as a squat man pulled himself on board.

Fireplug.

He scowled at the POWs, and then pointed to a high-walled facility behind him. "Criminals in new camp, Hỏa Lò. You no escape." He glared around the truck. "Listen to me. Your President Nixon very, very bad man for what he do. You die next time he try! Now you get off in Hỏa Lò." He turned and jumped from the truck bed to the ground.

Still standing at the rear of the truck, the guard motioned with his rifle. "Queek. Out of truck!"

Rod struggled to his feet, and once standing bent over to help his fellow prisoners. What had Nixon done that had caused them to be moved? Whatever it was, they'd have to wait until someone smuggled in the news.

Rod pulled a man to his feet and turned to look out the truck. It looked as though they were in the middle of town.

A crowd of several hundred uniformed Vietnamese soldiers shuffled past in the growing light, rifles over their shoulders and shouldering large backpacks. They carried coarse pillows, blankets, and sleeping pads along with heavy duffle bags; but instead of moving into the high-walled encampment, they were walking out of it. To a man, they narrowed their eyes at the POWs and scowled. They looked as though they were leaving the facility.

Were they giving up their barracks for the Americans?

Rod drew in a breath and steeled himself for what appeared to be the next phase of his captivity. Whatever was going on, it appeared the POWs had arrived at their new home ... and if it were truly in the middle of downtown Hanoi, then it would be impossible trying to escape from Hỏa Lò.

CHAPTER THIRTY-TWO

"Feelin' Stronger Every Day"

Two Years later
January, 1973

Hỏa Lò (aka Hanoi Hilton)
North Vietnam

There exists some evil so terrible and some misfortunes so horrible that we dare not think of them, while their very aspect makes us shudder; but if they happen to fall on us, we find ourselves stronger than we imagined, we grapple with our ill luck, and behave better than we expected we should.

Jean de La Bruyère, *Les Caractères*

Hey, Professor."

Rod turned from the makeshift blackboard he'd been writing on and looked over the nineteen officers sitting on the dusty floor in front of him. A young lieutenant, one of the newbies to Hỏa Lò shot-down during the Christmas bombing campaign, raised his hand.

"Go ahead," Rod said.

The man fidgeted as he shifted his weight, still unaccustomed to sitting cross-legged on concrete. "Sir, could you explain the difference between your Lagrangian and Hamilton solutions again? I still don't understand the kinematics."

"Sure." Rod nodded. "Maybe this energy diagram will help." As he turned to draw a graph on the area of the prison wall that he'd set aside as a blackboard, he felt a sense of accomplishment that so many officers were still following his advanced Theoretical Mechanics class. He'd originally targeted the content to a senior undergraduate engineering major, but with the men's enthusiasm, he quickly accelerated the content to the level of a first year graduate student.

Now that they were living 50 men to a cell in the big rooms set around the Hanoi Hilton courtyard, he'd quickly discovered that to a man, the POWs were quick learners. Their memorization skills enabled them to retain esoteric knowledge, and with the plethora of classes being taught throughout the camp—ranging from mathematics, engineering, social sciences, and foreign languages—he knew that the men would eventually validate some of the academic course at an accredited university once they returned to the U.S.

Rod started to explain the difference in the two energy approaches when he spotted the executive officer appear at the back of the large room. Rod motioned with his head toward the Exec.

The men twisted in their spots. Although the commander of the 4th Allied POW Wing was still being isolated from the rest of the camp by the Vietnamese, the officers strictly respected "plums," or Wing regs, established by the chain-of-command; and one of the plums was following military orders transmitted throughout the camp.

The men focused their attention on the Exec.

The Exec glanced around to ensure that no guards were present, and then cleared his throat. "Gentlemen, the commander wanted you to be aware before tonight's movie that there are scattered reports of officers being harassed over the alleged use of American germ warfare."

Rod rolled his eyes as a round of snickers emanated from the men. It seemed that once a week the North Vietnamese latched on to some wild theory of why they weren't winning the war, or why the American prisoners refused to meekly follow their orders.

"As you know," the Exec said, "biological warfare, as is chemical warfare, is strictly prohibited—"

"As is torture!"

"Correct," the Exec said, "and the Geneva Convention is the definitive protocol for the humane treatment of prisoners. As such, the commander wants to ensure all Wing personnel reply with the following language if you are questioned about germ warfare, and I quote: 'in adherence to international law, the U.S. does not engage in illegal activity.'

"In addition, immediately report any contact on this matter up the chain. Copy?"

The men murmured their understanding.

The Exec smiled. "One more announcement: tonight's movie is *Doctor Zhivago*, a film based on the novel by Boris Pasternak, directed by David Lean, and starring Omar Sharif and Julie Christie."

A few of the men clapped and whistled. "Is Julie making an appearance? Who's going to play her?"

The Exec smiled. "Tonight's show will be narrated and not staged—the original film was 3 hours and 20 minutes long, after all."

"Why not? They staged *The Sound of Music* last week!"

A fellow officer pushed him over. "Yeah, but remember our Liesl was more like 38 going on 39, not 16 going on 17."

"Gentlemen, gentlemen," the Exec motioned with his hands, then lowered his voice. "I'll be conducting an officer's call for the commander immediately prior to the narration of *Doctor Zhivago*, so please ensure your flight commanders are fully briefed on any additional intelligence you may have obtained." Hesitating, he suppressed a smile, "Or interest in this alleged use of biological warfare." He shook his head. "I tell you, this one is really beyond me. Any questions?" When no one responded, he nodded to Rod. "Carry on."

"Rog." Rod waited until the Exec left and the class turned their attention back to him. "All right, since tonight's movie is in here and we're running out of time, let's break for the day. Next time I'll go over the energy diagram in detail, so go ahead and report to your flight commander."

The men pushed up from the floor, and Rod started erasing the makeshift blackboard with an old rag. Although the North Vietnamese were keeping a distant eye on classroom activities, he wasn't about to give them the satisfaction of understanding what the Americans were studying—he never knew how quickly their situation might change, and no one knew if their academic exercises might somehow be used against them.

O O O

Later that night, the men congregated at one end of the large room on the concrete slab that served as their bed. They sat with legs crossed and armpits over their knees; some adopted the Philippine version of sitting in a "Filipino squat": squatting with their knees drawn up, their haunches mere millimeters off the floor.

Years ago, at the Zoo and other remote prisons scattered throughout the North Vietnamese jungle, some of the prisoners had been forced to kneel on their knees for days on end, and their kneecaps swelled to the size of balloons; so now, no one except for the very newest of POWs gave even a second thought of sitting on concrete.

The narrator walked to the front, and for the next two and a half hours the audience remained dead quiet, totally immersed in the movie. The POWs were entranced. Most of the men listened with eyes closed; others stared at the concrete floor; and a few gazed out of the big room and out into the courtyard, their eyes focused on infinity and ignoring the meandering of the guards.

As the narrator's voice rose and fell with inflection—ranging from a whisper to loud shouts—Rod imagined he was in the middle of revolutionary Russia. In his mind's eye he saw bombs falling, heard bullets whistling past, and stood next to Komarovsky as Julie Christie tried to assassinate him.

When the movie finally ended, Rod felt exhausted. It was as though he had been transported to a world decades in the past and thousands of miles away. After the sounds of clapping died away, the men rose and congratulated the narrator; it seemed to take a while for the memories of the movie to dissipate, as though the men had been given a temporary lifeline out of the North Vietnamese prison, and a respite from being in captivity. He'd never seen the 1965 movie, but after experiencing the mesmerizing narration, he almost felt as though he could have performed in the movie himself; it was executed that well.

As he fell asleep on his pad, Rod's thoughts drifted not to the Vietnam War, with its communist dealings reminiscent of the revolutionary scenes so expertly painted by tonight's narrator; nor even to Julie back in Colorado, who seemed to have been eerily described as Dr. Zhivago's own wife—but rather to Dr. Zhivago's lusty, passionate lover, whom Rod saw in his mind's eye not as Julie Christie, but Barbara Richardson, with her long, blond hair and ice-blue eyes....

O O O

Rod woke just before dawn. Scenes from last night's movie swirled around his head, and part of him was still caught up in the narrator's vivid description. He needed to move on, push the images out of his mind; otherwise, he'd be trapped in his head for days.

He struggled to his feet and left the cell to walk across the courtyard to the toilet—a hole in a raised floor with flat places to place his feet and squat. As he relieved himself, he looked out the latrine and surveyed the 20-foot high wall encircling Hỏa Lò; topped with broken glass and barbed wire, it made escape nearly impossible.

It had taken a year before news of Nixon's November 1970 Son Tay raid had been smuggled to the Hanoi Hilton, and the concern of another American rescue attempt explained their rapid departure from the Zoo, and their journey to the old army barracks. By placing the POWs in downtown Hanoi, it was obvious the Vietnamese were not going to risk another rescue.

Once finished with his bowel movement, Rod turned to leave, but pulled up when he spotted a small object lying on the floor, just inside the dark, smelly toilet.

"What in the world?" He peered through the darkness; the object was larger than his fist and was pushed up against the wall. He stepped over—it looked like a dead rat. It didn't surprise him. Everyone had seen the small creatures scurrying around the prison, and if he'd still been at the Zoo before their food started improving, he'd have tried to catch one of the rodents to eat.

He prodded the rat with a toe; it didn't move, but it felt slightly warm. The little guy must have kicked the bucket not too long ago.

He bent over and gingerly picked it up by its tail just in case it may have been sleeping or had been knocked out; the rat remained motionless. He started to toss the carcass down the toilet, but he was struck with a thought: The Exec had said the North Vietnamese had made a big deal about the U.S. exploiting biological warfare, and their paranoia was enough that the 4th POW Wing Commander had ordered the Exec to ensure that all officers and enlisted personnel were on alert for any harassment. So perhaps this little furry creature could serve as a way for the Americans to poke their captors in the eye, and maybe even show them how ludicrous their germ warfare claims were.

Rod walked across the courtyard holding the rodent and walked into his cell. A few of the men were awake; some of the officers prayed, others stretched their muscles. The sun had still not risen and no one seemed to notice what he carried.

He placed the rat at the foot of his pad, then turned and rummaged through his stash of old cloths he kept for cleaning. He held up a particularly tattered cloth that looked as though it had once been a T-shirt. He peered out of the cell—none of the guards were close, so hiding what he was doing, he tore several long strips in the cloth and worked his way around the edges. Some of the strips opened up without any trouble; he had to yank at others in order to pull them apart. All the while he tried to leave a circle of cloth untouched in the center of the rag.

Once finished, the swatch of cloth consisted of a circular center approximately a foot in diameter, with three-dozen thin strips emanating radially out from the middle.

He pulled out a smaller rectangular cloth, and tore two holes at the side and a larger hole at the top. He held up his work and nodded to himself. This should do the trick.

He found the pencil he'd been using to prepare his theoretical mechanics lectures, then bent over and meticulously inscribed a fictitious military service number onto the small cloth, followed by the words PROPERTY OF UNITED NATIONS.

Reaching over, he grabbed the now-cool rat, and pushed its head through the cloth's large hole and its two front feet through the smaller holes on the side. He tied the cloth ends together and held up the dead rodent. There. The rat now had a miniature harness.

Rod quickly fastened the long, thin strips from the circular cloth to the back of the rat's harness. He held up miniature parachute by the top and admired his work.

Someone snorted as if holding back a laugh; Rod glanced up.

Grinning, one of his fellow POWs propped himself up on an elbow. "That will drive 'em crazy!"

"That's the idea."

"Where's the landing zone?"

Rod motioned with his head. "The courtyard."

The officer pushed up and walked to the entrance; he glanced out of the cell and turned. "I'll cover for you. Are you going to toss it out the window, let them think he just parachuted in?"

"That will attract too much attention. I'd like to wait until exercise time, but it's dark enough now to just drop it near the center of the courtyard." Rod straightened and stuffed the rat and tiny parachute under his pajama top. "I'll follow you out—just be sure to distract them."

The officer nodded. He walked slowly out of the cell toward the toilet. Rod followed, keeping a good distance behind the man. The sky was tinged with a dull red as morning approached, but it was still dark enough that it was hard to make out any detail in the courtyard.

Two guards stood by a large wooden door at the far end of the compound, and another guard walked with his rifle slung over his shoulder as he patrolled the prisoners' cells.

Walking slowly, Rod reached the center of the courtyard just as his fellow POW ahead of him stumbled and loudly cursed; the prisoner made it appear he had tripped as he reached the toilet.

Immediately the two guards straightened; the other guard on patrol drew his rifle and pointed it at Rod's accomplice. The guard started running for the latrine.

Rod turned slightly so the bulge in his pajama top was hidden from view. He withdrew the rat and dropped the miniature parachutist onto the ground. He walked briskly away.

"You, halt!"

Rod kept moving toward the latrine. Only a few more steps....

"Halt!"

Rod pulled to a stop. If he'd been seen dropping the rat, or if he were still too close, then he'd be instantly punished; not only would his act of resistance be discovered, but also it might bring the wrath of the guards on the camp.

He drew in a breath and barely turned his head, expecting the worst....

But to his relief, the guards were challenging his fellow POW and not him.

A moment passed and the North Vietnamese stepped back to their posts, apparently appeased that the American officer had accidently tripped and was not attempting to perform any forbidden activity.

Rod slowly walked the long way back to the cell and waited for his co-conspirator.

His fellow POW shuffled into the big room, and seeking out Rod, he held his hand to his waist and gave Rod an innocuous thumbs-up.

Rod's shoulder's slumped and he felt drained of energy, and somewhat let down. This was weird. He'd thought he'd experience a sense of accomplishment, even a feeling of superiority for pulling one over on the guards; but now that his creative act of defiance was complete, his mind raced through the implications of any blowback or reprisals the POWs might incur. He hoped he'd done the right thing—

A chilling scream came from the courtyard. Rod bolted to his feet and looked outside. The men in the cell rushed to the door.

In the center of the courtyard, a lone North Vietnamese had his rifle drawn and pointed at the ground. He backed away from the parachute. From a distance the rat only looked like a small object lying on the ground. Guards rushed from buildings and surrounded the dead rodent, rifles at the ready.

No one moved. It was a standoff.

Fireplug strode from the central facility and pushed his way through the circle of guards. He squatted down, picked up the small parachute, and held it up for all to see. He whirled to see if any Americans had been watching as the POWs stepped back from the door. He started shouting. Two of the guards shrugged their shoulders and pointed up to the sky.

Several of the POWs stifled a laugh.

"Quiet!" Rod hissed. "Don't give them a reason to suspect it's us!"

Fireplug looked up and squinted. Not seeing anything overhead except for grey clouds, he shouted a command. The guards instantly brought their rifles to their shoulders and peered intently into the sky. A few of the men swept their weapons around, as though they were anticipating a horde of tiny parachutes to descend into the camp on a biological mission calculated to introduce germ warfare to Hanoi.

Several moments passed. Suddenly, even across the courtyard Rod could tell that Fireplug's face grew red.

The man shouted at the guards once more. They lowered their weapons, seemingly embarrassed. Fireplug held up the parachute, slowly turned, and moved his gaze from cell to cell. He seemed to visibly shake.

None of the POWs left their cells, and no sound came from any of the rooms … but it appeared to Rod that Fireplug focused his glare on his cell—and was staring straight at him.

O O O

Sunday morning, Rod stood in front of the church choir and directed seven fellow officers and two enlisted men as they sang "Onward Christian Soldiers" to a congregation of nearly 50 POWs. The men sang off-key. If he'd had his bagpipes he'd have been able to provide a strong lead, but just as the sermon had been given by an officer who hadn't been a pastor, it didn't matter that he'd never directed a chorale.

He'd only attended church sporadically before his own conversion, and he had never lived the life, or even taken religion seriously. His faith had grown only after long tap-conversations with Tom Ranch, and during impromptu discussions at Hỏa Lò, where some of the POWs had been able to recount an amazing amount of scripture from memory.

A week ago he'd stepped up and volunteered to lead the fledgling choir after piecing together the words to hymns remembered by various officers, as well as arranging the music for the camp's *a cappella* choir.

Some of the prisoners didn't participate in the service, and went about performing their camp chores; other prisoners sang along with the choir.

Outside the cell, a half dozen guards kept watch from the courtyard.

The choir completed the hymn, and after a final prayer, Rod raised his hands to begin the doxology when a loud banging came from outside the large cell. Rod turned his head.

Fireplug stood at the door. "Criminals no sing!"

No one moved. Rod felt his cheeks grow warm. Up to now, the North Vietnamese had allowed them to conduct church services and had not interfered with their worship, even when the service included the breaking of bread and passing of the cup—a tin of water, faintly colored from one of the rare pieces of fruit that one of the men had hidden away. The services had always been low-key, and the POWs tried not to draw attention to themselves.

But as if they were playing a psychological chess game, the singing seemed to have motivated the North Vietnamese to re-establish their absolute control.

Rod's nostrils flared. With all the headway the POWs had made, he wouldn't be the one that allowed that to happen. Especially not with Fireplug.

He brought down his hands and started singing.

Fireplug shouted, "Criminals. Stop!

Rod sang louder and a few of the prisoners joined in.

Fireplug stepped into the cell. "No sing!"

More POWs started singing, and Fireplug's face grew red. Gritting his teeth, he visibly shook as he strode further into the room. "Stop! Criminal no sing!" He drew back his hand and slapped Rod.

Rod's head whipped back. He touched his face and showed blood.

Fireplug motioned the guards to enter the large cell. Half a dozen North Vietnamese poured into the room, their rifles leveled.

The singing petered off as Fireplug glared around the open chamber. His eyes wide, veins bulged from the side of his shaved head. He pointed a finger at Rod. "Kneel."

Rod's heart rate quickened; he felt his chest constrict. Memories of torture roared through his head, all supposedly changed by the death of Ho Chi Minh; even the food had gotten better along with the treatment. Some thought that a truce and their release might happen soon ... but Fireplug's unrelenting presence had always tempered Rod's hopes. Especially now.

Fireplug took a step forward, his eyes locked with Rod's. "Criminal kneel!"

Rod breathed deep as he slowly sank to his knees. It had been years since he'd experienced the lashings, the beatings. But now he stared up at Fireplug and refused to look down at the floor in humiliation.

Fireplug walked past Rod and whacked the side of his head. "Take criminal to punishment camp. This man bad."

Two guards jogged up and grabbed Rod by his arms. They yanked him to his feet, and turned him around to handcuff his wrists.

The large room was quiet, and it seemed as though Rod could hear everyone's heart beat in the congregation. He saw Fireplug walk stiffly across the courtyard, toward the solitary confinement cells called punishment camp.

He heard several of the prisoners voice their encouragement. "Way to go, Lightning!" "Hang in there, partner." "Makin' us proud, buddy!"

As he was led across the courtyard to solitary, he heard singing start from the large room—a few prisoners at first, and then increasingly more, until it sounded like the entire camp joined in. Soon, the strains of "The Star Spangled Banner" echoed throughout Hỏa Lò.

And as the cell door closed behind him, Rod saw Fireplug standing off to the side, his face red and still shaking from the prisoners' united defiance.

Chapter Thirty-Three

"Tie a Yellow Ribbon Round the Ole Oak Tree"

February 12th, 1973

Hanoi Hilton
North Vietnam

I believe the struggle against death, the unconditional and self-willed determination to live, is the motive power behind the lives and activities of all outstanding men.

Hermann Hesse, *Steppenwolf*, "Treatise on the Steppenwolf"

Hurry. Quicky, quicky now," the guard urged. He set a plate of rice and fish morsels on the dirt floor of the small cell and pantomimed for Rod to start eating the meal. Something was up. Before he'd been sent to punishment camp for not obeying Fireplug to stop the church choir singing, the rumor was that they were being fattened up for release.

The guard forced an unnatural smile, but kept looking over his shoulder as he backed out of the cell. His face was covered with a sheen of sweat and his eyes darted from side to side, as if someone was watching him.

Rod waited until the guard shut the cell door before he moved to the food. He picked up the tin plate and flicked off a bug crawling through the rice before picking out the fish. He sniffed the meat. It didn't smell rancid, so he ate as he shuffled over to the small window to look out over the courtyard. Maybe the rumors were true. It was the second meal he'd been given today, so he knew something was up—something important enough that they wanted him not to appear malnourished.

Guards scurried around the courtyard, carrying large bundles of actual shirts and pants, and not POW pajamas. Others carried baskets of sandals, towels, and plastic jugs of water. Whatever was going on made their normally leisurely-paced tempo look as if a pile of ants had been stirred with a stick.

Strange things had been happening in the camp ever since the Christmas bombings.

Rod could still feel the rumble of the bombs, probably dropped by B-52s. The monster warplanes were flying too high for him to hear their engines, but from the quantity of explosives detonating around him, only B-52s, the BUFFS, could have carried that many munitions. The POWs had cheered with each rumbling explosion. They raked the metal bars with their tin cups during the week-long, earth-shaking bombardment.

The cell door swung open. Rod turned, still holding the plate of food. Clean pajamas and a pair of new sandals were thrown on his bed. Rod froze as the guard stepped in.

"You! Come quicky!"

Once outside they rubbed their eyes at the light. They passed the rock-lined well and trudged to a one-story, windowless building.

They entered, and shivering from the air-conditioning, he followed his fellow prisoners as they walked down a well-lit hallway. One by one they were herded into a room that was being run like an assembly line: nurses stripped their pajamas from them and tossed their clothes into a pile; the POWs stepped into a makeshift shower; once clean, they were methodically shaved and quickly inspected.

Rod called out to his fellow prisoners and asked what was going on; scowling, one of the guards strutted over, held up his rifle, and glared.

Rod stared back; but inwardly he shivered at the memory of having met the crew of German reporters the last time he'd been groomed—and was then severely beaten. He was in pain for weeks afterward, and his back was still tender.

They were given shoes, socks, a clean shirt, a light jacket, a pair of trousers, and then prodded through the well-lit corridor to where they were led outside to the central square. But instead of turning back for their cells, they were herded past the rope room, and for the first time since they'd entered the Hanoi Hilton, they exited the doors of the low-slung prison compound and set foot in the exterior world.

Rod's senses were overwhelmed at the chaos. He saw wood and concrete buildings, clothes flapping from clotheslines, dogs running in circles, yipping and being chased by barefoot children, and steam rising from cooking pots held on tripods; he smelled fish, onion, garlic, and rancid meat. He saw old men with long, stringy beards squatting at the side of the road, watching him while smoking a pipe, and young men in white shirts and dirty tan pants peddling Pedicabs. He heard horns blaring as small red and green two-seater cars weaved through traffic, people crossing the street ... the cacophony of noise, smell, and random images roiled throughout his body. He staggered backwards but was stopped by a metal rifle barrel pressed against his back.

Rows of old busses were at his left, filling the dirt street, thrumming with their engines running. Black smoke and fumes spilled out of the tailpipes. A double column of guards wearing rice paddy hats trotted up and encircled the prisoners. They pointed rifles at the ready, as if worried that the POWs were suddenly going to make a break for freedom.

Fireplug stepped to the front and faced the prisoners. For the first time that Rod could remember Fireplug wore a tan uniform with red shoulder tabs, his shirt sported aviator wings, and an oversized circular hat was set on his head. There was something else different about him. It took Rod a moment to focus, then it suddenly hit him—the uniform was not Vietnamese but Chinese, Red Army.

He'd always suspected that Fireplug wasn't Vietnamese. Was this why Fireplug had known so much personal information about him when he was first shot down? Was Fireplug being fed by Red Army intelligence? And he wore aviator wings!

During Rod's initial interrogation after he'd been shot down, Fireplug had known about him intercepting that Chinese Ilyushin Il-28, back during the Cuban missile crisis.

But that incident had never been declassified.

Had Fireplug been that Beagle pilot?

And did that explain why everything had seemed to be so personal to the man … or was Fireplug simply warped?

Fireplug's face was flush, his eyes narrow as he surveyed the American officers. "Criminals get on bus. Now. Move! Hurry, hurry!" He motioned with his arm for the officers to board.

The guards pushed the Americans forward. One stumbled and fell headlong into the dirt. The guard raised his rifle to beat the straggler, but a fellow officer bent and lifted the man to his feet.

The chaos in the street abated and a line of peasants gathered to encircle the busses. They silently watched as the POWs were prodded aboard. A white-haired woman, her spine bent forward so much that her shoulders were almost even with her waist, shook a finger at the officers, and admonished the prisoners with a shrill voice.

One of the POWs tried to pull himself up onto the bus but fell back, and had to be lifted by two of his friends.

Rod stepped up to enter the vehicle but he was suddenly yanked to the side. He stumbled and tried to keep from sprawling in the dirt, but someone held him upright roughly by the arm. Rod looked up and his eyes widened.

Fireplug's fingers dug into his flesh. He leaned close and spoke in a low voice. "Never forget me, Colonel. We will meet again. I promise you." He shoved Rod to the front of the bus and disappeared in the crowd of onlookers.

Rod breathed heavily. He looked around but no one seemed to have noticed the altercation.

He took a shaky step up, and pulled himself into the bus. He turned and looked outside, scanning the crowd, but there was no sign of Fireplug or anyone else in the distinctive Chinese uniform.

He carefully stepped to the back, taking time not to shove his colleagues as he moved past. He sat next to a POW not from his block.

Rod was taken aback at the condition of his fellow prisoner, and wondered if he himself looked as feral. He had sunken eyes, pale skin, an unruly look—but he held his head high.

A guard shouted outside the bus and waved a hand for the vehicles to start moving. Another guard ran up to the front of their vehicle, grabbed onto the rope at the side, and swung onto the stairs. He climbed aboard, turned to the men and glared, rifle at the ready.

The bus groaned as it ground into gear. It lurched forward with a jerk.

Rod pitched forward and held out a hand to keep steady. Although it was hot and humid inside the bus, for the first time in years he felt a breeze wash over him.

He turned to the man next to him. "Any idea where we're going?" He was surprised that he sounded so hoarse. He kept an eye on the guard, but the Vietnamese officer seemed more concerned about the men trying to leave the bus than talking.

"Don't know," the prisoner said. "Do you think we're being taken to another camp?"

"Not if we've been given these to wear," the man in front of Rod said in a quiet voice. Rod recognized him as the senior Navy officer in camp. "During the July parade back in '66 they didn't bother having us change. Why waste clean clothes?"

"Or food?" another prisoner whispered. "I've eaten more the past few days than I've eaten the entire month. Do you think we're going for a mass TV interview?"

"Why else would they want us looking well fed? And what about these clothes!"

An air of excitement swept over the truck as the men realized that the guard would not berate them for speaking. But still, no one said the obvious, or brought up the hope that they might be freed. It was as though it was bad luck to even speculate....

The convoy bounced through the streets and turned onto a wide road, where they gained speed as they drove through town. Dust boiled into the windows, causing the men to cough. They drove on, past houses, scattered huts, and lean-tos constructed with bamboo, all interspersed between a potpourri of buildings.

Sometime later the bus began to slow as they reached Gia Lam.

Slowing at a small gate, they drove up to a collection of buildings. A low whine filled the air and the smell of jet fuel wafted over them.

When the trucks turned, the men saw a vision of salvation: two U.S. Air Force C-141 Starlifter cargo planes sat on a tarmac. A crowd of Vietnamese in uniform stood opposite several USAF officers, as if the two groups were warily sizing each other up. Men in dark suits clustered behind a podium set up in front of the planes. Some held their hands behind their back and looked around the area while others spoke in small groups.

A murmur swept over the prisoners as they tried to contain their excitement, but not because they were afraid to cheer—as if they might be worried they may be rudely awakened from a dream, or at the last minute the Vietnamese might change their minds; but rather they stayed subdued, so as not to give the Vietnamese the pleasure to know they were ecstatic about being released. They forced themselves to remain unemotional, detached, and exuded a display of professionalism.

The bus groaned to a stop in front of the planes. Rod looked out the window and spotted several hidden cameras. The Vietnamese must want to film them celebrating.

The guards kept their rifles at bay as they jumped nimbly off the bus. The one in charge raised his voice at the officers. "Line up by height, short to tall. You do what I say. Quickly now!" The other guards began barking orders to the American POWs, as if they had to dictate their absolute authority over the men up until the last moment.

One POW struggled with a crippled leg and couldn't disembark. A guard ran up and impatiently drew back his hand to slap him. Another guard jabbered in a raised voice and excitedly pointed to an array of news cameras pointed at the convoy. The guard scowled, then pulled back. He motioned with his rifle for the man to hurry.

The POWs scrambled off the buses, and the senior American prisoner, a white-haired Navy captain, drew himself up. He raised his voice over the mayhem. "Gentlemen. Fellow Americans. Fall in, by order of shoot down!" He stood rigidly at attention at the side of the convoy, in total control.

Some of the officers limped and others had to be helped as the men lined up by the date which they had been shot down, the longest-serving prisoner standing at the head of the formation. With or without injuries, they tried to stand as straight as they could, hands held rigidly at the side, looking straight ahead. Feeling a thrill of pride, Rod fell into a brace that he hadn't accomplished since his basic cadet summer.

The guard in charge grew red in the face and ran up to the navy captain. Waving his arms, he screamed just inches from the captain's face, "Line up by height! You no do what I say! Line up by height!"

Ignoring the man's tirade, the captain waited until the last prisoner fell into formation. He then raised his voice even louder than the guard's. "Gentlemen, at my command. Forward, harch!" He executed a perfect about face and started marching straight to the crowd and toward the podium set between the two planes.

Apparently stunned by the POWs sudden audacity, the guards parted as froth on a pond swept aside by a preying alligator.

The POWs marched in step; ahead of them the crowd fell silent.

As they approached the podium the navy captain spun on his heel and shouted, "Formation, halt!"

The captain drew in a deep breath. He slowly nodded to the men and then mouthed, "Thank you." He slowly turned and lifted a shaky hand in a salute to an Air Force colonel standing behind the podium. "Sir, the American contingent reports ready to depart."

The colonel whipped his hand up in a salute. "Thank you, sir." He cleared his throat and raised his voice. "Gentlemen, parade rest."

The POWs stood with their hands behind their back. Rod felt his heart pound with excitement, incredibly proud to maintain his dignity in front of his captors. He wondered if Fireplug was watching and hoped that it would infuriate the man.

The colonel stepped away from the podium and a political appointee from the State Department stepped up. The message to the Vietnamese was clear that it was time for the military to move aside and let the diplomats to take over.

A Vietnamese officer stood and tried to shake the diplomat's hand, but the American ignored him. He swept back his long, blonde hair, withdrew a sheet of paper from his jacket pocket, and started to read into the microphone.

Something about the man's mannerisms struck Rod as oddly familiar. With the man's tanned good looks and athletic build, he resembled a young version of Jack Kennedy. But it wasn't his mannerisms that struck Rod the most; it was his voice.

It was the same voice that had traded stories in whispers after taps at the Academy, the same voice that had kidded him about falling for Barbara Richardson when they had visited San Francisco ... and the same voice that had denied that he had stolen his classmate's money, and then lied about being in an authorized location back when they both were cadets.

Fred Delante. His ex-roommate was now a political appointee in the State Department.

The words from the speech rolled over Rod, unheard as Rod squinted to get a better look. Was it really Fred after all these years? And in the heat and humidity of the Hanoi airport?

It was Fred, but only better poised. He looked as though he were a politician playing the crowd.

After Fred finished speaking, the colonel stepped back up to the podium and started calling the prisoners' full names, the longest held POW called first.

One by one the POWs broke ranks and walked swiftly to the podium. They stopped, stood at attention, and saluted. They then entered the C-141, swallowed out of sight.

"Lieutenant Colonel Roderick Jean-Claude Simone."

Rod didn't react at first, tuning out his name before someone whispered down the line, "Move it, Colonel!"

He realized in shock he must have been promoted while in captivity. Lieutenant Colonel Simone.

Fireplug had called him Colonel. How could he have known?

Rod walked stiffly to the plane, hoping to catch Fred's eye, but his ex-roommate chatted with a bevy of aides. They looked over a computer printout of names, and checked off the men as they approached.

Rod saluted as he reached the plane. He felt awkward; his eyes filled with tears as a beaming flight nurse stepped forward and gave him a hug and a kiss.

The colonel stepped forward and gave him a bear hug. "Welcome home and God bless," the colonel said. "We're all damned proud of you."

"Tom Ranch, Jeff Goldstein" Rod said, his voice cracking with emotion. "Are they here?"

The colonel quickly scanned the printout. He looked up and shook his head. "Sorry, their names are not on the list."

"Thank you, sir." Rod felt deflated as he limped to the back of the ramp and entered sanctuary, another world, light years away from hell.

Inside the plane the men talked excitedly among themselves.

Rod collapsed into a seat and closed his eyes. The last time he'd seen Tom Ranch was when he'd shaken his hand after he and Julie had been married, graduation day. And nine years later, he'd lived next to him in a cell, but had never seen him, never spoken ... only communicated by tap for two and a half years.

Memories replayed in his head: of being shot down, captured, and paraded through Vietnamese villages; of the operation on his leg, arriving at the Hanoi Hilton and the Zoo, the incessant torture and learning tap code; and most importantly, being forgiven of the wracking guilt of cheating on Julie and killing Jazz—all from learning about Christ's grace from the prisoner in the cell next to him. Although he'd never seen Tom Ranch the entire time he was a POW, he owed his survival and new life to his former AOC, the man who had mentored him when he was a cadet.

He tried to hold back but couldn't stop sobbing. The pain and stress of living through hell the past years engulfed him; tears ran down his face.

When the plane was in the air, he saw that he wasn't the only one who had expressed his feelings. Cheering erupted, fists pumped into the air.

He wiped his tears and stood. He searched the back of the massive C-141, but didn't see Fred Delante; his ex-roommate must have flown out on the other transport.

He collapsed back in his seat and someone next to him handed him a beer. Foam spilled from the top and the can was so slippery that Rod nearly dropped it on his lap.

Someone held up a beer high in the air. "To the United States of America!"

"Here, here!"

The cockpit door at the front opened and a pudgy officer in a flight suit stepped out. He wore gold-metal, straight-temple military pilot sunglasses; grinning, he held his arms high. "Gentlemen! I'm Major Sly Jakes, your aircraft commander and I'm pleased to announce that we've just left Vietnamese air space—we're now over international waters!" The men cheered again, and excited laughter filled the cabin.

Rod straightened. His old roommate!

The shouting continued and it took several minutes for Sly to quiet the passengers. "Men, I can tell you the entire nation is proud as hell. When we get to Clark, and after the docs get through with you, I'm holding an open bar at the Club. Drinks are on me!"

The men roared.

Rod struggled to his feet. "Sly! Sly, it's me!" His voice croaked from the excitement.

"Rod?" Sly pushed down the crowded aisle. As he passed, men stood and shook his hand, thanking him for flying them out. Sly grinned at Rod and made his way through the mass of excited officers. When he finally reached Rod he pulled him in a rough bear hug. "We've been hoping and praying for you, buddy! Man, it's good to see you."

Tears ran down Rod's face. "How's Julie, Nanette? Have you kept in touch?"

"They're fine. I'd have brought a letter from them, but no one knew exactly when you were going to be released." He looked up and down at Rod. "I need to give you some of the weight I've gained; you're thinner than a pitot tube." He turned around, then drew Rod forward by the arm. "Come on up to the flight deck, we have plenty of room. You can sit in the jump seat."

Rod followed his ex-roommate past the rows of men as excited chatter ricocheted throughout the aircraft. It was as if a party had erupted five miles above the ground.

He entered the flight deck and looked around; they had more space in the cockpit than he'd had in the cell he'd lived in for the first three years. And there were so many buttons, dials, and flashing lights that he felt as though he'd stepped into a space ship.

"Come on in, pull up a chair," Sly said. He turned to the three other men on the flight deck. "Hey, guys, my Academy roommate, Lieutenant Colonel Rod Simone."

Rod looked around. In addition to the pilot and co-pilot's seat in the front, there was an officer sitting at his left and an enlisted man on his right, each facing a bank of switches and various colored lights, with a walk space leading to the front. A smaller seat was positioned directly behind the pilot and copilot in the middle of the aisle, its back folded forward to save space. Sly wasn't kidding when he said he had plenty of room.

Sly pointed to the enlisted man on Rod's right. "That's Scotty, our flight engineer."

The man stood and shook Rod's hand. "Welcome back, sir. I'm honored to meet you."

Rod glanced at the man's nametag; the name plainly read Master Sargent Jay Hamilton. Rod shook his head. "Scotty?"

The flight engineer grinned. "Yes, sir—Chief Engineer on the *Enterprise*."

Rod blinked. "The aircraft carrier?"

"No, sir! Mr. Scott—from *Star Trek*, on television?"

Rod shook his head. "Never saw it."

Sly pointed to an older captain on Rod's left. "Waldo's the nav, our own Mr. Wizard; and the guy up here next to me is my co-pilot, Rock, a '71 grad."

Rock waved from the right hand seat and turned back to where he was flying the plane in Sly's absence.

The navigator stood and firmly shook Rod's hand. "It's great to get you back, sir. The whole nation has yellow ribbons tied around everything that doesn't move."

Yellow ribbons? "It's hard to believe I am back." Rod was at a loss for words, overwhelmed by the display of high-tech electronics and camaraderie after living in conditions reminiscent of the middle ages.

Sly gently led him to the front of the flight deck to where he erected the jump seat and eased Rod down. The ocean spread out in front them, dotted with cloud formations below; it seemed as though he could see forever. He felt suddenly disoriented in the vast openness after years of living in a confining space, demarcated by dank, musty, cell walls.

Sly squatted by his side. "How ya doing, Rod. Are you all right?"

Rod drew in a breath and refocused to the inside of the cockpit. "Yeah, though I can't put my finger on it. Things are going a little too fast. Everything seems so strange ... different." As if time had kept moving and the world has gone on ... and I somehow don't belong."

"Just relax. You have a lot of catching up to do, roomie. A lot of things have changed. I've got four kids now—"

"Four? I thought Carol wouldn't let you near her anymore after having the twins."

"That didn't last long. But I did get fixed after she had the next set of twins." Sly grinned as Rod's eyes widened. "Just take things in stride. After all, you were shot down a year before the Moon landing. But after that, even with the war protests, Kent State, the U.S. going off the gold standard, 18 year olds getting the vote, Watergate, Jimmy Hendrix and Janis Joplin dying, the Pentagon papers, Roe versus Wade, and the Beatles breaking up, this war ending is the biggest news in decades. And on top of that, your Nanette's not a little girl anymore; she's a young woman. You've got a lot of catching up."

Rod felt suddenly hot and had trouble breathing, as though the temperature in the cockpit had soared. He pushed up and almost fell.

Sly held out a hand to steady him. "Easy there. Can I get you anything?"

"I've ... I'd better get back and rest. I think that half can of beer put me under the table."

"That and culture shock, roomie. Let me help."

As Sly helped Rod leave the cockpit, the main cabin still vibrated with energy, the ex-prisoners still trying to grasp that they were really free. Rod reached his seat and slumped back. He closed his eyes and tried to digest all that Sly had told him, from his own family to the social upheaval rolling over the country. Even the language was somehow different.

He tried to make sense of the changes, the feeling of being left behind, and was overwhelmed. He felt numb, his head was like a huge balloon, while outside his bubble of focus, fellow POWs murmured excitedly as the huge cargo plane arrowed toward freedom and Clark Air Base.

CHAPTER THIRTY-FOUR

"Free Bird"

Two weeks and five days later
March, 1973

Mama's Fish House
Paia, Maui

Ah, pray make no mistake, we are not shy;
We're very wide awake, the moon and I.

The Mikado, II

Rod sat on a wooden bench next to Nanette and watched the waves roll to the shore. They broke a quarter of a mile from land just outside the tiny bay, and by the time they approached the beach they lapped quietly upon the sand.

It had taken three days after landing at Clark Field to push through a battery of grueling medical examinations, an incredible array of paperwork, and then fly *en masse* with the rest of the former POWs to Travis Air Force Base to meet his family in a heart-wrenching ceremony, followed by two weeks of debriefing. He was on his second day of a month of leave, and Julie had insisted that they fly to the small Hawaiian island of Maui to unwind near the obscure village of Paia.

He desperately tried to reacquaint himself with his family after six long years—five in captivity and one flying combat over Vietnam. Every few seconds Rod glanced at his daughter, a slender and dark-haired beauty, who at nearly fourteen seemed years more mature than her age. Sly had been right, she was no longer a little girl.

She sat next to him, wearing a white miniskirt and leather knee boots, a billowing purple shirt, and had a yellow orchid behind her ear. The last time he'd seen her was when she was eight years old, even before braces. He wondered if his sister would have looked like Nanette if she'd had the opportunity to grow this old.

Fifty feet behind them people sat at tables on the grass lawn outside the main dining room, eating dinner at the newly opened seafood restaurant in Kuau Cove on Maui's North Shore. A steady breeze blew in from the ocean.

Rod watched Nanette straighten as a large wave enveloped a surfer in frothy white foam. When the surfer's head bobbed above water she sat back on the bench, seemingly relieved.

"Pence for your thoughts," Rod said.

"Excuse me?" Nanette said, still watching the waves.

Rod smiled. "Your grandfather Hank used that expression, old even when I was your age. It was a way to break the ice, get people to talk."

She turned and gave him a look that showed more sympathy than understanding. "If you say so."

He thought about answering, but decided he really needed to get to know her better, not try to force things. He'd promised himself when he was a POW that he'd always give his family the benefit of the doubt, and after the last two days it looked like he was about to test his pledge, big time. There's nothing like being an instant parent of a teenager to stretch your patience.

He glanced at his watch. Julie had been gone for forty-five minutes. They'd arrived early at the restaurant and she'd wanted to do some quick shopping in the small hippie village of Paia before joining them for dinner. She'd insisted it would be good for he and Nanette to spend some quality time together, whatever that was, so after dropping them off at the restaurant she'd driven to the village alone.

Nanette fidgeted on the bench, seemingly bored at having to spend time with a man who was more a stranger than her father. After all, it had been six years since she'd even seen him, and that was nearly half her entire life.

The shrinks at Clark had warned him this would happen, so Rod tried to be patient. He tried another tack.

"Mom tells me you're doing well in school. What activities are you involved in?"

She rolled her eyes and recited a list, as if she was being forced to humor a retarded relative. "The usual stuff. Student government, cross-country, karate, National Honor Society, Keyettes—"

"Keyettes?"

She swept a strand of hair out of her face, a movement that reminded him of Julie. "It's the girl's auxiliary of Key Club, a service organization."

"I see," he said. What in the world is Key Club? He tried his best not to appear too out of touch. "Grandma told me you started taking karate lessons before I was shot down. How have you been doing?"

She lifted her chin. "It was really cool; the dojo was co-ed. I made Black Belt this summer—" She hesitated then gave a shy smile. "I was the first person in the class to earn it."

Although it was hard to believe that with her tiny frame she could have actually achieved so high of a degree, Rod was pleased he'd touched on something she was interested in. "That's great. I guess you're too old for Brownies—are you in Girl Scouts?"

"No."

"How's your model airplane collection?"

"Okay."

"Mom said you're taking cross-country. That's great. When did you start running?"

She turned away. "I can't remember."

So much for getting her to open up. "I used to take you to the cadet field house; we ran around the indoor track when you were little. Do you remember that?"

She kept her eyes on two surfers paddling out to reach the next big wave. "I guess."

"You'd run beside me and keep asking how much farther till we'd run a mile." Rod shifted his weight on the bench, his back growing sore. "I'd like to start running again, but it's going to take some time for me to get in shape."

"Yep."

Rod paused. "I guess you heard that I'm going to be assigned back to the Academy."

She turned to look at him. "So we don't have to move?"

"That's right. The Academy assigned me to head up their POW camp for the survival program. It's called SERE; they want me to make it more realistic. Maybe we can run some mountain trails when we get back."

"That would be fun." She was silent for a moment. "Were you able to exercise when you were in prison?"

Rod drew in a breath. It was the first question she'd asked about his time as a prisoner of war. "No," he said. "I was locked up and never really left the cell. The only time I got a chance to move around was when ... when they took me out and ... asked me questions."

"Questions?" Nanette frowned.

"They ... interrogated me. Asked me things I wasn't supposed to tell them." Which usually led to being tortured. "I had to cope with being confined every minute of the day and do whatever they wanted me to do—and not what I wanted to do. Five years of incredible boredom."

Nanette was quiet for a long time, and then she said in a small voice, "I know how you feel."

Rod leaned forward and put his elbows on his knees. He studied her for a moment. "You do?"

"Yeah." She brushed back another strand of hair. "Running makes me feel free. That and studying."

"Studying?"

She twisted her face. "I'd have to look after Mom if I didn't study."

Rod drew back. "You'd have to do what?"

She stood and straightened her miniskirt. "Nothing. I didn't mean anything. Forget it." She strode quickly away.

He watched her walk to the shore, but didn't follow.

She'd opened up to him, and he didn't want to cause her to clam up later; she'd expressed a common interest.

But what did she mean by having to look after Julie? Rod stretched out his arm on the back of the bench. Julie appeared to be all right. She'd gained weight, but she'd always had trouble keeping the pounds off. And to be fair, with his meager diet the past five years everybody looked like they'd gained weight.

He watched Nanette as she meandered along the shore. She squatted down by the ocean and picked up several shells that had washed up on the sand. The waves washed in as she leaned over and inspected them; her long, dark hair hung down until the tips almost touched the water. When a large swell suddenly rumbled in, she jumped up and squealed, then laughed as she darted away from the waves.

Safely on the sand, she drew up a leg, spun around in a pirouette, and threw out her arms in an exaggerated ballet motion.

Mystified, Rod watched her as she danced along the shore. She alternated between being poised and ladylike, conducting a mature, adult conversation one minute and then acting like a little kid the next.

Now a half a football field away, she resembled a beautiful young nymph gracing the shore, twirling lightly up to the water, as if playing tag with one of the most turbulent forces in nature.

He stared, mesmerized by his daughter's antics … and almost missed the man who'd staggered past.

The man stumbled out of the restaurant's grassy boundary, and stepped onto the sandy beach as he lurched toward her, weaving an uneven path. Muscular and tanned, the guy was barefoot and wore orange swim trunks and no shirt. His hair was matted, shoulder-length, and looked like he hadn't bathed in a week.

He stopped near the shoreline and wavered, watching Nanette.

Nanette giggled and ran back from a wave. She twirled and collided with the man.

Rod rose to his feet.

The man grabbed her arms and tried to pull her in, but she struggled to get away.

Rod started toward the beach. He limped quickly, shards of pain shooting up his leg as he tried to gain speed in the sand.

Staggering as if he were drunk, the man spun Nanette around to face him.

Over the waves Rod heard her sharply say something.

The man laughed. He pulled her close, bent over, and tried to kiss her.

Nanette quickly brought up her right knee to the man's crotch.

He grunted and released her left arm.

She kneed him again, twice more in quick succession.

He groaned and grabbed at his groin, doubling over.

Now free, Nanette reared back and gave the man a sharp kick to the head with her left foot.

The man reeled back and collapsed on the sand, sprawling on his back.

Nanette turned and started sprinting toward Mama's Fish House.

Rod pulled to a stop, breathing hard.

His leg hurt like crazy and his heart pounded from the sudden exertion of trying to run for the first time in years ... but he was more astonished than anything else. This was his baby!

Seeing Rod, Nanette slowed to a quick walk and glanced over her shoulder.

The man lay in the sand, clutching his crotch and moaning. He rolled over, his head doubled down.

Nanette stepped past and brushed back her hair.

Rod reached out an arm. "Nanette, are you all right?"

She nodded and twisted away from Rod's grip. "I'm fine." She continued walking up the path to the restaurant.

Rod looked from her to the man. "But he tried to—"

"I said, I'm okay. I can take care of myself."

Rod turned and watched as she strode past, acting as though it was no big deal that she had just taken out a man twice her age and size.

The shrinks were right—it was going to take some time getting used to being a family again.

O   O   O

Rod put down the *Life* magazine he'd been reading in bed when Julie finally came out of the bathroom. The restroom window was open as the utility fan pulled out the last remnants of smoke.

Although she'd covered the small opening at the bottom of the door with a towel, Rod could smell smoke seeping into the motel room. She knew he didn't care to be around anyone smoking, and he was struck by her thoughtfulness for not smoking in the bedroom. But she must have switched to a new brand of cigarette; it smelled sweet, like a heavy, burning rope.

Her eyes were bloodshot as she walked uncertainly from the bathroom and picked up her glass of gin and tonic. She drank deeply and collapsed onto the bed.

Rod admired the long curve of her back as she rolled over. "Six years," he whispered. "There were some days I thought I'd never hold you again."

"Was it worth the wait?" Her voice was slurred. They'd made love before she'd slipped into the bathroom for her cigarette; he still felt exhausted.

He thought back on the change that had come over his life, his newfound hope and the shifting priority of putting his family first. "It always will be." He stroked her shoulder as she leaned over to take another drink.

As he watched her drain the glass, he remembered the times when drinking had been so important in their lives, from hitting the Officer's Club for happy hour to the bottles of gin and vodka they'd kill over a weekend.

At the time it hadn't seemed a big deal—everyone drank, and getting blitzed was just part of a fighter pilot's life: You worked hard and played even harder.

The rationale was that you needed to keep your mind off the fact that the next time you went out to fly it might be the last your family ever saw you alive.

But as he watched her finish the cocktail, he realized that for as long as they'd been married their lives had centered on that next drink. Funny, he'd never noticed it before, but now it seemed so obvious.

He almost said something, but decided it wasn't the time to bring it up; there were more important things that weighed on his mind. Incredibly more important.

He grew somber, thinking that the last time he'd made love had been with another woman. He drew in a breath. Barbara. Maybe he should just blurt it out, confess, and hope that Julie would forgive him.

There shouldn't be any secrets between them ... but that was another potential hotspot the shrinks had warned him about: don't move too fast.

But what would have happened if he hadn't left his Flight at the Fire Empire that night?

Would Barbara have been killed by that kid's bomb?

If he hadn't felt so guilty about their affair the next morning, would he have been shot down? Would his reflexes have been fast enough to evade that SAM ... and would Jazz still be alive today? Would Jazz's wife Sally ever forgive him?

And would he have gotten back safely from that mission, finished his tour in 'Nam and come home to his family, to be around when his daughter had started running?

And would he have been home the years when Nanette had learned how to kick the snot out of some pervert who was stupid enough to think that he could fondle a beautiful young girl?

What else might have been different if he had only been faithful?

But as bad as things had turned out, paradoxically, if he hadn't been shot down, he knew that he would never have interacted with his ex-mentor Tom Ranch, and he might never have discovered his new found faith....

Julie rolled out of bed. She picked up her glass and padded to the counter by the bedroom sink.

Moonlight reflected off her smooth skin. Her stomach was rounded in a classic Rubenesque, and her arms were just this side of being plump. She hungrily munched on Maui chips and finished the container of French onion dip she'd bought at the convenience store.

She filled her glass with ice and sloshed some gin onto the floor as she poured herself another drink. She held up an empty glass to Rod. "Ready for that nightcap now, Lightning?"

He put his hands behind the pillow and shook his head. "Not yet." He had to tell her.

She replaced the bottle and sauntered to the bed. She shook the glass as she approached the bed, making the ice cubes clink against the side; she took a long sip. "Hmmm. You didn't turn into a teetotaler, did you?"

"I'm taking things one step at a time." How could he start? What could he say?

She cocked her head and looked at him oddly.

Rod rolled over as she sat on the edge of the bed. "How was shopping today?"

"Marvelous." A dreamy look came over her eyes. She started to say something, then hesitated. "Bought some heavy stuff. I don't suppose Maui-wowie means anything to you, does it?"

He furrowed his brow. "Maui what?"

She put a hand on his chest and gave a mischievous smile. "Never mind. You've been gone a long time. The world has moved on while you were in prison. Like you said, one step at a time." She sloshed her drink on him and the strong smell of gin wafted through the room.

"Hey!" He wiped off the booze. "I smell like a distillery!"

She leaned over and started licking his chest. She murmured, "I'll clean it up."

He closed his eyes, feeling increasingly guilty. He knew he'd been forgiven, but he still had to confess what he'd done. To make things right. He couldn't escape that.

He also knew the shrinks had warned him not to rush things, but it just wouldn't be fair to wait. Julie was his wife. He had to tell her, and the sooner the better.

But now?

It was crazy to bring it up, the very first night that they'd been alone after all these years.

But yet he had to. He loved her. It wasn't a condition of his faith, it was a result of his change … and it was the right thing to do.

He struggled to sit up. Julie tried to pull him back down, but he gently put his hands under her shoulders and urged her to sit with him.

Sighing, she gathered the sheet around her and plopped back against the pillow. The overhead fan softly swished as she settled in. Her eyes still red, she ran a hand through her hair. She looked annoyed. "What now? Do we screw one step at a time, too?"

Rod winced. "Julie." He drew in a deep breath. This was going to be tough. Really tough. He wondered how she'd take it, how he'd take it. "Julie, the last five years have been pure hell for me."

"You were a POW. What would you expect?"

Rod shook his head. "No, that's not what I meant. I mean, sure, I'd never wish that experience on anyone, but I've been carrying something with me that I've got get off my chest. I have to tell you, because … because, I feel so guilty and because you need to know."

Julie sat up and narrowed her eyes. "What on earth are you talking about?" Although her words were slurred, her voice was strong.

"First, you need to know that I've changed, really changed. Something's come into my life that's made me a new man. But I'll tell you about that later. You see, the day before I was shot down," Rod whispered, "I became an Ace, and by doing so, I killed a man, the Vietnamese pilot—"

"Everybody knows that. It was all over the news."

"But later that day, I saved somebody's life, a woman in Saigon. A woman who I hadn't seen for years and years.…"

CHAPTER THIRTY-FIVE

"Cat's in the Cradle"

**Three years later
December, 1975**

United States Air Force Academy
Colorado Springs, CO

The now, the here, through which all future plunges to the past.

James Joyce, *Ulysses*

After his experience as a POW, Rod was sure that nothing would ever shock him again.

That included his late-night confession to Julie in Maui nearly three years ago, when Julie had left the bedroom and refused to speak to him for the rest of the trip; and later, when he'd finally figured out that it was marijuana he was smelling that wafted under the bathroom door; and even when she'd left to live in Washington, DC with her mother, purportedly to think things over.

Throughout it all, he was impressed with the incredible resilience Nanette had shown, especially in diving into her school's extracurricular activities—which he suspected was a way of coping with his and Julie's separation.

But nothing prepared him for the two shocks he received that snowy night in December.

The first occurred before he left his fifth floor office in Fairchild Hall.

His small cubicle was located in the Military Training department, separated a mere fifty feet from the cadet library, but virtually light years removed from the academic faculty, although they were housed in the very same building.

He'd rediscovered what he knew as a faculty member back in the sixties: the distance between the academic and military training sides of the Academy was measured not in a physical measurement, but in degrees of culture. And the gap was getting wider, thanks to officers such as Colonel Whitney, who had homesteaded, and propagated their own interpretation of military customs. Perhaps someday he'd be in a position to change this place. At least now he hardly ever saw Whitney.

He started packing his briefcase to leave for home when the Commandant poked his head in Rod's office. "Hey, Lightning."

Rod pushed back from his desk and stood. "Good afternoon, General." The Commandant had a habit of popping in and shooting the bull, one of his many successful leadership traits that insured the moat dragons that guarded access to his presence didn't keep him isolated and out of touch.

"As you were." Brigadier General Beck eased into the office and took a seat. "You're staying late tonight, aren't you? The Academy was released an hour ago for the snow."

"My daughter called from Academy High to pick her up at six from karate practice. Besides, I needed to let the guys who live farther away than me hit the roads first."

The Commandant glanced out the window. Snow hammered against the smoky glass, swirling around and masking the ground from sight. "If you don't get out of here fast, both you and your daughter are going to end up staying overnight at the high school."

"Yes, sir." Rod snapped his briefcase shut.

"Your daughter is quite an athlete."

Rod looked up, surprised that the general would follow such things, but it wasn't out of the ordinary. "She's getting a third athletic letter this year."

General Beck smiled knowingly. "She'll go far, I'm sure. Just like her old man."

"Thank you, sir."

He abruptly changed subjects. "The ATOs. How are they doing, Lightning?"

"Very well. All twelve of them are ready to report early next semester, and are up to the task. Incredible talent. I've spent some time with all of them and I know they'll rank right up with the original ATOs." Perhaps with the exception of Tom Ranch; but then again, no one would be as good as him, though one could always hope. One of his extra duties had been to help select, interview, and prepare the female Air Training Officers who would oversee the first class of women cadets, scheduled to in-process next June.

"Outstanding. And I appreciate what you've done, Lightning. Damn fine job. But with that, I need you to stand down, recuse yourself of any further contact with the new ATOs, understand?"

Rod pulled himself upright. "Yes, sir," he said slowly. "May I ask why—"

"I've got another task for you, but can't talk about it now. You'll find out in due time. Until then I need you focused on the upcoming SERE summer program. So stand down and recuse yourself of all contact with any ATO, understand?"

Rod nodded, remembering a saying oft ill-quoted by cadets: Ours is not to reason why, ours is but to do or die. "Yes, sir. You got it."

The general smiled. "Copy." He hesitated, as if contemplating the next item on his mind. "Listen, Rod. One of the pleasures of being a commander is bringing good news to good people. Tomorrow morning the Colonel's List comes out and you're on it. Congratulations, Lightning."

Rod drew in a breath. "The Colonel's List?"

"That's right. You were picked up two years below-the-zone. Having one of my men marked as a fast burner helps the entire organization. Word about your early promotion will get around and attract more good officers to the Academy. It's a fact of life." He handed Rod an envelope. "Your line number is inside, and you'll see that you were nominated for senior service school—the Superintendent pushed you for National War College in Washington, DC. I was there five years ago and had a blast. I know you'll enjoy it, too. With that and your record you should get picked up for a star a few years down the road."

He clasped Rod's shoulder. "Listen, if the snow lets up, you need to take your daughter out to dinner, so both of you can celebrate." He winked. "I can't say more, but in any case, have a couple of beers tonight. You've earned it."

Rod was in a daze as he shook the general's hand. He sat at his desk after the commandant left, wanting to savor the moment, but he glanced at the clock and saw that he'd have to allow time to drive through the blizzard.

Minutes later he found himself in his car, driving through the snow, down the hill to Academy High. As the snow swirled around him, he kept being drawn to one thought—below-the-zone to colonel, once again being promoted before his peers. Sixteen years out of the Academy and he was on the full Colonel's List. He felt as though he were floating on air.

This promotion was especially meaningful. He'd always known it was the colonels who ran the Air Force; they were the go-to-guys who got the job done and who were in charge of the big, critical organizations. All Wing Commanders were colonels, and flying Wings were the backbone of the nation's air fighting capability. With this promotion he may even have a shot at commanding a fighter wing.

His assignment to National War College in Washington, DC couldn't have come at a better time. With Nanette ready to graduate from high school and head off to college, he didn't have any reason to stay tied to the Springs. Nanette was looking at schools ranging from Georgetown to Stanford, and with her gone he could move on with his life. His mother was still spry and doing well, so he'd make the trip to DC alone.

And moving back east would allow him to mend fences with Julie, make a real stab at getting back together. With him living in the same city as her, he could devote himself to reviving their marriage.

But leaving here also meant kicking the ball further down the road trying to understand what really happened that night his father died.

He pulled into the snow-filled parking lot at Air Academy High and Nanette met him at the car. He was still on cloud nine, so he moved over in the front seat and let her drive; she could handle the four-wheel drive jeep better than he. He also knew the more experience he gave her in hazardous driving conditions when he was around, the less he'd worry when she was out on her own.

As she drove she spoke excitedly about the karate meet. She'd placed second in preparation for State and was confident that she'd be competitive for a first place finish. Hearing her bubbling enthusiasm, and with the knowledge of his impending promotion, he felt more content than he'd had in years.

O O O

Twenty minutes later Nanette pulled into her grandmother's garage. The brick rancher had seen nearly twenty winters and still stood alone at the end of Candlelight Drive in Gleneagle, although a sprinkling of other houses dotted the land around the development. Snow blew across the open fields where plans had been discussed the past two decades of building a golf course.

It would be hard to leave this old house when he left for War College, but he'd return for good when he retired, and it would still be standing, silently standing vigil over the Academy, which was now socked in by low clouds and blowing snow.

His mother met them at the door as snow swirled into the house. She held a yellow envelope and wore a serious expression.

Rod pulled down the garage door and stomped snow from his feet. He gave his mother a peck on the cheek. "What's wrong?"

She held up a shaking hand. "They delivered a telegram this afternoon, lad."

Rod frowned and reached for the envelope. Had something happened to Julie or her parents? "Let me see."

His mother looked past him. "It's for the lass." She held it out to Nanette.

Rod raised an eyebrow. "Let's get inside. We don't want to waste all the heat warming up the garage."

They moved to the kitchen. Blue drapes covered the window; tiny pink flowers were on the wallpaper decorating the wall. Pictures of Hank and Mary lined the wall, as well as Hank's diploma from Texas A&M and an old painting of Mary's parents in Tyler, Texas, standing in front of a row of oil derricks.

Nanette pushed aside plates stacked on the long kitchen counter. A hint of cinnamon and clove drifted through the room, spiced tea that his mother ritually prepared. Snow beat against the western windows, obscuring the view outside.

Nanette ripped open the envelope and a smile grew on her face as she read the telegram. She carefully folded up the paper, plopped down on a chair, and nodded to herself, seemingly satisfied with the contents.

Rod detected excitement bubbling out of his daughter's usually poised demeanor. He waited a moment for her to say something, but when she remained silent, he said, "Is everything okay?"

"Yes, sir," she said. She seemed out of breath.

"Well?"

She bolted out of the chair and grabbed his mother by the arms. "The Academy! I've been accepted into the first class of women cadets!"

Rod stopped. His daughter? Accepted to the United States Air Force Academy?

His mother jumped lightly in the air as Nanette squealed. They hugged, and Nanette started crying. "I can't believe it!"

Rod opened his mouth but the words couldn't come out. Nanette—a cadet? He shook his head, incredibly proud ... yet sick to his stomach as a mixture of conflicting thoughts roared through his mind.

The thought was unbelievable. Nanette was fortunate enough to be picked!

He'd heard the competition had been fierce, as even women who'd completed three years of college had applied for the prestige of being chosen for the first class. The quality of applicants included Olympic hopefuls, Women-of-the-Year, and national scholarship winners. There was no doubt in his mind that Nanette deserved the honor, and he was certain she would excel.

Yet, he felt a deep dread that almost made him nauseous.

His misgivings weren't about the hazing or mental anguish he knew that she'd experience, or the overt prejudice he'd seen against opening up the Academy to women. Or even what was at the front of every male cadet's mind every second of every day: that three-letter word that started with s and ended with ex; he knew she could handle all that.

What worried him was what she'd face afterward, after she graduated, when she'd report to active duty and face the very real possibility of becoming a prisoner of war in armed conflict.

The past few years the Academy had sent all of its graduates to operational assignments, serving as pilots, navigators, or missilers. Working in an underground silo as a missile launch officer would be the safest career she could pursue.

But he knew that Nanette would only strive for the flying assignments. And from what he'd seen, by the time she graduated, he was certain combat positions would be available for women.

So his apprehension was that if there was ever another war— no, *when* there was another war, as we just couldn't seem to learn—she might be shot down and become a POW.

He wouldn't wish that on anyone. His own mental scars were still not completely healed, and he could only begin to imagine the atrocities an enemy might bestow upon a female.

It hit him why the Commandant had ordered him to recuse himself from dealing with the new female Air Training Officers: within six months they'd be serving as upperclass women to Nanette, and he had to insure he wouldn't place the ATOs in a compromising situation by forcing them to show Nanette any favor; his admiration for the Commandant soared at what the man had done.

He forced a smile and tried not to show his misgiving. He couldn't ruin her moment of happiness. This was her moment.

"Nanette ... I'm so proud." He hugged her, then stepped back and absently turned his class ring on his finger, the same ring that Sly had trumpeted so many years ago that "no one could ever take away."

He watched his daughter and mother hug each other, bubbling with excitement.

His mother held Nanette at arm's length. Tears ran down her face. "I remember the day your father was accepted to the Academy. He was so happy, and we couldn't have been prouder." She stroked Nanette's cheek. "He and Sandy celebrated by going to the malt shop, and word was out all over town that they were a couple. Remember Rod?"

Nanette rolled her eyes.

Rod smiled, trying not to spoil the moment. "Nanette ... this is quite the surprise. I didn't know that you were interested in the Academy. When did you apply?"

Nanette wiped away a tear with the back of her hand. "Before Thanksgiving."

His mother interrupted, as if a thought just occurred to her. "But lass, you're only sixteen. Don't you have to be 18 to become a cadet?"

"You can enter at seventeen with a parental waiver. My birthday's two weeks before my reporting date for the class of 1980."

Rod wondered what it would be like for a woman to go through BCT, ordered to undertake obstacles such as the assault course. He knew Nanette could handle it both physically and mentally, but there was a huge difference tackling BCT as a male versus being one of the first women at an all-male institution.

It wasn't BCT that worried him; it was what might happen to her years down the road....

He could always refuse to sign her age waiver. With her grades and athletic skills, she could get a scholarship to any school in the country.

But that would make her miserable, and it wouldn't be fair to her, or be the right thing to do.

He knew that Hank had never tried to talk him out of applying for the Academy, even though he'd been shot down in World War II and severely injured his leg, and even ended up having it amputated.

Hank had only wanted to make sure that going to the Academy was what Rod had really wanted to do—for himself and not for his parents ... or anyone else. That was what got Rod through the hard times, knowing that it was his decision to be a cadet, and not Hank's.

Rod tried to wipe his misgivings away, but he wasn't doing a very good job. He studied her eyes. "You really want to do this?"

"More than anything in the world!"

"Why didn't you tell me you were applying?"

She was quiet for a moment, but she straightened and held his gaze. "Because I thought you'd tell me that women don't belong there."

"I'm sorry you thought I had so little faith." He held her hands. "I don't doubt your ability at all." He smiled. "But you need to tell your mother."

Nanette's eyes lit up, "I'll call her!"

Rod nodded. "That's a good idea." He mused, "You know, this might be a way for us to spend some time together. Years ago your mother and I had dreamed of taking you to France, to visit Cahors and see some of your distant relatives."

"Really?"

"Absolutely. In fact, maybe we could spend the beginning of summer there, before I go to National War College ... and before you show up for BCT. A few weeks in the old country and you'll be more than ready for whatever they can throw at you."

She stood on her tip-toes and hugged him again. "This is the best day of my life!"

She and his mother left for the living room to call Julie.

Rod stood alone in the kitchen. He flexed his hand as he stared out the window. Snow beat against the pane, making a thumping sound that echoed hollowly throughout the house.

Who would have thought? Finding out he was promoted on the same day that his daughter was accepted as a cadet. But despite the accomplishments, without his wife his life felt as chaotic as the swirling patterns of snow against the window; what made it worse was knowing that in a few years he'd be worrying about his daughter embarking on her own military career, and the dangers she'd encounter when flying in combat.

In the distance he saw a shimmering light cut through the blizzard. For an instant the clouds lifted and he caught a glimpse of the Academy sitting on the far hill; the chapel lights burned through the night sky as the winter storm momentarily abated.

The sight reminded him of a sturdy lighthouse, simultaneously lighting the way while warning of danger ahead.

He knew Nanette would excel there. And there was no doubt in his mind she'd graduate. She always finished what she started—like the time she'd rescued him in the dark, after they'd hiked to visit Hank's downed plane in the mountains a few years ago, and he'd become pinned under the fuselage....

He just prayed that she'd be kept safe throughout the course of her career. As much as he worried about what might happen after she graduated, it wouldn't be right to discourage her.

Suddenly as it appeared, the apparition blinked away and snow once again swirled around the window.

He shivered, alone in the room. It was time to move on, not dwell on the past or what might have happened if things had turned out differently. He'd even ignored Barbara's periodic letters, urging them to get together. He was tempted to take her up on it, but he was scared where it might lead ... especially if he was serious about getting back together with Julie....

It also meant putting things to rest, such as what had really happened that night his father died. To him it seemed the events surrounding Hank's crash were so uncertain he might never find out what really happened.

Had George Delante been involved? He'd never had any proof, just a lingering suspicion, and that wasn't enough to go on. Just like the death of that *Denver Post* reporter before he'd graduated—the law may have been satisfied with the arrest of those drifters, but the whole situation didn't seem right to Rod.

And what about Colonel Whitney? The man had seemed to do an about face after General Beaumont had contacted the Superintendent about the lab analysis, and he'd kept a low profile after that. Still, there was something about Whitney's behavior that Rod couldn't quite put his finger on.

When he'd been reassigned to the Academy he thought he'd have the chance to tie up these loose ends, spend time uncovering the answers he knew were out there. With Julie leaving home and raising a teenage girl as a single parent, with the incredible demands of his job, he just hadn't had the time.

One day though, he would. He didn't know when, but when he did, he'd finally know the truth.

Even more importantly, he didn't really know what would happen to his marriage ... or his daughter, but he knew he had to embrace the new life ahead him.

They all did.

He turned from the window and padded down the hall, looking forward to the next phase of his life—as well as Nanette's.

EPILOGUE

"Only Sixteen"

April, 1976

United States Air Force Academy
Colorado Springs, CO

For hope is but the dream of those that wake.

Matthew Prior

Nanette kept off the dirt road as she ran up Quam's hill. Although there'd been a blizzard the night before, the ground was warm and the snow had already started melting. The spring runoff turned the soil into viscous mud, glomming to her shoes and making the path slippery.

She ran lightly up the rise leading to Jack's Valley, passing the mock POW camp on her left. The camp was mothballed for another two months until it would open up for cadet Survival, Escape, Resistance, and Evasion training. But this year her father wouldn't be around to run the cadets through the ersatz prisoner compound; he'd be off to Washington, DC immediately after their trip to Cahors and her report date for basic cadet training.

Her father seemed to be doing better now, having put his POW experience behind him. She just wished that her mother could do the same.

He certainly wasn't the same father she'd remembered before he'd become a POW. She wasn't sure what was different, but after returning from Vietnam he'd spent more time with her and he seemed calmer, as if he had found himself, as her hippie friends liked to say; to her, it was as though his priorities had radically changed.

She picked her way past tiny rivulets that flowed downhill. Every few feet water pooled in deep tire ruts, collecting the snow runoff in miniature swimming holes.

She'd parked her jeep by the cadet gym and run past the athletic fields on the crisp, April Sunday morning. She was glad that dad had waved off her offer to run and instead set off for church; she loved being in the mountains alone, where she could get away and think.

Aspen trees next to the road were interspersed in a grove of Douglas fir. Snow weighed down the fir branches, making the trees look like a picture on a postcard. No wonder one of the first things Dad had wanted to do after returning from Vietnam was to run in the mountains; it seemed to help put his POW memories behind him.

Too bad he couldn't have left his other memories behind as well. Whatever it was that he and mother had fought about that first night in Maui had driven a wedge between them.

Nanette had thought that things would get better once Dad returned to Colorado, but within a week, the constant fighting made her glad that mother had left to visit Grandpa and Grandma Phillips. But her one week's visit had turned into months … and then to years.…

At least it was nice to come home and not find her mother drunk, or wonder if she'd be able to get any homework done that evening because her mother would be ranting about some social glass ceiling. It was beyond her why anyone would worry about who was invited to what party or social event, anyway.

It wasn't that Nanette enjoyed living with her father any more than her mother; he just made her life easier. So after school, instead of finding her mother passed out on the couch, for the past three years she'd simply come home to an empty house. And when her father finally did come home, he was usually exhausted from running the Academy's survival program.

But he did take her to stuff that her mother never did—football, hockey, swimming, track, and just about every other intercollegiate game the Academy played.

And that's when she'd discovered the allure ... although she suspected that she had always possessed it, even when she was too young to know, such as in Maui.

Especially lately, when she'd be walking with her father on the Terrazzo and cadets would turn to give her that distant, longing look, one of incredible aching desire. They'd telegraph they'd give anything if she would only look their way, acknowledge that she'd picked them out from the other 4,000 cadets. She didn't have to show any leg or even bare a shoulder, she could simply swing her long hair around and it would cause them to stop and stare.

It didn't take much to bring on the look; it was heady stuff for a sixteen-year-old girl.

But since she had it, she tiptoed around this great power of becoming a woman; careful not to flaunt it, yet fully aware of the incredible possibilities. It was very different from the last time she'd been close to anyone....

Her thoughts drifted to Lukas Klein, the blond German boy in the house next door when they'd lived in Prattville, Alabama, while her father was attending Intermediate Service School. She'd only been seven, and although several years older than her, Lukas was the only boy who didn't treat her like a girl. And she never forgot.

They'd explored the woods behind their house, and despite their age difference, rode their bikes together to school. He was impressed by the collection of model airplanes her father had brought from his trips, and at night they'd blinked their flashlights in code from their bedrooms.

When the other boys taunted Lukas for playing with a girl, he'd fought them like a wildcat. His parents were constantly being called to school, but Lukas refused to yield, not caring what the other boys thought.

Word of Lukas' fighting spread and her father forbid her to see him; her parents had immersed her in activities to keep her busy—Brownies, piano, and dance.

Before they left Prattville, she'd met Lukas in the woods. They'd promised to write, but she never received any letters. She thought she had run into him a few years back, when her dad had been pinned by grandpa's plane; but she was too focused on rescuing her father to realize it at the time. Her relationship with Lukas was very different from the clumsy advances she'd experienced from the boys once she got to high school....

Her breath condensed in small puffs of vapor as she huffed up the hill. She put down her head and pushed herself to make the crest. As she rounded the top she thought she heard something over the ridge; she slowed and pulled up.

A jeep was stuck in the middle of the muddy trail. It leaned to the right, its right wheels deeply rooted in a rut.

Two cadets huffed as they tried to push it out of the muddy furrow. They looked up as she approached. One, a tall blond, wore a mud-covered shirt that read BLOOD, GUTS AND BEER: USAFA RUGBY. He straightened and wiped a hand across his face. The other, a squat dark-haired cadet who looked like a weight lifter, leaned over to catch his breath, his hands on his knees.

She slowed to a trot. "Hey."

"Hey," the blond said. "What are you doing up here?"

"I should ask you," Nanette said, jogging in place. "You guys didn't think you'd make it through this mud, did you?"

The blond looked defensive. "If we hadn't hit that last patch we could have made it to the other side of the Valley."

Mud was splattered over the nearby trees, looking as if they had spun their wheels trying to get out of the rut, but they'd only dug themselves in deeper.

From what she had seen, this was typical of cadets. They were presented with a plate full of opportunities at the Academy, yet some chose to dig themselves into a rut.

Just as there were plenty of opportunity to get out of this particular mud hole, for the most part the cadets ignored all what the Academy had to offer—the clubs, the running trails, the educational opportunities, the cultural events, touring Colorado, the amenities in downtown Colorado Springs or in Denver, the myriad athletic facilities, the access to world-class thinkers—but they wallowed in a rut of just surviving the Academy environment.

Living with her father outside the Academy gates and seeing what the Academy had to offer only substantiated her observation that the cadets took an awful lot of things for granted. She knew that in a few months, when she'd finally become a cadet, she'd fully exploit the system and wouldn't squander any opportunity.

Nanette stopped and put her hands on her hips. She breathed deeply, warily catching her breath. She was alone out here and didn't know these guys from Adam, so she watched them struggle with the jeep and remained on the far side of the vehicle, knowing that if they made a move, she could get a head start and easily outdistance them.

Or kick the crap out of them.

"Do you want me to call for help?" Nanette said. "I can run back to the cadet area."

The weight lifter's eyes bugged out. "No way!"

"That's okay," the blond said. "We can handle it." He put his shoulder to the jeep and grunted as he pushed.

"It's no problem," Nanette said. She was curious as to why the two didn't want any help. "It'll only take a few minutes. I'll flag down an air policeman." She turned to leave.

"Hey, wait a minute!"

Nanette stopped.

"I ... I don't think that would be such a good idea," the blond said. His face reddened; Nanette suspected it wasn't because of the exertion.

"Why not?"

The blond looked helplessly at his friend. The weight lifter threw up his hands. "Go ahead. Just go ahead. I told you we wouldn't be able to make it. I didn't want to come anyway."

The blond sloshed through the mud. He reached Nanette and said, "Ah, we're really not supposed to be up here. And this jeep." He motioned sheepishly back at the mud-covered vehicle tilting on its side. "It's not ours."

"It's not?"

The weightlifter avoided her eyes. "We borrowed it from a Firstie in our squadron."

"So?" Nanette said. She made her way to the front of the jeep. She couldn't tell its color as the mud was caked thick on the hood and sides.

"We borrowed it last night. The Firstie thinks we were going downtown to church this morning."

"You lied?" And this idiot is admitting it? Even civilians knew the Honor Code was the bedrock of the Academy; she'd be under the Code in a few months, and wouldn't dream of lying even now—it was too much of her as a person.

"No way," Weightlifter said. "We were just taking it out for a spin, testing out the four-wheel drive. We were going to get back in plenty of time to head downtown."

"Then what are you worried about?"

"He'd kill us if he found out; this is a restricted area. We've got to get his jeep out of here and cleaned up without anyone finding out."

She walked over and inspected the vehicle. Her dad still had Grandpa's old World War II vintage jeep at Grandma's, up in Gleneagle. They'd gone out four-wheeling several times, and just last week he'd taken her up Mount Herman, the small mountain north of the Academy, so driving a four-wheel stick shift wasn't a mystery.

"Tell you what." She pointed to a thicket of dead wood next to a National Forest sign on the west side of the trail. "Put some of those branches behind all four tires for traction. Then you two get back and push. I'll drive it out."

"You can handle a four-wheel drive?" Weightlifter narrowed his eyes.

"I've done it plenty of times. Now are you going to let me help, or are you going to wait for this mud to dry and catch grief for being late?"

The two looked at each other. Blondie shrugged and tromped into the woods. He started rummaging through the trees just off the jeep trail. Weightlifter watched him for a moment as if debating whether to try anything so radical. A long moment passed, then he trotted over to join him; he slipped on the muddy slope and held out his arms to keep his balance.

Nanette walked around to the driver's side. She reached inside the tilted jeep, found the handle, and opened the door. She had to boost herself in since the jeep leaned so far to the right.

Once inside she slid into the unpadded bucket seat. She ran her hands over the instrument panel. It didn't look that different from Grandpa's jeep. She worked the stick shift and found it even had the same neutral position.

Blondie dropped a pile of saplings into the rut and pushed them under the front and back wheels. He rapped on the side and said, "Are you sure you know what you're doing?"

Nanette smiled sweetly. "Ask me again in two minutes." She took the jeep out of gear and twisted the key in the ignition. The cadets stepped back as it turned over.

She revved the engine, and then placed an arm on the passenger's seat; she turned behind her and said, "I'm going to start rocking. Push as hard as you can when I move forward."

"Right." They sloshed behind the jeep and positioned their shoulders against the rear bumper.

She shifted to first and engaged the clutch. Just as the jeep inched slowly forward, she pushed down on the clutch and the jeep rocked back.

Quickly engaging once again, the jeep rocked forward, this time a little more.

Back and forth, with a growing, cyclic motion she patiently allowed the rocking to gain amplitude. She counted ten back-and-forth cycles and then yelled, "Push!"

She gunned the engine.

Mud sprayed behind her, but the jeep's wheels caught on the branches.

Using the saplings as friction, the jeep twisted in the rut, the wheels alternately catching dry ground, then slippery mud.

She fought the jeep as it fishtailed. It slid in the muck toward a large tree. One of the cadets wailed in horror, but Nanette coolly steered into the turn.

She gained control of the jeep as it shot to the top of the crest. She downshifted and coasted to a stop at the rocky summit. The trail plunged down in front of her.

Before her lay the northern end of Jack's Valley, covered in the snow. She saw the firing range two miles to the east and the top of Cathedral Rock jutting over a hill. She half thought about taking the jeep on down the slope, but she cut the engine.

Blondie and Weightlifter jogged up. They looked ridiculous covered in mud. All Nanette could make out were their eyes.

Nanette pushed out of the jeep. She slammed the door and started laughing.

"What?" Weightlifter demanded.

"You guys are going to be pressed for time if you're going to get cleaned up in time for church."

Weightlifter peered over the crest. The trail plunged steeply down. "No way we're going into Jack's Valley."

Nanette stifled a smile. "Good choice, guys."

Blondie stuck out a muddy hand. "Hey, thanks. You saved us."

"Sure," Nanette said. She returned his shake, then bent down, and wiped the mud off her hand in a pile of snow. "Later." She turned and started jogging down the steep slope into Jack's Valley.

"Hey," Blondie called after her. "What's your name?"

"Nanette," she said over her shoulder.

"What's your last name? Let me take you out to thank you."

She turned and started jogging backwards. She squinted from the sun in her eyes and held a hand up to her eyes. "I don't date cadets."

"Come on! I owe you one!"

"Don't forget me!" Weightlifter said.

"Then remember that when I need a favor." She turned and started running down the hill. She slid on the mud; holding out her arms, she kept her balance as she picked her way around rocks and brush down the steep slope toward the valley below.

"I will, beautiful!" Blondie's voice drifted down from above. "I'd do anything for you, anytime. And that's a promise!"

BIBLIOGRAPHY

Boyne, Walter J., Beyond the Wild Blue: A History of the U.S. Air Force 1947–1997, St. Martins Press, NY, NY, 1997.

Bruegmann, Robert, ed., Modernism at Mid-Century: The Architecture of the United States Air Force Academy, University of Chicago Press, Chicago, IL, 1994.

Contrails, The Air Force Cadet Handbook, United States Air Force Academy, CO, 1959 through 1999.

Fagan, George V., The Air Force Academy: An Illustrated History, Johnson Books, Boulder, CO 1988.

Head, Jim and Donna, Hiking the USAF Academy, USAFA Services, Marketing Division, 10th Services Squadron, USAF Academy CO, 1997.

Knaack, Marcelle Size, Encyclopedia of U.S. Air Force Aircraft and Missile Systems, Vol 1: Post-World War II Fighters, 1945—1973. Office of Air Force History, Washington, D.C. 1978.

Mock, Freida Lee and Terry Sanders and Christine Wiser, Tom Hanks Presents "Return With Honor", "The American Experience," distributed by the Public Broadcasting Service, 2011.

Monnett, John H. and Michael McCarthy, Colorado Profiles: Men and Women Who Shaped the Centennial State, University Press of Colorado, Niwot, CO, 1996.

Nalty, Bernard C., ed. Winged Shield, Winged Sword: A History of the United States Air Force, Volume I (1907—1950) and Volume II (1950—1997), Air Force History and Museums Program, U.S. Government Printing Office, Mail Stop SSOP, Washington DC 20402-9328, 1997.

Norris, Robert S., "The Cuban Missile Crisis: A Nuclear Order of Battle October/November 1962", Presentation at the Woodrow Wilson Center, October 24, 2012.

People Almanac, People Books, NY, NY, 1999.

Rasimus, ED, Former F-105 pilot, "The F-105 Thud, a legend flown by legends," http://www.talkingproud.us/Retired/Retired/F105ThudVietnam_files/the-f-105-thunderchief002c-the-airplane.pdf, August 30, 2005.

Shea, Nancy, The Air Force Wife, Harper & Brothers, NY, NY, 1951.

Sprague, Marshall, Newport in the Rockies: The Life and Good Times of Colorado Springs, Ohio University Press, Athens, OH, 1987.

The Air Officer's Guide, Military Service Publishing Co., Harrisburg, PA, 1951.

United States Air Force Association of Graduates, 25th Anniversary Pictorial Review of the United States Air Force Academy: 1954 to 1979, United States Air Force Academy, CO, 1979.

Watson, George M., Secretaries and Chiefs of Staff of the United States Air Force, Air Force History and Museums Program, U.S. Government Printing Office, Mail Stop SSOP, Washington, DC 20402

ABOUT THE AUTHOR

www.DougBeason.com

Dr. Doug Beason is the author of thirteen novels as well as two non-fiction books.

A Nebula Award finalist, Doug has published over 100 short stories and other work in publications as diverse as The *Wall Street Journal*, *Analog*, *Amazing Stories*, *Physics of Fluids*, and *Physical Review Letters*. A Fellow of the American Physical Society and Ph.D. physicist, Doug retired as the Associate Laboratory Director at the Los Alamos National Laboratory, where he was responsible for the people and programs that reduce the global threat of weapons of mass destruction. A retired USAF Colonel, Doug's last active duty assignment was the Commander of the Phillips Research Site and Deputy Director for Directed Energy at the Air Force Research Laboratory. He has worked on the White House staff for the President's Science Advisor, and was recently the Chief Scientist of U.S. Air Force Space Command. A 1977 graduate of the USAF Academy, he served on the USAF Academy faculty as an Associate Professor of Physics and Director of Faculty Research.

IF YOU LIKED ...

If you liked *The Officer*, you might also enjoy:

The Cadet
Strike Eagle
Five by Five 3: Target Vector

OTHER WORDFIRE PRESS TITLES BY DOUG BEASON

Assault on Alpha Base

Return to Honor

Strike Eagle

Wild Blue U: The Cadet

Kevin J. Anderson & Doug Beason

Assemblers of Infinity

Craig Kreident 1: Virtual Destruction

Craig Kreident 2: Fallout

Craig Kreident 3: Lethal Exposure

Ignition

Ill Wind

Life Line

Magnetic Reflection

Prisons

Trinity Paradox

Our list of other WordFire Press authors and titles is always growing. To find out more and to see our selection of titles, visit us at:

wordfirepress.com